LIGHTNING
& OTHER SHORT STORIES

INCLUDES
THE STUPIDEST STORY EVER WRITTEN.

By D.F. Williams

Published by Ember-Link International, Inc
Discerning Artists Division
dfwilliamsbooks.com

Edited by Catherine B. Johns.
Cover Design - Sol Terlson Kennedy

ISBN – 978-0-9919688-7-9 pbk.
ISBN – 978-0-9919688-6-2 eBook

10 9 8 7 6 5 4

BOOKS BY DFWILLIAMS

NeverEnding
Whiz, Natty & Me
The Blues

CONTENTS

JUMPING CATFISH

—————⊰⊱—————

*J*immy wouldn't know a jumping catfish if it jumped on his head but he said it at least 50 times a day. Different ways too, including a right holy one that Pastor Bob sometimes borrowed; it was impossible not to do that. But when Jimmy yelled it fast and loud, it meant only one thing. He was scared. And if he yelled it just once, he was scared severely.

Philly, Cal and me ducked down behind the pea trellis at the exact same time as Arly and Sam Petrovitch went flat belly in a carrot row. Then all of us counted the silence in our heads until we got to the number that told us if Jimmy wasn't already a goner, he soon would be. Bad news for sure but no time to be caught in wonderment about that; if we didn't move fast we'd miss his dooming completely and that's a pitiful way to treat your best friend when he's already doomed to start with.

Philly was the first to break cover but if you want my opinion that had everything to do with her being Jimmy's sister and nothing to do with being brave. She'd already waited her whole life to witness her brother being doomed and might never get another chance so even if she doomed herself along with him it would have been worth it to her. Real bravery was following her to the dooming but all credit to her anyway because she got us moving and in the perfect place behind the wood pile just in time to see the whole thing.

Jimmy was cornered. Fence on one side, chicken coop on the other and he was staring Witch Vargash right in the eye as she backed him up, severely long arms stretched out, skinny fingers waggling fast, flocking him into the corner. An excellent start to a first-class dooming but Jimmy wasn't giving up, no ma'am about that.

He faked right, dodged left, faked a duck under the big meat hook witch hand that just barely missed his hair standing straight up then he heel-spun half around, shot sideways to the chicken coop, planted one foot on the wall like he was going to climb all the way to the top but didn't and sprung back going headfirst into the ground with three lightning fast somersaults to the fence he'd better not hit or he'd be dead not doomed, but didn't and wasn't. Nobody could possibly guess what's coming next except possibly Witch Vargash who didn't fall for any of it and kept coming, waggling him like a gaggle, closing down his running room with every step.

For a sick second it looked like he just might try going between her legs, about the only daylight I figured he had left in the whole world, and probably the most dangerous escape move in all history, but after the last somersault he popped-up like a jack-in-the-box, faked left, right, left again, ducked low and charged super-fast right for a slender crack of freedom between the witch and the fence, watching for the grab and the trip, keeping his arms down and everything he had as skinny as possible, moving sideways, eye-to-witch and lightning fast.

She was faster.

Like a hen after a bug, her two fingers pecked down at Jimmy's stretched tight head and snatched his ear clean out of empty space. She was a witch all right; only a Mom can do that and Witch Vargash didn't have any kids.

Right now Jimmy started doing the Owweee dance and he wasn't faking it. Straight as a fence post but severely angled he jack-footed along beside her, she holding him out like a piece of meat the dog is jumping at. Jimmy's dooming was started and it started pitiful. Philly giggled.

"You little varmints skedaddle and don't you ever come back, you hear." She shouted over her shoulder at us.

Sometime in her witch career she must have gone to witch school where small varmints got eaten regularly and probably graduated with flying colors whatever that means. Not even an 'or else' or 'you'll be sorry' or 'I mean it' and obviously no dooming witnesses allowed either. She hauled Jimmy up the back stoop, through the squawking screen door and into the kitchen where for sure she had a huge black pot on the constant boil. We skedaddled before the splash. Philly stopped giggling. Her brother was a goner. It happens sometimes but it's especially bad when you can't be witness.

Down the road, in the ditch, we waited and waited until Sam Petrovitch had to go home, then Arly, then Cal until it was just me and Philly wondering if Jimmy had been cooked 'til the meat fell off his bones. Philly was braver than I thought and didn't cry once but she did yelp like a puppy when Jimmy came down the road and left the shadows. He looked pretty good, real good, considering the dooming he must have got.

"Jumping Catfish." says me when he gets almost beside us and Philly rushes out to severely gut punch him for the scare of a lifetime he gave her. Jimmy just smiled a crooked one, odd like, but keeps his trap shut and keeps on walking. Witch Vargash got his brain, probably.

All the way home he says nothing and when he does all he says is "See ya tomorrow." She must have left that part of his brain in him but the rest of it was long gone because after that night, Jimmy was never the same again, not even remotely.

In the first place, he stopped saying Jumping Catfish, stopped completely, like those pages were ripped completely out of the dictionary, out of his brain, most probably. Not long after that, the whole town got infected by not saying it.

Little by little, he stopped hanging out with our gang but it was not like he was hanging out somewhere else or with somebody else. He got less talkative too. Like he knew the answers before the questions got asked. And it went on like that until school started which is a guaranteed smart time to stop giving answers even if you know them and don't want to be teacher's pet but that didn't change him, the spell was so strong. That was when Arly, Sam Petrovitch and me knew it was up to us but not Philly because she was acting strange too and Cal moved to the city with his folks but not, he said, because our town was a goner and no point sticking around if you don't need to which is wrongful thinking and not like Cal at all.

Face it, if you don't save your own town no one will do it for you so it was up to us and we made that our #2 priority right after saving Jimmy, and Philly too, if she needed it. The whole town was acting like nothing had happened when a blind person could see it had. Little by little, the curse was spreading and somebody had to put a stop to it. No matter what, or how, but for sure as soon as possible, so we got started the next week after some tests and track and field day, my most favorite school day of all time.

The first thing we discovered was that witches can be pretty formidable enemies, something that witches don't have many of, for obvious reasons like getting burned at the stake if you get caught. The second thing we found was that powerfully nice witches who are on your side of immortal combat against the wicked variety of their own kind are never around when you need them. Maybe in the big city there are plenty of them but out here in the country all we had was Witch Vargash and she was the problem to start with so no help at all in the immortal combat department. After that came a whole lot of other disappointments.

Like so-called General Stores that don't even have basic spell-making ingredients let alone advanced spell-breaking ingredients. No bat's wings, which are almost impossible to catch by yourself let alone try taking the wings off without getting your fingers chewed to pieces. Not a single eye of newt which might be easy to catch, or not, depending on what a newt is. Spider webs we already had but not nearly enough to fill a pot big enough to break the size of the spell over Jimmy. What we needed, but didn't have, was a bulk supply store for witches, not farm seed. Even mail order would have been a big help but no such thing there so it was up to us to solve the problem without any help from anybody.

Sam Petrovitch found a moose rack but it didn't fit in the pot so we sawed it in half a couple of times, completely ruining it. Good bulk but impossible to cook tender. Arly made a bag of every spice in her mother's cupboard and I got tons of nettles, sawgrass, thistles, burrs and anything at all that itches like crazy but we still only had half a pot, mostly moose horn, and by now you couldn't see the spider webs at all so we needed more of those but by winter time fresh spider web was in hard supply so we had to settle for dusty ones from basements and such. That's when it came to us.

When you need witch ingredients, you go to the witch. Plus, and this was a big plus thanks to Arly's thinking, they also have the recipe book. Of course nice witches will give away this stuff for free but like I said before country-style witches of the helpful variety had left our town for the city so that left us with Witch Vargash as our only hope to defeat herself, a severe complication to be sure. But Jimmy was sinking deeper and deeper with every day that we waited and there was nothing we could do about that just like Dad said there's nothing you can do about the weather except wait it out and clean up after it's done.

Which is exactly what we did as we waited for the snow to melt down enough that we wouldn't get bogged down with our short little legs churning away hopeless against Witch Vargash's big old tree trunk legs not being slowed down one little bit. Then we waited for the ground to dry up for the same reason. Then we waited for a cloudy, moonless night until we figured that was precisely what witches waited for so we changed plans and waited for a clear, moonstruck-bright night which didn't come and didn't come and when it did

Sam Petrovitch had the measles and wasn't allowed to go out even though both Arly and me already had them and couldn't catch them again anyway. Immortal combat against witches involves tons of waiting, not to mention disappointment and loads of bravery, obviously.

Deeper and deeper went Jimmy and Philly too who didn't seem to notice like everybody else who didn't seem to notice, so the spell was spreading out-of-control and we had to do something more than just talk about it and gather cobwebs which were, thankfully, back in abundant supply again. So we decided to at least spend all our free time getting into top flight condition for witch evasion that you can never be too good at so you need tons and tons of practice which we made our #3 priority after homework and gathering ingredients for our witch pot.

Other than surprise ear-snatches, I was getting away from my Mom almost every time and so was Arly but not Sam Petrovitch because his Mom only ever used surprise attack, or so he said. Still, he practiced and so did we, getting into trouble on a constant basis and driving our parents crazy for good cause and any old reason. Pretty obviously by this time, the curse was spreading like wildfire and the whole town was watching every move we made, us being the only ones not affected by the curse and the only true hope for town salvation but they couldn't see that any more than we could tell them our plans and not get severely doomed for our good intentions, end of story right now if we did that.

Tons of practice later, Witch Vargash's peas were shoulder height and we knew it was time to make our move. Last resort we filled three spray bottles with our magic spell water which had frozen and thawed countless times, better than boiling for sure, and aged to a dark color with some green floaters that had to be strained out so as not to plug the spritzer. The night for immortal combat was promised moonstruck bright as day and early to boot, plenty warm and dry enough with no excuses for delay so off we went, dressed all in black with our best running shoes all ready for witch evasion come what may.

We waited in the same ditch as before and Sam Petrovitch hummed, not a tune, just hummed like a mosquito and Arly played with her spritzer, testing it on a bug which survived no problem, not a good sign but not a witch either. I watched shadows until there weren't any and that ended the waiting for immortal combat and began it.

We kept to the ditch until the last possible inch, squeezed under the broken fence, belly-crawled between the carrots to the pea trellis then squat-walked to the end of the row. The easy part was behind us and the hard part stretched out in front like miles of naked distance from a mountain top. A regular shooting gallery in front of us, open grass all the way to the apple tree outside the kitchen window, real close to the exact spot where Jimmy got doomed in the first place. A real smart place to put an apple tree if you don't want kids stealing them all the time.

We were just about to make a run for it when a shadow passed by the window. Witch shadow, no doubt about it and it made Sam Petrovitch bump into me and up the line to Arly. Close call and she sent an elbow to my guts and I sent a return elbow to Sam Petrovitch but missed. Maybe his Mom really was the captain of the surprise attack but no time for thinking about that as Arly took off without warning like a rabbit. Right on her tail, me and Sam Petrovitch rounded the pea trellis side by side, arms pumping high and chugging away like two old dogs in a race, nothing gonna stop us. Good thing nothing tried because by the time we got to the apple tree we were so over-ventilated, a duck cudda caught us, easy.

Wind back to normal, Sam Petrovitch boosted Arly into the apple tree for spy duty. Nothing boiling, she reported. We counted on that, moonstruck bright night and all. Quiet too. Graveyard quiet which made sense considering the territory but that didn't mean we liked it because we didn't. Everybody knows that witches can hear better than dogs, probably even good enough to hear my heart pounding and the blood squishing through my veins. Truth is, you can never truly be completely ready for immortal witch combat no matter how much you practice or how much you want to save your town in spite of them not caring or helpful in any way.

Arly hung from a branch with one hand, head tilted sideways with her tongue hung same-side-out and eyes bugged backwards, like we needed to see that but didn't when what we really needed was some distraction for the dog-eared witch and right then a good city witch must have heard our plea. Music started pouring out the kitchen window. Seriously big music, angry and itching to get inside your head where it could do some severe damage by bouncing around and setting off ideas. The first time any of us had heard witch music. Pretty bad and I wouldn't want to dance to it, or any music for that matter but it was already too late for Arly.

She started tapping her fingers against her leg and obvious as guilt caught red-handed the cursed music was blowing out the window and swirling around us like fog. We were getting stuck in it. Rooted solid like maybe that tree was some little kid who was cursed into the ground and had to make witch apples for all eternity. Witches do that kind of thing which is precisely why combat with them takes so much bravery.

Finally, Sam Petrovitch shook Arly's leg and broke the spell she was in and broke himself out of it at the same time. She dropped her hanging act and followed him around the tree, me too, up the stairs to the screen door where witch music was escaping in huge quantities, some of it bent like a rusty nail. Like sometimes starting over and over again because it lost its place in your head and had to go back to the beginning just to remind you to pay attention or else. Witch music, catchy as a cocklebur but bent horrible and that's an honest fact.

Arly went under Sam Petrovitch's arm and through the screen door sideways without making it squawk, then him, me after. Standing in the moonstruck kitchen, surrounded by witch music when we should have been intent on ingredients and recipes and mindful of the big pot on the stove but Arly got sucked out of the kitchen into the music like a moth to the flame, Sam Petrovitch right after, me last, we were goners, I knew it.

Goners being pulled down the hallway by evil witch music like a doomed fish on the line being pulled to the surface, seeing the line held in one meat hook hand and the fishing rod in the other meat hook hand with everything getting cleaner and clearer until the water breaks over your eyes and you're forever doomed in the bottom of the boat or in this case standing at the kitchen door looking into a witch's parlor.

Philly saw us first. Sitting on the piano bench beside her brother who used to be Jumping Jimmy Catfish but now the whole town just called him Philly's big brother. She severely gut punched him so he stopped playing witchy music and turned to see us. His eyes bugged out and his cheeks turned six shades of red, the pitiful picture of caught-red-handed in his own doom and even worse when the witnesses are your best friends.

Then you-know-who saw us, stood up and poured apple juice squeezed from you-know-where. She pointed a crooked finger at Arly to sit beside her on the sofa and she did, Sam Petrovitch next then me too on the arm, pitiful goners all of us.

Jimmy looked me in the eye with the plain and simple truth, the only kind of truth there should be. Then he looked at her sideways so she couldn't catch him doing it. Plain and simple, she stole his name, cursed him into a terrible piano player and made his little sister brilliant to spite his nose.

No doubt about it, she's a witch. A mean one.

THE TRINITY

—————⟫●⟪—————

Three, blood red rubies sparked fire on the wall as they tumbled from the bony, outstretched hand. Unlikely the hand of their rightful owner, when it released the gems it made a tight fist then recoiled with a quick vicious salute to a sunken chest that was more skeleton than flesh. In the crack of that act, a crack open for no more than a second, the expression of pain indistinguishable from pleasure betrayed the seller's addiction to his ritual.

As the rubies came to rest on his velvet, Armand Wilhelm completed his first impression. Two trips a year for twenty years, forty trips to Bangkok during which he had never witnessed a presentation so curious, by a person so equal to that curiosity nor had he ever seen the color, caret and cut of the gems which cast those brilliant sparks on the dirty walls. Never before, and, he was equally certain, never again would he see such perfection or witness such a performance.

Where those gems were unearthed or how many hands had held them was of no immediate concern to him. What was inside them became his only interest and in short order his loupe would, as it always did, answer that question. He thought he had a moment to consider his approach to the transaction when the seller hit him sharply on the arm. The business of bargaining had already begun and it would be serious.

There would be no dance or drama with this transaction. No push or pull toward a value which both buyer and seller deemed acceptable but to which neither, out of contempt, greed or pride would admit as fair. This transaction would be fast, a minor error in judgment would be fatal; the failure to agree would condemn and abandon the deal just as quickly as a successful negotiation would be denied and forgotten when the money went into one pocket and the gems went into another. That was the code of the market but Armand sensed this was an unusual transaction and the urgency of time, not trade, was driving it.

The old man, Chinese from anywhere in the world, perhaps but unlikely even China herself, looked about vacantly, carefully avoiding the gems' glow on the black velvet. He was either an expert with jewels or had spent a lifetime dealing with thieves. In either case he could not be cheated and would not be robbed.

Time, Armand reminded himself, was driving the old man's need to sell what had to be his life treasure and he best not wait to be reminded of that fact again. The old man was becoming anxious, perhaps questioning his decision to sell.

"And who is the rightful owner?" he asked as he, and every buyer like him would open each and every negotiation. Sellers expected the question so it was not taken as an insult, but a lot was vested in the quality of the answer. The better they could lie the more they could make. From the brief appraisal Armand had of this seller, he expected a large lie, well told.

"Of no import." uttered the old man, words spoken with as complete a deception as the face which expressed them. Slightly British in pronunciation, they could have been the only English words he knew just as equally as he could have spent a lifetime practicing them, waiting for this precise moment for their release. Neither truth nor lie evident to his eye or ear, Armand dismissed the evasion. Ambiguity of question and answer fit comfortably within the few rules of the market.

"Seventy-five percent retail, perhaps less depending on flaws." he responded to the obscure answer of ownership and reflecting the degree of deception he thought he saw and heard. It was a generous offer. Legally owned or illegally acquired, he could feel the gems heating his desire to possess them, however temporary that ownership would be. 'Of no import.' were as true words for the seller's ownership as they were to his cost. Whatever he paid for them, even as much as the full retail, he was in the cheapest place in the world to buy rubies. He could depend on having that price returned fifty times over when the stones were set and sold on the continent. Full retail or one half of black market was significant to be sure, but largely irrelevant to his final profit.

Once he examined the gems and made his final offer, he would hear the seller's counter-offer, if there was to be one. The gems would be his, that much he knew, that much he sensed, they both knew.

The old Chinese dropped his head, agreeing to proceed; his gaze was frozen on the velvet, eyes bright with desire, as if it were the first and not the last time he would see and hold this life treasure. Armand followed the old man's fascination to the source of his pleasure and pain.

The gems laid naked on the black velvet in a circle of display as fine, as vain and as deceptive as any setting he had ever seen. Had he not witnessed them drop haphazardly onto the cloth he would have sworn they had been cleverly arranged by sleight of hand too quick to see. Absurd or natural as that thought was, he realized with sudden clarity that what a few seconds ago had been a tantalizing desire for profit had been transformed into the final triumph of his life's work. He had to have those gems as his own, yet he feared disturbing them. Even more curious and completely contrary to his nature, he feared taking them to his loupe as if he had no right or reason to see inside them, let alone touch them. It was a hesitation to the negotiation which could have been taken as a sign of weakness in the bargain yet he sensed the old Chinese understood why he could not touch them until his eyes had completely absorbed the naked beauty of a perfect trinity for the very first time.

Three rubies, brilliant round cut, lying with their crowns pointed outwards, their generously faceted pavilions closing the inside of the circle, drawing light and visual acuity with such convergence as to provide the illusion of being a single stone, a solitaire which might once had been their nature.

Had some fool, some grossly incompetent fool of a cutter made not just one horrible mistake but two? Two mistakes to birth three gems from one which should never have been divided, from which nature had never intended division?

The glowing red iris with its fixed black pupil stared back at him.

Inconceivable. Ridiculous. Impossible.

He had to concentrate, he had to focus, he had to start before the old man changed his mind.

Numbers, start with the numbers. How many carets?

Nine point six, ten points even, ten point four, thirty carets total, he gauged by sight alone before selecting the smallest stone for viewing, raising it slowly and turning it into the loupe held close to his right, near-sighted, eye. Flawless but equally compelling to that triumph of chemistry was the sheer perfection of the cut. So astoundingly proportionate overall but with facets so subtle in angle and generous in quantity, he realized he had foolishly over-estimated the carets. The cutter's genius had reversed the law and logic of division by which a flawless stone, when cut to its true nature, creates the illusion of being larger than its true weight. The mind of the cutter who understood those laws, whose eyes saw into the heart of an uncut, unpolished, dirty rock and the hand which set its beauty free were as far beyond Armand's knowing as was the intensity of the heat, the enormity of the pressure and the persistent, immeasurable time it took to give birth to the crystal. And to have cleaved a trinity from a perfect, unflawed solitaire was insanely contrary to the nature of every cutter since the first gem was chipped and polished into existence yet he knew that was exactly what had happened and it was not a mistake, at least not a worldly one.

Under his loupe, with each turn of the gem, his discoveries multiplied. The surfaces were as clean and perfect as if they had just left the wheel. Not a bruise or a chip, a burn or a nick, he wondered if the stone had actually been cut or if, by some miracle, it had been created as he held it, without the intervention of chisel or wheel. Internally perfect and without a single knot or needle, let alone a flaw or a fracture, it was a solitary wonder.

Then, like his misjudgment with the gem's weight, the certainty and science of internal perspective cratered as the brilliant focused clarity which is only born from the exactitude of mathematical refraction, failed to appear in the depths, in the heart of the gem. Impossible, yet true and that truth came with fresh expectations and demanded deeper penetration into the eternal mystery of creation. He saw the light of a single blazing sun in the center of the perfectly cut ruby shattered into beacons of light from all the stars in the universe. Stars so countless he could barely distinguish the end of one galaxy from the beginning of the next no matter how deeply or at what angle he looked. Every ray guided him to its source before fading into the brightest star of the galaxy behind it, taking him deeper into space and bringing powerful thoughts and wonderment of order and chaos to the forefront of his mind. One galaxy hot with creation pointing to another, collapsing into red giants of dying stars. Tempests of violent primordial force released by the acceleration of a spinning vortex heralded the genesis of light, mass and matter governed by laws made at the beginning of time, in the first nanosecond of the universe. Perfection upon perfection, galaxy after galaxy, star after star. Never before had a crystal displayed and preserved the dawn of time like the one in his hand.

Breathtaking, until he saw a cloud. A monstrous flaw. A terrifying, milky cloud of inclusions too tiny to be seen individually; nature's refusal for utter perfection and a warning to intruders on her sacred domain for a creation as unique in time as in shape and structure. The cloud condemned his exploration and flooded him with anger. Anger which rose to blind rage then sank to disgust with such speed and intensity he tore his eyes from the gem to confront the seller with a vicious insult. Only when he met the eyes of the seller did he realize it was the old man's hand crossing behind the gem, cutting its source of light and interrupting his journey. That realization instantly settled his anger and forced an immediate retreat into his mind and moment. How long had he been exploring the universe and the stars within it? A minute, an hour, longer? What had he seen? Never mind what he had seen, what remained to be seen and how long would it take him to see all that was there? And lastly, most importantly, what would he give to see it, to bear witness to life itself?

He was held captive by his thoughts and knew, they both knew, those thoughts were shared. There would be no bargaining, no offer with counter-offer, no pretense of insult by seller nor feign of interest by buyer. Like the dreamer does not own his dreams but belongs to them, so too was this the way, the only way, to proceed with the transaction.

He reached into his breast pocket for his leather billfold, still full and fat in anticipation of a long, productive day at the market and handed it, unopened, to the old man, for taking what he wanted. They were just numbers on paper for which Armand had little interest let alone the time or desire for worldly distraction. Perhaps he should have been surprised when the wallet disappeared, unopened, into the sleeve of the once rich and elegantly embroidered silk tunic but he wasn't. Nor did he care.

"Sometimes you only find what is lost when you too are lost." said the old man as if the sale would not be complete without an obscure Chinese prophecy. Armand only half listened to him as he placed the gems onto heavy white linen paper, folded stiff creases to form an envelope from which they could not escape. When he looked up, the old man was gone.

"That's enough for today." he muttered to himself, ignoring the two young thieves in front of him and the handful of glitter they dropped onto his velvet. "That's more than enough days wasted in pursuit of money. There is more to life than this." he muttered and walked away without a backwards glance at the sparkle he had pursed for most of his life.

Sooner or later all things must end, he reflected of his career and the now singular accomplishment of those years, a trinity of blood red rubies. He felt his life purified, compacted, crystallized and mysteriously returned to him, fresh, new and compelling. It was secure in his pocket; his hand clutched the envelope maintaining constant contact with his future. He had seen but one of the gems and had to see again. And then there were the other two which, if they were anything like the first, and they had to be, he had a fortune in his pocket. Three fortunes to be exact.

★ ★ ★ ★ ★

Three fortunes which refused estimation, no matter how many times he looked or how much he saw as he went farther into the universe. Not that day or the one following or the night in between which he spent looking into the heart of one stone before being driven to look into the soul of the next. Hour after hour without eating or sleeping, sending away the maids who ignored the sign to leave him alone and tapped on his door, afraid, perhaps, that in the quiet of his room, he had died. "Go away. Go away now. Leave me alone." They weren't wrong with their fear for his life and he knew it. If he didn't break his ritual with the gems for food or sleep, death would most certainly claim him and it would do it quietly, stealthily, like a thief in the night. If he learned anything in those hours alone, he learned that.

As he had done more times than he could remember, he put the gems away, carefully folding a new sheet of the stiff linen paper to replace the one whose edges had become curved and soft from so many attempts to give the stones, and himself, some rest from each other.

So many attempts for a peaceful separation which ended, once again, with a broken smile of defeat and the opening of the envelope as he attempted to convince himself he retained the power of choice by saying aloud: "Just one more time, just one last time." He emptied the envelope into his hand and dropped The Trinity onto new velvet to reveal, as it always did, its glowing red eye looking up to him. It was always the same, without fail or change, an outcome completely inescapable, even if he wanted to escape it, a desire which, with each drop, he saw becoming more distant and less important.

His hand clenched to a fist and recoiled in a sharp, snapping salute to his chest, pain and pleasure indistinguishable from each other. With each time, he was getting faster, but not as fast as the old Chinese, whose hand was across his chest before the stones had come to rest to the cloth. Perhaps, when he could do that, he would rest. Perhaps then he would be able to rest.

No longer using his loupe for magnification he didn't need, he examined them again, starting, as always, with the smallest. Each stone was different but equally compelling, he would be lost in one until he desired the next and then the last until there was nothing left to do except drop them again and start over. Sometimes viewings would take seconds, sometimes minutes or hours, each time was unique but always concluding with the same tortured finale signaling an impetuous, hurried beginning for the next performance. One more time and he would rest, just one last time and he could rest, he promised himself and two more days passed.

It was another promise for rest that he couldn't keep on the 12 hour flight to Amsterdam but then because of the profound, paralyzing fear his treasure would be lost or taken from him. As before, he held the envelope in his pocket and couldn't release it, not for a second. So intense was this fear and so uncertain was his mind of any reality without his treasure that he couldn't rest from all the fearful thoughts coming unbidden to his mind. Was that fear to be the price for the wonderment of his treasure?

Only when he was locked safely in his home and the fear of loss or theft was no longer rational did he have the answer to that question. From that moment forward the gems never left his eye or his hand and the promise of rest was only achieved when he succumbed to fatigue so great, he could not resist it. When that happened, it occurred with such an abrupt collapse of his mind, body and will that he never slept in his own bed but instead fell into unconsciousness with his arms outstretched in readiness and his head resting on his table or his body fallen back onto his couch like a rag doll. The Trinity would be held tightly in his left hand because in his right he would most certainly drop them onto the velvet and start the ecstasy from which he could no longer willingly escape.

With time becoming meaningless and irrelevant to him, he secluded himself with his forever changing, always inspiring universe, refusing to question his fortune as good or bad just as he refused to acknowledge his insatiable desire for more of it. He refused when his legs became too weak to carry him up the steep, spiral staircase of his canal house or when, pounded time after time by a vicious, hard fist, his battered and bruised chest became skeletal just like the old Chinese. He steadily refused to admit his addiction when his right eye became too nearsighted to see anything except the ruby which had to be held so close it almost touched his pupil. He ignored all the signs his body sent him: his discolored skin, his swollen feet and the pounding headaches which only retreated with the sight of the gems.

He refused to stop when he knew he was killing himself just as he refused to stop when he knew he was going to die, and quite soon. That only forced him to search harder and longer because by then he knew what he was looking for so he continued his relentless pursuit until, in the largest ruby, he finally found the galaxy and the star within it which he knew to be his star. He knew it the moment he saw it. With each drop of The Trinity, he hurried to his star. His search was over and soon too, would be his life. A life, he reflected, that was finally in cosmic order but in earthly disarray.

His little house on Leidsegracht, not far from the diamond merchants with whom he was no longer known or welcomed, was dirty and in disrepair both inside and out. Garbage had piled up from food delivery. He had no electricity because he didn't pay his bills. He was shunned by his neighbors, estranged from his family and isolated in a time which no longer accepted or wanted him. His star was becoming fainter and harder to find. He understood what the old Chinese meant when he said sometimes you must be lost to find what is lost.

That was not all he knew. He knew the end of his earthly time was pursing him.

With pain and pleasure now completely indistinguishable from each other, he dropped the gems onto the buyer's black velvet, pounded his chest and answered her question with words freshly resurfaced from a distant memory. "Of no import."

Wherever Emily de Ruyter looked, deep or shallow, side to side, they were there. Sunrises and sunsets over islands from tropic to arctic, over desert oasis, jungles and forests primeval or seas from azure to black. Sun setting over mountains, hills and valleys; sun rising across lakes and streams, through trees and flowers, some scenes she recognized, others she had never seen but which were impossible for her to have imagined. Spectrums of color streaming forth and colliding in squall and calm. All unique, each sunrise or sunset making a pure simple statement toward a tranquil moment before propelling her on to the next vision, her next mortal thought.

Anger, rage and disgust vanished with the realization that the cloud in her loupe came from the old Dutchman's hand passing through the light behind the gem. How long had she been looking at her visions? A few minutes? An hour? Longer? Of no import rang true for all. She emptied her safe of its cash and gave it to him.

"Lost is not a place. Lost is a time. A time when every direction is unknown."

She heard him but his words didn't register in her mind.

He didn't expect a reply. She had much, much more on her mind than the simple warning of a profound truth she would only learn when she lost herself and discovered her destiny.

Quite the opposite of himself. He took the money he didn't need and couldn't use. His mind and body were wasted, nothing would bring them back. All he wanted was to get home before his star collapsed so he could die in his own bed.

No Stranger

―――⟫●⟪―――

"All Aboard."

"All Ahhh-Board"

"How did they ever convince me to do this?" she muttered while putting her favorite old traveling hat on the overhead bin. They didn't hear her, she could have said anything and got away with it. Just like they hadn't heard a single word she'd said all morning. She dropped into the seat across from Bud, his 6-year-old face plastered against the window, a miniature copy of the grown-up 31-year-old child sitting across from him. Why she married Josh was a mystery of the first magnitude.

"She's gonna go, she's getting ready to blow and go." said Bud, building the excitement for his father.

Like he needed to do that, she thought.

"She is, she is, she sure is Bud." Josh encouraged.

Like he needed to do that.

They pulled their faces from the window, leaving greasy imprints of noses, chins and foreheads and sat straight as rails, shoulders not quite touching the backs of their chairs, arms crossed but not touching their chests, anticipation building for 'the gravity-busting event'. They had spent at least 20 minutes talking about it, how they would sit, what it would feel like, if it would come with a creak or a groan, arguing over each minuscule and irrelevant detail. Staring at each other intently, they were concentrating on each other's reaction so hard that if the train didn't get rolling pretty quickly, they were sure to explode, and that, she understood only too well.

"Clank!"

"Thunk!"

"Bump." she said before their imaginations produced every train noise on the planet. One more argument settled by not taking sides. Not that it mattered whether she agreed with Bud's clank or Josh's thunk. They would re-live it and argue about it for hours on end anyway. If that's what they wanted to do, for certain they would find a way to do it but then at least it wouldn't involve her, they wouldn't argue her 'bump' and they wouldn't ask her again, which was just fine as far as she was concerned.

"Gravity is busted."

"Sure is."

"Is he going to blow the whistle, Dad? Will he?"

"Sure he will Bud, sure he will."

The whistle didn't blow but it didn't matter to the two boys who had already returned to their window-face-plastered position. She cringed with the thought that outsiders would see through that childish display and blame her for such undignified behavior. Or worse yet, someone might recognize them and sometime when she was not expecting it, she would have to explain their foolish behavior. If only they could be normal, at least in public, but she had wished for that too many times to wish for it again.

She looked out the window and saw what they didn't see.

A little family was standing quietly by the wall, waiting patiently for something or someone. A husband and a wife, a son and a daughter, standing there all prim and proper like completely normal people and not tearing around looking for a silly adventure or arguing over every little thing. What a joy of a life they had, what a joy to be just a normal little family like that.

Joy that came with a shudder attached to it because Josh still talked, only wishfully now, about having another child. As if the four years of waiting for Bud and the last five years trying to get pregnant with a brother or sister for him wasn't enough wishing, waiting and hoping for one lifetime. She knew it wouldn't happen. It would never happen and she was resigned to that reality even if her childish husband refused to accept what was obviously his reality as well.

"Hey Dad, let's go exploring."

"Which way? Want to come with us Maggie?"

"That way. Come with us, Mom."

"Not right now boys. You run along, I'll wait here."

Bud was already half-way down the car before he turned and waited for his best pal, her childish husband who was standing in the aisle, looking like he was asking for permission to go outside and play: "You sure? It'll be fun. We won't be long." he said.

She nodded out of habit. The fun part wasn't at all in doubt and that they could be gone for hours and still claim they were only gone for a few minutes was nothing new but also fine with her. At least she might get something out of the trip. A few precious hours to be alone with only her thoughts was something she didn't get very often.

The carriage door closing on their backs was the sign for her mind to do the same thing and get on with her fantasy of an ordered and normal family life. Her alone time was precious; she didn't want to be interrupted and she didn't expect to be.

"Would you mind if I sat with you for a few minutes?"

The question and the stranger who asked it shocked her out of her solitude even before she had become completely lost in it. She wasn't pleased with the interruption and didn't attempt to hide it.

"Just a few minutes?" He asked kindly. She looked up to him as he sat down beside her without waiting for her answer. She really didn't expect him to do that, but he did. Sat right beside her like an old friend or favorite uncle. It was an intimate act and he quickly explained himself.

"I like to face the direction I'm going. You too?"

For some reason, the question calmed her, perhaps because of its innocence: "I suppose so. I never really thought about it."

In truth though, it was the second time that day she had never really thought about it. The first was when the boys argued that exact question. Both of them wanted to sit beside the window facing backwards because that was the best position for the 'gravity breaking event'. She had, as usual, made the final decision. Bud would face backwards on the way there, Josh would get it on the return and that way they both had a turn beside the window. It was the usual absolutely pointless argument and her completely irrelevant decision because neither of them would stay seated for more than a few minutes anyway and besides, they always took turns at everything, they always shared even before their turn was up. She really didn't care which direction she faced and didn't even think about it for herself until the stranger asked and all she could say was that she didn't think about such things. She wondered if that was a mistake and what he would think of her.

"Outbound or inbound, which is it?"

"Pardon me?" she asked.

"Do you prefer the trip to your destination or the trip home?"

Weren't they the same thing? It's not like the train had a choice; the track was the same and sitting backward one way and forward the next, the scenery was identical so wasn't this question the same as the forward/backward seating question? It was slightly irritating to have to think about it. "Aren't they the same thing?"

"Not to most people."

"Then I'm not most people."

"No, you're not."

A most peculiar introduction, she thought. Not where are you going? Not what do you do? Straight to the heart of the matter, what do you like, who are you? She wasn't sure she appreciated it but now she could no more tell the stranger to leave her alone than she could change seats without being rude. Had it been planned that way?

"I suppose one place is as good as the next." He said.

His eyes were dark, almost black. Her immediate thought was that the stranger would not be easily shocked. "Or as bad." she replied, hoping that would end the conversation on an equal note.

He wasn't put off by that. He seemed to take it as an invitation to continue. "Too true. The bad is always there, you can always find it around the next corner."

"Too bad." she said before suddenly realizing the words could also be taken to mean she wanted something bad right now instead of around the next corner. As that thought passed through her mind it came with the odd realization that the stranger wasn't the kind of man who would think that. He wouldn't joke about anything bad or evil. He didn't, in fact, look like the kind of man who joked at all. Not like Josh, who couldn't be serious about anything for more than a couple of minutes. As if to prove her thoughts, the stranger continued.

"It's all part of the balance, Maggie. Good and bad, you have to make choices."

"You know my name?"

"Your husband said it."

She remembered. It was when Josh asked her to join them exploring the train like he was asking permission to go outside and play. And that embarrassment wasn't even 5 minutes after he left his greasy face print on the window, a larger but mirror image of the print made by his 6-year-old son. She remembered the silent embarrassment of possibly being seen by a friend and winced a little. She seldom allowed anyone into those feelings, into that part of her life but the man beside her was a stranger so she didn't try to hide her feelings or her thoughts. He could read them if he wanted to read them.

He was looking out the window, not seeming to mind the slums, the decay, the dirty industrialization on the edge of the city through which so many railway tracks in so many countries were laid. Not easily shocked was a very good first impression and she silently complimented herself for her intuition. His silence and peaceful contemplation of what she didn't want to see gave her a moment to study him. He didn't seem to mind.

His hair was longer than the fashion, at least the fashion for someone his age, about the same as her own, she decided. He had a slight beard, not well tended but not neglected either. He was slender but well-constructed, sturdy in a way. Dark, dark eyes which were concentrated on what was passing in front of them and that interested her. When she looked to see what he was seeing, she caught both their reflections in the window. He looked into her reflected eyes and smiled. It could have been an embarrassing moment but it wasn't. She didn't know his name but knew he was no longer the stranger he was only moments ago and wondered when that changed and how it had happened. She saw her own reflection return his smile and was pleased; it made her feel good to be honest.

"It isn't that complicated." He said.

"Maybe not for you."

"If you think it is complicated then it will be complicated. If you think it is simple then it will be simple." He explained.

It sounded like something Josh would say. And the way he would say it too: innocent, simplistic and non-threatening. That was Josh and the way he was with her, the way he had always been with her. She had to agree so she did: "True. I suppose it isn't all that complicated."

"It's good you feel that way." He said.

As the world outside her suddenly became less complicated, the world inside her became more and more peaceful. Her sense of calm intensified, exactly the opposite of what calm should do but exactly right all the same. Intense calm, it was an unusual feeling and it gave her a sense of amazement but without an object or a reason for it, just the stranger's presence, it was a strange amazement. Strange for a stranger, she thought then put her hand over his, certain that it was right to share her amazement after such an important agreement had been reached. He didn't react to her gesture.

"Your son is very curious, very adventurous." He said.

"He will be the death of me."

"Don't be too hard on him."

"I won't." It felt good to have that settled too. How long had she been thinking about Bud and his insatiable curiosity? Not long, she decided. Mostly she thought about Josh and his inability to be an adult, to be serious and to take things seriously. Why she married him was a mystery of the first magnitude, but not a bad mystery, she decided. It was good to have that settled too.

"Josh is a good father." He said.

She couldn't remember saying her husband's name. Perhaps she said it in the train station while she was waiting for them to decide the best way to sit for 'the gravity breaking event'. But names were not that important, she decided. "Yes, they are good friends."

"That's the way it should be."

"Yes, it is much better that way." she said forgetting her complaints about Josh as a husband and a father and seeing him as the stranger saw him and as the man she fell in love with and married.

He gazed out the window and she followed his lead.

The slums had given way to the countryside. Not real countryside but elite countryside with large, imposing estate homes plunked here and there like big mausoleums in an old cemetery somewhere in Europe where the wealthy were buried inside the wall and the poor were buried outside. The rich with their polished, inscribed marble headstones; the poor with crude rock markers or wood crosses with names and details disappearing or missing completely. Both of them were dead. She didn't like the image and she didn't like it coming to her the way it was.

"I think I'd like to look backwards for a while."

"That's a good idea, Maggie." He said.

She gave his hand a little squeeze, certain that it was the right thing to do before getting up and taking the seat opposite him. And, she decided, she should sit down like a lady and not plop herself into the seat like a sack of potatoes falling off an old farm truck. And she should make a habit of that too, she decided.

Facing backwards was different from what she had imagined it to be. Had she ever tried to imagine it? Did she even try to understand what her boys were arguing about when they were arguing about something that didn't interest her? No, no she hadn't. She had thought it too trivial, so she dismissed it, as usual. It was silly of her to do that, but she wasn't embarrassed about it now because it was in the past and too late to worry about. Simple, just like the stranger said.

He looked forward, she looked back. The past stretched out as far as she could see while the present came up beside her, came up in the corner of her eye for a mere second before it joined the only place it had ever been or ever would be. Strange, but it fit together perfectly. On the spur of that moment, she decided she would take a brief nap. Just a few minutes, that would be enough. The stranger wouldn't mind. He might even take a nap himself. Wouldn't that be nice?

"Mom. Mom. Wake up, wake up."

The seat across from her was empty but she wasn't surprised or disappointed. He was on the train and they would meet again, she was certain of it, it had been that kind of day and it would continue that way because, well, just because. "And how are my two favorite explorers?" She blinked the sleep from her eyes, brought a smile to her face, still feeling very dreamy and enjoying the sensation.

"We saw everything, just everything. There are seven cars that way and..."

"Twelve." Josh helped.

"...that way. There's a diner car with two floors, the top floor is all windows, like a, a..."

"greenhouse."

"...like a greenhouse. That's where we have dinner. You can see everything, just everything. Front and back and both sides, just everything. It's awesome but you have to look fast or it's gone." Bud jabbered away at top speed, his usual state when excited.

Standing in front of her, she took his face in her two hands, gently pulled him forward and kissed his forehead. She had often wondered what her son would become when he grew up, and sometimes, as she knew mothers only ever admitted to themselves, she also feared it. Silly, she thought, he'll be just like Josh, how could he ever be different?

"What else did you see?" she asked while staring into his eyes, feeding her own soul with his excitement, his rapture with life which at that moment, was a train.

"Lots of people. All kinds of people. And we saw the club car where people have drinks, but I can't go. And the sleeper car. We found our beds…uh, they're really small, Mom." Bud said with some hesitation.

"Really small?" she asked with pretend concern.

"Cozy, very cozy." said Josh, then asked: "Are you feeling ok?"

"Fine. I had a little nap. I'm just waking up is all." She reassured him and watched his face begin to relax with her words. She loved the feeling that came with reassuring him and knew it came from their love.

"Can we have dinner now, Mom? Can we please?"

She smiled and moved his head up and down in her hands letting that and her smile become the answer he wanted to hear.

"In a minute, Bud. Mom is still waking up. We can wait a minute, can't we son?"

"I'm fine, Josh. Who's going to be the leader?"

"I will."

"I will."

They waited for her decision. It wouldn't matter to them who she picked but it wasn't a pointless exercise; it was a precious gift. She felt a tear forming but knew it wouldn't puddle and fall; she knew it would stay and that she had to hold it. She looked at her son: "You can lead us there and Dad can lead us back." It was the perfect order, which she only recognized after the words left her lips.

"This way. Four cars this way and we'll find dinner. Follow me." Bud said as he walked confidently to the sway of the car.

She got up and when she didn't see the brim of her old hat she stretched and searched the back of the luggage rack but still couldn't find it. Josh looked too. Not important, she decided, so she squeezed under her husband's arm, put her hand around his waist and pulled him tighter to her like he needed reassurance when he didn't and neither did she. They took their first step forward at exactly the same moment, not a touch, a word or anything to signal it, just knowing the precise time the other person would move. It had always been that way with him. A mystery of the first magnitude but not one, she decided, she wanted to understand because that might change it, that might ruin it for all time; knowledge did that sometimes. The magic and its mystery were better, she concluded thoughtfully.

Four cars down, all counted by Bud, they found the diner. She didn't see the stranger anywhere along the way but when she thought of him, or looked for him, it didn't distract her thoughts from her family. It wasn't at all like being a person with something else on their mind as they try to talk on one topic and work their private thoughts or agenda into the conversation at the same time. It was just a simple feeling of the stranger who rested comfortably behind all the other thoughts and words in her mind but which didn't interrupt their flow. He said it was simple, so it was.

"Mom, which way do you want to sit?"

"I'd like to see where we are going." she said without hesitation.

"Me too."

"Me too."

The three of them squeezed onto a bench meant for two and didn't care what people thought.

Cozy, close and comfortable were nice words with a nice feeling behind them, she thought. The way it should be, and she didn't have to try and make it that way, it already was. It was just another moment or another game or another exploration all stitching time together until it was as real as grass blowing in the wind.

"It's getting dark." she said, almost to herself.

Unbelievable. Where had the time gone? Like someone had reached into her mind and stolen it. Hours of rambling discussions, little jokes, observations large and small, imaginings and side trips to here and there. Sometimes a small hand, held in her own, sometimes a big one. She didn't see the stranger, not once in all the journeys she took but she didn't doubt she would see him again. She could feel his presence just as surely as she could still feel her hand on his.

"It'll be bedtime pretty soon." said Josh.

"I want to see it get totally dark. Can we do that? Please, Dad, can we do that?"

"We can do that." replied Josh while looking at her and this time he wasn't asking for her permission, this time she understood he was answering for everyone.

She wanted to see it too. No, it wasn't that she wanted to see it, she had to see it. It might be the same as every other night and every other sunset and that would be just fine with her, but she had to see it, she just had to see her day, their day, this exact day turn into night. She squinted her eyes as the light disappeared outside the window, slowly merging into night, perfectly accompanied by the sound of iron wheels sounding on iron track.

Bud's eyelids kept drooping, fluttering like little bird wings but he wouldn't give up. He could hardly wait to go to sleep on the train, that had been a frequent topic of conversation, but he didn't want to miss anything either. His day was fading and just like he didn't want to miss anything, she wanted to keep him in her arms for as long as she could. She knew it was the same feeling because it came from the same place in her heart.

Other children were in the same predicament of holding on and not wanting to let go. Little families like the one she had seen standing at the station. Every now and again an exasperated voice rang through the air or a sob or a cry drifted down the aisle. But not so much as a peep of complaint came from Bud. Josh wouldn't allow it. He would change the topic or start a game or pour love into the empty space that was crying for attention.

The only complaint Josh would tolerate was that life was already too short and complaining about it only made it shorter. She wondered if that piece of advice came from his father. Probably not, at least not directly, she concluded, because his father died when Josh was quite young, but it came from somewhere, perhaps it came from within. That could happen, didn't the stranger tell her that?

"What do you say, Sport? Is it dark enough for you?"

"Ok Dad, I'm ready. Are you coming too, Mom?"

"In a minute, Bud. I'll be there soon."

She didn't think he'd make it to the end of the car before falling asleep and he didn't. Safe in his father's arms, eyes shut, arms limp and dangling over his father's back, they passed through the door to the sleeper car. But this time she didn't close her thoughts on them. This time she watched every step until the door was shut and then she locked that memory away where she could keep it safe for as long as she lived.

This time the stranger didn't ask for permission to sit with her. He just sat down, facing her like she was looking into her own future. He was wearing her old, floppy traveling hat.

"It looks good on you." she said.

"Thank-you."

"It really is simple, isn't it?"

"I was hoping you would find that way." He said.

"But I'm not certain about the facing forwards or the facing backwards part."

"Then you never will be." He said.

His eyes were even darker at night. No doubt now that her first impression about not being easily shocked was true just as she understood to the depth of her soul that this day was perfect and complete. There were no questions and there was nothing left to wish for or to explain.

"I must go to my family."

"Sarah." He said, "You should name your baby daughter Sarah."

"Sarah." she agreed.

Certain that it was the right and proper thing to do, she knelt and took his left hand in both of hers, kissed it lightly on the back and then held the palm to her cheek. It caught the single tear which fell into it.

DUKE

Rose-Marie Ancora is the most persistent person in the world and until someone actually teaches a buzzard to sing, a vulture to play the banjo or a condor to recite poetry her place on the persistence pedestal will never be challenged. Not that she ever actually got even one precious chirp out of her own Neolithic spoiler of souls and their dreams, but she never stopped trying. Not until the gruesome end, which for every one of us should have come a lot sooner than it finally did.

When it happened, Rose figured the cantankerous old buzzard just gave up and died, but that isn't the only explanation for its death. It could have died because it was just too mean to live with all her love and affection or it could have died because of its own disgusting ugliness, which was, by itself, more than enough to do the job. Maybe both are true. In any event, except for Rose, no one mourned the passing of Duke and more than a few of us figured that she wasted good money on the box she buried him in. Setting his dead carcass on the centerline of the freeway to become the desiccated roadkill that was his nature, would have been a far more appropriate ending. She might even have made a few dollars out of his passing; most of us would have paid hard-earned money for the privilege of running over his ugly corpse. At least I certainly would have.

Why she ended up with him and called him Duke or why she insisted that he sing is a mystery but why she loved that vile and contemptible chunk of primordial vomit is clear and uncontested logic.

Rose-Marie is spring and summer combined into a whole set of glorious, sensuous, warm and wonderful days, one after the other, every last one of them guaranteed to be bright and sunny. Hope, optimism and joy all mixed together with laughter and wit into a small, willowy package that is as close to mother earth you can get. That's the woman. She loved that naked lizardly head with the mean, beady eyes and sharp nasty mouth because she could love it when no one else could. That's why the rest of us put up with it and no one ever asked her what in the world she was doing by keeping such a repugnant and repulsive thing in her house and in her life. Clearly, and obviously, Rose-Marie is more than life itself, mine included. She is a reason for life, she always was, and she always shared that gift freely, even with something as vile as Duke.

She was sharing her precious life with that rotting, ungodly miscreant when I met her five years before and it had been there for a while before that. Duke was almost always sitting on its own armchair in the front room, poking about with its stupid head, swinging it around on the end of its half-naked, bony, serpentine neck. Watching and waiting, waiting and watching, death and decay always in those keen, black, suspicious eyes.

"He's really quite intelligent." She confided in me, warmly. I believed her. That tar-headed hunchback didn't trust anyone except Rose and that was pretty good thinking on its part. Unfortunately for her, that trust was about the only good thing it ever gave her. He wouldn't be happy for her, wouldn't sing for her and what voice he had was like the brittle nails on the end of those deformed bony claws scraping and clutching a rusty drainpipe. It may not have been a sound intended to wake the dead, but it damn sure would make certain whether or not something was dead. It was loud, vicious and totally indifferent to everything save one thing, itself.

"Now, now Duke, you don't have to use that voice with me. Why don't you try something soft and sweet?" Then she would hum a little tune. Smiling away like nothing had happened and that one day the dirty vulture would actually be happy for her. More hope, more optimism, endless quantities of joy and persistence, always the persistence, her bold signature below all the other fine and noble qualities she wasted on that gross, genetic miscalculation.

Once in a while she would take Duke with her on this or that social occasion. She always asked her host if that would be a problem and it never was. No one could really refuse the only request she ever made and even if they thought they could refuse her they wouldn't take the chance of missing her even if it included the regurgitating mutant. No one ever got used to seeing her with it on her arm, or anywhere else for that matter, but especially holding onto her arm which turned the world to madness with both heaven and hell staring you right in the eye at the exact same instant. She, so bright and vivacious and he, watching and waiting, waiting and watching, death always around the corner. Unnerving just about describes it. Unnerving in the physical sense of the word like when the spinal cord is cut by a sharp, wicked beak and the nerve is yanked clear, sparking and popping as it empties the vertebrae.

But somehow, somehow Rose never really noticed the effect Duke had on other people, although why she didn't is probably more due to her gentle and kind nature than it was to her complete innocence of suspicion that anyone would ever lie to her about him. Then again maybe she just attributed the revulsion to Duke's bad breath which even she admitted was 'not one of his more charming attributes.' That stink of old decaying flesh went together with his ugliness and his meanness so perfectly that it spawned the darkest and most grotesque of thoughts. It was a stink so strong that you could feel droplets of it condense in your nostrils from where those putrid abscesses of decay would work right into your brain, where they became thoughts. Monstrous, unclean thoughts. His thoughts, and when he stared at me, it was as if all my senses were being raped and impregnated with death and morbidity.

Not that I was any different from anyone else because he stared at everyone that way, always watching and waiting, all the while hanging onto her with the most ungainly of postures. Always thrusting his head and rubber neck toward anyone who came too close to him before emitting that awful noise and the deathly odor that produced it. But it was the eyes, always the eyes, which were the worst. Eyes which were always fixed on his victim's heart as if he could actually see it beating beneath the skin before fluttering wildly as he thrust his torpedo-like head into the cavity to take a bite. Duke was no intellect but no dummy either. He would always attack the heart, the emotional center of his victim, first. That much we all knew.

"One day you will be happy, won't you Duke?" Her smile would melt the fears Duke created and the topic would be changed. Spring and summer would temporarily triumph over the darkness and despair of cold, dark and endless winter.

When he wasn't on her arm, he would take possession of any other place, or object, that he desired. Sometimes he would walk around. That is, he walked when he didn't spring suddenly forward in a lopsided, crooked hop which was his usual and surprisingly quick and menacing way of getting the attention of someone who tried to ignore him. His true walk was worse. It was a drunken, obnoxious and challenging gait. Were he not so disgustingly obscene in both appearance and temperament it might have been comical, like a penguin's walk is comical or maybe a bear when it walks on its hind legs. But there wasn't anything funny about his loathsome, drunken swaggering challenge of a walk. Best to avoid being the target of that walk just like it was best to avoid the eyes and the breath.

At one of our gatherings, he was walking around the Crawlers' pool, head jabbing and thrusting like an insane deformed turkey, when I first wondered, can that beast swim? Can it swim with something on its back? Something like, say, a heavy chair? Good for nothing, obsolete piece of detestable Paleozoic puke, can you swim?

For sure it couldn't sing, Rose's metaphor for happiness, and she tried everything. She bought canaries and finches but if Dude didn't threaten and pester them to death they stopped singing of their own accord; silenced by the screeching devil they were supposed to cheer with their lovely, romantic birdsong. Then she tried modern music, then flute and piano, the harp and other strings. She sang to him and she sang along with all the music she bought to make him happy. At least five years of this and not one lousy note of joy ever came out of him.

Persistence doesn't always pay off. Thank heavens you can still count on some things, like the grim reaper, the sickle man, the ultimate solution to everybody's problems.

Next to Rose, I knew Duke better than anyone and that was because she is so special and precious that I would put up with the malevolent bastard when her other friends wouldn't or couldn't.

'I just have to run out for a moment. Be a dear and keep Duke company until I get back. He doesn't need anything, just some company.' she would ask and that usually got me a hug and sometimes a kiss on the cheek. When that happened, I always tried to get some of her sweet floral fragrance on me and then I would store the sweater or shirt in a plastic bag to keep the scent fresh and keep her near to me for all the days it lasted. I did the opposite with old vomit vapors and stayed respectably out of range and hoped he would be quiet and keep the air from being fouled with his degenerative, digestive stench.

"Was he happy?" she would ask when she returned and always spoken behind his back so not to embarrass him, like that would make a difference. Always that question but I knew if the worthless creature ever showed one ounce of happiness for her, I would deny it. After everything she had gone through, I wouldn't deprive her of not being the one to see his happiness first-hand. No, I wouldn't deprive her of being the one to see him happy any more than I wanted to be the only one to see it and be responsible for that memory forever. No, I wouldn't deprive her of the momentary pleasure that by some fluke, some reversal of nature's gravest error, that Duke could actually be happy for an instant or do something nice just once in its life. I couldn't do that to Rose.

To anyone who has enjoyed good fortune and avoided knowing a creature like Duke, this recital might seem like an unduly harsh and critical condemnation of nature and her periodic folly with fatal, deforming diseases. It isn't. You can't imagine how bad it was.

Was. What a beautiful word.

Duke Ancora is finally stone cold dead; now Rose needs a new husband. Someone to shower with all her love and I'm going to swallow every last drop of it.

THE STUPIDEST STORY EVER WRITTEN

➤➤●◄◄

The stupidest story ever written is about the oldest living clan of idiots and imbeciles in England and possibly the entire world. They still live on an estate just northeast of Lanehead Crossroads on an oxbow of a tributary to the River North Tyne called Tarset Burn. Or at least they used to live next to the tributary. Sometime in the 12th century, the local villagers got together and dug a channel across the narrow end of the oxbow, like the open end of a horseshoe, and diverted the water with the hope that thirst would drive them away. No such luck. Either they didn't care, or they couldn't be bothered damming the diversion but most likely they were just too dumb to figure out what stopped their water. So, they dug a well, levelled the dry creek bed and invented the game now known as croquet.

All clan sports use sticks but the idea of a mallet was a rare stroke of genius for these morons and that made body armor mandatory. Back then, old armor was a shilling a dozen; now they use a random assortment of Canadian hockey and American football pads and helmets which makes the game much faster so it's more dangerous to play and really thrilling to watch.

Written records do not exist as far back as the Horrorfish have lived on their land, consequently, there aren't any actual deeds to prove when they first settled there, nor is there any mention of them in the Domesday Book of 1086 which was commissioned by William the Conqueror. The purpose of that survey, which included all of England and most of Wales was to record property ownership (via the book), assess taxes (via hide count) and collect arrears (via any means necessary). How the Horrorfish avoided being included in Domesday is anyone's guess, but a whole lot of alcohol and naked bodies would be a good place to start guessing. Unlike most everything in this story which is totally unimportant, the fact the clan didn't pay taxes in 1086 or after winning the civil suit in 1342, one of the more ridiculous parts of this story which will be told later, it is almost worth the words wasted writing it.

Anyway, sometime in the 7th or 8th century, the 3 Horrorfish brothers responsible for this literary landfill of stupidity, claimed by virtue of eminent demesne (domain), a very large estate. Using the only topographical mapping system available during the early medieval period, their estate was demarcated by natural landmarks like big rocks, hills and streams where they existed and where they didn't, the brothers clear-cut a wide swath outside the boundary of their property and stole the wood. At the time, the land was heavily treed and sparsely populated and while the motive for settling where they did and building the estate which came to be called MiddleWoss Manor might be of some interest in this otherwise pointless story, regrettably, unknown.

Whatever their reasoning, if any at all, the brothers were basically wood choppers and as mentioned there were plenty of trees and not enough people to prevent three big incorrigible assholes with axes so through a variety of means, they claimed right to vast tracts of woodlands which over the centuries the cult mercilessly exploited in furtherance of a progressively perverse and unconscionable lifestyle without an ounce of care, concern or conscience, of any kind, for anyone.

[In the interests of full disclosure, there are some late 12th century records of so-called timber rights on display not even a mile away from MiddleWoss at a boring little museum in a garage just north of Charlton, on the edge of Linthole Burn. However, as with anything Horrorfish, these records must be taken with a grain of salt because they are undoubtedly forgeries. Not even a Horrorfish would argue their authenticity but best not make that challenge without a sturdy helmet and a strong stick.]

As important as anything in this stupid story can be (and there is precious little of importance available for the telling of it), it is worth noting that it was the brothers' greed and larcenous depravity which provided the financial wherewithal necessary for centuries of clan survival. Very unlikely they intended to create this legacy (they were barely capable of planning lunch let alone a legacy) but the woodlot is the only reason the clan survived when by all right and reason, they should have either imploded or been brutally murdered before the end of the medieval period when that was the popular way of dealing with assholes like them.

Unfortunately, neither of those events occurred and every succeeding generation of Horrorfish has become progressively more proficient at unrelenting selfish indulgence without boundary or hesitation. Of course, one could argue that wanton selfishness, greed and complete lack of impulse control is the true legacy of the founding fucktards and you won't get into a fight with that statement. To a Horrorfish, those are hard-earned compliments.

In any event, while it took several hundred years for this collection of bovine shitheads to cut and sell nearly all the trees to which they claimed title, the first 3 trees were selected from the estate's own woodlot. These were used to build MiddleWoss Manor, an architectural catastrophe in every way describable and a disgrace to this day but one with a unique construction, unique being interpreted in the broadest possible sense which in this case means no other builder in the entire world has been dumb enough to copy it.

Aines Horrorfish, the youngest brother, is generally held responsible for this architectural brain fart but it is a brain fart which must also be acknowledged for having significantly influenced every generation of Horrorfish since its release. *[Purely by accident and to be discussed at length later, this mental misfire might actually deserve credit for the origin of the term and concept now known throughout the world as 'Family Tree'.]*

For whatever reasons but which no doubt included far too much alcohol and far too little intelligence, Aines decided that chopping the branches from a tree was unnecessary so long as that tree was going to be used for vertical support. To communicate this moronic idea, Aines is said to have waved his arms around his head like he was being attacked by a swarm of bees, which perhaps he was. Whatever the reason, his dumb-ass older brothers agreed with him and 3 huge oak trees were selected based upon the structure of their canopy. These were then stripped of leaves and small branches and the canopy was trimmed to the approximate apex shape for a plain gable roof. When so readied, the trees were dug up and dragged to the building site where they were replanted side-by-side-by-side to become the 3 center support pillars for the west 2/3rds of MiddleWoss Manor.

Needless to say, this asinine idea from the dimwit Aines made for an extremely complicated rafter system and rendered all space above the lowest limbs useless for everything except climbing. It was the descendant of this design dementedness which was to become Aines' contribution to future generations as climbing and living in the canopy became a vital survival skill for Horrorfish children. As soon as they could crawl or bum skoot, they would wait until the coast was clear then go straight to a tree and shinny up the trunk if they could. If they couldn't, older children would come down from the canopy and haul them up, saving them from parents and clan alike because children caught on the ground or knocked off a branch during a roundup were enslaved. *[One child in the 14th century is said to have lived in the canopy until he completely matured before his feet touched the ground for the first time. There are no facts to support this claim, but it is entirely believable.]*

Children were in constant danger of enslavement until the age of 12 or 13 when they were generally safe and could escape capture because both their fitness and intellect had fully matured making them faster and smarter than the adults who were easily tricked with a fake move or a colorful rock. Regrettably, but predictably, once the child mingled with adult insanity, all skill and intellectual development ceased and the steady decline into the Horrorfish cycle of stupidity began. Once that started, these juveniles were no longer welcome in the family tree where elite platoons of their former friends and family would relentlessly pursue and violently expel them with thrashing sticks and projectiles, like shoes.

The east 1/3rd of MiddleWoss Manor which was not occupied by towering oak trees was a conventionally framed apartment-like structure using dimensional lumber and a box design that produced 3 floors of 24 to 36 different sized rooms per floor with standard 12' ceilings. There is no proof that the British system of Measurement (the BM system) which so aptly converts 1, 2, 3, 4, 6, 8, 9, 10 and 12 foot increments into practical squares and rectangles was invented by the idiot brothers but MiddleWoss Manor is ostensibly the first and definitely the oldest known building anywhere in the world to employ it. The 2'x24' room on the third floor is still used for captured children.

Of passing interest on this topic was the clan's baffling desire to patent and own the BM system. Like so many ridiculously impossible initiatives, they actively pursued this claim until 1610 when the Addled parliament was dissolved by King James VI and I (James VI, King of Scotland was demoted to James I when he became King of England and Ireland on March 24, 1603). This had nothing to do with the clan but for anyone inclined toward obscure and irrelevant British history, it is a convenient way to remember the exact date when the clan finally ceased its inane attempt to own the BM system. Who knows why they wanted it or what they would have done with it but the pursuit gave them something to argue about and occasionally produced spinoff benefits, such as the invention of the highly addictive dice game, 'Duck'. Duck was invented to use the leftover numbers from the BM System, so 7 and 11 became key dice throws (forerunner to craps) and 5 became the official length of the Duck stick.

In any event, like the reason no one uses entire trees for vertical structural support, no one knows why the 3 bovine brothers built so many rooms, but they weren't wrong because there hasn't been a vacancy for centuries. On the negative side, reflective of the mentally vacant state of these vegetative jerkoffs, all the rooms are boring and suffocating because, except for the shit shoot room in the northeast corner of each floor which for obvious reasons has a window, all the other rooms were windowless cubbies. This, possibly because window glass had not yet been invented, but most likely it was simply a design deficiency resulting from limited intellect. No matter about that now but an excellent time in this stupid story to use a pointless cliché to introduce a profound irony.

Contrary as hell freezing over, it was this conversion of square footage into random cubes and rectangular cuboids, that was to become the source and raison d'être for the only clan politic which exists to this very day: namely, who got a cubby and who had to sleep under the trees and risk getting pissed on by the kids.

[Not wishing to be boring or pedantic or include even more useless information in this accounting but it is important to underscore the pervasive negative contribution MiddleWoss Manor has made to centuries of persistent regression in clan intelligence and the relentless retardation of behavioral

norms. It was a huge, vastly uninspired, chicken barn with 2/3rds of its space filled by 3 massive trees for juvenile habitat and 1/3rd dedicated to random-sized cubbies for the adult asshats. It became the perfect petri dish for generations of vacuous Horrorfish morons in lifetime pursuit of becoming vapid Horrorfish shitheads and vice versa.]

Some of the cubbies on the ground floor, at the back, became kitchens and storages and as poor and ill-fitted a design as that was, it has never changed. The shit shoots were modernized with flushing water in 1551, (45 years before Sir John Harington invented the toilet) and were quite likely the forerunner of the current system for the disposal of human waste. *[The other BM system, but for which, odd as a three-footed goose, the clan did not seek patent when they should have persevered to their advantage].*

Electricity was added in 1988 but only one outlet so they could watch the Jamaican Bobsled Team compete in the Calgary 1988 Olympic Games. The original TV is still in operation in the family room where it broadcasts around-the-clock pornography on channel 12 or BBC3 on channel 24 when some brave child risks slavery with a mad, open floor dash to change the channel.

Needless to say, construction of MiddleWoss consumed a great deal of timber and kept the brothers busy for years, no one knows or cares how many. It was a long time ago, there are no written records, and the brothers were old and despised when they were locked out of their own manor and froze to death. Of course, they didn't actually freeze as their blood-alcohol level would have prohibited that but dead they were and missed by anyone they were not. Especially not by any son or daughter born over their decades of thoughtless fornication.

Notably, since them, every Horrorfish has been born out of wedlock and none have ever expressed a desire to know their *pater or materfamilias*. This disdain of parents by progeny is fully reciprocated by the total lack of care, concern or love from parents. This is most likely because from top to bottom everyone knows the whole family shiteree is in a constant and serious state of degradation and want no blame for their part in it.

[Later on, in 1485, this reciprocal detest was to manifest itself and become both an obstacle and an opportunity for Aineley Horrorfish. This anachronism will be explained after the civil suit of 1342 although there is no connection between the two events so like everything in this story, the order of telling it is irrelevant because the content is complete shit.]

To swiftly conclude and succinctly summarize several hundred years of the astonishing regression which occurred following the hypothermic death of the founding fucktards, the clan concentrated on exploiting the woodlots along with supporting businesses of blackmail, bribery, booze and brothels. As a result of this feudal system and its underlying systemic depravity, MiddleWoss Manor earned a mild reputation for being the English equivalent of Babylon *[remembering this was the Middle Ages so that wasn't much of an accomplishment].*

The High Middle Ages (1100 – 1250) did not, however, come completely without challenge because they came with a lot of church building and this came with priests and like religious hierarchy all of whom condemned everything the Horrorfish stood for and so they should have. But, as is so often true with human nature wanting to go where it doesn't belong, more than a few of these righteous men and their nuns risked their chance at Heaven just to see the trees and experience first-hand what they planned to condemn in next Sunday's sermon. Naturally, taking advantage of this momentary lapse of virtue in favor of curiosity with sins and sinners, the clan profited obscenely as church-building requires a lot of wood and the religious aristocracy were easily blackmailed into paying over the market for Horrorfish timber which was often poorly cut and always short-counted. Even today, at a time when morals are quite relaxed and open in a Horrorfish direction, the clan takes great pride for their part in restraining the one-sided morality of the church before it could push the price of sin out of reach for the average peasant.

[Note on Pride: not a single Horrorfish has ever renounced his/her birthright or the lifestyle (Greed, Lust, Envy, Gluttony, Anger and Sloth) which came with it. More than 1200 years have passed and not one of them has a birth certificate, been married or gone to school or church or taken a driver's test. Nor has a Horrorfish ever held any kind of public office - although several have been hung from public gallows or died in a fight outside the public house and not a month goes by without a whole whack of them celebrating something senseless and ending up in jail together. Twelve centuries and they continue to divide public opinion. Some believe that jailing or hanging a Horrorfish is progress while others believe nothing short of total extermination, like bedbugs, counts.]

By the beginning of the Late Middle Ages (1300 – 1500), the cult was losing its ability to change or adapt to anything because everything was allowed. Clear and obvious to them and long before Darwin plagiarized them, they understood that without change there is neither evolution nor devolution because there is no need for either. They understood their way of life was remarkably resistant because it didn't resist anything. Nor could it. By then, all team sports had been abandoned due to severe interpersonal trust issues so if they had to mount a defense against an outside threat, most likely they would have ended up being responsible for their own genocide. That MiddleWoss was never conquered by Viking, Roman, Anglo Saxon or Germanic hordes is a real mystery but somehow it escaped being burned to the ground with all inhabitants inside. As unfortunate as that may have been then, now it is as good a time as any to explain the civil suit of 1342, a time of great expansion in England.

After the water diversion attempt failed to drive them away, the nearby villages sought another way to rid themselves of the Horrorfish and came up with a new plan. They figured if they could stop, or even severely curtail the clan's income, that would put a damper on their obscene lifestyle and maybe drive the whole perverted collection over a financial cliff, like lemmings. To accomplish this, they took them to court by challenging their woodlot title, or lack thereof, using the Domesday Book as absolute proof they had none then, and deserved none now.

It was the one and only time anyone used legal means to oust the Horrorfish and this resulted in another absurd Horrorfish claim, this time for the right of ownership to the legal principle of Stare Decisis (whereby courts must abide by precedent decisions on similar cases). Once again, who knows why or what they would have done with the ownership of a legal concept but practical details like that seldom enter into the orbit or ambit of Horrorfish thought and do not require speculation here.

Worthy of clarification, however, is that no legal authority has ever recognized so much as an inkling of contribution by Horrorfish v. Crown for this vitally important development in the Due Process of law. The key argument (and it is a moral argument, not a legal one) against attributing any part of Stare Decisis to Horrorfish is the appalling contradiction in logic which it implies. In brief, Common Sense must sustain Common Law and Common Sense dictates that the only recognition a Horrorfish should ever expect from Common Law was a quick trial and a short rope. Nevertheless, and regardless of whether or not the clan was responsible for the invention of this crucial foundation of western civilization, it successfully defended its right to MiddleWoss Manor and all the insanity within.

The reason the prosecution failed is alluded to in the seldom quoted and shamefully candid Obiter Dictum of the presiding Judge and Chancellor, Thomas Grenacre, who many believe to be founding father of the village of Greenhaugh, not too far distant (population 161, 2006 census). Judge Grenacre's dictum cited the intense confusion and conflagration which arose by virtue of clan testimony (the meaning of conflagration has changed over the centuries but essentially it meant then that the evidence was destroyed in conflict whereas today it means that it went up in smoke). Some of the regulars at the Boar's Head reported Grenacre shaking his head and uttering a new, hyphened word, *cluster-fuck*, to describe the testimony and those giving it.

In essence, the clan's sole defense was that 'all this shit' was an accident of fate resulting from hundreds of years of every imaginable human flaw and the complete absence of morals, ethics, standards and the lack of any measurable governance of any sort, manner or kind on individual or collective behaviors. This defense produced a hearty and complicated objection from the Crown Prosecutor which was immediately overruled as 'moot' when centuries of 'all this shit' landed squarely in Judge Grenacre's courtroom as every Horrorfish from young to old showed up like they were going to the circus.

Everyone knew the clan to be notorious liars, especially the young children who constantly invented and then elaborated strange stories of clan behavior which were randomly interspersed among days and days of wild and completely conflicting testimony including 4 rounds of Duck (one of which lasted 6 hours and sent 4 innocent bystanders to hospital). All under oath and all without a single Horrorfish ever once claiming ownership or stewardship of anything which is the whole point of title and the reason for the lawsuit in the first place. It was dim, dumb and daft with every lie, rumor, conspiracy or threat spoken as absolute truth and sworn with both hands on the bible, the first time any of them had ever touched a book. In short, they collectively responded to every charge with conflicting testimonies, contrary accusations, obscure deflection, irrelevant fact, unbelievable fiction and countless outright lies. 'A cesspool of illogic.' was the court reporter's conclusion after more than one Horrorfish left the stand, which had to be nailed down so they wouldn't steal it.

In the end, which couldn't come soon enough for anyone who wasn't a Horrorfish, Judge Grenacre had no choice but to rule that since the Horrorfish had always lived where they always lived and always done what they'd always done, no matter how anybody felt about that, they had precedent right (Stare Decisis) to continue doing it as long as they stayed on their own property or in prison if they got caught trespassing outside. The clan was delighted with this ruling and threatened to expand their domain, but this threat was not executed for the usual reasons.

Needless to say, the verdict was a devastating loss for the Crown and every citizen who owned property within a hundred miles of MiddleWoss but it was one which was neither appealed nor relaunched on new grounds due to the arrival of Black Death in June 1348, in London and everywhere else soon then after. Black Death claimed an astounding toll of every second person in England but not Judge Grenacre who was stabbed to death outside the Boar's Head in an argument with a drunk Viking. *[As if there was any other kind of Viking except a drunk one after their pillaging heyday in the 8th century.]*

Luckily for the clan, in spite of the massive death toll claimed by this pandemic, MiddleWoss Manor was sufficiently isolated by Judge Grenacre's no trespassing rule that it survived cycles of plague with the death of only 1 very stupid child attempting, against all advice, a gravity defying plunge to a much lower limb on the next tree.

Paradoxically and posthumously, it is that tragic event which provides the perfect backdrop for introducing the earliest recorded use of 'Family Tree' which Grenacre so starkly defined as 'Horrorfish inherited traits of gross and belligerent stupidity in pursuit of their own nonexistence'. To elaborate on this observation, his Obiter Dictum cited countless generations of legitimized deceit, perseverant delusion, abject drunkenness, an absurd governance system of no rules/no punishment, the ridiculous invention of combat croquet and the psychotic game of Duck. With that evidence, he concluded the case by granting the Horrorfish eminent domain, a vast elevation over mere title, practically making them a sovereign state. He defended his decision with the incontestable logic that the clan had all these horrible attributes yet were completely immune to the influence of the societies surrounding them even if the opposite was far from true. 'They behave like they are on their own island and should be treated accordingly'.

Furthermore, he made it abundantly clear that the whole pathetic entourage would only retain their eminent domain status with a diligent, unrestrained quest for totalitarian stupidity or self-annihilation, whichever came first. It was a proud moment for the clan but one which was to come with the usual unforeseen consequences.

After generations of lying, cheating, stealing and fornicating with complete abandonment, the concept of leadership became extremely obscure and this obscurity impeded their ability to maintain the absolute minimum of a socio/political structure needed for existence as a society, however inane and disorderly it was. In brief, given the absence of a credible system of rules by which to elect a leader, or a legitimate lineage of descendant-based heredity by which one might conveniently emerge from the birth canal, they had no hierarchy or hope of developing one. Random everything may be loads of fun but, as Darwin was to later postulate, chances are excellent it will lead to random extinction. Realistically, someone had to rule against rulemaking, someone had to get the big room across from the shit shoot room and someone had to impose temporary moratoriums on a long list of divisive disputes like owning the BM system.

In response to this existential threat to their existence, 143 years after the lawsuit, on August 22, 1485, when Henry VII finally won the War of Roses by killing Richard III at the Battle of Bosworth Field, Aineley Horrorfish (distant, distant relative of Aines) remembered Judge Grenacre's Obiter Dictum Re: The Family Tree. It is said this profound inspiration came to him as he laid drunk on the floor staring into the branches where numerous children were waiting until he passed out so they could steal his shoes.

The next morning, a shoeless Aineley proposed that whoever had the most Horrorfish blood in him/her should be the leader of the pack and he set about determining that mathematically. The first Horrorfish, say Aines, was given a factor of 1. His child would be given .5 (unless he procreated with his sister, but he didn't have one). Thereafter it was a matter of assigning fractions which Aineley invented but for which Simon Stevin (a Leiden University dropout) later took credit.

In pursuit of leadership for himself and to show off fractions, he used a very complicated and contradictory set of rules, conditions, allowances and assumptions to calculate 'The Dilution' and proclaimed that whoever had the smallest number on the bottom of the fraction had the least amount off contamination and should become the number 1 leader at the top of fraction. He named this process: 'seeking the lowest common denominator' a term still used today but with a different meaning.

In a sideways gesture of support for idiots proposing ownership for the BM System (remember the Addled Parliament was in 1610 and this is 1485) and complicating Dilution unnecessarily, denominators had to be cleanly divisible by 12. *[Aineley was contemptuous of vague rules unless he made them and couldn't finish a piss before getting trapped in a loop of his own bizarre idiosyncratic thought. Many still consider him to be the only Horrorfish genius ever produced.]*

Regardless, he couldn't trace his roots back to any of the founding fucktards because so many generations had birthed and departed without record, but neither could anybody else. Knowing this and utilizing his advanced understanding of fractions, he created a barely credible history of ancestral incest giving him a Dilution of 1/72. He then challenged everyone to the impossible feat of beating him using his own rules.

Naturally, this didn't impress anybody and being an argumentative bunch of inbred dipshits, criticism came in torrents which he fully expected but to which he astoundingly persevered, eventually triumphing. He did this by admitting to some vagary in his formulas and a few holes and overlaps in his incestry but mostly he succeeded by adding a newly invented process called Selection, to be held every 24 years, (or sooner if the incumbent died). Abdication was prohibited and that remains the only rule Horrorfish have ever consistently allowed which doesn't mean much because nobody has ever tried to abdicate. Why would they?

With the promise of providing an enormously entertaining spectacle of deceit, insult, infight, alternate reality, Duck challenges and all kinds of abnormalities and perversions, Selection was unreservedly adopted as the clan's process for determining leadership and Aineley was forthwith Selected to lead the cult's retreat into this unknown. Three years later he died under mysterious circumstances and the first 'no rules' Selection was held without his annoying, high-pitched voice whining about this rule or that rule like there was a difference or anybody cared when no one did.

That first Selection was an immediate success and since then it has grown in drama, tempo, stupidity and in every way and direction imaginable. It takes 12 months of hard campaigning with no fixed rules except every candidate making them and accusing the opposition of breaking them. All fiscal, social, sexual, legal, illegal and entertainment platforms are allowed with any kind of promise made but none ever kept. Bribes are made openly, voting irregularities are so common there is no regularity, alliances are made with passion, broken with a croquet mallet or a Duck stick and everyone takes sides against everyone else. It is a Roman spectacle with the lions and gladiators being the referees and judges.

With 276 months between Selections in which to recover and think up new campaign strategies, novel ways to cheat, create rumors or uncover incriminating facts to screw or defame the competition, Selection became firmly and unquestionably institutionalized in a society which would immediately condemn a simple agreement if one ever happened. Why the system hasn't been adopted by modern democracies in spite of the fact that so many strategies and irregularities are the same is yet one more Horrorfish contribution to the world which has wisely been ignored.

Obviously, to anyone with half a brain, Selection produces a total shit governance model with an extremely high risk of manipulation and zero chance of accountability, but it is those very qualities which make it uniquely and completely Horrorfish to this very day.

[As promised, just when you think this story can't get any stupider, it does, but sometimes it is hard to recognize a little extra stupidity when it is buried in massive amounts of it so this is just a reminder it won't get any better.]

To conclude and compliment the wisdom of Judge Grenacre's insistence for clan pursuit of totalitarian stupidity, the democratic process of Selection was combined with the hereditary process of Dilution. Naturally, both processes have been systematically degraded and contaminated with every Selection, of which to date there have been 22 but no one cares about that. Truth is, no one can care about that. There is no governing body, no appeal or adjudication because those procedures imply taking sides and everybody lies about everything but especially about whose side they are on.

However, to give credit where it is due, even if occasioned by fluke of his diminished short-term memory, Aineley truly metamorphosed day-to-day life into a full-blown political ideology that gave the clan the direction it sorely needed. Or, as he summarily concluded: 'That which cannot be resolved due to a pathology of mendacious duplicity (lies, damn lies and campaign promises), and that which cannot be prohibited due to the absence of rules, must be acknowledged as the uncontested direction of leadership.'

Which is the essence that makes Selection so exciting. Absolutely anything can happen at any moment and that is the way a successful campaign is waged. Horrorfish do not like to wait for anything. Surprise attacks. Instantaneous Duck challenges. Promises of more, faster. Free beer. Any and every indulgence, right now, with the completely random possibility of being elected and getting the cubby on the second floor next to the shit shoot, the sole benefit of clan leadership with no defined responsibilities.

[The current head of the clan, Lesbian Margethe, stage-managed a brilliant move from 1/512 to 1/60 Dilution in the last 21 days of the 21st Selection and captured the crown, so to speak, because there is no crown. She accomplished this feat by bribing the children with scones, having them tie 21 colorful ribbons to the largest limbs and claiming them to be a sum-combined fraction of her direct descendants resulting in an impossible dilution of 1/24. To counter scorn for this absurd nonsense, she immediately amended her calculation to 1/60 and created the campaign slogan 21 IS THE NUMBER TO WIN including the rare tactic of supporting it with two actual facts. It was the 21st Selection and she was 21. Then, to cement her name-recognition, she got everyone hooked on Blackjack by turning it into a drinking game called Margethe. Anybody who got a Blackjack, yelled 'Margethe' and got a free drink. That pretty much made her an automatic pick on the ballot which she had printed to look like a scratch-and-win lottery ticket.]

Fortunately for Horrorfish and unfortunately for the rest of Britain, Selection was well rooted when the first and only schism to visit the clan landed on its doorstep, a mere hundred years after Aineley was thrown onto the burial mound with his ancestors. True, a hundred years is a long time to blame him for a schism he knew nothing about but Horrorfish time passes differently because so many days are wasted the same way. Point being, nothing requires a leader more than a schism and Dilution and Selection were stark reminders that thanks to Aineley, schisms and leadership were inseparable.

The decades of recurring plague following Selection/ Dilution were a time of constant building and burning of hovels, new churches for the Reformation and England's emergent demand for ships to rule the seas and colonize something before the Dutch got all the good stuff. Altogether, this created strong demand for Horrorfish timber and the clan's diminishing woodlot was being harvested at a furious rate. Even the stupidest Horrorfish intent on pissing away this windfall knew they were running out of the legacy which kept them in pursuit of the lowest common denominator.

A replacement source of income would soon be needed so the clan entered the commercial alcohol business and not just because it was their biggest expense. Alcohol is a highly lucrative trade providing you can control the competition and avoid taxation (which they could on account of eminent domain sovereignty) and of all the stupid things to happen to a clan without any rules to begin with and whose entertainment always started with chugging a boot of lager and 2 shots of Jager, it was alcohol that created the Schism.

This was a real shocker and it happened after Selection 5 under the leadership of someone so stupid no one can remember her name, but this particular halfwit divided the clan into product lines. Wood and Booze. A totally unnecessary and extreme perversion of fractions that almost brought down the whole dynasty from the inside and further demeaned the abject repulsiveness of MiddleWoss Manor when the Boozers built an annex to it.

In the middle of the long wall on the south side of the now old and dirty black, windowless giant hovel, they erected a tall, octagonal, limestone turret with a central spiral staircase surrounded by 12 rooms, 8 floors of them. It was twice as high as the sagging gable roof and no one wanted to live in it due to the inherent danger of ascending or descending the narrow spiral staircase when inebriated or other diminished capacity. Visually, Boozer Tower gave MiddleWoss the appearance of a stubby white erection with two square, black, testicles.

Fortunately, Schism didn't last very long but not due to the halfwit's leadership which caused it but because woodlot operations ceased abruptly in 1558. The reasons for this are not exactly certain as some of the clan's woodlot was still uncut but the date is precisely coincident with Elizabeth I's claim to the throne of England. The morning after Her Majesty's November 17th coronation, the last stand of trees to be felled was left to rot. With that, the boozers became the uncontested and dominant clan force which they relished until Yuletide, a celebratory time of inordinate indulgence at MiddleWoss. Then, without hint or warning of any kind, cohabitation and copulation between groups was restored and the Horrorfish legacy of no rules, no punishments, no excuses and 100% pathological lying was back in full force.

Fittingly, with the end of Schism, Horrorfish society returned to its former glory of chaotic stasis and to recognize this event, the most incompetent and delusional Horrorfish of all time, Ainthe, was Selected, by bribery assisted acclamation. He rewarded the clan with 24 years of gross incompetence, absolute incorrigibility, abysmal ignorance, profane arrogance and terrible personal hygiene that would have got him hung if he was ever sober enough to leave the Manor, which he was not. He was the model leader, the absolute best of the pathetic worst and from him to the present day, almost no change has occurred nor is it expected to occur because clan and cult politic had finally embraced all the absurdity and stupidity possible and that was all of it.

For sure, a lot of shit has happened in the 500 years after Ainthe blew himself up in the still but as mentioned before, MiddleWoss time is reduced in a peculiar fashion. Outside it passed normally but inside was basically the same day and week repeated over-and-over again so while the rest of the world moved into the 20th and 21st centuries, MiddleWoss remained unevolved, like the Galapagos. A real achievement and a remarkable tribute to an absolute shit system of governance which negates not only the rule of law but rules altogether.

And, to compound this unbelievable accomplishment further, not only has the clan survived but it flourishes and continues to do so. People want cheap booze and the clan's extremely popular Abbey Spirits brand is very well established in the basement of that industry. (Clan strategy for producing any kind of success has always depended on the immediate exploitation of a momentary triumph of vice over virtue and Abbey Spirits has never failed to live down to that expectation.)

In truth, the brand is a perfect testament to the scavenger theory of capitalistic survival and the Monk's line of misnamed Digestive as a therapeutic tonic is the often-quoted example of the failure of that system of economics and competition.

Therapeutic it was not, but the clan's love of gin and laudanum, (raw opium) it was. By complete accident of fate, the concoction was introduced just days after the Great Reform Act of 1832 when the riots in Bristol were the worst ever seen. These riots, the closest to civil war ever experienced in England had nothing to do with Monk's Digestive or laudanum which has a very calming effect (until withdrawal occurs). By so-called accident and blamed on a simple spelling mistake, the label asserted the product to be a cure for civil unrest when it should have said colon unrest. With that error and the quick endorsement of parliament who were rightfully nervous about more rioting, Monks Digestive became the opiate for the masses (a term later borrowed by Karl Marx). Years later when laudanum was made a controlled substance and available only by prescription the clan removed the ingredient from the label (but not the bottle).

Lesbian Margethe, is extremely proud to say that other than this minor change which was deemed advisable due to the irrational public fear of highly addictive narcotics, no other material concessions to the outside world have been made. Every now and again a child falls out of a tree but most of the time someone catches it and puts it to work in the kitchen. The system is working perfectly.

She readily admits the clan has slipped in every category used by the International Quality of Life Survey but blames that poor performance on the narrow and biased scale of happiness used by the Survey. The survey fails to recognize the clan's unique position on the spectrum of societal norms where it fits well on both extremes but not at all in the middle.

"And it will never fit in the middle so stop judging it." she says haughtily. "People can be happy with some laws and unhappy with other laws and the clan is extremely happy with no laws. They're just too damn argumentative to acknowledge it." she says proudly.

Anyway, not her problem, it was Selection, and she wasn't running again.

Not that she didn't want to run but she already broke the rule against being Selected twice and she only got away with that by telling everybody the one-time rule (which she made up) was only for men because men only need one chance to royally fuck-up anything. As a result of this clever ploy, she got a lot of male respect which is not easy for a lesbian, and that respect came with the votes she needed to be re-Selected. It was a complete cow move except a real cow is a lot smarter.

She hated the thought of having to sleep in the family room but after almost 46 years of luxury in her cubby on the second floor next to the water-fed, gravity-powered shit shoot, chances of anybody feeling sorry for her and giving up a spot elsewhere were nonexistent, and she knew it.

Her day in the sun had set and nothing short of Armageddon was going to stop Selection from evicting her. The whole lunatic clan was divided into fractions of tards and turds and all of them were primed and pissed to the gills with double-distilled Digestive and the recent acquisition of a suitcase full of premium Mexican peyote buttons. It was going to be down and dirty, the craziest Selection ever and she accidentally provided the extra octane needed to send it over the top. When she figured, after a 63-day binge on Digestive, that if society thought a little bit of laudanum was a bad thing then obviously more was needed. She doubled the quantity, sales took off like a rocket and that created the most dangerous situation any Selection had ever faced. Money in the bank.

Promises were being made like tomorrow would never come and only a Horrorfish knows where that can lead and how to get there.

One of the turds was renewing the pursuit for ownership of the BM system but wasn't telling anybody which one.

A weak-minded, bowlegged tard was promising world domination, starting with the immediate occupation of the roofless 400-year-old ruins known as Black Middens Bastle House, just north of Tarset Burn and maybe had a good idea. Without a proper foundation, Boozer Tower was in danger of falling over, possibly onto the Manor.

Another collection of anarchistic asshats were arguing about rules for a combination 30-day Croquet/Duck tournament.

Children were extremely wary and impossible to catch; the dishes were piling up and if anybody wanted to avoid another round of food poisoning, it was time for a roundup.

Just another day for the idiots and imbeciles of MiddleWoss in their search for a rich vein of un-plundered stupidity.

LIMITATIONS OF THE FUCK-IT PLAN

Jake's dark moments were like all dark moments where there is a gut-wrenching portent of impending death whose sole purpose is to spawn yet more darkness so the moment can go from frightening to depressing to profoundly depressing to pointless and from insanely pointless to suicidal. Nobody wants to think, read or especially write suicidal, but that's where Jake's darkness was taking him.

Without doubt, he regretfully acknowledged, death fit perfectly into the realm of darkness. It was undeniably logical because dark means no light, which means no life. Dark equals dead, period. It doesn't take a lot of words to get that point across and the dot after the word period is both ironically irrational and ridiculously redundant. The end is the end and there are no periods, there are no dots and there is no light after the end

At first, Jake ignored this dark because he could and because when he subscribed to the Fuck-it Plan he thought he was safe from it. Morning, noon and night were the same. Morning, fuck-it. Noon, fuck-it. Night, well, that's when dark happens so fuck that twice. It made perfect sense. Just like not asking questions for which you don't want to know the answer makes sense or the last thing you want when you are begging for death is more pain.

So he ignored the dark closing in on him by rationalizing it as a minor side-effect from his once-in-a-lifetime, no guarantee, no trade-in, no return and no cancellation subscription to the Fuck-it Plan. Once he did that, nothing short of the coming of Jesus Christ Jr. was going to change his mind or convince him that all the meticulously manufactured metaphors about darkness and death were anything more than bullshit existentialism so fuck philosophy on the way out the door.

He accepted there wasn't a choice or a chance of backing out because once he made that momentous decision, when it came to taking sides, evaluating options, or making choices, he was 100% committed to Fuck-it Rule #1. This rule, the only rule in the whole jambouree, owed its existence to the single, over-arching and over-riding principle that after Fuck-it, no other rules were needed. No sides, no exceptions, no dot, no period, no stress, no need for agonizing over this choice or that choice and definitely no need to be vigilant or concerned about anything except Rule #1. It was a complete and beautifully closed system which made his life pleasantly and permanently unaccountable to everyone including himself.

Initially, it was a completely neutral and benign system because taking-no-sides means neutrality but it also eliminated the process and values needed for thought, or more accurately, it resulted in the abandonment of any contentious or difficult thought, or decision, along with the concomitant defense of the adverse consequences which might arise from it. A double win. The Fuck-it Plan automatically provided impenetrable cerebral armor against wasting time or energy on subjects that have sides to them, which is most of them. So easy, and the little bit of dark which came along for the ride went away if he ignored it long enough. It was a virtually perfect plan although there were a few limitations, like dark, which are immune to Fuck-it, but he didn't see that in the beginning.

From the moment of sign-up, it was an extremely convenient, low cost, universal solution for dealing with life's issues and predicaments, which Jake already had more than he wanted, which was none. The Fuck-it Plan provided a complete defense that any logical person would ever need for anything with just one simple rule and, better yet, it didn't matter when he used it so he used it a lot. After all, sooner or later everything blows up so why wait until it does and go down with that ship? One well-placed Fuck-it and he was done, dusted and ready for whatever came next. Nothing wrong with that, maybe a little content-lite on account of real-life experiences being cut short, but so what? Something always comes next, why stress about a little missing content when next replaces it anyway?

As a result of that thinking and the constant and frequently premature application of Rule #1, the Fuck-it Plan became Jake's complete, only and highly efficient alternative to any spiritual, intellectual, philosophical, ethical, moral, mindful, political, sociological, scientific, religious, psychological, you-name-it system for life and living including all the knowledge, beliefs, skills and especially governance which came with those systems. There simply wasn't a competing methodology or ideology which stood even a remote chance against the easy to use, always available, no-questions-asked, equal opportunity Fuck-it. Morning, noon or night, on trains, at rock concerts or funerals with friends, family or complete strangers, if you didn't get the desired results with the first Fuck-it, simply repeat. Eventually they either figured it out or they went away. It always worked. Maybe not exactly good for long term relationships and maybe a little extra dark got through on account of that, but a relatively small price to pay considering all the bullshit and baggage avoided.

Unfortunately, and exactly like dark was unforeseen, the failure to make meaningful and sensible life and lifestyle choices came with some unintended and unavoidable consequences to Jake's emotional well-being. This side effect gradually manifested itself in unpredictable emotional turmoil and irrational outbursts due to normal feelings and emotions not being completely felt or fully experienced before being killed off by a random Fuck-it. Without consummating and then logically internalizing real-life experiences, his emotions, sentiments and passions got all mixed-up with a ton of resentment and frustration which then escaped at inconvenient and sometimes inappropriate times.

A necessary evil, he figured, and an outcome which, ironically, was when Fuck-it was needed the most. Sometimes several of them before the problem went away but who's counting? Seriously, what wrong to anyone, anywhere or anytime did one Fuck-it ever make so no point in being stingy with them.

Accordingly, after an unlimited number of Fuck-its, his emotional conflicts were temporarily shelved but after a few years of unsatisfied and undifferentiated emotional states which were not attached or confirmed by any kind of shared reality with anyone, he couldn't smile or interact socially without looking and behaving like a fool if he was lucky and some kind of undiagnosed mental deviant if he wasn't. The Fuck-it Plan made him so completely insincere he couldn't even fake a feeling so eventually he just looked down at his shoes like a guilty child and twisted his lips into the best rendition of a smile or a frown he could manage and which even he knew looked absolutely hideous.

But he had to suck that up and acknowledge that the Fuck-it Plan didn't work perfectly all the time, or every time, or even on time, so looking hideous now and again had to be accepted because overall there wasn't anything he could do about it.

Nor did he want to, so he stoically accepted the inconvenience which he reasoned to be the causal force of the Fuck-it Plan in the first place. Obviously, Fuck-it made just as much sense when it worked as when it didn't and because absolutely nothing ever works all the time, Fuck-it saved a lot of time, energy and unnecessary thought otherwise wasted on figuring out what worked, what didn't and why it did or didn't. A little more dark crept in there but just like so many plans that don't work out exactly as expected, or stay worked out when they do, nothing is always light and bright forever so why fault the system when it's working perfectly as designed? Seriously, if that isn't just the perfect time for a massive unconditional Fuck-it, then when is?

All things ill-considered or ignored, Jake's emotional mayhem eventually became an obsolete side effect and in spite of the Fuck-It Plan turning him into a shallow and untrustworthy person who was often rejected and shunned, Jake remained a staunch advocate and didn't consider himself any worse off because of it. He accepted his isolation and embraced his hideousness with pride and the idiom that appearances are deceiving at the best of times and especially at the worst of times, which eventually happens to everyone. No one escapes ageing and nothing condemns appearance more than having birthdays so the whole issue was about timing, not process, so Fuck-it. With that defense, every rejection or insult simply put him ahead of the curve because sooner or later everybody gets old, isolated and unattractive so no sense in blaming the Fuck-it Plan for the relentless march of time that it was never designed to counter or fix in the first place.

Furthermore, it wasn't his fault or responsibility what anyone else felt or thought about him or his actions. Absolutely not his problem and obviously no need for guilt because if they weren't doing what he was doing to keep their life from going into the crapper or getting strangled by someone else's problems or emotions, well, they should have been so Fuck-it, good lesson and they should thank him for it.

And he wasn't above telling them that. If somebody objected to his behavior or his attitude, he judged their actions as either beneath him or worthy of a distained rebuttal. Then he told them straight up and in detail that it was his right to

Fuck-it just like it was their choice to suffer stupidity and be ignorant for the rest of their lives.

That was extremely satisfying so with time and practice, he excelled in reducing whole arguments to tried-and-true clichés and platitudes. Then he twisted definitions, diminished content and impugned the character of language so as to render every principle into meaninglessness with the supreme and unconquerable arrogance that came with the Fuck-it Plan. Ultimately, and he always proved it, there wasn't a solid reason for anything because whatever the opposite of that anything was, somebody was doing or believing it and that justified the existence of everything in general and defended the existence of nothing in particular. No one can fight facts like that.

Then, as happened with his emotional implosion, he found out the hard way that there were unexpected consequences with the demolition of language and logic. The more he excelled at the deconstruction of ideas and thoughts, the more his understanding of life and his ability to live it in any kind of orderly manner fell apart, and that's when dark stopped being noir or goth or the Warlock he wanted to be. That's when he began to understand the Limitations of the Fuck-it Plan because he couldn't go backwards or forwards and not just because of Rule #1. Those choices were eliminated by his own deconstruction and there wasn't a Fuck-it for that. Eventually he realized, he had to accept responsibility for the choices he didn't make as well as the ones he did and that put him at the bottom of deep well where he experienced Dark for the first time in his life.

This Dark became a trap, an implement of torture, and there wasn't an escape because after years and years of using and abusing Fuck-it in order to build defenses that were clever and strong enough to destroy everything outside, he inadvertently forgot about being inside. Argument by argument, principle-by-principle, belief-after-belief, he cut off all the light and the avenues for his own escape by ignoring, denying, refuting, condemning or failing to acknowledge any sides or choices to everything through thousands and thousands of Fuck-its. Vulnerability has its faults but so too does invulnerability and after years of zealous commitment to Rule #1, Jake was certifiably invulnerable. He was impervious to intercession, impenetrable to alternatives, immune to logic and without compassion of any kind. Excellent qualities for a trap, unless you are in it.

Clearly, what he needed to escape the Dark in the well which became his life was something far above and beyond the simplistic liturgy of Rule #1. He knew it wouldn't be easy, perhaps not even possible to undo what he had done, and not done. He was ready to give up when it occurred to him that if the thoughtless application of free will and the complete abandonment of conscious choice got him into Dark, then maybe a supreme Fuck-it of Deniability would get him out. In other words, double-down on the Fuck-its which he did, but that only deepened the well until he finally accepted that the cause could not become the cure.

Obviously, another approach was needed and he knew better than anyone that a hole is also a well if you want to call it that so instead of thinking Dark and dark, he searched for an escape word and lightlessness came to mind because it put a nice positive spin on what he was trying to eradicate by any means possible. But that didn't last very long before he had to admit he was jousting with a made-up-word, just playing a dictionary game of definitions he had long ago reduced to meaninglessness. He had no option but to face defeat by his own arguments and decided not to waste any more time making up new words but to remember lightlessness as a reminder that words were not only malleable and fallible but also useless. They were useless for getting him out of the trap he built with them just like adding more concrete doesn't get you out of a concrete coffin. And they were just as useless for getting help. Whenever he explained the hopelessness of his situation all he received in return was a look of resignation and a wave goodbye. Only he could un-dream his nightmare; he had to get out of it himself.

With words being taken off the anvil for forging an escape from his ever-deepening well, Jake hoped he could still use them for thinking up a good idea because for sure his emotions weren't going to help him. So he thought harder than he had ever thought which still wasn't very useful because he had become quite incompetent with the practice of identifying alternatives and resolving contradictions in order to find a solution which didn't end with a Fuck-it.

Using his simplistic reasoning, eventually he concluded that a viable solution required evidence that the presence of dark and the absence of light were two different things. If he could do that, then a Dark thought might be changed back into a dark thought, one which has light on the other side of it, like day and night. Then life would begin to flourish again.

Flourish meaning his life would be worth living and Fuck-it wouldn't be needed except perhaps for special occasions. For sure, this was a very simple solution to a really complicated problem but after all, he reasoned, if thought made Dark then more thought should be able to turn it back into dark.

Jake truly hoped that contrarian logic would produce an answer to the riddle burrowing in his brain and he thoroughly explored his entire universe of self-deception before finally admitting that either it didn't work, or his brain was hardwired to the Fuck-it Plan. Every attempt to think Light attracted one Dark hole after another, each one deeper and darker than the one before until there were holes everywhere and what was keeping them apart was a huge mystery, but one for which he didn't have the time, or the inclination, or the ability, to understand. Which was when Dark became DARK.

With such hopelessness now accompanying every waking thought, he decided to stop saying Fuck-it aloud or in his mind because, he more or less accepted by now, Rule #1 had to be at least partly responsible for the dark holes everywhere. But to do that, he had to eliminate all the people in his life because they were the cause of so many Fuck-its.

With no other choices available, Jake retreated deeper into the well he dug into the middle of his barren consciousness. He did this in spite of the fact that he was running away from the light and the people in it but the Fuck-it road was impossible to un-plow with them on it. Maybe when he got DARK back to being Dark, or for sure when he got it back to just plain dark then some people could come back.

That was a big maybe plus it was also using words which he knew were not only useless but also consuming what little light he had left, and which was also in constant danger of being sucked into an enormous and powerful Black Hole where nothing could escape its immense gravitational pull, not a single photon. Truly the worst-case scenario at the bottom of his ever-deepening well.

But he could still think, and he was pretty sure that thoughts were not subject to gravity, so he kept thinking and believing that as long as he could work the problem, he still had a chance even if words had to be his medium. A bright thought was his only hope for getting some light into his well and if that failed, he wasn't sure what to do next.

This was a truly ugly consequence which was starting to look very probable and even more troublesome than DARK had become. After all, if he couldn't use words to think he was doomed because thoughts need words including next coming around the corner which he had taken for granted for too long. If the Black Hole got next, then being doomed had to be right after that and that would be a real fucker of an ending to this paradox. Even though Jake knew he wasn't thinking very well and was scared shitless by what his own brain might think next, he had no alternative except keep focused on making light.

So, he reasoned that while photons were subject to gravity on account of their velocity and could therefore be sucked into a Black Hole, thoughts had no mass or velocity and couldn't be seen so they couldn't be sucked into a Black Hole. Therefore, thoughts using words should be safe, which protected next. That made complete sense, for now.

For now. Time was also a major concern. If all the Black Holes combined like the DARK was combining, then everything including the end of time would be sucked into one huge DARK MATTER BLACK HOLE until another big bang occurred. That was something which had probably happened many times before and explained why time didn't have a start or end date, it was just a loop of Big Bangs, but luckily, he heard somewhere, that was not on the verge of happening any time soon. The universe was expanding and that meant there were still plenty of photons from trillions of stars available if only he could capture enough of them for some flourishment.

It was a damn good scientific postulant with great potential except Jake had disagreed with every scientific principle on account of the Fuck-it Plan so he was a longways away from figuring out how to capture light, even a single photon of it. He needed deep, reasoned, scientific thought in order to extend his postulant into theorem and from there into practicum. Except he didn't have deep, he didn't even have very much shallow in spite of the fact he'd spent a lifetime wallowing in it.

All he had was a boatload of simple and not all of that was reliable so he decided to start with the absolute minimum science which he knew for sure to be true and maybe that would lead somewhere. He identified the smallest thing he knew to be matter and applied that to the largest maximum available field of mass. If he could get that right, chances were good he'd catch the truth somewhere in the middle of those extremes and that would either be the source of light or set him on the way to it.

Hydrogen.

1. Atomic Number 1 and 75% of the baryonic mass of an expanding universe with all its billions of galaxies and mega-trillions of stars and planets. (Enormous)

2. A single, spinning, negatively charged electron bound to a nucleus of a positively charged proton by the Coulomb force and forever orbiting that nucleus with a relationally-equivalent galaxy of distance and time between them for a lone gamma ray to flash through on its random trajectory across a vast, vast sky of black celestial space. (Tiny).

3. Dammit. Jake found the original Fuck-it Plan.

No one could really blame the boys for digging where they did. After all, nobody had been buried in that cemetery for a long time and they were digging far from gravestones and into prairie grassland that had never been turned. Or so everyone thought, until they found what they found.

At first glance the cemetery wasn't much different from any other abandoned prairie boneyard, of which there are a lot more than most people think. History-wise, it made sense to have so many graveyards because back in the old days, and most of them weren't good old days, especially before the railroad came through, folks wanted to be buried next to loved ones where they might be remembered on special occasions so every town, no matter how small or poor, had its own boneyard, most often attached to a church, which this one once was.

Also history-wise, if you know how to read the names and dates and sentiments on the crypts, crosses, markers and headstones, sometimes a cemetery is the only place you will find it recorded. A common date on a single headstone for a whole family might just be the only reminder of a disease, disaster or massacre that today would be photographed and recorded where it could never be forgotten. No doubt about it, the graveyard endures long after the births, deaths and marriages in the family bible are abandoned with its words or eroded by the vicissitudes of time.

Naturally, not everyone sharing dirt is family; strangers got buried along with kin and kind too. Too on account of too far from home, too bad or too late to ask forgiveness and get back in time to be buried beside the loved ones with whom they were feuding. In some cemeteries, strangers were put in a low spot or in the tangle of roots under a big tree but in conservative Orthodox cemeteries like the one the boys were digging in, strangers were given ground specifically reserved for eternal fellowship and communion with those of their own kind. Families, town folk, and especially the faithful, they had their own real estate. At least most conservative Orthodox cemeteries were like that but, as the town discovered, a graveyard full of strangers wasn't the only thing no one thought about before the boys dug up what they dug up.

Still and all, to be fair and honest about bygone burying practices, while segregating strangers may not sound right as far as equality and discrimination is concerned today, there's no sense getting upset about that because at the time it was perfectly acceptable, only a little different from now. And, just to even out the appearance of judgement and prejudice a little bit more, some of those strangers were family and good folk. They were just unlucky enough to die in someone else's town but their earthly remains were respected enough to be given a proper burial even if the surrounding company wasn't family or the view wasn't so nice.

Anyway, point is, regardless of burial practices or whether Christian, Orthodox, Hindu or heathen, in a church cemetery or in a public graveyard on the edge of town the graves of strangers are easy to recognize by what is on their marker, but especially by what is missing from it. Some have a first and a last name, but others have just a single first or last name. Very few have an age, if they celebrated a birthday before that clock stopped running, and most have the year they were buried, all of which adds up to being a stranger long enough for somebody to wish them good morning but nothing more worthy of their life to record at the time of their death. Just another person who was passing through town but who didn't finish the passing part the way they planned.

Of course, in the interests of complete honesty, there is also another factor to consider and one that no town is proud of but worth mentioning because it is true as often as it isn't. Fact is, some of those strangers were as unworthy as they were unwelcome. In the days before a town needed or could afford a Sheriff to keep the peace, it wasn't at all unusual for the burial year to be the only thing written on a marker. People got killed for various reasons and no point advertising that to relatives who might come looking for them and be tempted into revenge.

Except a violent and untimely death isn't the only reason for only a year to be scratched on a stone. Some qualities and characteristics of strangers haven't changed over time. Just like today, some folks, good and bad alike, had their reasons to disappear and use a made-up name or somebody else's name, so no point in confusing the past or upsetting relatives with something that might not be true. Absent any real identification or a trustworthy witness, a marker to show the year the earth reclaimed its resident was more than enough recognition for those who didn't want any to begin with and that is the other thing graveyards do besides keep history. They keep secrets.

Like the stranger the boys dug into; the one doing his eternity without a name, a date, a sentiment, a marker and as it turned out, more secrets than all the dead buried around him combined. He was planted in prairie dirt with absolutely no evidence left as testament to a short life above ground and now more than a hundred years returning to the dust from whence he came. All the trivial facts of his existence were in full and final decomposition until the boys put a shovel into his chest and found a man buried in a hole like a dog. Well, maybe not exactly like a dog but in an anonymous grave completely alone at the very edge of consecrated ground where it would never be disturbed and that raised some questions, created some uncertainties and ignited a lot of curiosity.

Curiosity which some folks called a revelation, others eventually labelled a resurrection and a few figured was nothing more than the past coming back to haunt the present like a bad curse but once the facts of this stranger became known, everyone agreed that planting a shovel in his chest was a tiny mistake compared to feeding the curiosity that came up with his bones. Putting the whole works back in the hole and forgetting about it like a forgiven sin would have been the smart thing to do but sometimes people get as greedy with their curiosity as they do with their money so that didn't happen.

No sir, or ma'am, before the boys uncovered him, his resting place was forgotten in time and abandoned in history and not just because the cemetery was in the middle of nowhere or because some of its residents were Russian settlers and nobody understood their alphabet. Those weren't satisfactory reasons or logical explanations and once folks started thinking about what they didn't know, they wanted facts and not supposition or imagination to get past their fears.

But not facts like the Cyrillic writing on Orthodox crosses which still bore names like Petr Ruchechnik, Radivil Osesovich and Lula Lutochna because that was just a reminder these people were abandoned and forgotten by everyone in past and modern history. That was just one part of the mystery which got people wondering about things they never wondered about before and worrying about what else they might be missing.

Towns come and towns go but cemeteries don't and the fact there wasn't a single common name on any of the 32 headstones, crosses or markers in this one was a genuine curiosity. Boneyards without a single husband and wife, a set of brothers beside each other or a mother and child buried in the same grave are almost impossible to find. Even a prison graveyard has relatives so a boneyard full of strangers is enough of an oddity to spawn a lot of dark speculation. There was more.

The oldest of the strangers rested below a stone marker with, for one of the reasons explained above, just a year scratched onto it: 1856. The last person committed to the earth was beneath an upright, orthodox cross which was carefully cut from a piece of hard prairie sandstone and it belonged to:

Lula Lutochna,

An Angel Reborn

17 Years, 3 Months

1865

That meant the graveyard was active for 9 years, which is a pretty short lifetime for a boneyard and that was mildly curious whereas being in the middle of the prairie wasn't a curiosity at all until people asked themselves why they never really thought about who put it there so thoughtfully and then abandoned it so completely that it took two small boys digging in it to bring it back to life, so to speak. That was another minor detail which got folks thinking maybe they should have been curious about those questions before and wondering if there was a good reason, or most likely a not-so-good reason, why they hadn't thought about a graveyard full of strangers abandoned so methodically and secretly there wasn't a single living memory left to explain it.

Six of the residents had simple Christian crosses with English writing on them. The names on three of the crosses could still be read: Hadensack, 1862, Mary Hopper 1863 and Rodensteen, his date of commitment not recorded. Maybe he froze to death while passing through the township and his remains were found scattered on the prairie, and nobody knew for certain the year to put on his cross. Or maybe nobody knew any other detail of his life so the year he died didn't matter to those who buried him just like it didn't matter to him.

Regardless of those details, or lack of them, the strangers could have been religions of any kind but no matter or concern for that, whoever buried them, buried them Christian, not Orthodox. Four others like them had flat stone markers like the resident under 1856. Their names were thinly scratched and all but erased over the next a hundred years. The remainder rested beneath Orthodox crosses, or with Orthodox crosses on their marker but if any were family it was only because they prayed together as a congregation and were now spending eternity with those prayers.

The only trace of the church which once held the cemetery in its shadow was the river rock footprint of its foundation. A foundation that bore no sign of being scorched by its own embers as penance for standing stubbornly in the way of the wind-whipped prairie fire which was feared even more than winters so cold they froze everything but the bison and the devil. Nothing else was left of God's house, not a sliver of timber, a shard of glass or a bent nail, just like there wasn't a page written or a memory passed down to explain why or how a righteous, God-fearing Orthodox church vanished so mysteriously and so completely that it left only the foundation and its dead as evidence it ever existed.

For sure, the destruction was not an act of God. The order and cleanliness of it was not the result of one of His disasters, no doubt about that. Only people destroy so neatly and with such precision and the reasons behind anyone doing that added even more oxygen to the curiosity unearthed with a body buried anonymously in a graveyard of 32 strangers. In the end, folks had no choice but to believe all these questions were related and that maybe the truth was even worse than what they imagined.

Just a little over a hundred years in the past and no one had a single fact about a church being raised from its foundation and its memory exorcised from consciousness, which are hard things to accomplish together. A hundred years is not much time as far as churches go or as far as memories go either. Homesteads, by comparison, appeared overnight and disappeared just about as quickly and lots of those stories were still active in the collective memory of the community and its descendants. So how does a church appear out of nowhere only to vanish into thin air and if that doesn't challenge belief and persecute the faith behind it, then what does? Prairie farming doesn't but it should.

Surviving the northern prairie takes guts and faith and not of the kind or in the quantity that prays for survival in a tent or a barn, so churches were sometimes built even before the faithful knew if they would survive to spring. For sure, some churches were abandoned the same way as whole hamlets and villages just up and quit or were driven away. Even the most stubborn of farmers can be broken by years of hardship, starvation and the constant fear of massacre. But abandonment is different than wiped clean off the surface of the prairie, which nobody thought about until the boys dug up what they dug up and then people started asking questions about who would tear down their church so completely and abandon their dead so shamefully.

To the believer, leaving that river rock foundation, which would only have taken a day or two to break up and return to the creek bed from which it was taken, was viewed as an article of faith not yet lost. A way of keeping hope alive that eventually someone would rebuild the church and tend to the dead as if they were their own. To a skeptic, leaving it was a warning never to build anything on that ground again. At least that's what some people thought and then believer, skeptic or otherwise, no one really knew what to think, which is the ripe and fertile ground for the kind of speculation that keeps curiosity alive and growing.

The boys started digging on the morning side of a densely thick hedgerow of Siberian Caragana, one of the few non-native plants hardy enough to survive the heat, cold, drought, fire, flood, insects, beasts and other general threats to life on the northern prairie. Over the next 100 years it became a tall, thick tangle of brush and bush that encroached the cemetery on 3 sides and hid the boys from the road, not that being hidden mattered. The road wasn't much more than a back-country dirt path to some nearby fields and hardly anyone was ever on it. Even if somebody came by they wouldn't have cared anyway. There might be something wrong with digging in a cemetery if you are taking something out of it but there's nothing wrong with just digging a hole in abandoned land, which is how everybody thought about that cemetery until then. So, nothing at all wrong with what they were doing until they discovered what they discovered but that's exactly where Chief started his interrogation because he liked to start his questioning around the edges and sometimes even completely off-track. He was friendly-like because at that moment making the boys fearful of the badge on his chest wasn't in his best interest.

"Why were you boys digging that hole?" The questions about what they dug up could wait; he'd get to those in due course. It was his way and even the boys knew he would take his time. They knew that when they fetched him, just like they knew nobody ever outsmarted Chief for very long even if that was exactly what they were planning to do.

"We was just digging." answered Jimmy Wiser.

"Looking for arrowheads." added Ronny Becker.

"Uh huh." Chief responded but didn't nod his agreement. He wasn't expecting the truth but he expected a better lie than digging for arrowheads.

Jimmy and Ronny weren't bad boys, but they were both 13 and at that moment they were trying to look like 9 which was the last time they could tell lies that dumb and fake enough innocence to maybe get away with them. They might have fooled some folks but Chief had been the law in Grinrod County for so long everybody called him that, just Chief, and not much fooled him.

Hardly anybody knew his full Christian name but he knew theirs and their children and their grandchildren, just like he knew innocence the second he saw it. Fact was, it was the first thing he looked for, even before he thought about circumstance or motive or opportunity or anything investigatory and that was a good way to keep community relations, so he kept doing it and kept getting re-appointed to his job. Innocent people appreciated having their innocence recognized right-off-the-bat so he always started slow and looked for it until he couldn't find it. Then he would change his tack and use his slow, roundabout questioning in a way that gave the suspect plenty of opportunity to practice their story and build up their confidence. When he got enough story, and they got enough confidence, he'd go hard at something in the middle of their pack of lies until he found a crack which he'd needle at and worry loose and split apart until he got a real good conflict with the facts. It didn't have to be anything important it didn't even have to be related to the crime, but once he started winning and they started losing, the truth was never far away and Chief ran it into the ground like it was wounded prey.

It was his way but he didn't tell anyone why he did it any more than he told them he knew guilt and innocence were nothing more than two sides of a coin spinning in the air with nobody ever always innocent or always guilty at any time or all the time. More than one person got away with their misdemeanor because they were good most of the time and not generally mal-intentioned and Chief believed they learned their lesson. He could dispense that judgement without a twinge of conscience that he wasn't upholding the law to the letter like he was paid to because he believed his discretionary powers were in everybody's best interest. Fact was, he had a much harder time accepting the same latitude when the judge failed to deliver just punishment. In that case, light sentences were encouragement, not deterrence, and 99 times out of 100, those were the ones to reoffend and a little prison time just made them harder to catch and convict.

He knew the boys weren't telling the truth, but he was just getting started, so at the moment, the truth wasn't as important as the fact they weren't telling it. They needed a slow, nervous lesson in what happens to boys who decide to lie to the law, so he helped them get their web of deceit started.

"Find some?"

"Naw." answered Ronny so Jimmy shook his head. So far it was going good, they fetched him when they should have and Chief wasn't blaming them for what they dug up.

"Think maybe you was digging too deep?"

It was either a real good question or a real good trick question but either way the boys had worked out a plan for that in advance, which included not looking at each other when they answered because that was how their parents knew they were making up lies on the spot. "We was looking for old ones. Deep buried 'heads." said Jimmy.

"And maybe a spear point too, cause they're heavy, you know." Ronny added just like he and Jimmy and gravity had agreed all along. That was the plan, whatever the first guy said, the second guy backed up and made it into his story. No fighting over an answer, good or bad, true or not, stick to one story, like glue. Fighting over details would only result in a winner and a loser and if they got separated like that then pretty soon both of them would be up to their eyeballs in explanations and not just to Chief.

Chief knew their plan, just like he knew the boys were hiding something because you don't need a plan for telling the truth. He decided to play along and see how much innocence they could fake. "So who has the best collection?"

Jimmy forgot the plan and looked at Ronny but Ronny didn't so he looked at something over Chief's shoulder and said quickly: "We was just starting."

"Yeah, just starting." confirmed Jimmy positively, happy with that and reminding himself to work it into his next answer or use it again if he got stuck with a question he couldn't answer.

"So you decided to start digging here?" Chief asked in a no-account voice to neither boy so both of them shrugged and nodded and looked around at other places they maybe should have started and hoped Chief was still buying their lie but getting plenty nervous that maybe he found a loophole somewhere. What they didn't know was that Chief didn't really care what they were burying or the lie they were trying to bury with it; he just cared about what they found. Boys their age were always burying something, sometimes to get rid of it and sometimes just to keep it safe for a while. If it had been night then digging in an abandoned cemetery would have been on a dare. For sure it had nothing to do with a troublesome behavior because that would have been digging in a grave, not finding one by accident.

Ironic. In the process of trying to hide something, they found something that had been hidden for a hundred years and was now so close to the invasive caragana that in another 10 or 15 years it would have grown over the grave and stopped anybody from discovering it until after the next ice age swept the prairie clean again.

Chief dusted the irony out of his thinking, most crimes had some irony to them and as far as he was concerned finding a skeleton while pretending to look for arrowheads was about the only irony to this crime. Assuming there was a crime to begin with, an assumption he figured was about as likely as sunset but for sure the boys were innocent of it. They didn't put the bones in the hole and what they were planning on putting into it was on the side of the coin he wasn't there to investigate.

"So, what did you find first?" Chief asked and the boys were relieved that the questioning got on the topic of digging and away from burying.

"The gun." replied Jimmy.

"Then the cross." explained Ronny, "gun on top." he added quickly, like it would have been wrong to keep digging if they found the cross first and wanted Chief to know he wasn't raised like that.

"Some bones was sticking out but we didn't see 'em at first 'cause they're all brown, like roots. But we stopped digging after that. After that, we stopped 'cause we didn't know what to do *with this* but you would know so we fetched you." Jimmy pointed at the cross in the hole and emphasized '*with this*' to keep Chief on track with the discovery and not the reason for it.

Based on the excavation, which was small, 2 feet square and about half that deep, Chief knew he was hearing the truth, or at least the part of it he cared to hear about. The sod had been removed in one neat piece and cut at an angle so when it was replaced it would sit right back down in the hole like a plug. Done like that and after the next decent rain, all traces of the hole would disappear for another hundred years. The plug was sitting sod side up on a tarp with the dirt from the hole piled neatly beside it. Whatever the boys were going to bury had left its impression on the grass beside the tarp. Square shaped, smaller than the hole, it was either an animal getting a loving burial or maybe something the boys would dig up later, providing they had a way of remembering exactly where they buried it. No matter, innocent on the first count and nobody's business on the second.

Chief examined the gun in his hand. It was only a gun because a couple of inches of barrel stuck out of the hard-packed conglomerate of rust, dirt and clay that had grown over the weapon after decades of rain, drought, snow and more freeze than any prairie farmer will ever confess to outside of church.

The cross which the boys were respectful of, maybe fearful of, was still stuck in the hole, partially covered but glittering gold where the dirt had fallen or been knocked from it. The thick gold chain attached behind the cross was held captive by undisturbed ground and was likely wound around the neck bones of the person buried with it. The cross, part of an amulet, rested on caved-in ribs and looked like maybe a hand was once underneath or maybe holding it, the ground was too disturbed to know which. Against the side of the hole were a couple of bones which had been broken by the shovel as it exposed the Cross of Christ to the first sunlight to shine on it in more than a century.

Chief put the gun on top of the sod plug and got down on his hands and knees for a closer inspection, starting with the amulet. He took a good long look at the red glow of ruby at the center and the bright sparkle from the diamonds radiating from the spokes behind the Orthodox cross. He picked it up the few inches which the captive chain would allow, blew some dirt off and examined it for a minute or two, finding it hard to tear himself away from the lure of his own curiosity with an artifact he was certain had to be a lot older than the bones buried with it. He put one hand on virgin prairie grass and bent over for a close look around the hole. He finished his examination then made a small depression and put the cross into it.

When he took his eyes away from the amulet and got to his feet, his first free thought was that robbery wasn't the motive for this murder, if indeed it was murder. His second free thought told him it was definitely a murder. His summary thought was wondering who could bury such a beautiful piece and when that question drove him to examine his own motives, he knew with absolute certainty he couldn't have done it.

Not only *wouldn't* have done it, but *couldn't* have done it. It was a simple realization that first intrigued and then concerned him, and it seemed to come from a part of him that was as buried and foreign as the amulet which produced it. Like ethereal or mystical, which was unusual for him because he was a practical and direct man. Strange but acceptable because there wasn't choice with that. It was an odd sensation and he figured it would likely stay with him because all too often an investigation ended up with the same feeling with which it started. Feelings of revulsion or disgust at the outset of an investigation always portended horrific, inhuman crimes, just as sad and pathetic feelings always ended with tears and remorse for the guilty and the innocent alike. The only feeling he really approved, if approved was the right word, came with crimes of revenge because they ended in revenge and he was the official instrument of that vengeance.

He stood up, picked up the weapon in one hand then put his other hand in his pocket. For a full minute, he stood like a statue in reflection of the moment and the thoughts he had and the details he observed. It was another of his methods, he interwove his personal thoughts with the crime scene in a memorable tapestry so he never forgot, and could easily find, even the smallest detail.

"Dig him up, Jesper." he said to the short, slightly pudgy man standing off to the side. "I'll see you in the morning."

"Do we get the gold thing? Finders-keepers?" asked Ronny.

"Maybe but probably not." answered Chief.

"How about the gun?" Jimmy chimed in.

"Nope."

"How come?" asked Ronnie.

He looked at the boys for a few seconds, long enough to give them a life-long message about who asks the questions when Chief is in the conversation.

"Cause it ain't no arrowhead." and the boys knew better than to argue with their own lie because Chief was just a minute away from the truth, and they both knew it.

He waited and watched them until they figured out the next part, which they did when they hung their heads and couldn't look at him. Next time, they'd tell the truth because now they were stuck with arrowheads for a lie and Chief wouldn't let them forget that, ever.

★ ★ ★ ★ ★

When it came to John Doe #58, Jesper realized he had a first on his table. For a change, exhuming the body was not at all unpleasant, laying out the bones for examination was textbook simple and the cause of death was determined the moment he cleaned the skull with its neat .45inch hole in the center of the forehead and the absence of most of the posterior cranial fossa on the exit side of the bullet. After that he extracted the easy information which the skeleton gave up to his practiced eye and forensic acumen: male, 45-55 years old, dead for a helluva long time which might as well start with the patent date on the Colt Dragoon buried with him. That was the earliest date that the murder could have been committed with that weapon and Jesper figured it should be good enough for Chief to do whatever he wanted to do with John Doe #58 because what difference does 10 or 20 years make to the time of death when you've already been dead for more than 100? Then, hopefully, that would be it. Just a quick, quiet reinterment because almost anything Jesper had to do, especially the fishing trip he had planned with his granddaughter, was better than getting tangled up in tests and arguments over the time of death of a 100-year-old cranium with a hole on both sides of it. That wouldn't prove anything to anybody or mean anything to anyone regardless of true, false or undecided.

The body had been clothed when it was put in the shallow grave, but what remained of the cloth turned to dirt when he touched it and he had to do that in order to exhume. A couple of patches of it survived, more or less, and mostly because they were held together by gold thread, the real stuff, in a design which might once have been some kind of an emblem or a crest but that was just a guess because the wool was so badly deteriorated even with the gold thread holding it together none of it would survive straightening.

The amulet was another matter. Covered in dirt, it was one-in-a-hundred-years spectacular. Clean, it was awesome, in the true dictionary meaning of the word. It radiated fire and brimstone.

Made of rubies and diamonds, it was a work of art and endurance. The gold which framed it was more than thick enough to secure the gems but didn't over-power them, the creative legacy of a master goldsmith. Gold spokes radiated from behind the dimple-hammered gold orthodox cross like rays of the sun. Those spokes rested on the chest of the priest and elevated the cross from his flesh. In the center, the rays were studded with rubies which gave way to diamonds as the spokes radiated out.

It was unmistakable in its symbolism. A simple cross with a blood red sunset behind it, if that's what you wanted to see, it was there. Blood, light and crucifixion, a message as eternal today as the moment the piece was hammered into being.

Jesper knew right away that the cross illuminated by this inspiring and elaborate setting was more than just symbolic because the diagonal, oblique part of the cross representing the second article of Orthodox faith was sculpted with an irregular hollow channel and had small prongs at each end and in the middle. Those prongs probably held a relic; a fraction of bone from a revered Saint, a fragment of human ivory that to a believer was more precious than the gems and the gold which held it, which presented it for reverence. The boys had dug into a priest, and not an average one.

"What about the amulet?" was Chief's first question.

"It was around the neck, or what used to be the neck." answered Jesper before adding: "Shot in the forehead, .45 caliber at close range, damn close range based on the neat entry and not-so-neat absence of cranial fossa at exit." He paused then added his irony: "The priest saw it coming."

Chief looked at the bones loosely arranged on Jesper's autopsy bench but wasn't focused on anything in particular, including the skull in Jesper's hand. Given that the cause of death was about the only thing they knew for sure about John Doe #58, Jesper found Chief's disinterest in the best, AAA prime-cut, evidence of murder he was ever going to get to be out of character. He knew Chief was good at solving crimes but found it odd he wasn't that interested in the evidence staring back at him with two blank eye cavities and a neat hole in the forehead.

As if to reply to that unspoken irony, he was asked: "This all of it, Jesper?"

"There was a little bit of cloth held together with gold thread. Could have been anything, embroidery on a scarf, a vestment, who knows, it's over there with the cross." Jesper pointed at a tray at the end of the bench but didn't need to. The amulet was the first thing Chief noticed when he came into the room and now that it was clean, it heated his curiosity with even more intensity than it had when he first saw it in the grave.

He picked it up. It was warm. The room was not.

"Know anything about this?" he asked.

"Looks like a reliquary, kind of odd being on a piece of jewelry but maybe not for an important priest back then, or maybe somebody higher up, somebody who travelled to visit each parish, provided governance and collected the tithe, if there was anything to collect. See the prongs where a relic might have been held and how the channel is odd-shaped, like it was designed to house a fragment of bone? Who knows? It's just a guess." Jesper didn't figure anything he had to say would add a clue to the murder and for sure he wasn't worried about compromising the science of his autopsy with absent-minded conjecture because as far as he was concerned the results spoke for themselves. His job was done. There were no forensics left to apply or any evidence on which to apply them. Cause of death was a bullet through the brain and not damn likely that was postmortem, which reminded him: "I'm missing most of the posterior cranial fossa so he had that hole in his head when they laid him in the ground. They didn't throw him in the hole and they didn't lie him down and shoot him there either, if that means anything to you."

"Not much." With that, Chief put the amulet into his pocket. "Box him up. I'll get back to you later."

Again, Jesper shrugged at Chief's attitude. He didn't seem to care about the facts, but he was obviously interested in a murder that had been lost to the sands of time. Then again, maybe it wasn't a murder or a murderer driving him. It could be the victim's story or the victim's family who needed justice but one helluva long time too late, if that was the case. Jesper wrote it off as idle curiosity or as occupational hazard from being Chief for so long. Either way, if he intended on solving this murder it wouldn't be for justice because the guilty were already several decades into their death sentence.

★ ★ ★ ★ ★

In bright sunlight and under clear blue prairie sky where he could gather and order his thoughts, Chief struggled, and failed, to add another clue, motive or identifier to the victim or his executioner, or, more likely, executioners. The only clue he had to unearthing the identity of the priest, if he really was a priest, was the reliquary, minus the relic it once held, and that was a pretty solid lead. The only clue to the killer, or killers, had to be Lula Lutochna who was buried in 1865, but that was just an educated guess based solely on her being the last person officially buried in the graveyard plus the sentiment on her marker. 'An Angel Reborn'. That was it. End of the trail. If Lula Lutochna didn't have anything to do with the priest being shot in the head and laid in a shallow grave on the far edge of hallowed ground, then by God none of the strangers buried around her would be any more help.

The Dragoon wasn't any help. It was a .44, not a .45 as figured by Jesper but that was plenty close enough. If by some miracle it wasn't the murder weapon then whoever buried it with the priest must have had their reasons and after all this time, who could possibly care what those were or on which side of the coin they sat?

To his way of thinking, if the murder was anything more than a simple case of cause and effect, it wouldn't be solved while he was walking the earth. The cause had to be Lula Lutochna and not because she was the killer or even witness to the priest being put in the ground. No, she had to predecease him. It only made sense the priest was the last to be buried in that cemetery, he was the effect, the conclusion. That made her the only cause worth investigating. An Angel Reborn meant something to whoever carved that into her headstone so that made her the cause, because angels are innocent and don't go around shooting people. Nothing else would explain the priest's execution and burial without marker, coffin or a ceremony unless pissing on his grave was the ceremony, and somebody probably did that.

Then, just to make sure the whole and unholy episode would be erased and forgotten before time could take care of that and all the sin which went with it, the same congregation of murderers tore down their church and every last scrap of it was carted away, leaving only the foundation. Lord only knows why they left that, other than they didn't dig up their dead and move them so why dig up the foundation? Maybe because the ground was consecrated and the foundation was part of it? That was all he had to work with and the first time anything, big or small, surfaced to disrupt this line of reasoning, no matter how irrelevant or uncertain, the investigation was officially over.

Not even 24 hours into it and he wasn't sure he should have started it in the first place but now it was on everybody's mind and too late to stop without satisfying their curiosity. Anything less than the best facts, conclusions or plausible cause he could unearth was no longer his choice and besides, he had to admit, he couldn't stop. His own curiosity wouldn't allow him to invoke a statute of limitations that expired even before his own parents were born. He had to know what it all meant as much as anybody and that wouldn't go away, that wouldn't be forgotten and that would definitely haunt him forever if he tried.

It was a crime where everybody above ground was innocent so now they had to know everything about the murder, the murderers and the murdered and it was his job to deliver it even if it made no difference to anyone's life. Just another irony, but one that was completely irrelevant and besides, it wouldn't be the first crime or curiosity he regretted investigating. Sometimes the truth came with reward and sometimes it came with punishment but that was the nature of the job which had become his life so no point analyzing his own motives to death.

In the final analysis, he would investigate because Lula Lutochna was An Angel Reborn and angels don't kill priests, even when they deserve it. She died and went to heaven and the priest died and didn't. All done and forgotten until the boys dug into him and curiosity shone the bright light of day onto something which was never supposed to see the light again.

His boundaries as clearly defined as they could be, he summed up the murder as he summed up decades of keeping the law and untangling the crimes and the minds of those who committed them. Good meets bad then bad meets Chief. That was enough to justify why he took seriously a crime so old that most lawmen would have ignored it. He had pursued wrongdoing for too many years to ignore a crime just because the guilty were dead and had gotten away with it.

He wondered, then doubted, if priests felt the same way about sins and sinners.

★ ★ ★ ★ ★

Chief was good at finding things that went missing and the people who went missing with them. It took only two days to find Sylvia Katrina Lutochna's record of marriage. That record showed her to be the daughter of James Lutochna, the probable bastard son of 17-year-old Lula Lutochna and the priest. At least that was how the mother and son were connected on paper, the part about the priest fathering a bastard child was nothing more than an extension of logic from the simple cause and effect theorem of being the last 2 people buried in an abandoned graveyard. The rest was a matter of public record.

Sylvia Katrina Lutochna married Brian John Mathison in 1925. She lived her 67 years in Wegerville where she died but was buried in Velim, about 100 miles from where her grandmother Lula was resting in the churchless graveyard. The family business, Mathison Seed, Feed and Implements, was still going strong in Wegerville. According to tax and licenses, the current owner was the one, and possibly last, living connection to the case so one way or another, in all likelihood, perhaps and maybe, the investigation would end with the Lula Lutochna's great-great grandson who was still minding the store and possibly keeping the secret of a murdered priest.

Chief had never been in the store before, but he'd been in lots like it and knew from the smell of the air and the sound of his own footsteps that the place had the history he needed to find the piece of puzzle he was trying to solve. All that remained was to determine if the owner knew about the murder of a priest who might also be his great-great grandfather. A simple request, assuming all that shame was passed down and assuming it wasn't too soon to talk about it. All priests die with secrets but priests who are executed by their own congregation create even bigger secrets and a hundred years may not be nearly enough time to discuss those over the price of a bag of oats.

To complicate the matter even more, the congregation of murderers who tore down their own church and scattered it and themselves without ever talking about it again had to hide their secrets and the priest's secrets too. It was a perfect case of double jeopardy so if any of it was passed down, it was only passed down to prevent it from ever being discovered. It was a secret that went from grave to grave.

As he walked to the counter, Chief acknowledged the duty and cost of secrets like the one he was trying to learn. He had a few of his own and gave silent respect for anyone who had not just to keep a secret but to protect one.

The man behind the counter looked to be in his mid-fifties. He had the wide face and ruddy complexion of a field worker but when they shook hands, his were the small soft hands of someone who didn't do a lot of physical labor. Chief introduced himself, asked the shopkeeper if and how he was related to Sylvia Lutochna and watched carefully as the man's response unfolded with a sense of trepid innocence mixed with cautious curiosity.

"Yes, I'm Greg Mathison. My father is Peter Mathison and he is the only child of Baba Sylvia. She was an only child too, her father was James, just like you said from the marriage certificate and he was Lula's only son. Before her is Russia and we don't know about that, never looked into it, to tell you the truth. So, the blood order is: Lula, her son James, his daughter Sylvia, her son Peter who is my father and then me. To be honest, none of us know a lot about that side of the family. All Baba ever told dad or me was that my great-grandfather James was a pious and faithful man and his mother Lula died as a young woman. We didn't know where she was laid to rest and assumed she died in childbirth, quite common back then." He paused his recollection then expressed his curiosity: "Why do you ask?"

It was a common question from someone being interviewed, and it had two equally common but divergent motives. Sometimes it was motivated by innocent curiosity and sometimes it was motivated by nervous guilt wanting to know what facts were already in play and which needed to be wound into the lie that was coming. Because of that, Chief always had two answers ready. One answer was the truth which he always used if what he saw, heard and felt was innocence and which he sometimes used if the truth or facts he possessed were so powerful, he could use them like dynamite to blast out the truth. Failing innocence or dynamite, the only worthwhile alternative remaining to him was to respond with question after question until the prey got caught in its own trap.

With Mathison, he didn't get the overwhelming feeling of innocence and he didn't have a fact powerful enough to blast the truth out of him so he replayed what he heard and the body language he saw and got nowhere. Sometimes nowhere meant he was on the right track but with the wrong crime and sometimes it meant there was nowhere to go.

This was not quite a nowhere case. Mathison wanted to know why he was being asked about his great-great-grandmother and his concern came with an undertone of curious anxiety. It was not the easy-going, friendly openness of the moment before. His family had a secret and either he knew it or he was defensive about it because what he didn't know, he feared. That left Chief with no alternative but to bring out the bait and see what kind of reaction he got when he dangled it in front of the great-great-grandson of an Angel Reborn.

"We found some jewelry that might have belonged to Lula Lutochna. You ever hear about something like that being lost or stolen?" Chief told the lie with considerable innocence. Silence followed as Mathison thought about it and around the only fact given him and whether it fit with anything he knew or suspected about his family.

"No. Can't say as I have. What kind of jewelry? How?"

Good questions, asked innocently. The boys dug up the past and now Chief was obligated to continue the dig. He accepted the irony of unearthing something that was never intended to be seen again and that he was going in completely the opposite direction to that intention. And for what? To satisfy a whole lot of curiosity, some of which was his own?

It was too late to go back; he had his shovel in the dirt and was committed to finding out what came up with it. Be patient, he told himself. Sometimes big things are discovered one small piece at a time, so he slowed his actions and concentrated his observation. Innocent reactions or otherwise, he'd sort that out later.

He took the amulet from his pocket, unwrapped it from the blue velvet cloth and handed it to the storekeeper. That is, he tried to hand it to him. Mathison's eyes showed interest but as his hand moved forward to touch the piece, his interest and then his curiosity vanished as he pulled his hand back and crossed his arms at his chest. It was a classic defensive posture but without fists so non-aggression. Not innocent, not guilty.

After that, Chief couldn't get a read on him, so he took the direct approach: "Mind telling me about it? It was a long time ago, I'm just searching for an owner before I give this to the finder. No crime here, and this didn't come from her grave, that hasn't been touched, which you'll see if you ever go there."

He didn't expect an answer or expect to believe it if he got one, so he focused on Mathison's face and looked for a tell, the sign that lies were overtaking the truth and a mind in the background was working furiously putting those lies in a particular order which was logical and airtight. That was the first decision the guilty person made, which lies to tell and the order in which to tell them. The innocent don't have a clue what you are talking about and behave that way, clueless. Sometimes they behave a little guilty because they think they should be able to answer the question, but that's ego and not guilt. To his surprise, that was Mathison's reaction. Some innocent guilt charged with personal curiosity for something hiding in his family tree. Something which might explain a behavior which had caused decades of speculation.

"I don't know much, and nothing about that cross. Maybe Baba knew something about it or the past that goes with it, but she never said anything to me and if she told my father, he didn't tell me. No point asking him now, his memory is gone and so is his language; he is completely incompetent. I do believe there was some history on Baba's side of the family, and it had to be dark because it was never talked about and we are a close family. Only Baba knew what she knew and as far as I know she took it to her grave."

As he talked, Mathison's eyes stayed with the amulet, but that didn't mean anything. It was a completely natural reaction to that golden cross with the blood red and white light radiating from behind it. Chief felt the same way and found himself wondering if the way it reflected light was what made it feel warm to his touch. Warm as blood. It also produced a metaphysical sense of reverence, but he wasn't sure of the reason for that reverence. Was it a truth? A belief. A law? A murder? And for whom: Christ, his disciple, his priest? And then, what came after that? Penance for whom? A resurrection for Lula Lutochna, 'An Angel Reborn'? All kinds and natures of doubt arose about what was in play, but no doubt Matheson was telling what little truth he knew and was being just as honest and openly curious about what he didn't know.

Oddly though, in spite of his obvious curiosity, he continued to distance himself from the amulet and to continue that separation he deflected: "You might want to talk to the Father in Velim, if he's still alive, and still there. Orthodox, do you know the church? The one with the white shingle, onion-skin dome? It's the last one of its kind in these parts and it was Baba's church. Truth is, it was more than a church to her, she was more than just a member there."

He reflected on his words for a minute like they stirred dormant memories which might explain his grandmother's connection with her church and the ground in which she insisted to be buried. "It was more than just Sunday services for her, if you know what I mean. She was bonded to her church in a way that was beyond the liturgy, beyond the gospel, beyond congregation, if you know what I mean. She never insisted we go and she never missed a mass. The Father might know something about that cross, it's as Orthodox as he is, or was. Sorry I can't be more helpful." He extended his hand without saying good-bye.

Chief wondered, and not for the first time, whether anyone's curiosity would be satisfied and if so, whether or not anyone would accept the answer which satisfied it. So far, the investigation was going in the wrong direction, but no surprise there. Find a murdered priest and sooner or later you end up in church and if the trail doesn't go dead right then and there, it's only a matter of time before it does. It wasn't his first run-in with the church and their secrets. Fear of death is a compelling reason for the faithful to go to church and that makes it an equally compelling reason for the church to maintain that fear.

A quid pro quo which had been silent until a Colt Dragoon and two small boys exposed it and now it was taking Chief down a road he really didn't want to travel.

Velim was 60 miles in the wrong direction but it was the forwarding address of a priest who had his brains blown out 100 years ago and he had no choice other than to follow the clues he was given. He accepted not having a choice with the investigation or control over his curiosity or where it would end, but he didn't have to hurry so he took back roads and tried to enjoy a day which started out with the likelihood of being a dead end and which was now sending him to a graveyard in Velim.

It was a nothing church. Any kind of fire and it would be ashes before you could throw the first pail of water on it, but in spite of its humble, paint-peeling façade, it seemed orderly and well-tended. Parking was a small windswept gravel lot to the side with deep grooves in the three spots nearest the door. An old, yellow Volvo station wagon was parked in the shade next to the fence.

Inside, the floor was worn by thousands of footfalls, the pews were rough-hewn with a distinct patina of worship and the windows were clean and streaming bright light inside. Garden flowers decorated the altar, the same as the ones in the graveyard, evidence of a parishioner getting two blessings out of one bouquet. Baba's church as much now as it was then, no doubt.

Chief absorbed the past in which he stood. Years of faith given, prayers said, hymns sung, baptisms, weddings and funerals celebrated. Life and lives reduced and concentrated by the power and presence of words written hundreds of years ago and bound in a black book with gold lettering.

This profound, perpetual repetition of doctrine and dogma and its infusion with human destiny were marching through his mind when an old, white-haired priest in a black woolen robe came out of the vestry. He bowed at the altar, turned slowly and approached with an unhurried step and constant gaze. His eyes were grey and the lines radiating from them were unreadable as to their creation, but not to their character. They were not from laughter or pain and they were not the lines of man who has spent a lifetime with worry or uncertainty. A true man of the faith.

Irrelevant detail in facial identification, but what was important was the accumulation of time. Although he couldn't have married Baba Sylvia, he was definitely old enough to have celebrated mass and heard confession for most of her life. Maybe that included the secret of a murdered priest buried in an unmarked grave, a church torn down and an abandoned graveyard full of strangers, but not likely she confessed that to him. That's the kind of secret which is only ever shared when the priest is already part of it.

"Good morning, Father. I'm Chief from Grinrod, cross-county. I was hoping you could help me. Did you know Sylvia Matheson, born Lutochna? I think she was married here."

Priests don't have to answer questions about their congregation and most of the time they don't, especially when the law is asking but this wasn't one of those times. Maybe the statute of limitations for silence had expired or maybe Baba's purity or atonement exempted her from such privacy, like a saint. Whatever the reason, the Father answered quickly and business-like, his eyes not searching, not penetrating, not challenging, not yet. Chief recognized the tactic; the priest was looking for sin just like he looked for innocence.

"She wasn't married here. She was married Baptist, because of her husband, but this is her church, and she rests with us."

Chief did the odds and came up with even. Whatever he knew, the church wanted to know too, so the betting window was open. As long as he was prepared to speak truly and ask his questions with care and respect, they might trade some facts before the window closed and then death itself wouldn't wrench it open again. It wasn't his first experience with priests who thought they had the power to absolve sin and then keep secret the crime.

He decided to play the exchange the way the priest was playing it: quick response, to the point, and with as few, carefully chosen words as possible. He unwrapped the velvet from the reliquary and displayed it. "I have questions about this."

The Father glanced at the amulet for a second, no more than that, before abandoning eye contact with it and Chief. He drew his elbows close to his body, pressed his palms together and held them to his chest, fingers pointed to heaven in a quiet precise ritual of subservience toward the cross.

HONOR.

He genuflected.

RESPECT.

He turned toward the pulpit and said over his shoulder, words that seemed not directed to Chief but to the open door and with no mistake that Chief should follow them. "Someone will call you."

He stepped into the first pew, knelt and prayed in silence.

PENANCE.

Penance for what? What crime can a piece of jewelry commit? Or perhaps it was the other side of penance - a prayer of thanks for a prayer answered?

Chief felt on the wrong side of his own investigation but had no choice except to leave with even more unanswered questions than he came. It was the unmistakable sign of a curiosity about to be satisfied with punishment and not the first time he'd been there.

He didn't like it. In fact, he hated being made to wait on the other side of his own investigation, but all he could do on his way back to the station was to reflect on that turnabout in fate plus the fact that somebody knew a lot more than he did and most likely he was no longer in charge of his own damn investigation or whatever fate came from it.

★ ★ ★ ★ ★

After more than a century in her grave, Lula Lutochna sent him to a church in Velim and true to the old priest's words, 10 days later the church came to him from, they said, Moscow. Three of them and except for white collarless shirts, their shoes, socks, balloon-legged pants and knee length coats were as black as their wide-brimmed Homburg hats. No other adornments, no rings, canes, crosses, bibles or anything, but all it took was one look to know that religion as strict and as pious as any ever practiced on earth was standing in Chief's station and demanding to see him. It was the kind of religion you don't question, because there was only one answer to everything.

The only thing distinguishing one Brother, if that's what they called each other, was that only one of them spoke and he didn't mince words or look anywhere except into Chief's face.

"You have property of the church and the church demands its return."

"Fair enough." Not even a cheap lawyer would argue that with them. Chief opened his desk drawer, picked up the amulet, unwrapped it from the velvet and laid it on his desk without losing eye contact with the Russian. It wasn't easy to do because he was certain he would never see the amulet again and had grown possessive of its warmth. He didn't like that feeling and he liked the arrogance with which he was being treated even less and didn't try to disguise that as he stared into the dark eyes of his adversary. It surprised him how fast that relationship happened: he'd taken a lot longer to reach the same conclusion with some murderers and molesters. What Chief noticed next, because of its absence, was the complete lack of doubt, question or any weakness in character of the man facing him. Maybe that's what drew the line between them so quickly; they were the same and neither were prepared to share.

The moment he removed his hand from the amulet, the Brother spoke, and it was as clear a statement of fact as night follows day. "Church property."

"Fair enough." repeated Chief. "You'll have to sign for it." In spite of his desire to challenge the authority, which was being shoved down his throat, it was neither prudent nor politic to get into a pissing contest over who was in charge of determining the ownership of a cross. Those contests are not worth losing.

The Brother nearest the amulet picked it up, looked at it for a moment and after some foreign, guttural, half-whispered words spoken into the ear of the speaker, quickly wrapped it in a white linen cloth before it disappeared into the robe under his coat. Chief immediately wished he had taken a picture of it and then was glad he hadn't. A picture would only have reminded him of the loss.

With the next statement, the Brother's arrogance turned to insult bordering on accusation. "The relic is missing. This is nothing, it is history, nothing more. Without the relic, it is nothing. Find me the relic." he demanded with the tone and attitude of an autocrat used to giving orders without any need to be nice about them.

Chief felt the accusation behind the words and that brought his anger to the surface. Fast.

"It's your cemetery, you find it." He replied eye-to-eye and expected resistance of some kind to his anger but got nothing unless you call the empty space around a stone wall a reaction.

Just as quickly as his anger came to the surface, that empty space was filled with the realization that the men in front of him were all business and whatever that business was, they had been at it for a lot longer than he had been Chief. The last couple of hundred years of being Orthodox in Russia wasn't for sissies and Chief knew they could give as hard as they got. If he started a fight with them, it wouldn't be fair or fast but loss was an absolute certainty and Chief disliked that even more than everything else he disliked about them.

As if in defiance to an ultimatum they neither heard nor would heed had they heard it, the Brothers turned and walked away. No backward glance, no short footfall, no stub of the shoe, not a breath distinguished one from each other. They were one, united against sin and Chief was only a fraction of their concern with their mission to recover 'church property'. If it was intended to be demeaning, it worked.

He expected to see them again and knew they wouldn't make an appointment.

★ ★ ★ ★ ★

The day after the grave had been dug out to virgin ground and sifted into prairie dirt no bigger than a grain of rice, they were back in his station and if he thought they were determined before, he was about to see that word redefined.

"We did not find the relic. Where are the bones? Who touched the cross? Give me the names. The relic belongs to the church and the church demands its return."

Chief doubted the church could do much more than threaten him, but he had absolutely no doubt it could make life very uncomfortable for whoever it chose to make it uncomfortable and that would flow downhill and land squarely on his desk where it would stay until he made it go away. He had no interest in defending himself in a hopeless fight and even less interest in being on the receiving end of a political shit show. If it came to that, he was still outmatched, and knew it. This was not now, nor would it ever be, a simple case of bible-thumping but whatever came from it, it would come in biblical proportions. Power comes in many forms and the one in front of him was of unrestrained and unrelenting variety. They had waited a long time for this moment and weren't about to leave until they got what they came for.

"Maybe the boys who dug it up touched the cross, for sure the coroner did when he exhumed and cleaned the bones and it's been in my possession since then. That's the list and none of us are thieves. If you didn't find the relic, it was never in the grave. Why don't you start by telling me who was in the grave with it, and why somebody shot him in the head?"

Chief immediately regretted the impulse in his confrontation but only for the second it took him to realize he was speaking to the masters of confrontation with the truth. He also knew there could only be one truth, they were on opposite sides of it, and if he learned anything from them it would only be because they wanted him to know the honest-to-God truth and who was in charge of it.

Stand-off. To him, all questions were legitimate, he was the law. To them, all answers were optional, mortal law was irrelevant to the crusade. They ignored his question.

"We will talk to them. We demand to talk to all of them."

"Fair enough, come back in the morning and you can talk to Jesper, he's the coroner but understand this, no matter what or who you talk to, I will be present. In this country, nobody interrogates anybody without a witness and an authority of the court and in this case, I'll be both. That's the law and there will be no exceptions."

"Tomorrow morning. Tell him to bring the bones, all of them. The boys are next."

"We'll see about the boys. In this country, minor children have more rights than anybody. If you aren't satisfied with Jesper's answers, we'll talk about the boys. But not until then." Chief wasn't about to negotiate those ground rules now. Once he'd witnessed the interrogation with Jesper, he'd know what to do and what to allow, if anything, with the boys. Some fights are worth losing because if you don't fight at all, you lose even more.

★ ★ ★ ★ ★

When Jesper walked into the station, they were waiting for him in a small interrogation room which was between the station on one side and the jail on the other. Bars on both sides, one way in and when the bars to the station were locked, no way out.

Jesper didn't like it; it made him feel like a criminal and he wondered why Chief picked that room and not somewhere more dignified, like the mayor's office. His stomach growled and he felt a flush as his blood pressure went up.

Chief was waiting at the door outside the room and watching the churchmen who were inside and standing behind a table, their backs against the wall. Chief motioned Jesper to sit at the table facing them then shut the door and stood behind him with his back to the door and his eyes on the Russians. The temperature in the room went up almost immediately.

No introductions were made, but Jesper wasn't surprised about that; Chief had already warned him the church wasn't on a fishing expedition and the Brothers, as Chief called them, were intense. He placed the box of bones on the table and sat down to what was supposed to be an informal inquest but looked like an interrogation and felt like an inquisition. In the steady, unblinking glare of all three Brothers, he squirmed in his seat.

"Is this all?" asked the Brother standing in the middle but leaning into him close enough Jesper could smell the odor of a strong disinfectant on his clothes and garlic on his breath.

"That's the works." he answered and hoped his voice sounded calmer than he was feeling.

"The works? What meaning is that?"

"That is all. That is everything I found and took from the grave."

The Brother nodded. "Church property." and the one to his left took the box of bones under his arm.

Jesper looked back to Chief who shrugged, obviously indifferent as to where the bones ended up. Maybe he was even happy to see them leave his jurisdiction along with any responsibility that came with them. Maybe he was even hopeful the murder investigation, if it still existed, would leave with them. A lot of maybes which just happened to fit perfectly in the uncertainty of what might happen next because it damn sure wasn't over yet but not at all obvious where it was going. Jesper sat forward in his seat, his back drenched by a sudden sweat.

"How was the body laid?"

He thought for a few seconds and then became flustered as he worried his hesitation might be misunderstood. He was looking for simple words and phrases which, due to the intense scrutiny to which he was on the receiving end, he couldn't easily find so he talked slowly and louder than he normally would have done. "He was on his back, his feet were straight out, one hand by his side, the other was on his chest. The chain was around his neck. A piece of cloth with gold thread was there too, it's in the box with the bones. Everything else was dirt or turned into dirt when I touched it."

"Which hand was on his chest?"

Jesper straightened, imagining himself as the body, and his left hand moved to his chest as he spoke: "Left."

"It was under the cross?"

"I think so."

"You do not know?" the Brother questioned in a demeaning voice.

That put Jesper into defense, the kind of defense which is sourced from too many experiences of self-preservation on the witness stand and that instantly made him think about surviving the entire interview and not just answering the question. Before he could get back on topic and deliver his response with indisputable science, the next question was spoken, and it was just as harsh.

"Were the fingers holding the cross?"

"I don't know. The phalanges, the finger bones, were all there but by the time I got to them, they had been dislocated on account of the digging, same with the ribs on the left side. And both the left radius and left ulna, those are arm bones, had been hit by the shovel, the ulna was broken in two but both pieces were recovered, you will see that when you examine the bones."

"The cross was on top?"

"I've already told you that. Yes, by the time I got there it was on top."

"Was it hit by digging?"

"I don't know. Perhaps, it may have been hit but I didn't see any damage to it. All the gems are present and intact in the setting, I saw that when I cleaned it."

The Brother put the amulet on the table and pointed to the third oblique arm of the cross where the relic had once been attached by the gold prongs. He put his fingernail under one of the prongs and sprung his finger up sharply. It made a dull metallic sound but didn't move. "The relic was there, where is it now?" When he asked that question, he leaned forward and the tip of his Homburg almost touched Jesper's forehead. Eye-to-eye interrogation and the priest was good at it. Nothing slower than a cobra strike was getting past his attention. Not a blink or a pulse was missed.

"I don't know. Maybe it is in the box, I didn't assemble the bones to exact anatomical detail, but it wasn't in the cross when I took it out of the grave. That I know for sure." Jesper stuttered.

"How can you be so certain?"

"Easy. First of all, it was evidence and I recovered it that way, very carefully. Second of all, that thing has to be worth some serious money. All those rubies and diamonds and probably hundreds of years old. Believe me, I treated it very, very carefully so no part of it would get lost or damaged and nothing did."

"You cleaned it?"

"That's my job and it's exactly as I pulled it from the grave, just without the dirt."

"Nothing left it? Nothing more?"

"I told you, I was very careful removing it from the grave and I was just as careful cleaning it. If the relic isn't in that box with the rest of the bones and you didn't find it sifting through the grave, then it was never in the grave to start with. Sorry for your loss but that's the honest-to-God truth."

"It wasn't there." said Chief from the background before adding: "I saw the cross when it was still in the grave, still attached to the skeleton. I guarantee you, what is in your hands is exactly what Jesper took from the grave. Nothing is missing now that wasn't missing then."

"I will talk to the boys next." the Brother demanded.

"Of course you want to speak to them and I told you before, the boys' rights are what I give you. First you see if what you are looking for is in the box then we'll talk about another interview."

"I will talk to the boys." he demanded like he hadn't heard a word.

Chief wasn't born yesterday and loved to threaten his suspects into confessing using the same bullying tactic they were using and suddenly he wanted to teach these so-called churchmen some law, particularly the part about who was in charge of it. "I told you before. The boys' rights are what I give you."

"We will talk about rights some other time. Now, we are looking for a priceless relic, not negotiating the right to question the truth." The Brother's tone changed from arrogant to flat and unemotional. Like he had a gun pointed at Chief's head and felt no qualm or uncertainty with pulling the trigger. His message was obvious: divine authority versus a tin badge.

Chief knew something had just changed, like he had just had his bluff called, but he wasn't bluffing, and it took him a minute to figure out exactly what had happened, what had changed so quickly. The expressions on the Brothers' faces were frozen and not a single vein showed a pulse. He even thought they were holding their breath which didn't make sense but that was when he figured it out. They weren't going anywhere. They would stand there until they starved to death and then no doubt the next batch would show up. It was the most intimidating case of stalemate he had ever experienced. Only 4 seconds into it and he knew they wouldn't negotiate any more than they would walk away and not come back until they got what they wanted. Anything he did and every moment he waited would only increase his loss and his time being shamed with it. They won and only a fool would deny it.

"Thanks Jesper, if there's anything else, I'll call you.

Jesper was more than happy to leave and if he never saw those eyes and faces again, he would be grateful for that gift for the rest of his life. With every step he felt his stomach come back to normal which was good because for a few seconds, he was on the verge of losing his breakfast, which is not something that happens very often to a coroner.

"Talk." Chief took the offense, and he took it without reservation. He wasn't in control of much, but he was in control of his own interrogation room and wanted to let them know he could still put up a fight even if losing it was a dead certainty.

"Property of the church is missing. The church will have it back."

"That's your problem, but you have no right to tear this town apart because you don't get what you want when you want it. This town is my responsibility and that includes the people in it, so you follow the law and that law is me. If you don't like that, talk to the people who appointed me and the people who elected them and see where that gets you." It was only half bluff. He knew his constituents and most of them, maybe all of them, wouldn't put up with the brute arrogance of the Russians for more than a few seconds.

"The boys were first to open the grave. I demand to know if they saw property of the church."

Chief knew the time for talking was over and the time for questions was almost over. It was either time for answers or time to get stonewalled into the next coming of Christ. "What has Lula Lutochna got to do with this? Tell me that."

"Who?"

"Lula Lutochna. After she died and was buried in your cemetery somebody put a bullet into your priest's head, buried him like a dog and tore down your church." He waited a second before dropping the next question on top of the confusion Lula Lutochna obviously created: "And why is your graveyard full of strangers?"

Unexpectedly, the answer came quickly.

"Sometimes fate takes a turn, a twist."

"A twist, you say. Does this twist have a name?"

"No more he doesn't."

"What will happen to him now."

"His bones will be ground to dust and the dust will be thrown in the gutter. Not like a dog; less than a dog."

"So, let me take a stab at this. The twist with no name was a bad priest, probably got her pregnant, maybe even killed her." Chief hoped for a nod, some kind of acknowledgement, even a denial would have been a clue he was on or off the trail but there wasn't a reaction from any of them, he might as well have been talking to a rock about the weather.

He waited but they didn't break so he waited a little longer, two can play that game, even if they were writing the rules. When the response came, it came as a surprise because he wasn't expecting it and he definitely wasn't expecting such an undisguised truth from a man of the cloth about the sins of his own church.

"Lula Lutochna wasn't as special as you make her. Not the same as the rest but not special. The priest was responsible for most of them, maybe all of them. He is the one thing these strangers have in common. Sometimes a priest gets obsessed with sin, it happens. You should know that. Sometimes the police get obsessed with the law the same way."

Chief figured they believed their own pitch about confession being good for the soul because they didn't waste any time getting to it or put any perfume on it when they did. Then, as he replayed the words in his head, he realized they weren't ashamed either. Right and Wrong. Good and Evil. God and the Devil. Good priests and bad priests. Pairings. Contradictions. Spectrum extremes. The necessary boundaries within which life is experienced, within which life exists. Or ceases to exist, he reminded himself.

It made sense, which was disturbing because it meant they had to accept their own priest was himself a murderer who was shot point blank in the middle of his forehead before being thrown into an unmarked, shallow grave where he would be forgotten for eternity. Then his church, their church, was torn down by its own congregation and everything was abandoned except the cemetery and the foundation which, all things considered, was starting to make the most sense.

They accepted all the contradictions of life, death, fate and and not because of forgive and forget because they didn't forget anything; they waited a hundred years and would have waited a hundred more for this moment. He wondered what they would say about the priest's punishment on and off the earth but didn't have time to ask that question before it was answered.

"Many priests have been shot in the head. Sometimes for political reasons, sometimes for other reasons. It is not so shocking. It still happens. A bad priest doesn't make bad faith any more than bad police makes bad law."

"And you don't apologize for that?"

"I have already said. The priest was responsible, that is my apology. Give it to whoever seeks comfort."

"Then we're done here." said Chief.

Brother must have thought it was a question or maybe he just wanted to remind Chief who was in charge and wasn't about to leave until he got what he came for. "Property of the church is missing."

"Fair enough but it's your property, so look in the box. We're done here."

"I will talk to the boys and then we are done."

The air turned stale with conflict neither resolved nor settled. The kind of stale which is often followed by the smell of burnt gunpowder. It was another loss and should have been expected, but it was tough to swallow because for the brief moment when he was in control, Chief forgot the utter determination, complete conviction and absolute power of those he was facing. He used the same tactic to break a suspect and knew he wasn't going to win.

"Fair enough, tomorrow morning, 9 o'clock."

★ ★ ★ ★ ★

In deference to their stature as juveniles, the location of the interview was changed from the station to a small room in town hall. No other concessions were made because Chief didn't need to make any. He opened the interview, which had grown to include the boys' parents. Other relatives, friends, spiritual zealots and interested parties were not allowed in the room, or in the building, so it was just Chief, the Brothers, the boys and their parents in a too-small room. It was tense, crowded, immediately too warm and exactly 9:00 o'clock.

Chief started assertively and not just because he was temporarily in control and wanted them to know it, but because overnight he had developed a deep distaste for the Russians and their arrogant piety. He convinced himself that a combative attitude was in the best interests of a level playing field and wanted to make damn sure they knew he didn't like them or give a damn about their property or their problems. After this was over, and as far as he was concerned it would be over quickly, if they didn't like it they could rot where they stood and that would be the mayor's problem. He told her that before he told her she wasn't going to witness the proceedings and she didn't put up a fight over jurisdiction, methods, procedures or consequences, which didn't surprise him. You can't be a politician without having a run-in with religion at some point and she had no interest in repeating the age-old battle of church versus state with a bunch of Orthodox Russians who didn't know the meaning of the word, compromise.

"To start with, and to make sure everything is as fair and as quick as needs can be, there's going to be some rules. So, parents Wiser and Becker, you are here as parents and not to testify, so to speak. I say, so to speak, because this isn't a trial so unless somebody asks you a direct question, you don't volunteer anything, you don't say anything. Do you understand that? It's got to be a direct question asked to you, saying your name out loud. Don't you worry, I'll look after your boys, you know I'll do that don't you?" The parents nodded at both questions. They knew and trusted Chief, a point which was not lost on the Brothers when he directed the second part of his opening statement to them.

"Now, on the church side of things, I think you know your business and that's good, but it also has responsibilities and consequences too if you aren't respectful. That's not a threat or a warning but you need to understand this part clearly. You know your business and I don't. I repeat, I do not know your business, but in situations like this I don't need to know everyone's business, so here is what I am going to do about that. I'll allow you 10 minutes and three questions. If you know your business like I think you know your business then you can get your business done with that and no argument about this, that's all you get. This isn't a negotiation so don't waste your time or your first question on me."

The Brother who did the talking moved forward and captured the boys' attention by gathering his arms into the sleeves of his robe and relaxing his expression, but he did not smile. It made him look like a statue, yet he was completely open and unthreatening. "What did you take from the grave?"

Jimmy couldn't believe his ears. That's what this was all about? Taking something from the grave? "Nothing. I took nothing. He took it." pointing to Chief.

Ronny was right behind the story: "Me neither. I got nothing."

Like they planned all along, Ronny didn't look at Jimmy so when he looked around, he accidentally caught Chief watching Jimmy like a hawk then Chief caught him and he got embarrassed, so he looked away again and saw one church man also watching Jimmy and the second one staring right into his eyes like he was reading a book. The third church man was watching Chief with a blank face and blank stare, like he didn't see anything, but no way was that true. All of sudden, without any clue or cause or reason they all broke their staring at the exact same moment.

"No more questions." The Brothers left without a word of departure or a backwards glance.

Minutes later, when Chief walked onto the street, they were gone. He figured the old priest from Velim took them away in the yellow Volvo.

He also hoped that was the end of it and he would never see them again but knew that was just wishful thinking. Church or law, they both understood right and wrong, but neither of them gave a damn about differences or definitions when it came to the one and only thing that mattered to them: their principle existence. He understood that and so did they, but his side of the coin was clear and uncontestable. Without justice, the world would be unlivable for everyone except those who should be damned, not forgiven and absolved of sin. All the prayers and all the salvation in the world wouldn't make up for justice and they knew it. Their hypocrisy was blatant.

★ ★ ★ ★ ★

After entering the plain, red brick, 3 story building on a poor street in the Moscow Kitai-Gorod neighborhood, 2 Brothers scrubbed their shoes on the rough mat while they unbuttoned their coats but didn't put them or their Homburgs on the rack inside the door. They wouldn't be there that long.

The hallway was clean but battered by age and poorly lit.

They walked up 3 flights of stairs in harmony, breath-by-breath, step-by-step, then down a narrow hallway to a large room with windows overlooking rooftops. It occupied more than one-half of the floor and was the largest room in the building. The walls were covered with shelves laden with carefully arranged books and the room was haphazardly furnished with desks, tables and chairs. It was neither a school nor a library, but a place where both learning and knowledge were sacred.

The smell of tobacco was enticing but served only to remind the Brother he was there to report and not to pursue soteriology, the study of salvation, his academic virtuosity. The Counsel had waited decades for his report, and they wouldn't be happy with it. Four of them were at the far end of the room where two sets of leather armchairs were tucked into a bay window. The chairs encircled a low table with small glasses of sweet coffee and ashtrays on it.

An incense burner in the center of the table threw a thin column of smoke into the air. The two old, long haired and bearded priests sitting with their backs to the window stopped their reading and watched the Brothers approach. Weak light filtered through the dirty panes behind them. The other two, facing the window were in quiet conversation, which ended when the amulet was placed on the table. A wave of silence slowly overtook the room as the amulet was passed from hand to hand. A gathering formed behind this brief ceremony and enveloped the Brothers like a protective cloud, everyone wanting to see what had not been seen in lifetimes of study of which the amulet was a revered, but missing, part.

The relic of St. Sergius was secure in its station and held by the prongs on the oblique arm of the cross. It had been sifted from the dirt and was broken in two places which were temporarily bound with virgin linen thread. Later, that would be replaced with gold and never again would it be lost to the profane world.

When the last at the table finished his prayers and touched the cross to his forehead, he asked: "The crucifix of St. Sergius is found. Where is the ring?"

"Found but not yet recovered." replied the Brother with anger tempered by his failure to deliver both artifacts to the counsel. "No word from my Brother or Father Paul from Velim has been received for two days."

"Dead." said the one sitting next to the window and looking out as if he received that answer out of the sky through divine inspiration.

"The Chief is playing with fire." predicted the next.

"Church property and the church will have its return." said the one looking at the sky, but not said by way of command, rote, ritual, or dogmatic wondering. Said simply as a fact that had not yet occurred.

The Brothers nodded acceptance of their orders, turned and left. This time their mission would be different. This time they would break a commandment and Chief would die in a ditch like a dog and the ring would be taken from his dead hand.

Sometimes power is good, sometimes it is corrupt; sometimes one commandment is broken in order to save the rest. That wasn't a theological premise, theory or argument. Truth and power were there to protect the sanctity of death and for that there were no commandments, no good or bad morality, no religion, no politic or temporality. Just earth to earth and dust to dust mortality.

When the faithful are unafraid of judgement, they are unafraid of death. That was the promise of the church.

Where right has no power – there power likes to be. The curse of the ring.

Chief was playing with fire and now fire was seeking him.

★ ★ ★ ★ ★

Chief looked in his rearview mirror as a black plume of smoke rose from the onion-skin dome. His shoulders were pushed back against his seat; the palm of his right hand guided the wheel; his left forearm rested on the open window and sunlight caught his hand. It reflected on the ring so with every bump and vibration the rubies cast a dancing spectacle of small red droplets around the cab of his cruiser.

He was unhurried because he had yet to decide his destination. He also wanted to watch the church burn to its foundation but wouldn't have time for that before he went over the hill so he drove slowly in order to see as much of it as he could.

Within seconds the black plume was consumed with heat so intense it burned the smoke to white. Then the flames licked through that and turned the dome into a raging fireball with the iron Orthodox Cross at the peak. A perfect imitation of the amulet. He regretted surrendering it but had no choice.

Nor did he have a choice with the ring and as long as he was alive it wouldn't leave his hand again.

When he first realized the power of life over death that came with the ring, it was minutes after it left the bones of a priest shot in the head a hundred years ago. He felt its heat when he picked up the amulet, so he searched it out and pulled it from the finger bone. Then he covered the depression and placed the amulet on top in order to conceal his theft.

He couldn't resist the temptation to hold it, to explore the source of its heat and didn't think about keeping it until he walked past Lula Lutochna's grave. By then it was on the ring finger of his left hand and he felt its power and understood, with innate clarity, how an angel can be reborn.

After that, the more he wore it, the more he understood the futility of actions without consequences and that made giving it up impossible to consider. When he refused, they were just as determined to take it from him. The old Father died quickly but the Brother fought with his last breath.

It was unfortunate but unavoidable. Unavoidable and as inevitable as death. The ultimate contradiction: living to die. They understood that.

Completely logical and completely acceptable considering the futility and the foolishness of contesting opposing states of mind including states of grace that always conclude with a fall. Adam and Eve. Heaven and Hell. God and the Devil. Good Priests and Bad Priests, Crime and Punishment, Pleasure and Pain, Guilt and Innocence. Being and non-Being. With the ring, those states which were on polar opposites of the spectrum merged and became an inseparable, unconquerable force when unified. Like coal and diamond are both carbon only separated by time and relentless pressure.

Chief knew they would be back, likely even in greater numbers and when they returned they would be unstoppable in their intent of recovering church property, only to destroy it. This time they wouldn't think life and death, or life after death, not even life or death. This time Chief and death would be synonymous and he accepted that judgement so completely it might as well have been his own thought because now he was what they would become. He was absolute law. He would arrest, prosecute, judge, convict and execute and it would stay that way until they stopped him. That was the state borne from the resolution of all contradiction; singularity is godliness.

The fireball engulfed the dome as the roof collapsed, the walls would be next to fall. Just another churchless graveyard. It wouldn't end the dogma or the hypocrisy any more than death can stop time or change the fact that the only strangers in a graveyard are the ones walking on it.

LIGHTNING

<hr />

That no one knows everything is patently obvious to everyone but seriously, who really believes they truly, actually, know all they think they know? And don't confuse the verb *know* with the noun *truth*. If there is one thing everybody really does know it is that for every knowing, there is more than one truth. And if that isn't serious and sufficient warning about some major problems with the verb, then use a faster one to seek cover because knowing becomes a whole lot more unstable and a whole lot more difficult to believe after it has been struck by lightning.

That single cataclysmic event provides over-ample evidence that knowing is untrustworthy, unsupportable and unsustainable. One simple bolt is all it takes to change that egotistically contrived asset into a fragile temporary state at best and a highly dubious state, at very best. Then there's the disappointment of seeing all that hard-earned knowledge, perhaps a whole lifetime of it, instantaneously put to the test and implode in a record fail.

This is a serious charge against reality and not to be confused with any old near-death experience which causes some re-thinking, some reevaluation and some adjusting to the temporality of life. Lightning is a total game-changer, and the old game was a lot more defined and a whole lot more fun to play before the catastrophic destruction of self and perception was hit with the unparalleled aftershocks of questionable belief and flexible realities.

Realities that are unlike any before experienced and not even close to what you get when you put 5 people in a near-death experience, like a plane crash, and end up with 5 different memories, 5 different truths, 5 different explanations of exactly the same thing. Those are just screenshots of an event which was uniquely processed and recorded in millions and millions of neural connections weaving silvery threads into a web of false belief called knowledge. Five people, 5 differences, 5 knowings, 5 wrongs do not make a right.

And to condemn this fantasy of belief even further, all so-called knowledge is colored, filtered and enhanced over time by the retelling of it under different emotions with varying motives using the latest lingo and fashion. Bad enough but superimpose a layer of awareness from another major life loss, cloud the optics with a couple of decades of aging and then see how much of this so-called knowing is still intact, let alone accurate. So, not only was it an incomplete version to begin but the longer it survives, the less true it becomes and there is only one thing, just one thing, that is exempt and sacred from this fault of how humans blindly experience and incorrectly record their entire lives. The one knowing which absolutely and irrevocably is always true and always the same, from its nascent spark to forever hereafter, is the unknowing which comes from being struck by lightning.[1]

Admittedly and just to be sure we are all on the same page here, it is absolutely true that everyone who has experienced a direct hit has a different story to tell about how or when or what they were doing when their life was changed in a nanosecond[2]. The colors which were registered, the smell of hair singed, or skin burned will be different and the location and sensation of the pain will vary as widely as the reports of the plane crash but every single victim of electrocution by natural sources has the same image in their mind's eye. It is the image of a jagged

---

1   A bolt of lightning, that is. Sheet lightning is like being inside an old-fashioned cathode ray tube for a couple of seconds. Hardly worth the words to describe it.
2   On average, a lightning stroke only lasts about 30 milliseconds, but the impact is instantaneous so a billionth of a second is about right.

hole ripped out of a dark black sheet of midnight sky through which a very, very, bright light shines. Every day and all night, it shines.

No matter what the circumstances of before or after, they were blasted inside-out through that hole and what they found on the other side is not only known by them but sometimes known in a language they never learned to speak or which no one else can speak. That can't be misunderstood; that can't be denied; that can't be fantasized; that won't be colored or filtered over time and it absolutely cannot be forgotten.

Also, in the interests of clarity, just like the circumstances surrounding the strike are different, the aftermath is bound to be different. Post-blast symptoms vary dramatically, even within a small population, but what is on the other side of that jagged hole is the same for every person who lightning puts on their knees and it stays that way forever. And no, it isn't God. It definitely isn't God. Maybe God made the lightning but getting hit by it has nothing to do with the concept of a supreme being, although the corollary is likely true. That unfathomable energy, the sheer immensity and the suddenness by which it simultaneously triggers every thought, emotion and sensation ever experienced or imagined could certainly lead to the revelation of a god.[3]

I know this. I truly know about this knowing, about what is the same and what will never change, never become filtered, decayed or distorted. I know this because I have been hit 6 times and before I start the stories of my fractured life, I want to begin with an apology.

The truth is, no one, including me, can tell or write or explain what is on the other side of that jagged hole. It defies language just as it defies a comparable life experience but maybe through these stories and their details, a hint or a glimpse of what it is like will get through, will sneak past all the logical and illogical filters and barriers and sink a tap root into raw consciousness. Perhaps a piece from this strike or that aftermath will join together like a jigsaw puzzle and show part of the pic-

---

3   Many cultures, from primitive to modern have either given lightning god status or put it in the hands of a supreme deity like the Greek Zeus, the Hindu Indra or the Norse Odin.

ture. Maybe an image of what life is like after it has been massively, horrifically electrified and the jagged hole is opened once and forever will appear out of the fog. That should be possible.

After all, everyone accepts how some learnings and wisdom are created that way, when completely random events become connected over time as experiences of good and bad build on each other or are dependent upon each other like cause and effect. Events that happen over years which suddenly collide and create the Aha![4] moment that watermarks the rest of life's pages. Hopefully that will happen with these stories and that is the reason for writing them because there is a lot to learn about being human after being struck by lightning. Like, for example, how the entire construct of a mind must be rebuilt after it is blown into countless random 3-D fragments which are scattered far and wide and can never be reassembled the way they once were because the master plan and its creator was blown-up with them.

Still, I am sorry I can't provide a simple and direct vision into the jagged hole, one that can be comprehended but which won't shine into your life, every second of it, until the end. That would be the most convincing truth of all but, for sure, you don't want that no matter how curious you are.

Nor can it happen; the jagged hole is not implanted in the mind like false knowing is implanted but perhaps these stories, these segments of a rearranged existence will provide something valuable. Some insight into something else so powerful and foreign that it can't easily or properly be described in words because it didn't happen in words. Something above and beyond day-to-day life and living. Something like a super-consciousness or a higher level of meditated mindfulness where none of the physical and metaphysical states are discovered by logic or bound by words. Something sudden, surprising and staggeringly obvious once the curtain of disbelief is lifted.

If you are thinking that might be like having another entity implanted in your mind, like the hallucination from psychedelic drugs, then maybe that's a place to start. A little confusing perhaps, because that other entity is you, but with a little bit of imagination, it is a metaphor worthy of exploration.

4 Eureka for Archimedes.

After all, everybody suspends their disbelief long enough to read fiction or watch soap opera on TV so why not do the same with the fiction in your life? Give that a try and suppress the fear it could send everything you thought you knew about yourself into question. Simply make knowing and truth subject to the same interpretative values you use for many other situations and people in your life. Ask yourself why you allow your life to be governed by these ambiguous memories of childhood, implanted norm values of your culture or generation, peer pressure requiring daily validation or a host of random experiences and faulty memories which are mostly important to, and only understood by, you.

Suspend your disbelief with your own life like you are watching a movie and see where that takes you. Start with an easy example, your childhood. Forget about how far in the past it is and test the strength of those silvery threads you always use to initiate and hold that memory together. Ask yourself how much of it is true and how much of it has become your story. How much of the person in that story do you truly know and why is that person always appearing to you in third party? Is it because he/she/it feels foreign and abstract, like someone else, someone who you once knew quite intimately but with whom, over the years, you have lost touch?

Could it be that person has succumbed to becoming a manufactured memory? Is the background of that child painted-in, are the colors faded and is the texture of that life, the immediacy of the moment which separates dream from wakefulness gone? Admittedly, there will always be sufficient residue to know it was once real but now that you think about it, how strong is the sense you have grown apart and the marriage, so-to-speak, is over?

Still not quite sure about the fatal fault of this thing called memory and knowing?

Then up the voltage; supercharge it. As high as you can take.

Become the moth when it flies through the fire and falls to the ground on the other side of the flame with its burnt legs and scorched wings as it simultaneously becomes moth and non-moth. Now understand and admit there is no knowing to that because knowing does not exist on the razor edge of being and nonbeing.

That is the landscape when 100 million volts[5] hits a bio-electric thought generation utility that normally runs at .00001 volts and 0 amps to produce 1 million synapses just to get out of bed. Hit your childhood story with that and see what is left.

Just surviving, just coming out the other side of that massive assault to the senses, which means the brain, is one of lightning's greatest[6] mysteries. Perhaps not the greatest of life's mysteries because that would be not coming out the other side, but unlike other phenomenon, lightning becomes more impressive with inspection, with facts obtained, agreed and then passed into science. It also becomes more mysterious with contradictions, hidden questions and illusions.[7]

Science says lightning strikes earth about 50 times a second[8]. A second. About half the time to take a breath.

It strikes all over the planet including lots of places where no one is around to witness it. Like in the far Arctic or on an atoll in the middle of the Pacific, although statistically, those are both very safe places to be when it comes to being struck by lightning. Statistically, there are also some very unsafe places to be.[9]

Unfortunately, there is also no guaranteed safe zone and you can just as easily get blasted out of your shoes on the 8th hole of the golf course as on a beach walk with your dog. Just minding your own business and without a single conscious thought of lightning is when it will strike. That is, the first time it strikes. After that, the absence of a single conscious thought is replaced with a very bright light shining into your mind, day and night,

---

5   It can be as great as a billion and as hot as 50,000F, 4 times higher than the temperature of the surface of the sun.

6   And arguably, for many victims, the most devasting.

7   The smoke and mirror behind the flash.

8   Not including lighting which never makes ground contact.

9   Like Catatumbo lightning which occurs at the mouth of the river of the same name where it empties into Lake Maracaibo in Venezuela. Every second night or so, it rages for 10 hours with as many as 280 strikes per hour, sometimes with a frequency as high as 25 times a minute. It is the most lightning prone place on earth and it is well and truly feared.

until it finally stops shining because that mind has stopped thinking.

The destruction of innocence[10] is the first and most devastating of lightning's consequences to a simple protein-based life form and its cerebral pilot. After that, innocent thoughts are difficult to find and they are always found aloof and alone; the familiar gathering spots for life's fiction either no longer exists or has been sucked into the jagged hole and cannot be accessed.

After that, DNA is wound a little tighter, but you think about lightning a lot and not just when you want to think about it. If you still have the courage and the coordination for golf, it fractures your focus at the precise apex of your backswing or the fraction of a second it takes to miss a 1-foot putt. That might not sound serious, but it is. Golf you can quit.

Now, with the jagged hole open and the moth lying on its back with its burned wings and scorched feet struggling to discover what purpose those things serve non-moth, if you are beginning to think there might be more to lightning than pictures on the weather channel or some science faction about being zapped through your telephone line, you are on the right track. Tracks, statistics and science are interesting beginnings in the understanding of this phenomenon so here are some more, together with some questions which are hiding behind those facts. Questions which are seldom asked and never answered.

Fifty times a second is 1.5 billion bolts a year, enough to electrify every 4th person on earth so, like the Olympics, every 4th year, it could get you. By extension of simple arithmetic, if you live to the ripe old age of 80 (and you may not want to) you will have been hit 20 times. Of course, that's monkey math because lightning strikes aren't distributed equally anywhere or amongst all things including humans, but it is a reliable statistic hiding a question, an interesting one.

How many people do you know who have been hit even once? How many cocktail party conversations or lectures have discussed that statistic or thought that thought, done that math or mentioned the jagged hole? Easy question because it's an

---

10 Traditionally, destruction of innocence means greater awareness of evil, pain and suffering but in this context means the destruction of knowing.

easy answer. Zero, right? Except by now you are probably beginning to suspect, with the kind of knowing which can survive
any question, in any language, there are no simple answers after
being struck by lightning.

Yes, there are survivors, most people do survive[11] so rare exceptions on the cocktail circuit will occur. It's possible a survi-
vor is standing silently beside you with a wine spritzer in her
hand and the light from the jagged hole shining brightly in her
mind, illuminating all the pointless chatter surrounding her[12].
She doesn't want to talk about it because why and how she
survived are two very personal questions, just like before and
after are two different lives and that kind of discussion is not
polite cocktail conversation. Mostly though, it is just plain not
appreciated to remind those who are 'innocent' that they don't
actually *know* what they are yapping about.

No, polite lightning conversation stops well short of the jagged hole. It stops at claiming to having been close to a strike,
like when a tree or a lightning rod is hit or the story of Alfalfa,
a horse down Longview way who was witnessed as having been
struck twice (2 different storms) and survived to the ripe old
horse age of 31. She was a terrible ride. Her gait was random
and bizarre. Like riding a buggy with 4 different sized wheels
and none of them properly round.

How can this be? How can such a force of nature with such
consequential ramifications to the human understanding of
conscious life be so quietly ignored when entire TV channels
are dedicated to floods and fires and their physical devastation?
How can a billion strikes a year miss so many people and yet so
secretly destroy the ones it picks to electrocute?

And on that question, if you jump to the conclusion that
lightning is selective with its targeting then you are jumping in
the right direction.[13] Impossible to prove, but just as impossible not to believe the millisecond after you join that exclusive
group of human lightning rods and horses with metal shoes
that make them excellent conductors. Once that happens and

11 70% of people survive but with serious side effects that never go away
    and are incurable.
12 Although most likely a male by a 4 to 1 margin. Chauvinist that.
13 Science says it is not. Science doesn't know everything.

it only has to happen once, you know just as sure as the bright light shines down on your every thought that lightning picked you and that anybody bragging about being hit is lying because being picked by lightning is a lot of things, but it is not a compliment or an accomplishment.

It is not cocktail party bragging rights and you don't reboot your memory and internalize the experience like being in a plane crash or having a Class V heart attack, revived, just in time, by some pissant defibrillator.[14] It isn't a virus to which you develop antibodies and get lifetime protection. You don't forget it because you can't forget it. You do your best to live with that bright light shining through the jagged hole knowing that as much you hate it, when it stops shining you are dead.

Now, to add a little flavor to this preface of fact and unknowns, to explain it a little better or perhaps complicate it even more, hard to say which way that will go, but the experience and aftermath of being struck by lightning is significantly confounded by the happenstance of life. For some it destroys an otherwise peaceful and productive existence while for others it destroys a past which deserves what it gets and that is the happenstance. That is not the jagged hole and not even close to becoming non-moth.

That is linear thought in straight sentences colored with adjectives and adverbs just as each of the stories which follow have been colored with my happenstance. Expect them to be different and inconsistent because they are different lives or different versions of a life that has been blown apart and put back together, 6 times.

For example, the 1st time I was electrified is the hardest to describe but not because it was the 1st time or because it was a long time ago but because of my biological stage at the time. At 17 years of age, the juvenile brain is filling-in, in search of the adult it is to become. It is processing an enormous number of possibilities while simultaneously reprocessing the entirety of its own history into a new story, into a credible narrative.

---

14 Which produces a mere 3000volts for .0001 seconds – enough to light a 100 watt bulb for 20 seconds – the equivalent of one breath in a lifetime compared to the real thing.

Every past experience from infant on is dissected. Those which happened after time was discovered and those which happened before self-awareness and political subterfuge became causa prima are chopped into puzzle pieces for reconstruction, for version 2.0 assembly.[15] All those thoughts, learnings and memories are reorganized and restructured, some moment by moment, some image by image, others experience by experience but all in a process of genetically-driven forgetfulness designed for the creative re-emergence of a new and unique individual. Caterpillar to moth. Values, ethics, emotions and behaviors from pathetic to prodigy are split apart and recombined, crystalized and stored, trapped actually, in the defensive zone of the pre-frontal cranial lobe. This becomes you, the one that lasts until it is either unfused by the gradual disintegration of the brain cells which gave it birth or defused in sudden death by natural or unnatural causes.

Unless, of course, it is stuck by lighting and blasted into a billion pieces and must start all over again.[16]

For a person already going through this process, being struck by lightning may already seem like a normal, knowable event. If not entirely normal at least not completely different from some other very powerful first-time experiences, one in particular. But afterwards is a different story, a different life. This version includes a jagged hole as a signature of the chaos which separates knowing and knowledge in a way they were never intended to be divided.

Like how do you explain before and after when everyone else views before and after as numbered boxes on a calendar or the position of hands on a clock? Just another fork in the road and when one is taken the other disappears because everyone knows you can't go back and relive time or forwards to avoid it.

---

15 Which is one of the reasons childhood memories are either not carried forward at all or are carried forward incompletely/inaccurately. They are reconstructions.

16 And this is true with every hit. Some chunky bits might survive but every hit requires a re-make, a complete re-do. After a couple of hits, a lot of past isn't reassembled and not just because it can't be found but because there is no point.

Complete, true and honest knowing until you survive lightning then simultaneously and suddenly true and false, moth and non-moth.

Once that jagged hole is ripped into being, time, all kinds of it can enter and surround sentient life just like water and air. Before and after become indistinguishable bookends. Then you begin a life with strangers and the next page starts the story of the youngest, and most innocent, of the strangers with whom I have shared life.

LIFE ONE

It was just another day in the last semester of high school. Nothing special about the day, other than I was with Kitya, my first love since March 2 of that year. Kitya made everything special because when I was with her, everything was either special or on the way to it.

She was also 17. She was overall skinny, even her short colorful hair was skinny, but not twig skinny which would make her joints look swollen or her eyes look bug-like and she didn't hang with that crowd. She was svelte, slender, feline. She was the only person in the whole school who could walk through the yard and not get noticed. Magnetic when she wanted to be, especially her eyes, which mostly she kept hidden behind round glasses that made her look like a pixie. They had the kind of lens which darken in sunlight and masked irises with so many shades of blue and green it was like looking at Caribbean waves reflecting the sky.

The rest of her she dressed in loose clothes, mostly dark colors but with a scarf, a hat or shoes of some unpredictable color or texture that made you wonder not about her fashion, but about her choices and the more you thought about that, the more you entered her world and realized she was alone in it. She didn't like goth, noir, or any cult and she didn't belong to, or want to belong to, the yearbook, debate, chess or any kind of club, clique or crowd who would have happily accepted her. They would have genuinely accommodated her quiet but certain individuality except she didn't express any need for inclusion, so they respectfully left her alone. It was their way of accepting her without having to confront her, which would have resulted in the exposure of false pretenses.

Flowers have pretenses[17] as do butterflies[18] but Kitya had none and she was both of those and more.

Before her, I was a loner, an unknown, somewhat reclusive, living by my own choices, covered with my own wallpaper. Av-

17 Venus flytrap.
18 Several species of butterfly mimic the poisonous Monarch.

erage in every respect. Waiting for my brain to finish filling-in and a little anxious about the future. Not a crisis of confidence in either direction but not strong in the middle either.

We met in the one class we shared. Our introduction was eye contact and a shrug before she turned and left the image of a blaze orange scarf burned in my mind, like looking at the sun too long. The scarf framed her face and looped under her chin with each end thrown over the opposite shoulder and down her back receding from my sight as she looked over her shoulder to see if I was still held captive. I was. It is the first memory I have of her; it is always the first to appear with her name. After that, memories of her come like boxcars pulled by a locomotive, always perfectly in line, always connected and moving at the same speed, each car holding a collection of Kitya wonders. A long, long train of Kitya memories defining the landscape of my life.[19]

She was new to the school, so our life together began as the result of politics and economics as the lives of students were rearranged with the budgets of school districts. Some students stayed put, like me, and others moved, like her. Fate can be tricky that way, it leaves some things alone but makes them bear the consequences of the things it decides to uproot. This time it was generous and for that I am to this day, and have always been, grateful.

The day after she shrugged at me, I sat next to her. She smiled and blinked slowly with a warm, mildly seductive greeting partly veiled by her slightly tinted lenses; it immediately infused me with uncertainty. She ignored the flush in my cheeks, and they began to cool. The first 17 years of my life were about to change which she knew because she was in charge of it.

---

19 You wouldn't be wrong thinking that that moment was a lightning strike because that's how most people think about it but the actual experience is far different. So different in fact, that when people use 'being struck by lightning' as a metaphor, it only serves to demonstrate how little talent they have with metaphors because the only thing that is like being struck by lightning is being struck again. Even then there can be some significant differences like one bolt blowing you out of your shoes and next one melting your eyeglasses not their frames but believe me, those are just minor issues compared to the neuro residue. Unquestionably though, whether or not Kitya influenced my lifetime attraction for lightning is a question I have asked myself many, many times without answer.

Yes, that fast.

She blinked again.

"Kitya." she introduced herself.

"Petrov." I replied and she smiled. In those formative years I often disguised my name, so often in fact that my parents stopped using the one they gave me without my consent and would only introduce me as their son, leaving me to name myself if I felt like it. Contrary to what they thought at the time, this had nothing to do with being a contrarian teenager. I'd read somewhere that excess of self-identity was the surest way to block or alter reality and was determined not to make that mistake by associating myself with something as selfish as a name. It was a total guess and is still pretty much a guess although a more reasoned one now that I have more experience with the concept of identity formation.[20]

Ridiculous as it sounds, it is clinically impossible to adopt a new identity and keep the old name.[21] If you want to change your identity, you change your name, period. Of course, that wasn't what I was attempting to avoid, meaning, excessive self-identity due to naming conventions but those two things are logical entanglements of each other. Almost everyone experiences reality through their identity; I was trying to avoid that because a bear doesn't need a name or an identity to walk in the woods and be a bear. It doesn't even have to know it's a bear; nature doesn't care about names, maybe that's why so many people don't care about nature. Their name keeps them from belonging to it.

On her side, Kitya was mostly intuitive. About half her intuition came from common sense, another half came from So-

---

20 Identity concepts are incredibly important constructs when your mind has been blown away and you need to rebuild it. Obviously, it's important that you choose your concepts with care but you should also take them with a grain of salt because not all concepts are true or useful every time your mind gets rocketed into space. You need to restart with concepts useful to the life being restarted.

21 A cognitive behavioral psychotherapy called Reality Therapy focuses on present needs and wants and not the understanding the past like other psychotherapies so it's basically the same thing as a name change and it works, for some people.

cratic logic and the rest came because she understood solitude and didn't get preoccupied with other people's thinking. Some people thought she had a gift, others thought she was a white witch, some believed whatever their crew told them to believe but no one thought she was evil. She moved so gracefully and smiled so genuinely she could make anyone uncertain of their emergent being. Totally disarming for someone already questioning reality and that was just one of her powers.

Some girls can ruin a boy's reputation by being good and she had that power. Anybody who wanted to be big man on campus had to respect, protect and defend her in order to remain unchallenged in their own image, their own perception of themself. Reality in high school is divided between subjective and objective classifications and she transcended both. Everyone knew she was the genuine, authentic article and had been that way forever. She was Australia, an island and a continent on its own journey through time.

"I'll call you Augustus." she whispered to me as class was starting.

Augustus. Damn fine name, I thought, and decided to research my new identity but not too deeply for obvious reasons. Anyone who bridged the gap between BC and AD and once led the Roman Empire was certain to have great strength and I didn't want my ego to succumb to that in the unlikely, but always possible, event it would conflict with a future identity and create civil war.

Augustus? Where, or when, in the world did she come up with that? No point in asking though because her most likely response would be to counter: 'You don't like it?' and from that there is no recovery. 'Yes' would demonstrate infatuation with an unearned reputation and 'No' would be the rejection of a gift and the relationship which came with it. Being given a name with such monumental history was a huge compliment and if there's anything more important in high school than history it is the avoidance of creating a bad one. High school doesn't last forever so waiting for bad history to vindicate itself is not an option, just like revolution with an uncommitted, unmotivated proletariat isn't an option. If Petrov taught me anything, he taught me that.

It wasn't long before Kitya and Augustus became a known pair and were, by virtue of sociological division, completely ignored. Before we became we, neither of us belonged so afterwards we automatically became half of what we were, so, almost invisible. Everyone was relieved; they were free to define their reality without having to fit us into it.

We maintained invisibility by not drawing attention to ourselves, by not having an opinion on school politics or by engaging in public displays of anything personal. No kissing, no drama, no dependency, no problem. Once Kitya taught me how everything is better when it is a secret, it was easy. She encouraged secrecy in general but when it came to love and affection, she was insistent upon it.

"Augustus?" She asked as the front door of the school closed behind us and anything she had to do with that world was locked inside and she was asking me if I felt the same way. By way of reply, I touched the hand holding my arm at the elbow like an Italian Contessa but didn't look at her.

We entered an extremely bright afternoon and her glasses shaded to dark almost immediately. I squinted and took a long, sweet breath of freedom mixed with happy anticipation. It was Kitya time, the time Einstein proved as Kitya time but didn't name for her because if anybody knew more about secrets and how to reveal them it was him. He wanted the world to discover her on her own terms and not be prejudged by astrophysics.

"Augustus. I don't want you to become a Doctor. Not any kind of Doctor, not even a PhD doctor. That would be a waste."

"Fine with me."

"Promise?"

"I promise."

That's the way it was. Whole conversations were shortened to their essential being. Complications galore were abandoned on a path never taken, ignored, condemned to nonexistence, denied, buried in a graveyard of dead or dying ideas. Commitments of a lifetime were made in seconds. It was done. No doctor in my future, ever.

Perfectly acceptable to me but also in conflict with the university application forms held hostage by my userid which I recognized as my only form of legal existence. Not that any decisions on higher education had been taken and especially not doctoral decisions but conflict nevertheless. Completely random education is generally unacceptable by institutions which pride themselves on producing football victories and educated units suitable for mass production.

Still, not a problem for me and creating conflict was certainly not her purpose even if that was the result. She was merely suggesting selectivity over the future content of my brain and besides, I never planned on becoming a doctor. With a name like Augustus, that would be retrograde if not downright barbaric.

But something else was in play and I didn't know what it was. Maybe it was something which could, should or must be learned elsewhere. Or possibly just another step on the path or another drop in the stream of Kitya moments which always ended up in the same place but always got there in a different way. Regardless, no point in trying to figure that out, a promise is a promise.

Regardless and besides, no harm and no foul. Becoming a doctor wasn't a decision in the first place so not becoming one wasn't one either. It was merely an elimination, Kitya's logic worked that way. If she said I had to become a plumber that would have changed history but deciding not to become a doctor didn't alter anything.

She lived her life that way too. When she eliminated a potential, she eliminated the thought that went with it and that greatly simplified her life and mine too. Not becoming a doctor was just one example of how Kitya didn't change the natural order, didn't interfere with anything but made room for more important things to happen with the spontaneity and joy with which life and love should always be pursued.

Love was a singular quest in her day; she was always perfecting its meaning, always purifying its existence and because of that, everyone thought we were just friends. Even our parents believed, or wanted to believe, that. If we held hands it was like children crossing the road or helping an old person get on the bus with a bag of groceries under one arm. When we talked to each other, we shared all kinds of surface words but kept the deep ones unspoken. We never kissed in public. We made love every day.

Kitya perfected that too. She perfected touch, sound, the intense heat of transcendental passion but most of all she used love to perfect, and protect, time. She made every second count and every second unforgettable.

"Love is the expression of the universe and you won't find it by running after it and trying to grab it. It will come to you, but you must make yourself open to it, you must lean into it." she explained. Our love was bigger than both of us and not because we nurtured it or forced it to govern our lives. It was bigger because we submitted to it.

"Augustus, promise you will always love me."

"I promise."

"Promise you will never fall in love with me."

"I promise."

"What do you think is the difference?"

"Love is spaghetti is in the box. Falling in love is spaghetti tangled on the plate and covered in sauce."

"That makes perfect sense."

Of course, by then it was too late, and I knew it; I had fallen in love with her and I absolutely lived to love her. She was pure and sweet and defined my self because she was all I wanted. I kept our memories in a vault and never discussed them with anyone. It was a completely selfish act of love which I couldn't resist. When we were apart, I relived our moments together as a conquest. She was my Rome; I was her Augustus.

We spent glorious measures of time in our collective agreement to stay apart no matter how close we became. All kinds of conflict were eliminated because the past and the future were treated with respect but not allowed into the present.

"Kitya, would you like to go to the beach again?"

"Again?"

"Yes, it's supposed to be a nice day. Would you like to go back?"

"Augustus, that is impossible, both of them, you know that."

In the end, I had to agree with her but without understanding how she could stay so present. For me, the past was just as much a mystery as the future, but I couldn't live either of them the way she did. Sometimes I hoarded the past, other times I feared the future and those two secrets I had to keep from her.

"Augustus, what are you thinking?"

"I'm just trying to remember something."

"Is it something you need this moment?"

"The formula for buoyancy."

"You mean the formula for buoyant force and you know perfectly well that objects of equal volume experience equal buoyant force so what are you really thinking about?"

"I'm not entirely sure."

"Do you have one thought that is more dense than another? Is that the problem? You have a thought that is sinking?"

"Maybe that's it."

"Then you're wasting your time, both will sink. Dense thinking always does that. That's why Archimedes discovered the physical law of buoyancy before he invented the water screw. Thoughts need to be floated the same way, without a principle under them, they are doomed."

"I understand." And it was true but for reasons I couldn't explain to her. Some days my memories were pulling me under and other days my anxiety over their place in my future was on my back, submerging me. Falling in love hurts; she warned me about that and said there was nothing I could do about it except not to allow it, not to let it happen. Don't fall in love. But unless your name is Kitya, being in love without falling in love is hard no matter how old you are, or were, or want to be.

"Augustus?"

"Yes Kitya."

"Please don't talk to me today. I don't want words."

Silence.

"Thank-you. Knowing you won't tell me how much you love me is telling me how much you love me."

Every time we made love was the first time. Each touch was new and exciting. She became more beautiful every day and more desirable with every moment together. That deepened the joy with every meeting and provoked a bottomless fear with every parting.

For all my faults with falling in love, and no point in making that list now, at least I was never jealous. That I could avoid because her love for me didn't leave room for it. She protected me from myself. I knew that from the very beginning, it was one of the reasons I fell in love with her; her strength caught my weakness like a net catches the flyer from the high trapeze. It seemed right at the time, but it wasn't Kitya right. For her, love shouldn't be shared that way. Each person had to keep their weaknesses because those were as much a foundation for love as were strengths. Take away one or the other and love went with it.

The semester drifted by like a boat without a motor, always downstream and occasionally getting beached on sand or caught in a tangle of stumps and branches stretched across the banks by some academic flood called midterms. Tests which were really just institutionally induced revenge for not listening to warnings that a hurricane was forecast and only constant learning was going to prevent catastrophic failure.

"The air is becoming thick." Kitya observed as the jocks worried whether Bernoulli's law would fly their football next week. Faces were lined with panic as books were cracked and pages were scanned in hope of vestigial memory. Simple arithmetic was routinely performed: X pages unread divided by Y days remaining equals learning per day. Memorization ruled over knowledge. Study groups were formed, alliances were made, and grievances were suspended as the grade curve became the common enemy.

This amused Kitya who was immune to the threatening consequences of not having answers because she understood that power came from knowing, not knowledge. 'Better to be a knowing entity than a known quantity' was how she expressed, and lived, that life concept. She treated knowledge, fact, theory and history the same, equality ruled in her universe and because of that she never forgot anything. Of course, it didn't hurt that when she needed help she could tap into Archimedes or Da Vinci for help. She reasoned if their thinking survived, so did they. Out of sight did not mean out of mind to her.

"I like to learn how a mouse learns." She would say when anyone asked her how she remembered a formula, how she extracted philosophic etiquette from raw ideology or the date a battle started and who fired the first shot. Teachers were baffled by her ability, but they didn't pursue the enigma of her intelligence. They knew she was super smart and the last thing they wanted anyone to know was how much smarter she was than they were. They feared being accused as hypocrites who taught what they could not learn.

Kitya loved to run and to run fast, setting the pace and then destroying the competition with a kick at the end which left them gasping while she soared over the finish like a peregrine coming out of deep dive. Maximum speed. But she couldn't be convinced to join the track team.

"That would make it a race, Augustus, and you know how I feel about races."

I didn't know but nodded. Sometimes the explanation came later and for one reason or another, later was just as good and sometimes better. Later allowed for mystery but not like a murder mystery because in Kitya's world, the butler always did it so there was no hurry, no rush to get to the ending of anything. Not that anyone would suspect the butler, and sometimes there wasn't a butler until the very end, but it was always the butler and that discovery always came as a pleasant surprise, like a flower newly opening.

It wasn't just me who felt that way. Teachers, students, even parents felt like that; they never questioned the order into which she put the world. They knew it was better her way, especially my parents, who loved Kitya because if they called Augustus, I would answer.

Her parents, both of whom were Sam - Samantha for her mom and Samuel for her dad probably wouldn't have made it through the day without Kitya reminding them that at least part of it wouldn't happen until tomorrow or next week. Both Sams were lawyers and had their own firm: Snell and Lockerbie which they said was the reason they never married. They didn't like the sound of Snell and Snell and Lockerbie and Lockerbie sounded like boat builders. I thought it was because their first names were already the same but Kitya said the real reason was because married lawyers who keep their names are more successful with divorce cases.

One day Ms. Sam asked me if I could survive without Kitya. I didn't think so but said if trees survived the ice age, I might survive for a while. Kitya overheard.

"Do you love me, Augustus?"

"Of course I do."

"More than anything else in the world?"

"Of course not."

"Good, then everything is fine just the way it is."

But it wasn't and I couldn't tell her it wasn't. I couldn't tell her my world was getting bigger every day and starting to fold over me. Falling in love was catching up to me, and fast. In a few weeks and after a few pointless exams the future was destined to unwind, or unfold, or explode. A rose or a thistle, it didn't matter, it was going to bloom and there wasn't a thing I could do to prevent it so I held onto the present with all my strength and denied the future with my mind shut tight.

I stayed as close to her as I could without being caught in love and locked every word, touch and smile into my memory because if a day without her came around the corner, I wanted to remember her to the smallest detail. That way, I reasoned, I could keep her with me forever as I blindly refused to acknowledge what I knew to be true. When love becomes greedy, it isn't love anymore.

TUESDAY

Etymology:

Middle English Tewesday meaning Tiw's Day,
the day of Tiw, the god of single combat.

One thing I can say now but didn't know on the day of single combat was that the bigger your world is, the more ways it has to trick you. I'm sure that's why old people get so fed up they never leave their house. They are sick and tired of being tricked by an outside world that has become too big and too full of tricks.

The whole of Tiw's Day was spineless chaos for vertebrates. Final exams were less than 2 weeks away. Exams that lasted anywhere from 2 days to forever. The brainiacs were weirded more than normal as normal entered a highly questionable state of surreal on account of too many tricky questions requiring precise answers. The teachers were smug, knowing the time they warned us about on day 1 was just around the corner and their words of wisdom couldn't be ignored or denied or shrugged away with the unapologetic disdain toward someone who has forgotten everything about being 17 except the number.

Tiw's Day was even more intense than the Monenday[22] which just barely preceded it and that meant even more chaos was invited to the party. The battle was on and there would be no prisoners. Victory or defeat were the only available outcomes. All retreat was cut off at the pass. There were no favorites, no exemptions, no excuses, nothing left to do except match enough answers with the correct questions and escape into the future.

Kitya was unaffected, as usual, and that meant she was surrounded. She was the safe port in the storm and the storm was a class 12 hurricane. She was a magnet, and they were the iron filings on the paper above, drawn in circles around her positive and negative poles making the sign of infinity with everyone

---

22 Middle English, the second day of the week. The Day of the Moon. Worshipped in many pagan cultures but has a bad rep in the work ethic of Western Culture which just goes to show you that progress isn't always a good thing.

hoping beyond all reasonable hope infinity would last long enough to learn what had to be learned.

I knew differently.

Tīw's Day she was more beautiful than ever, truly radiant. Black leggings, a hip-tight, flared, knee-length dark blue skirt and a knit top with black, pink and grey horizontal stripes that started wide at the waist and became narrow at the neck where it rolled over and glowed pink. Red shoes. Pink hair. Rouge on her cheeks like an elf. She was gorgeous and I had to be close to her but not because she was so calm and lovely or that chaos was raining down on everyone. I had to be close to her because she was my sanity. I had crossed the bridge of obsession.

"No passion tonight, Augustus. The moon. You understand?"

"In the wane, passion succeeds to reflection."

"Close enough."

Then she told me her parents were going to Europe for the summer and were taking her with them. It was a graduation present for everyone because Sam and Sam never had time or money to travel before.

"Augustus, the Sams are going to the continent and I must go with them. It has nothing to do with us but they are getting older and need to be surrounded by history. As ridiculous as it sounds, I am a link to their past and must go with them. They are too old to do this without me. You understand, don't you?"

I was holding the hand of the cutest elf ever in one hand and opening the tall entrance door with the other. I remember the outside light looking very different from the inside light and wondering if I had just never noticed that before or if there was some other reason like the Sams taking Kitya away from me had changed the orbit of the sun.

There were a few clouds, lots of mid-afternoon heat, high humidity and what meteorologists call 'unsettled conditions' when they don't have a clue what could happen next, but which could be violently destructive, so unsettled conditions covered their guess in case of a lawsuit.

Light blinked.

The first pulse of sheet lightning made everyone look up and remember that lightning comes in different forms and that Intra-Cloud had just made a brief appearance. Cloud-to-Cloud could be next so look up or you'll miss something impressive like St. Elmo's Fire, Red Sprites, Green Elves or Blue Jets displayed as spiders or super-bolts. Benign and passive entertainment until Inter-Cloud becomes Cloud-to-Ground and then say good-bye to life as you know it if it's a negative bolt and goodbye to life altogether if it's positive and uses you to ground itself.[23]

It was an almost perfect day, even the scattered clouds[24] looked like a beach day. The light blinked again or perhaps it was just the mirror reflection from the windshield of a bus which was a possible explanation that didn't complete analysis because in the next instant the smoking, ripping, searing, red-hot jagged hole that was to change my life forever was brazed into my innocent mind. I didn't see it coming or going and the edges of that jagged hole didn't stop burning for 2 days.

In that instant, which is a plodding word for the speed of lightning[25] but fast compared to the speed of thought, the bolt hit the top of the brass door and travelled down the edge to my hand where it separated into streams. One of them continued down the door where it had to jump an inch or so to the granite step. As lousy a conductor as I am compared to a brass door, most of the voltage went through me because it didn't have to jump that inch but chose instead to melt and weld the soles of my runners to the granite they were standing upon.[26]

I became the cartoon figure who is made to look funny by some animator who thinks getting hit by lightning is funny.

23 Positive lightning produces at least 10 times the amperage as negative lightning which is a lot of current and as many as 10 billion watts which is a lot of energy but only for 5/1000 of a second so it isn't as much power as you think until it decides to use you on its way to the well.

24 A few clouds overhead don't predict anything. Lightning can strike from 20 miles away.

25 While the light from lightning travels at the same speed as light from the sun, 186,000 miles per second, a lightning bolt is slow, 3.700 miles per second.

26 Those footprints are still there, burned black with a fuzzy outline. Parents take pictures of their kids standing in them like it's a joke. It isn't.

Arms and legs fly out at opposite angles because they can't stand being close to each other. The face displays unreal shock with protruding eyeballs and a mouth wide open with a scream that can't escape because the tongue is stuck far out. A contorted primordial scream expression without sound except for a raging thunder which seems to come from within. Then absolute silence. -273°C Absolute Zero Silence. Quiet. Quiet like you have never heard before, so quiet you know you can't be deaf. Everything stops in that silence except for the collision of a million thoughts which are instantly, simultaneously, triggered. Neural pathways are created, destroyed, recreated, redestroyed. Pathways for sight collide and join with pathways for hearing; every hair on your skin stands straight-out like little antennae broadcasting pure electricity. Memories, knowledge, all kinds and sorts of the imaginable metaphysical melt and meld into ethereal glass before shattering again.[27] Medieval history is re-enacted in the background of the Grand Canyon being eroded into nonexistence. Things you think you cannot think join with thoughts you never had or that don't belong to you and the beaker of reality overfills and boils over.[28]

I speculate that the instant I completed the cloud-to-ground circuit with the several hundred million volts using me for that purpose, I was automatically programmed for future strikes. Maybe it made me a lightning rod instead of the burnt-out stump you would expect from transmitting that much energy through a resistant, low ampere life form but that's just conjecture. What isn't conjecture and what isn't unique is that the human body is a lousy conductor and suffers greatly because of that design deficiency.

So lousy, in fact, the bolt didn't pass straight through me and then ground itself like common sense would dictate but it encountered enough resistance to lift me up, leaving my shoes welded to the concrete. Maybe it was just a few inches but when you aren't expecting it and your arms and legs are trying to leave

---

27 Petrified lightning occurs when a bolt hits a beach and fuses silica sand into glass, looking like trees with branches. The same thing happens to thoughts and experiences which are exactly like sand, just not sand you can hold in your hand.

28 Generally, no 'concept' of reality is worth preserving. It doesn't stand up to the real thing. See the footnote on concepts worth preserving.

their points of body attachment in order to escape the electricity raging through them, even a few inches of instantaneous vertical life is enough to convince you the next stop is Heaven.

That wicked jag of current held me in space for an instant, the longest imaginable definition of instant containing a super-charged awareness of chaos, before letting go and dropping me like a jellyfish. I landed on my back, paralyzed, eyes wide open and unblinking, like being very suddenly and very violently awoken from a sound sleep by a gunshot beside your head. That kind of an awakening; shocked into graphic awareness, but senseless.

When cognition returned, it returned with spasmodic jolts to a brain that was swimming in an excess of electricity, some of which was being pumped up from arms, legs and guts where it was momentarily stored. Then the silence opened to a rolling thunder that came from inside, deep inside and the first complete, rational thought came up with it: 'Is this a dream?'

That was the question and more than any other time in my life I prayed for one answer: 'Yes, this is a dream. This is just your brain playing tricks on you'.

But it wasn't a dream. It was a gradual, haphazard awakening from death and no mistake about that. It might only have been a few seconds but those few seconds were not life.[29]

Which answered the dream question by substituting a much more serious one: 'Am I dead? I don't want to be dead. I can't be dead. I can't feel anything, but I hurt everywhere with a pain I have never known. Am I dying; is death next?'

I stared into space not searching for an answer but trying to avoid one answer in particular and saw the fragments of my life which had been blasted into superheated air rising above me like ash from a fire. As they disappeared into space, they formed images like smoke or clouds and the first image to become clear and real was Kitya standing over me, watching me, waiting for me.

---

29 Returning to life and living after a horrifically large shock is neither quick nor complete and comes with damage to a lot of cerebral baggage, some of which will never reach destination because it is burned beyond recognition.

People circled around to look while she kept them back.

"His hair is smoking." someone said.

"He has to breathe. Give him space. Give him time." She said it over and over and I knew she was talking to me but they listened to her so I looked into the hole in the sky they opened above me and waited. Not knowing why or for what, just waited. Maybe for a bus. Maybe an idea. Maybe until my body had discharged like a battery leaking excess energy into the concrete which felt beautifully cool on my back. I waited for the nothing to stop so the something could begin.

Kitya later told me that it didn't take long for me to find and assemble enough pieces to think but it felt like a year and I remembered seasons pass over me, starting with early summer and ending when the first tulips of spring made an appearance. When those tulips bloomed, I stood up to a world, my world, that had just been rearranged without my permission, without my input of any kind. All I knew for absolute certainty was that I had been blasted inside-out a jagged hole of intensely bright, white light and I was never going anywhere without it. That one certainty has been beside me ever since.

She moved to my side and put her arm around my waist, maintaining my balance without anyone realizing that was what she was doing, like it was affection. She waved her other arm in a gesture that meant: 'It's all over, you can go home now.' Like a royal wave or a casual dismissal and that is what they understood. It was over. He fell off his bike and got banged up a little but no blood, no tears, nothing to see. Happens all the time. Everybody back to what you were doing. They obeyed her as they always had.

She took me to the Sams' house, removed my clothes and examined the damage, asking me if I could feel her hand on my chest which I could not. While examining my forearm, the one holding the door, she said "Lightning Flowers"[30].

---

30 AKA 'Lichtenberg Figures' named after Georg Lichtenberg, caused by an electrical charge rupturing capillaries beneath the skin. Sometimes known as 'skin feathering'.

When she was certain nothing was left burning, she put me into her bed and lay down beside me. I fell into a deep and troubled sleep with a brain that had forgotten how to dream.

LIFE TWO

A 17-year-old brain is already going through a reformatting process similar to what it must go through after being struck by lightning.

It is a time of life when the world is constantly enlarging because the identity, personality, individuality and self are making more and more connections with each other and those connections are being stitched into a long-term plan for reality. It is an intense, time-consuming process, often accomplished during sleep and several years in the making. All those processes and connections are unique to the individual and take time to find, define and put into practice. That's what Doctors understand.

Lightning, they don't understand. Lightning stays with you, you don't grow out of it or into it, it doesn't heal, there are no drugs for it and you shouldn't talk to them about it. They don't have a book for it and no matter how interested or compassionate they may be, that doesn't compensate for what they don't know which is practically everything about being a human lightning rod. Suggesting they go stick a wrench into an electrical panel or fly a kite into a power substation won't be appreciated either. They are pretty much opposed to that kind of learning on account of the Hippocratic Oath and the Darwinian desire for survival.

Lucky for me, Kitya knew what they didn't.

"Augustus, you've been enlightened. It was bound to happen sometime, you knew that, didn't you?" she asked and then explained why a particular thought or behavior I'd once had or done was a result of either being enlightened or on the way to it.

And I understood. Enlightenment was jail and endless space, combined. And everything she said was right on target because she always made sure the entire spectrum was represented with every explanation, every possibility. Kitya accepted contradictions because she knew that without them, life had no color, no texture, no harmony and no freedom.

Stop/go. Hold/release. See it, feel it, touch it or ignore it, just don't try to outrun it and you can't hide from it.

And don't spend too much time or effort trying to nail down firm answers. Definitely don't look into the jagged hole for answers. Don't do that and don't apply logic or seek an old reality; that won't prevent or stop the unknowing from chasing you like a cat chasing a mouse with absolutely no doubt about what is going to happen to the mouse. Follow that path and false knowing will build and build and then shatter into even smaller and more uncollectable and unrecognizable pieces. The old way is neither the new way nor on the path to it.

Day-by-day, hour-by-hour, this week, next year, all quantities of time were scorched and burned. Out of focus, out of sequence, unstitched and unbound. I couldn't figure it out but Kitya knew. She knew my clock took a direct hit even before I did.

"Let me feel." She put her hand on my chest where my heart once beat but which I couldn't sense no matter how hard I tried. "Not yet." she said without concern.

Her heart was a different matter. I could hear it from across the room. It was so beautiful and soft I decided to make it mine since I no longer had one which was the exact sequence of thoughts in which I had an important and singular moment of duality.

I accepted that my clock was totaled and might never heal itself. Without it I couldn't run away or be free, so I used enlightenment as a challenge and accepted a reality to which I didn't belong alongside a reality to which I belonged but didn't understand. I decided to take someone along for the journey and that someone was me. I was in one place, twice. Me, listening to myself think. Asking questions and wondering who would answer. The absence of time makes for strange bedfellows and you had best like yourself because getting through days when time comes and goes against your will requires all the help you can get.

Kitya was ok with that. No clock? No problem. Two versions of Augustus? No problem, everything else seemed to work. But before getting too excited about this being any form of recovery, I had to accept and understand the basics of being without a clock.

Was it never knowing time in numbers or in the boxes on a calendar? Was it going to bed in the morning and getting up at night? Was it an event suspended until being randomly triggered into being or are the hands of the clock frozen because it is a millennium clock, and takes 83 years to tick through an hour? Do fast and slow exist in a timeless state?

It is none of those. Nor is it a rock on the seashore which has been sculpted smooth. That is merely the presence of time disguising a jagged boulder and the dust it will become on its way to being a mountain again. You can hold all time in your hand with one rock. Its clock has not stopped; it never will. Maybe because it doesn't have a spark in the plasma that will run out of fuel and completely cease its cycle forever.

And that is the start, middle and end of an explanation of where and when you live without a clock. One moment is medieval and the next is random. Except, of course, you aren't there, you aren't present because you are everywhere on the spectrum of time from what was to what will be. No clock is a severe impediment to, if not the complete absence of, the present. It is anytime all the time.

And it doesn't include a get rich scheme where you can go back and make the bet because you know which horse is going to win the race or which numbers will be drawn in the lottery. Even if you could find the window in time to make the bet, chances of finding it after the race is run are almost zero and forget about spending your winnings before money was invented. Try finding that exact needle in an infinite field of haystacks of identical needles.

"Sergio is going to die." I told Kitya. She was the only person I could talk to about life without a clock and this is a good example of why. She looked at me like I had more to say.

I repeated: "Sergio is going to kill himself. Street racing. Tonight."

She thought about it and held my hand. "I should tell him, shouldn't I?"

"And wonder if you were the cause of his death for the rest of your life? And if he tells anyone, what will they think about you afterwards? You can't change this, Kitya."

Official Time of Death was when the paramedics got there but Sergio really died the second he wrapped his 280hp Civic around a bridge abutment and his mantra came true: 'Be the Civic.' It wasn't an accident. He was 4 lengths ahead of the Integra and should have braked. Nothing was going to change what Sergio had already decided.

That prediction may sound somewhat innocent even if it is dark and sinister, but a stopped clock also manifests itself in ways which are not so easy to explain or accept. It is hard to explain for a couple of reasons, the first of which is that some things you don't need much when you have a clock, but you need a lot when you don't. Courage for example. And not just the kind of courage it takes to look at a cloud which is hard enough but the kind it takes to face the next moment, not knowing what it will contain. So many surprises.

Which is another thing that is very hard to explain about a dimension without a clock. I'll call it a portal and you will call it crazy. You are probably right.

A shimmer is how a portal presents itself. A vertical shimmer of light with glowing, fuzzy edges. They are not everywhere but there are a lot of them. I almost passed through one out of curiosity before pulling back but I got a peek. Both sides of the portal were in the same space at the same location, but the time was different. The buildings were gone, the temperature was hot and the humidity was high. There were no dinosaurs, no flying saucers, not a single person but there was no doubt about where I was. I just didn't know when I was.

Then again, it's possible those glimmers are nothing more than vestiges of electricity smoldering in my brain like a forest fire waiting out the rain in the root ball of a big tree and perhaps I shouldn't have chickened out. Except there is only so much courage available at any one time and I'll never have enough to pass through a portal and face the uncertainty of not being able to return, being unable to find the exact shimmering portal with Kitya on the other side of it. Sure, it's crazy and hard to believe but that's not the thought at the moment because just like Sergio before he drove into the concrete bridge abutment, thoughts don't count when they cease to have control over the next moment.

Maybe it was a dream. Sure, let's go with that. Portals? Seriously? Let's just say some photons were jumping around in the sun, got kind of fused together, created a shimmer and leave it at that.[31]

Regardless of neurology, philosophy or physiology, my clock was stopped and there wasn't a thing I could do to get it restarted including wait for it to heal itself. Stasis. Limbo without equilibrium. Disorder with constant and continual chaos which might sound like it could normal but restful it definitely is not.

As a byproduct of timelessness, a number of difficulties are presented particularly with learning and recall because so many contrary truths exist simultaneously. Kitya explained it to the teachers by telling them that without a clock it was impossible for me to answer specific questions with a correspondingly specific answer, but my overall knowledge was around 83%.

If they wanted, they could make up a test where each question included answers from different centuries and specific points of view and influences. Clearly, a multiplicity of correct answers would be required, and I would answer with the one which had the greatest referential integrity for the data provided and the attending attributes over the implied time horizon. She explained that without a clock, this could take a very long time involving tedious explanations which would look a lot like trial and error and perhaps even then I would come up with a correct answer no one had considered.

For example, she told them, a question on gravity has diametrically opposed but completely correct answers before and after Newton, and either of those answers might be correct, or not, depending upon the conjugation of the verb or verbs used to frame the question. To complicate matters even further,

31 Or it could be physical, vision. Neurons in the primary visual cortex are arranged into distinct columns having similar specific properties. These columns are collected into assemblies called modules which analyze one small area of the visual field. Many modules complete the visual scene as they populate it with color, movement, depth, orientation etc. and this is the raw data for a picture. Fuse a bunch of these modules together and who knows what the brain will think it is seeing. Like a hallucination, things don't have to be physical to be seen just like pain can occur without touch. The brain is in charge of all the realities it wants.

unless the gravity being questioned specifically excluded subjective answers or interpretations, then multiple nonscientific
deviants[32] were also possible.

I received 83% for every course and didn't have to write my
name.

The next day Kitya left for Europe.

★ ★ ★ ★ ★

She was gone and so was my clock.

It was a very sad time; I didn't want to go out, didn't want
to talk to anyone and after visits with several kinds of doctors,
understood why I promised I would never become one.

I was on my own, living in a basement where I was immune
to lightning. It was an unpleasant time, (or a time without any
pleasant experiences), but it was a thoughtful period because
Kitya ordered it to be so. "Whatever you do Octavius, keep
thinking."

"What happened to Augustus?"

"That is what you are here to discover. Take your enlightenment seriously, Octavius[33]. And there's no point in me telling
you when I'll be back because your clock is stopped, you understand that, don't you?"

"Yes." I lied.

Being struck by lightning rearranges everything and time is
a worm hole so of course it can get rearranged like furniture.
No different than looking at a rock and seeing a clock because
they are made of the same thing, just a lot of subatomic building blocks arranged differently, like Lego. Any Buddhist[34] will

---

32   Biblical prophetic gravity vs Newtonian gravity vs Einstein general
     theory of relativity which coterminously denies gravity to be a force be-
     tween apple and earth but a consequence of space/time curvature caused
     by the uneven distribution of mass, post Big Bang.

33   Gaius Octavius Thurinus was born 63B.C. and given the name Augustus
     (exalted one) by the Roman senate when he became leader of the empire
     in 26B,C. This was Kitya's way of saying I was reborn older.

34   So too would Salvador Dali when he painted the melting clocks in The
     Persistence of Memory.

tell you that but when you are stuck at the molecular level of enlightenment, rocks and clocks make for a lonely society.

On the other side of this subatomic, the society of time is never alone and is always busy. It knows the difference between a short while and a long time and stamps everything with a best before date. This society takes its job seriously and provides boatloads of irony to keep everyone on task with expensive watches that tell the same time as a sundial. Schedules and durations govern everything. Hair turns from black to grey to white while waiting for trains and buses. Turn around and a new decade meets you on the other side. Everybody has experienced that shock.

So how do you explain timelessness and existence together? See the spaces between the words? The part of writing that doesn't make sense on its own, but you can't read without it. Blank space which is needed to bracket and separate the words and allow them to attain their collective meaning, to a livelihood on the page. Taking away those spaces is like taking away time. That is where time hides when it is off. It is a state within a state within a larger state, but everything continues because when time is off, it is shared with the time that is on.

Which can be confusing because when it is off for you it isn't necessarily off for everyone so when it is back on for you, things have changed. Drastically, sometimes but you can't stop time. How many times have you said that and didn't think about what it meant just like time could be tricking you right now and you either accept that or you deny it, knowing in your heart that both are true.

Could it be that you are walking in your tracks? Maybe you didn't make those tracks in the snow yesterday because it didn't snow yesterday but it is snowing right now and you are watching the person making those tracks, knowing that person is you. For sure that exists and yes it could be déjà vu but without a clock, déjà vu is nothing more than a fancy French word for the past happening again. All very interesting but not very practical and if life is anything, it starts with practical.

Practically speaking, when your clock has been shattered, everything in your head needs to be reorganized. If you want any hope of ever finding anything, including where you left your shoes yesterday or next Friday, a replacement time management system is a necessity.

No one sells this like a software program so I had to figure it out for myself. Not wanting to be called crazy, or become that way, I started the only way possible. I started with the past, which was once in order and specifically, I started by putting my Kitya memories in order. At first, I tried putting all the memories of our love in one place but when I got to our secrets, I realized some of them were the same so I developed a cross reference between love and secrets until I realized she would never accept them being separated. Conflicts like this grew and grew until I had so many unique moments with such a complicated system of references and indices but no continuity, I had to give up.

After that failure, I defaulted to putting all Kitya memories in one place, the things she planned to do went beside the things she would never do. All the things she did repeatedly were combined with the things she did once. It was messy and impossible to find anything but that didn't matter because the process was lovely. It isolated her from all the other fractions of memory and brought her close to me in a way she was never close before.

It was at this intersection where I realized how much I needed her help, so I wrote and told her how much I missed her and the trouble I was having without a clock. She was too far away for the beating of her heart to be my clock, but perhaps her words would set me on the right path. She replied and said she would try but that I had to find a way to keep it straight, she could not become my clock. She said I should write a journal of my days and my most important discoveries.

I followed this advice. Some of it is exactly as written and some is summarized. Incomprehensible and unbelievable entries are excluded although that is a fine line so if something reads that way then obviously my editing wasn't very good.

DAY 1.

Because I am writing to myself, I will use a sequential numbering system of days instead of calendar dates which have become random. Obviously, there is an inherent weakness with this approach because if I don't write anything for a day, that day will be lost like a grain of rice in the sack. It's an outcome I have to accept but believe that as long as I write down the important stuff, whatever I lose is something not worth keeping anyway.[35]

After a great deal of thoughtful introspection which always seems to lead to uncontrollable random thought, I will continue collecting Kitya memories because it is the only activity that gives me any joy at all. I will limit myself to 3 memories per day which I will send to her and ask: Did anything important happen before or after this memory and which should be attached to it?

Each memory and her response will be put onto cards that can be organized and reorganized like playing cards where hearts are Kitya memories put into a 1,2,3 time sequence and another suit like spades can be locations and clubs could be a person or the weather. Cross references and other relational attributes will be entered on the back of the card for re-processing into a more sophisticated system later. Eventually, this baseline will become validated historical time and either that will kick-start my clock into the present or I will have accumulated a lot of information for another attempt at assembling past time and keeping it in a solid form.

Conventional wisdom gives this approach pretty good odds. People constantly spend time reliving their past because it is predictable, easily accessible and a rich source of material for creating vignettes of amusing narratives by which to avoid the present. Of course, it can be instructive too, but all too often, past mistakes are repeated, not corrected, so I must be careful to avoid that wasteful failure. This isn't a game.

---

35 This is an extremely controversial duality when viewed by the Butterfly Effect and the Chaos Theory. These two theories propose that a very small action like the flapping of a butterfly's wings in the Amazon can result in very large changes like a hurricane destroying New Orleans. No argument that the flight of a butterfly is always important to the butterfly or that a single shot can be heard around the world but you have to pick your beliefs and concepts just as you carefully as you have to pick your enigmas.

DAYS 2-4.

I sent my questions to Kitya and spent the rest of the day in the future. I believe I must become more comfortable with this horizon, but it is not easy because it requires being and non-being. It is as close to walking through a shimmering portal as I can get. It is, basically, a gigantic search for meaning or confirmation of order. Some insights come quickly and others I am still waiting for and might never arrive. Predictability is at the heart of it.

Movie dialogue, for example, I can correctly predict, in advance, with significant accuracy. I can finish a line of dialogue before it starts. Not a great achievement but one which takes a lot of concentration because some actors are not very good; they send out contradictory messages which must be ignored. People acting as themselves are easier to predict providing their world view isn't threatened. Once they get into that territory, emotions prevail and then the script can go anywhere.[36]

Predicting movie dialogue and predicting real events are different in process but similar in outcome. Both of them start by concentrating on the subject but movie dialogue comes with tons of clues like body language and a plot while finding a train wreck starts by listening for the sound of steel wheels braking on steel tracks, a very specific sound in a cacophony of sound. Airplane crashes are impossible to find that way because the sound of crunching metal is the same for so many collisions and manufacturing processes. Better to listen for the screams of the passengers who are about to die.

In conclusion and as a passive observation, the shimmering portals are probably an even quicker way to discover past and future events but only for the space and time and in which they exist. In other words, a portal in Goa is good for a train wreck in Goa (in 3 days), but useless for a plane crash in Dusseldorf (in 4 days).[37]

---

36 The obvious inference to this is that with a little bit of effort and control a whole lot of life events are predictable and therefore, if they are bad, avoidable so predicting the future has some real benefits.
37 Going through a Goa portal and ending up in Dusseldorf would be teleportation, which is clearly, and only, science fiction.

DAYS 5-8.

I continued selecting and high-grading past memories and sending them to Kitya and exploring the future some more. Unfortunately, it doesn't look like I'll find a clock this way because there is so much future it is almost impossible to put days in a row, but I'll keep trying.

Exactly as found on Day 3:

The train wrecked in Gao, India. Twenty deaths, none of whom were passengers.

Lufthansa LH921 to Dusseldorf crashed on schedule, no casualties.

DAYS 9 TO 11.

I found a window, a gap or a warp through which consciousness can pass. It is very exciting, as exhilarating as free fall, as captivating as an arrhythmia and as awesome as space without the stars and it makes tons of sense. I can disappear then in the blink of an eye return but only with a residue of the future, not the real thing.

It is a contra-aging-window, the body stays in rhythm with the planetary waves and the mind acts as a stabilizer. Space-time continuums can be accessed by this thought process because thought is non-particle based even if reliant upon physical neurons.

It is like being stuck at an age from which the past dictates how the future will be experienced, and most people do this. They pick, or find, or get stuck, in a time from which the rest of their life will be experienced. For some that sweet spot is 20, for others it is 40 but for both of them it is the time when they were the most open, the most present, the most in concert with their own existence. At 80 they will tell you they are still 40 and will always 'be' that age. That is the age, the values and intellect at which they have experienced the last 40 years. Very simple, at first. The simple stuff is always first.

Day 12.

Trees make one choice in their life. Place in space. Put down that tap root and that's it, done. Don't put it down and that's it, done. Risk doesn't enter the equation, enlightenment isn't considered, not even a tiny particle of thought, a completely determination-based existence. A hundred years in one spot isn't boring to a tree, it's a good life and for some trees, 100 years is a young tree.

Human beings do not like to admit to non-orbital time. They rationalize hours and time zones as the causa prima for keeping a little blue planet spinning around a middle-aged, average-sized star in so-so galaxy on the outer edge of a universe filled with billions of galaxies containing trillions and trillions and trillions of stars. As long as everything is revolving around everything else it makes sense. The fourth dimension, time, is vital to experience what cannot be comprehended without it.

That dimension holds the others (length, width and depth) stable in order to establish boundaries. Without time, the scale and scope of even one of the remaining dimensions exceeds the parameters for knowing.

If you can bring something with you, you are in time. If you can't, you are in space.

Day 13.

Some experiences are so intensely personal they cannot be admitted, even to ourselves. This was one of those days.

Day 14.

Something has gone wrong. The Day 13 memories which couldn't be shared were triggered when I cut myself shaving and today, I have a week-old beard. What am I missing? What did I forget? Where did those days go, were they spent in the future and will I run into them later? Has this happened before? Now I understand why Kitya said I had to write everything down. A cosmic drift seems to be happening and I'm caught in it. I need a second reference point, an anchor of some kind that will prevent leakage and possibly leave me in a time zone or in an experience from which there is no escape.

I put a 1liter bottle of water on the windowsill. It is almost full; I've drawn a line at the water level and written 14 on the line.

Aside from the fright it gave me, this has taught me I really need to understand the present while it still has a working definition. Words and ideas that are time sensitive (which is almost all of them) are becoming increasingly difficult to process. They are becoming blurry and undefined at the edges; the center is becoming increasingly shallow. There are a great many circles and loops including some vortices which are consuming or redirecting thoughts before they can complete.

Day 15.

I poured a little water out of the bottle, drew a new line and labelled it 15. So far, so good.

I have over 300 cards and spent the day putting them into many logical sequences and made notes. Each sequence is becoming more difficult to resolve and taking longer to accomplish. It seems that Kitya is feeling the same way as she is taking longer to respond, and her answers are getting shorter.

The entire system is becoming unruly and needs more discipline so from now on:

1. References and cross references will not be completely eliminated but will be severely limited. They are creating their own memories and making matters worse.
2. Only the positive side of any contradiction will be maintained as the negative side can be figured if necessary and I don't need any more negatives.
3. Building block experiences (hearts) and the memory/ event chains (spades, clubs and diamonds) used to define them will be deleted and only the outcome will be retained (10 of hearts).
4. All descriptors will be replaced with a numerical classification of 1 to 5 with 1 representing ordinary and 5

being extraordinary. This might be eliminated later if there are too many 3's.

DAY 16.

The water was where I left it on Day 15 when I realized the stupidity of this system. Extreme time leakage could exist for weeks before enough water evaporated, and I detected the leakage. My thoughts and logic are manifesting themselves as tricks and none of them are mission critical to survival.

I am missing Kitya terribly. My clock is busted and so is my heart.

I have to escape the confinement of this loop so I'm going outside hoping that the loop doesn't follow me.

Damn the consequences. I am tired of being tricked and I don't care what happens.

LIFE THREE

Consequences don't care either. I turned a corner and met the Sams. They were back from Europe but didn't bring Kitya back with them. They gave some reasons which I knew to be excuses. Kitya was a prisoner of time and she chose France for her exile, probably with Leonardo da Vinci in Amboise.

We talked for the minimum polite time and said goodbye. I watched my shoes walk. My mind was completely lost in time and space, something which was occurring with increasing, uncontrollable frequency and I knew this was being accelerated by a heart which was running out of love. It wasn't anyone's fault my clock was dead, but it was my responsibility to figure it out and I was failing so I watched my shoes take one step at a time hoping they would reset a brain which was stuck in a paradigm of its own creation. It seemed to be working, for a few steps my shoes emitted a light blue haze; like the way Sergio's car glowed from the blue lights he had underneath it. That was a warning, but I missed it so instead it became a first-hand introduction to leaders.[38]

The bolt hit the left side of my head and some of it exited my right elbow targeting a metal light pole 2 feet away. It was a bright white band of extremely straight electricity which, for inexplicable reasons, travelled up the pole and blew out the light fixture in an explosion more brilliant than an arc welding torch but eerily silent like being inside a vacuum tube with not even a pressure wave as witness to the destruction.[39]

The explosion was followed by a mist-like rain of tiny glass and silver particles which were so airy and light it took a full

38 A leader is a bidirectional channel of ionized air between oppositely charged regions. Each region seeks the other with the positively charged ions wanting to fill a negative well and vice versa. The leader will start/ stop in a process called stepping, collecting more charged ions at its end with every stop before it spurts toward the oppositely charged leader which is doing the same thing. When leaders join, lightning follows the path they established.

39 Maybe because phonons are energy and like photons they are subject to the same laws of relativity so under specific conditions of temperature, velocity etc, they either cannot exist or present themselves in a form other than sound.

minute before they settled on the ground where they were all but invisible, just a sheen of silver wetness. I'm pretty sure if I hadn't absorbed some of the energy before it found the bulb there wouldn't have been anything left of it, just a puff of protons looking for some electrons with which to dance.

Other than that, the strike was pretty much the same as the first time. Arms flew out and I was lifted off the ground, sneakers included this time, maybe because the pole absorbed more of the hit and didn't need to melt them. I did another jellyfish landing and while my body reacted the way it did before, my mind was much more observant, if that's what you want to call it when all your thoughts and memories are being exploded in an aerial pyrotechnic show. I thought with spades and clubs like: 'I want to keep that' or 'That's not something I should try again' and then watched that thought and memory rise like a Roman Candle as far as it could go before disappearing into the dark. With every explosion I became emptier and the light in the jagged hole grew brighter, filling the spaces in my mind vacated by the escaping thoughts, memories and me.

It took a while to come around, which doesn't mean my clock started. I knew it took time because an ambulance came before I could escape; ambulances are not instantaneous, and it didn't come alone. It came with a news crew and the last thing anyone who has a jagged hole erupting magma in their mind wants or needs, is any kind of publicity about that mental state.

Samuel Snell and Samantha Lockerbie, local lawyers, witnessed an individual they know as 'Augustus' being struck by lightning last evening. They were out for a walk and had just finished a conversation with him when they noticed what they called a 'blue aura' at his head and feet. He was walking south down 8th Ave and was ejected several feet into the air by a bolt of lightning so bright it blinded them for several minutes. The thunder triggered car alarms for blocks around, rattled windows in nearby buildings and exploded a nearby streetlamp.

'Augustus' refused to be interviewed and threatened THE TRIBUNE with legal action on grounds of invasion of privacy but sources say this is not the first time he has been struck. He refused hospitalization and one of the paramedics who attended him reported that his only statement to them was that his 'clock was still busted'. Evidently, his only injury was the loss of a patch of hair on the left side of his head.

"Weirdest thing I've ever seen. Not shaved, not burned, no redness, swelling, not even a smell, it was just gone, vaporized." said paramedic Peter Lincoln.

Continued on the bottom of page 12

Electricity is relatively simple, the human mind is not, even if that's what runs it. Like the ability to predict the future will not necessarily give way to the future and this is not a contradiction it is a trick because once you know something it is no longer the future it is the past. But that's knowing and we've been down that road before and don't need to go down it again.

From some things you can run and maybe escape. From some things you can hide and maybe escape. From some things you can't run, hide or escape and not because they follow you but because they become part of you, like the jagged hole which was larger, and with a brighter, more intense and angry light.

My clock was still busted but something was definitely different and I couldn't get a handle on it. Maybe because I was looking for it[40] but something significant had happened with this strike and whatever it was, it wasn't done with me. Some serious rearranging was in progress and watching it happen was the only available option even if that contributed to the problem.[41]

DAYS 18 – 24.

(Day 17 is filled with incomprehensible expressions and drawings, several pages of them. If they made sense then, they don't now. One of the drawings is of someone who resembles me looking out of a tunnel or a cave. While I don't know exactly what sourced this drawing, it is familiar and familiar with

---

40 The disturbance of an observed system by the observer is known as the Observer Effect. Nor does the observer have to be a conscious system in order to invoke a change in what is being observed. It can be a machine – see the 1998 Weizmann experiment. AKA was what I sought hiding from me because I was seeking it?

41 Being early in the second strike I knew that a life had been blown up but didn't yet realize another life version was starting.

the sudden, shocking sense of familiarity. Like seeing a twin you never knew you had come around the corner right up to your face. Or turning into a mirror you didn't know was there and shocking yourself.[42] A simple mistake, until you look in the eyes and realize you are not looking at yourself and the person looking at you feels exactly the same way but both of you nod and agree it is you.

I am convinced that something of major importance has occurred and maybe because of that, equally convinced something serious is about to happen and there is nothing I can do to prevent it if it is bad or accelerate it if it is good. Such dilemmas and ambiguities are huge obstacles to recovery and they come with major uncertainties. What if my own beliefs are the problem? Could it be that my clock is broken only because I think it is broken? Am I authoring this into destiny? Am I actually outside this body?

There are many questions like this which are interesting on their own but collectively terrifying. How can you live in a reality which is nothing but questions? Can that confusion get worse and if so, what can be about it? Are all thoughts in a timeless state non-sequential by definition? How close is that to being the definition for insanity?

This must stop.

It must stop now!

Accordingly, all investigations for restarting the clock are hereby and forthwith abandoned. All plans for sequencing the past are discontinued, in their entirety. No more exploring the future. The Aftermath will be accepted as it must be even if it is incomprehensible. It makes more sense to accept what has happened than to question it with logic or emotion. Either way I am involved and if there is one thing anywhere in this tangled morass of potentialities which is true, it is the mandatory

---

42 Or it could be Autoscopy which is the experience of seeing or perceiving the environment from a different perspective, from a position outside the body. Heautoscopy (seeing your own body) is a derivative form of autoscopy and thought by those who don't know any better to be the source of doppelgängers. More than one you may be quietly acceptable but keep it between the two of you if you know what's good for either of you.

acceptance of what has happened because the past can't be undone, or denied, so live with it.

SUMMARY: Strike One was destruction and Strike Two is advancing the destruction.

Severe neurological damage has been sustained. Some systems are shutting down in a time delay fashion which is horrific to experience or predict. Smell diminished to nonexistence and taste followed it. Tingling in the extremities was followed by pain, then tremors then numbness. Running is impossible and stairs are difficult. Hearing in the left ear is gone but the right ear can hear the beat of the hummingbird's wings; every beat, every feather moving the air. Balance[43] is severely compromised.

Sight in both eyes is intense, better than a hawk.[44]

Perceptions are now multidirectional and instant.[45] This makes a stimulus feel like it is inside my head or like my head is inside a drum with someone outside pounding on it. Things are too real to be real.

Maybe I am becoming a hunter, although probably not a good one. Prey, more likely.

Thoughts hurt. Nothing makes sense except the nothing which is the space left when all the galaxies have collapsed and been put away like toys in a toybox. With every acceptance of more possibilities, confusion grows. Writing is becoming harder and producing less. Extreme fatigue is setting in.

---

43 The vestibular system of the inner ear has 3 semicircular canals filled with fluid and small hair cells. When the head moves, the fluid moves and the hair cells send signals to the brain for further processing and instructions to muscles which keep you from falling over. The 3 canals respond to different motions of the head: tilt up/down; tilt left/right and turns. Two otolith organs measure acceleration. It is impossible to know if lightning impaired these functions or if it impaired the transmission of the data they send via nerves to the cerebellum but either case the result is the same. Stand up – fall over.

44 A hawk can see 8 times better than a human being which means it can see a rabbit 2 miles away.

45 Most people need 50 milliseconds after seeing a word to perceive it which is pretty fast. Instant is a different realm of knowing.

Day 25.

It is one thing to procrastinate because you like where you are or don't want to do what you must. It is another thing to be in limbo without a clock and incapable of action. A completely contradictory state, a paradox, a riddle, a conundrum. How can you have limbo if you don't have a clock? Such is the territory of profound confusion where reality hides in open spaces, taunting you.

I have no choice but to employ cliché's like wait and see. Perhaps I will regain the faculties I lost and perhaps I will lose the enhancements I gained but I must accept that profound confusion is sown with maybes between rows of uncertainties in a misplaced field of unknowns. This is in conflict with logic, which demands that perhaps or maybe introduce a statement of questioning or wonderment.

But questioning requires a focused memory. If you can't find or remember the problem, you can't solve it, you just get to keep it. Some of this confusion may be real but separating that from what has been confabulated is impossible. Countless thoughts are triggered by countless unrelated thoughts until profound confusion ensures the equality of everything and denies the certainty of nothing. Profound confusion is a cancer which inhabits every word and obliterates its meaning along with all its adjectives and qualifiers.

And yet, one image keeps flashing through this minefield of anarchy and every time it does, it comes with a sense of familiarity in spite of the fact it is always different. I don't know what it is except it is not Kitya.

Days 26, 27.

I am fearful of outside in all its meanings. Time is gone and space is soon to follow. The very special and hugely important knowing which comes from having an address on earth, a place where knowing can rest undisturbed, is fleeting between illusional and delusional realities. The sense of being lost is palpable and it is not the kind of lost where a stranger can give directions but the kind of lost which consumes all directions and all destinations. Where I am is losing when I am and leaving both of us in a state of aloneness and emptiness of everything but unresolved conflict.

I have programmed my phone with multiple alarms to a schedule on a piece of paper I carry with me so I don't induce anxiety by having to look everywhere for it, sometimes forgetting where I started and having to start over and over again. The idea of having a schedule is based on the questionable assumption that in the absence of any external structure, I should impose some discipline and not allow myself to go entirely with the flow.

I follow this schedule diligently. At 8:00am, the alarm sounds so I look at the schedule, and brush my teeth. Other needs, like eating or sleeping happen spontaneously and I try not to think about the origin or consequences of spontaneity. Those needs are driven by bio-rhythm and I don't want to speculate on the origin of that either, or what will happen if it stops.

Of only one thing am I certain and is unquestionable. This is the worst time of my life.[46] It is the most alone, solitary, withdrawn and reclusive existence possible for which there is no understanding or solution. Words for it exist but the order in which to put them does not. Days are only distinguished by the numbers given them in this journal.[47]

All but one thought, that recurring thought which is not Kitya, is condemned in this wasteland of dead, dying or decomposing ideas. It is the only entry worth mentioning. It is a thought and a vision and is accompanied with sound and most important, it seems to contain a meaning, a message. It is not something I can control or analyze; it comes when it wants to come and stays for as long as it wants to stay, like an apparition. Its origin might be the jagged hole.

---

46 As contradictory as time is without a clock, the feeling and knowledge of impending doom (or death) must be vestigial. In other words, it is known but not because it has occurred before. And it doesn't inhabit the mind, it haunts it.

47 Not to be confused with The Groundhog Effect which is a single day looped. These days are differentiated and probably sequential, but the contents are indiscriminate and there is no way to predict what will occur the next moment let alone the next day.

Day 28.

The sight, the sound, the scent, the idea and the persever-
ance of thought collided.

Finally, I have a destination and perhaps from there, a destiny. The address is:

Staroměstské nám. 1, 110 00 Josefov, Czechia

The Prague Orloj

Located on the southern wall of the Old Town Hall in
the Old Town Square.

This clock was created in 1410 by the great clockmak-
er Mikuláš of Kadaň and Jan Šindel, medieval scientist
and Catholic priest respectively. It displays Babylonian
Time, Old Bohemian Time, German Time and Sidereal
Time[48]. It also displays moon phases and the passage of
the sun through the constellations of the zodiac. Its calendar movement shows the day of the month, week and
feast days. These movements are surrounded by autom-
atons of rotating apostles and a skeleton ringing a bell,
a warning that your days are numbered so add up your
sins and pay your indulgence[49].

Legend holds that City Counsellors, fearing that Mikuláš would build a bigger, better clock for someone
else, blinded him. This drove him mad and he threw
himself into the clockworks with the curse that all who
tried to fix his clock would become insane or die.

The motivation behind this apparition, was one word: obvious. Some answers should never be questioned; this was mine.
It made perfect sense to go to the oldest, working astronomical
clock in the world which still accepted sacrifices and see if that
rebooted next or shredded it.

There was a problem.

---

48 Sidereal time is the angle measured along the celestial equator the me-
ridian to the great circle that passes through the March equinox and both
celestial poles. Measured in hours, minutes and seconds.
49 No doubt this was Šindel's contribution to the Orloj. An indulgence is a
fee paid to the church in order to reduce time and torture in the afterlife
for specific sins. It was a real money-maker and a real conflict of interest
which the church chose to ignore as it basically sold tickets to Heaven.

My dear Kitya,
   I believe I have found a solution, but I need your help. I am
going to the Prague Orloj. Either that will start my clock, or I
will stop that one. Nothing makes more sense than this.
For now, Octavius

My dear Octavius,
   Of course it makes sense but it won't be easy. The Orloj was just
recently restored and everyone in Prague is on tenterhooks because of the curse. They have made it almost impossible to
throw yourself into the clock, but I have a friend who might
help. Please send me a picture of your ticket so I know time is
not playing tricks on you.
Kitya, as ever and always.

   Thank-you Kitya. I am a complete wreck and couldn't possibly
throw myself into the works without your help.

   I know.

Days 29 – 31.

The days since Strike 2 have seen improvement or regression
to somewhat normal states in almost all functions except clock.
Sight has gone downhill but hearing and balance are almost
restored. I still don't know when anything will happen but have
made a decision and programmed my phone with it. That fills
the void created by the myriad of uncertainties which inhabit a
world without time. Even though knowing can't be trusted, not
knowing is exhausting.

Travel will be challenging; I will need help at airports but
will be safe in the plane as I can't get lost in it and the chance of
lightning rerouting my plan is remote.[50]

My ticket is booked and waiting to leave is just as difficult
without time as it is with it.

Days 32, 33.

I walked into the silver cocoon with wings and emerged,
twice, LHR followed by PRG.

It was light and appeared to be midday in Prague. I looked

---

50 Aircraft are frequently hit by lightning but the last confirmed crash in
    the United States which was attributed to it occurred in 1967 (catastroph-
    ic fuel explosion).

everywhere for Kitya but followed the plan we set by following the crowd. She found me when I walked into the Arrivals Hall.

She wasn't alone and the way he had his arm around her shoulder, holding her tight like she was his plush toy made him more than just a friend. She didn't look happy. She didn't even look like her, like my Kitya. I was shocked. I suspect she was too.

Had years passed? Did I write in my journal everyday like I thought or had some weeks or months leaked out? Had the second strike caused some collateral clock damage when it blew up space?

She introduced him as Francois and he sneered when she said his name, like he was an aristocrat and she forgot his title. He was tall, too tall for her, skinny as a drug addict and dressed in black. His hair was also black, straight, too long and it fell over a narrow forehead to hide eyes which were not kind. He was here against his will and that was our first common ground.

There was no hug, no scent of her hair, no squeeze of her hand in mine. He wouldn't let go of her and she didn't struggle. All he wanted to do was get to the Orloj and leave me there and that was our second, and final, common ground. With or without help, one way or another, if the Orloj was to be my final destination or my ultimate destiny, I was ready for either. This life was going to stop.

The only conversation on the train to City Center was his. Mostly he spoke in French and if she responded, it was with a oui or a non as she looked out the window. This didn't seem to bother him but it tortured me.

For me, hearing Kitya speak her thoughts was like being in a Utopian dream but he didn't care, only his thoughts mattered. He asked me what it was like to be struck by lightning but didn't wait for an answer. As long as I validated his question by not denying it, he didn't care to hear the answer.

It was raining when we got to the tower; I hadn't touched her, and she barely looked at me. Francois took charge. He wanted a coffee so he sent me into the ticket line as they watched me from a café. She had tears in her eyes, tears which stayed in puddles which would not fall. I looked for her trademark splash of color, her signature style but it was missing. What happened to her?

The tower is 50 meters tall and the viewing platform is accessed by climbing 172 steps up a narrow, spiral staircase. It was a mind-numbing, repetitive ascent. One foot rose after the other, eyes seeing only another step in the spiral, the repetition at first comforting, then fearful as my line of vision broke over the threshold and was forced to confront a great expectation which could go any direction.

When I stepped onto the platform, the rain stopped because the world stopped. Raindrops were suspended in time; the Orloj was doing its job.

Fairy tale and horror film played simultaneously. Distant thunder didn't bother me. One way or another it was over. I could feel Kitya's eyes on me but couldn't return the look.

Only two choices were left: Now or Never.

LIFE FOUR

I spread my legs for balance, raised my arms over my head and stretched them as far as they would reach, palms facing each other, fingers also seeking maximum extension. Then I looked up to the sky, closed my eyes and defied the jagged hole. There was pain but not real pain, not the kind of pain to be feared or avoided but it hurt. It was encompassment, it was incisive, it was a necessary part of the moment, it had to be sought, endured and accepted. Light spilled from the jagged hole, spreading slowly into the corners of my mind, like a time-lapse movie of a sunrise, a bright one and getting brighter by the moment.[51] The jagged hole pulsed, slowly at first, then erratically. The edges softened, melting like marshmallow, revealing a bubbling well of light.

Kitya cried from below: "No! Please don't take him."

It was a most peculiar experience. As it should have been because ball lightning[52] is extremely rare and there is no written record of a person ever touching one let alone having one suspended between their palms. This one was small, about the size of a tennis ball, extremely erratic and highly energized, like the ball in a fast pinball game with lots of bumpers.

A bolt of ball lightning was captive between my hands.[53] It sent orange leaders to the fingers of one hand then to the

---

51 Lightning rods are installed in all tall buildings. They provide a low resistance conduit for the positive and negatively charged ions to equalize without blowing walls and innocent bystanders to pieces and they work perfectly unless there is a conduit which offers even lower resistance or a bigger well of oppositely charged ions requiring equalization. The odds against getting hit when a lightning rod is an available option are astronomical, like the clock.

52 There is no commonly accepted explanation for ball lightning. First-hand reports vary significantly, with the size of the ball ranging from a thumbnail to a large beachball. They have irregular shimmering edges. Red, orange and yellow are the most common colors with a life expectancy from a second to over a minute before the ball mysteriously disappears or explodes.

53 On July 10, 2011 ball lightning with a 2meter tail entered the control room of the local emergency services in Liberec, 90km north of Prague. It entered a window, bounced to the ceiling then to the floor then back to the ceiling where it rolled around for a few meters before dropping to

fingers of the other with an exchange that seemed to keep it suspended, caged, between my open palms. The leaders were cool to the touch, but the surrounding air was hot.[54]

It departed as quickly as it came, after only 10 or 20 seconds, and fortunately it did not explode but innocently disappeared like magic. I have my suspicions where it went because the moment it disappeared my clock started. I felt it. Why I do not know, but there was a vibration as the rings of my clock began their rotation. The wheels engaged the cogs turning the splines and moving the second hand with a tiny jerk as time started in motion again.

Tick after tock, one second followed the next in perfect accord with the principle of original design. That rhythm came with joy, with the reprieve of a life sentence and a mortality which would now conclude it naturally. No mysterious chatter in between thoughts or experiences. No more shimmering portals. No more fear for a radical, bizarre next. Just the steady beating of my heart and the commotion of a lot of people who witnessed something they only wanted to know was true if it didn't upset all the other truths in their knowing. Bless them for that innocence.

In a statement, an act of faith over science that would have made Jan Šindel proud, I rubbed my hands together and smiled my best trickster smile. *Just an illusion folks. Just a little bit of flash powder from the magician.* A little girl clapped and laughed and that was enough to convince the others to return to the fiction with which they were most comfortable.

My palms were hot like a sunburn and they would stay that way for days, but I only wanted one thing and that was to hold Kitya's face with them. I started down as the Orloj began announcing a new hour. By the time I walked out the door, everyone was watching the dance of the skeleton remind the congregation of its duty to pay and pray. It was enough of a distraction for me to become lost in the crowd, unnoticed by a curious few who were still struggling with what they had witnessed. Un-

---

the floor and disappearing. It knocked out all the telecom systems and destroyed 1 computer monitor.

54 Lightning has no temperature but it heats the air and water particles around it pretty hot.

noticed, that is, by everyone except the one person who would ever matter to me. She came up beside me and placed her hand gently on my arm, mi Contessa Italiana.

"I see you are back but who have you become?" she asked quietly, almost in a whisper, as she guided me into a side street and out of the square.

"Max." I replied, spontaneously, with great happiness to once again feel the immediacy of life in my voice and the spirit driving it.

"Maximilian from the Roman Generals Maximus and Scipio Aemilianus? You have lost some stature, Augustus."

"I know. But I don't want to be emperor anymore. I just want to be whoever the next minutes allow me to be. And now, more than anything, I want something I can't have, Kitya. I want you back."

"You can have me here and now Max. I am sorry for the greeting you received but you had to do this yourself, I had to keep you from clinging to me. There really was no way I could help, no way of knowing if I would make you better or worse. I couldn't bear to see you ground up in that clock but if that was what it took, I had to let it be. I couldn't tell you that any more than I could tell Sergio not to race."

"And Francois?"

"He was part of my disguise, Max, but he saw what you did. I warned him so he couldn't deny it, like he denies everything with his arrogance and perversion of knowing." she laughed with her pixie voice and my heart mended with every note. How amazing that something so small and unique as a melody from that one precious instrument in the entirety of life's orchestras can become everything to the one person who loves it.

"You scared the shit of him, Max. He ran. Not even an Au Revoir. I suspect he thought you were Thor or some such deity and would slay him with a bolt for the disrespect he showed you. I wouldn't have blamed you if you had." Her eyes were bright and mischievous, studying my face.

"What now?" I asked as her thoughts were once again comfortably appearing, completely unbidden, in my mind. I was back in her world.

She smiled. The mischievous Kitya smile which stops time. "Now or now? Which one do you want?"

"All of them."

"Let's go, I have a room. I need to get out of these dreadful clothes and be with you. I am so proud of you, Max."

"I know it's wrong, but I can't keep it from you. I am in love with you Kitya."

"I know and I told you this would happen, didn't I?"

"You did."

"Well, let's not dwell on it. Your clock has started, now let's put our hearts back where they belong."

* * * * *

Fifteen years of extraordinary followed that singular, defining day and night in Prague.

Fifteen years of day following day like waves breaking on a beach. Everything in perfect sequence. The past stayed put, the present didn't flicker and the future unfolded. The cycle of time held us captive and wouldn't let us go.

Kitya became a PhD Psychologist. I opened a shop and fixed things like appliances and computers.

Titus was born shortly after Kitya graduated and Lili was born 2 years after him. Life becomes very fulfilling when children are part of it. Their innocence, perhaps. Watching the development of character traits and personalities. Watching individuality attach its anchor lines to the innumerable possibilities with which life begins and then weave that sacred tapestry of a unique and beloved human being. It was a time of inordinate happiness.

The jagged hole shone brightly through it all, a constant reminder that lightning strikes the earth 50 times a second.

LIFE FIVE

LIFE SIX

I entered consciousness with the thought that burning all the trees on the mountain doesn't change the mountain along with a shocking extrospection that I didn't recognize my own body. It was as if somebody put pale old skin on me and my insides didn't feel right either, muscle mass was not what it should have been; my gut was bigger than it had ever been.

Aftermath was my immediate and most hopeful thought because it was in opposition of, and wholly in preference to, my greatest fear. A fear which was suddenly in play as years of worry about accidentally walking through a shimmering portal became a brutal possibility.

By the complete virtue of immediate survival, I had to escape that possibility along with the consequences of it being a one-way trip or even a return trip but without Kitya at the other end. I looked around the hospital room for the portal through which I must have entered. The search ended on the eyes of a man in the bed beside me. He pressed the call button in his hand.

"Where am I?" My voice frightened him. Considering what was sourcing it, a valid reaction.

He answered and looked away: "Ich spreche kein Englisch."

A nurse was the first to arrive and before she said anything the man said: "Er ist Englisch." She shushed both of us then took my vitals, checked my IV and scrolled through pages on the monitor. She was unhurried and it was clear she didn't like interruptions while she did her job. Fine. The last thing I wanted to do was engage with anything or anyone and accidentally get trapped in a time when I did not want to be.

A young doctor was the next to enter. The nurse said "English." and he smiled and said: "Nice to see you have decided to join us. Please wait for the others before we start." The nurse spoke to him in a quiet, subdued voice which sounded ominous and which had to be the result of the machine's assessment of my wellbeing.

It didn't take long, and it didn't take a genius. It wasn't a dream. I wasn't dead or dying. I hadn't walked through a portal. I'd been hit again. Damn. Starting all over.

Just as they finished speaking, two more doctors and an older nurse with a very severe face entered the room. The younger nurse drew the curtain, separating me from my curious roommate, and 'my team' introduced themselves. The young doctor then said a few words in German, no doubt updating everyone on my condition before asking me if I knew how I came to be lying in his hospital. They were gathered around the bed, like it was story time so I cooperated by explaining to them where I left my car and hoped they would quickly release me so I could get to it and back to my own world.

I told them I was leaving Sunnyside Nursery on highway 17 with a cart full of pansies, daisies, begonias, nasturtiums and a half a dozen other flowers and herbs for spring planting. It was to be a surprise. Our first planting of the year, the beds were warm and ready for plants and seeds. If the rain held off, at least some of the plants would go into the ground that afternoon, if it didn't, the next day. For us, spring planting was a ritual that continued into early summer as the beds around our small house filled with bloom. The children had their own gardens as Titus preferred the order of an Italian garden and Lili preferred the chaos of the English. I was walking to my car, pushing the cart and that was my last memory.

They looked at me in disbelief and unless you are lying to them, a doctor's disbelief is never a good sign.

The young doctor told me I was in a hospital in Hamburg and it was winter. I was admitted 7 days ago and had been in a coma since. He told me I was struck by lightning while walking the path around Lake Außenalster and that was the totality they had of me. He emphasized totality and then went on to define it: no name, no documents and no one had enquired about me or reported anyone like me missing. "Did I know die identität?[55]

---

55 Sometimes, and this was one of them, it's a toss-up whether it is better to know where, when and why you are compared to who you are. Some social disciplines like law and medicine, value identity over content, which they assume.

I gave them my name and told them I'd been struck by lightning before, 4 times, and I would be fine in a day or two. They were unconvinced of my certainty, perhaps even my sanity but asked little more.

It wasn't much but it was enough for the police to find my belongings at a budget hotel where, they determined, I had been staying for the last couple months. Before that, no one, including me, knew where I had been or what I had done. No police record so that was good and no charges pending, also good. Evidently, being struck by lightning in Germany is perfectly legal. They came with a few possessions which I didn't recognize but it was more than enough for me to put the pieces together.

One second, I was pushing a trolley full of flowers for my family in Canada and the next I was blasted into a hospital bed in Germany.

Not easy to accept but that was the starting point of a reality which was only to became more terrible with time and as it did, my greatest fear of walking through a shimmering portal became my greatest desire. At least with that, I might find a way back, a return from a hell which was just getting started. Unfortunately, reality has a way of kicking you when you are down and however unreal those portals might have once been, they had also been gone for years and were probably gone forever. Either way, not something about which to talk to a doctor, any kind of doctor.

It didn't take long for them to figure out a fraction of what they didn't know, which was a lot, but it was as true as my passport was real. Somehow, between pushing a trolley full of flowers out of Sunnyside garden center and landing in a Hamburg hospital bed, years of my life disappeared. Completely disappeared, not a single memory for over 12 years.[56] No memory of being struck twice, like they happened to someone else. Not the strike at the greenhouse when I was 36 or the strike a week ago, while walking around a lake in Hamburg at the age of 48. Interesting?

56 Retrograde amnesia is the inability to remember specific and/or general details before a certain date which could include months or years of memory. I lost everything in a specific time period.

Fascinating. All memories erased between two totally unique sets of events is more than enough to create a blizzard of academic investigation into a physical phenomenon which everyone thinks they know yet few have experienced and fewer still can explain. But there was to be more to this than academic fascination.

The doctors were immediately beyond curiosity and just as immediately initiated a battery of tests by which they hoped to discover something about the way the human brain remembers and recalls.[57] In effect, they had a human primate on their laboratory table and were reluctant to let him go until they learned all they could learn[58] about the impact of supercharging a delicate neural network beyond its breaking point. What they didn't say, but which didn't take long to figure out, was that this learning, this curiosity was in opposition to any therapy that might accidentally close the door on the mystery of memory suppression. This was what they truly wanted to understand so they could market it.[59]

They used a variety of techniques to keep me engaged but the application of Teutonic guilt predominated. If only they could understand the reason for memory loss for a very specific period of time, anyone suffering from memories they did not want would benefit from this discovery. Lives would be restored, saved in some cases. Memories obliterated without lightning, a scalpel or a medicine cabinet would be a precious gift to all humanity. Anyone with PTSD could be treated, perhaps they could even fix me.[60]

With this as their stated motive and having a brain on their table which had already achieved this objective created the

---

57 Physically, they want to know what is going on with the medial temporal lobe, especially the hippocampus. Chemically they want to know about biomarkers, especially RbAp48 protein deficiency and its genetic consumer, the RBBP4 gene.

58 Brain surgery I declined.

59 Electroconvulsive therapy I also declined on the basis of having already experienced this treatment at extremely high levels and no desire to find out if it was possible to turn a scattered memory into a vegetative one.

60 It is already being used but with limited success, as is memory interference which means injecting new awareness into an existing tortured memory in hope of disrupting and destressing it.

perfect psychogenic storm and I was the center of it. Except I didn't matter, nor did the last 12 years of my life which had disappeared in flash. That was my problem. Twelve years had been stolen from me and were being analyzed like a symptom or a side effect and not a crime or a profound loss that had to be recovered.

For them, and me, after days of MRI, CT, PET and SPECT scans, not a clue surfaced as my patience was drained along with vials of blood. Dozens of interviews while connected to all manner and kinds of measurement devices yielded nothing for them.

For me, if I learned anything about the life missing from my time, it was that it was gone and the only way to get it back was to go and find it. Maybe if I went back to Sunnyside and finished pushing that trolley full of flowers into the parking lot, by the time I got to my car, 12 years of my life would be returned like a boomerang and spring planting would continue as planned. Unlikely but at least I would be back home, a little older and definitely no wiser, but home and safe.

I had a credit card and a passport, so I borrowed my room-mate's phone and made a call.

Two days later I showered, shaved, put on fresh clothes and without saying goodbye to anyone left by way of the back staircase. I took a taxi to the airport and was in the air before I could be missed by anyone.

★ ★ ★ ★ ★

Fourteen hours later, I was in the place I knew as home, 12 years and 25% of my life ago. Except our little house was gone. Heart stopping. Was that life a dream and was this was the nightmare? Too real for anything except panic. The neighborhood had changed but not extraordinarily. The family across the street no longer lived there but I remembered their names and faces. Ikbir, Charanpreet, their son Manraj and daughter Chuni were the same ages as Titus and Lili.

Next to them were Josh and Lani, newlyweds back then and very friendly with Kitya. Perhaps they could explain what happened? They remembered me but did not invite me inside, preferring to answer my questions as I stood on their doorstep and based upon the questions I was asking, I couldn't blame them for that. They didn't have many answers and what little they knew was not comforting.

Kitya and the children moved away 10 years ago, and the new owners tore down the little house to build a bigger one. They didn't know where they went, hadn't heard from her and didn't know if she had another man in her life.

My old shop was a nail salon.

I called Kitya's employer, Island Health. They told me she no longer worked there and refused to answer any questions.

The Sams would know. I went to their office; they refused to see or talk to me. Security escorted me from the building and told me not to come back and to expect to be charged with trespass if I did. What had I done? Was my family alive? What happened in those 12 years?

I had to find home. I was experiencing my life with guts that felt like I was standing on a crumbling cliff.

My parents would tell me what had happened, what I had done, no matter how bad it might be.

The house looked the same and so did the yard. The first reassuring memory of a day I wanted to forget.

A memory is a treasure when all is lost but it is a torture when there is any hope it can be revived. I had to find Kitya and the children. It was the territorial imperative and it came with the knowledge it came with a price. A price hinted by the neighbor's caution and by the Sams' refusal to see me. I was not welcome and that could get worse.

The children would be grown. Titus would be 21, Lili, 19. I missed most of their lives. What would they think of me? What would they remember? What of my dear Kitya, my one and only love? Some questions you don't want answered because some answers you cannot bear to hear. What was hiding in the jagged hole? It looked different, ominous.

With feet dragging on a concrete sidewalk I helped pour, I struggled to the door, rang the bell and waited in fear. A stranger answered and the fear froze into dread from which I knew there would be no relief. Dead. Car crash.

A world which I didn't believe could become smaller, shrank almost out of sight. Stunned to almost non-existence, to thoughts so slow they almost lost themselves before completing, I wandered until finding a quiet bench. Overwhelmed with profound sadness, I sat and grieved until empty of all emotion and nearly all thought.

Blank and extremely heavy, I had to go, but where, why? Was this the time to quit? Could I take anymore?

I wandered and wondered. Who was I and what had I become? All the markers of my life were being erased and taking me with them. Without someone to witness your life, individuality is optional; being a person is reduced to words on a document or a userid on a screen. Just another alpha-numeric trying to survive.

I had to find my family before I lost that sense of being. Every thought, memory, experience and emotion was dying with no order or place to rest. Knowing was disappearing and nothing was replacing it. Profound emptiness, sadness and regret were strangling me. The last of my species searching for a place to die.

I found myself at the school, went to the Entrance Door, found my footprints and stood in them.

Tiw's Day and Kitya was more beautiful than ever before, truly radiant. Black leggings, a hip-tight, flared, knee-length dark blue skirt and knit top with black, pink and grey horizontal stripes that started wide at the waist and became narrow at the neck where it rolled over and glowed pink. Red shoes. Pink hair. Rouge on her cheeks like an elf. She was gorgeous and I had to be close to her but not because she was so calm and lovely or that chaos was raining down on everyone. I had to be close to her because she was my sanity. I had crossed the bridge of obsession.

Someone said: "His hair is smoking."

She took her hand from my arm. With tears in her eyes, she shook her head and quietly said "No." then disappeared into the crowd and was gone forever.

MARNIE

"This is not gonna end well." she said under her breath, but he was thinking about something entirely different when he replied: "Nothing for you to worry about yet."

Yet? Like what could possibly add to her problems with this hillbilly town when it had been nothing but problems in spite of the fact she had only been there for a few days, all lousy, and now about to get worse, not much doubt about that.

Try the rent. Try the truck stop mentality. Try the only entertainment being The Hound and its pathetic collection of misnamed regulars. She pretty much figured those boozers took turns getting pissed on the basis that sooner or later, by simple elimination of no other choice combined with blind luck one of them would get lucky so what difference did anything make, have another drink, it was all random anyway. Unfortunately, that came true often enough to keep the theory alive. Some poor little chiquita would have one too many glasses of Chardonnay and then one of the hounds would tell her his pathetic life story hoping to get a pity fuck. And if that didn't work, they'd put a few doubles in her and take what they wanted, however they wanted to take it. Then chiquita would be left with scars for memories and nightmares for the blank spots with no hope for justice because with a cheap lawyer and the good old boys' club of wing men testifying to her so-called consent, justice was not only blind but deaf, dumb and as extinct as a Dodo.

It was a town for good old boys just like the one at her window, only this one had a badge. SHERIFF. Like in the old fucking west. Sheriff Bridget Durman. What the fuck kind of name is Bridget for a man?

"Ma'am." "Ma'am." he repeated softly.

She kind of snapped into the present. "HMMmmm?".

And that little noise, which he asked for with his nice voice, for Chrissake, that was what ratcheted everything up to a grand fucking federal case. He probably figured she was making a pass at him because he was wearing a gun and if she wasn't scared of it then she had to be wanting the hips wearing it. Seriously, WTF, she wasn't even close to being in that mood and even if she was, he wouldn't be her first pick unless he was her only pick.

Then again, she had woken up with worse memories than him, but she'd set her New Year's resolution at zero tolerance for one-nighters and all the macho bullshit and ridiculous drama that went with them.

True, she didn't exactly make their life easy but what did they expect? She never hid the fact she'd kick ass without a second thought. Or that they'd only get one warning so pay close attention because the warning will only hurt your pride but what happens next is whole different hurt, and for longer.

A couple of them were even dumb enough to get physical just to see if she was telling the truth and ended up in hospital where they learned the stupidity of a surprise attack and that sometimes even a ton of therapy won't make things as good as new.

No matter, no excuse and no deflection allowed either, also part of the resolution. It was her fault for picking them in the first place, so she always made at least one visit to the hospital and always felt genuine sympathy for them, even if it was their own damned fault because they had absolutely no goddamn excuse or reason for provoking her when she was always being perfectly nice and honest. And she reminded them of her words. 'Go ahead and play rough if you want to but understand that if you start pushing your weight around and it stops being fun for me, the consequences only go one direction.'

But that was then and this is now, she reminded herself. Without being asked, she passed her license and registration out the window.

Then she waited for him just like he waited for somebody in his radio to tell him what to do. Her first impression with the law in Loserville was not very flattering and unfortunately that usually meant that trouble with a capital T was coming down the line. Shit. Like she needed trouble when she really didn't but no matter who started it she wasn't the kind of girl to run from a fight so he better not start one. Dammit she was in a bad mood. Like foul with a capital Fuck.

"Ma'am? Marnie Hill? You are Marnie Hill?"

She was happy to admit that any old time but foul is foul so she challenged him right off the bat. "Yeah, I'm Marnie. What did I do wrong?"

"Nothing Ma'am."

"Then what fucking difference does it matter who I am?"

"You've got a point there, Marnie."

She was tempted to flip him a response about his pointed head thinking like the dick in his pants, and if he didn't have a badge, she would have said it but decided to hold back a little. Another New Year Resolution only this time in the form of hold back *a lot*. She had to stop being governed by her emotions and that included, no, that especially included, making decisions based on a flood of feelings and that was damn difficult. She'd had a lifetime of running on pure logic, on perfectly calculated cause and effect, of tactics, strategy and the minimization of collateral damage and she absolutely loved the thrill of letting her emotions rule for a change. Unfortunately, they had been bottled-up for so long they just about always made bad things worse and sometimes much worse. Oh well, at least she was doing something by her own choice and didn't feel like a goddamn machine so why was he treating her like a criminal? Good question.

"So why did you stop me?"

"Routine. Well, not routine for you but for me it's a routine confirmation of a suspected stolen vehicle which it isn't. Just checking, thanks for your cooperation."

"So, when you're wrong what does that tell you about your suspicions or is this just random bullshit like everything else around here?" Yeah, let's play games, see who had the worst day maybe.

Before he could answer, a matching prowler with 2 wannabe lawmen pulled up, close up, in front of her minivan and when they got out it, it wasn't exactly friendly but at least no flashing lights, lucky for them. She'd had enough cheap intimidation to know that whatever happened next was only going in her direction if there was a fight.

"Well Marnie, in this case it means you aren't a suspect. Have a nice day."

Some things never change but not being a suspect was always nice to hear even if it never stayed that way for long. Unfortunate truth of it was, her nickname was Trouble with a capital T and that came in more forms than most people imagined but they all agreed on one thing. Get as far away from Marnie as possible. Physically, emotionally, psychologically, financially, spiritually, you name it, but run away and run away fast. Don't look back and if anybody asks if you know Marnie, any Marnie on the planet, plead the fifth.

It wasn't goddamn fair, they'd start it and then whine and cry when she had them backed up against the wall fearing for this body part or that body part. Like that is on their mind when Cause of Death or the fear of seeing their whole pathetic life flash in front of their eyes would be a way smarter thing to worry about. But no, not this time, this time they picked the wrong chiquita to blame for something she didn't do and which they started. Like Sheriff Bridget and his .454 magnum attitude. It just wasn't fair, but she always warned them.

She sensed a bad day getting worse and maybe a resolution or two going into the crapper, at least temporarily, and that pissed her off some more. She just made that resolution and when she failed at herself, everybody got punished.

"Who names a boy Bridget? Honest to God, what kind of moron did that to you?"

"Yeah, not my Mom, she named me Bridge."

"That's only a fraction of a difference. You're goddamn lucky she didn't like asphalt, how'd you like a name like Asphalt for the rest of your life, Bridget?"

"Yeah, it's confusing, I guess. Could you step out of the car and give me a breath sample."

"Blow yourself. I didn't do anything wrong, you said so yourself."

"That was then."

"And this is then too. Don't play that game with me."

But it was too late; she knew it by the body language of the 2 wannabe's who were looking at her like she was Dillinger or Capone. They should be so lucky.

What happened after that definitely wasn't her fault. Maybe some innocent civilians don't mind being handcuffed but Marnie wasn't one of those and she told them NO at least a couple of times but did they listen? Hell no they didn't, not even after she told them what was going to happen if they didn't back down and get civilized, right fucking now.

★ ★ ★ ★ ★

Which was pretty much how the whole stupid episode played out in court as Sheriff Durman, limping slightly, accompanied her down the aisle to trade words with Judge Fifth who was reading charges before she even got to sit down. Kangaroo court.

She let him finish with "How do you plead?"

"Not guilty."

"You plead Not Guilty?" Judge Fifth repeats, somewhat incredulously.

"Yeah, in other words, I'm innocent."

"So, if you are so innocent, how do you explain two deputies going to the hospital with cuts, bruises and trauma, 5 stitches for one of them."

"Maybe they don't know how to do their job. I didn't do anything. They attacked me."

"Attacked you? They are officers of the law and you didn't obey their orders."

"Hell no I didn't."

Judge Fifth looked to a couple of faces in the courtroom then to Sheriff Bridget who immediately started talking about failure to cooperate, resisting arrest, damage to a police car on account of it being used as a landing platform for an airborne deputy, general wear and tear on uniforms and the people wearing them plus additional costs associated with putting Marnie in her own cell, of which they only had 3 but she had to have one all by herself or she'd kill whoever they put in there with her and this time they believed her.

She'd had enough. "Bridget, did you tell me I was innocent? Yes or Yes?"

"Yes."

"Did I tell you I was leaving?"

"Yes."

"How many times?"

"Three."

"There you go Judge, innocent all the way."

"So why didn't you cooperate?" Judge Fifth asks with undisguised curiosity. Somehow it took 2 deputies and 1 Sheriff to put 1 Marnie in a cell but only 1 Marnie to put 2 deputies in hospital and give 1 Sheriff a painful looking limp. Not only that but she didn't have a scratch on her. In fact, she looked like she was ready to do it all over again, just bring on some new deputies if you got'em. There had to be some wisdom there, somewhere.

"Cooperate? Who says I didn't cooperate? You think he put me in that cage without my cooperation?"

Judge Fifth couldn't quite map it. "So, was that before or after the deputies drew their weapons?"

Sheriff didn't wait on that answer. "She cooperated."

Judge still didn't quite get it but it sure sounded like somebody should have drawn a weapon and it wasn't her because that was about the only charge missing. "So, is anybody going to tell me what really happened?"

Marnie liked the way it was going, Judge Fifth was coming around to her way of thinking. "What happened was all the stuff he's talking about plus 2 days in a cage for me plus my inconvenience all of which is worth at least $5,000 and it goes up $500 a day so you decide what you can afford but you might as well pay it now when it's cheap because you know you're gonna pay it. Make it easy on yourself."

It wasn't a complete bluff, she left some room for negotiation and hoped Judge Fifth would see and appreciate that. The last couple of days had given her a lot to think about. Teaching Sheriff Bridget a lesson in failing to arrest guilty people instead of trying to arrest innocent ones was one of the things she thought about quite a bit. Add to that her opinion of him wasn't improving on account of him trying to accuse her of some minor felonies for which he ultimately was responsible. Two whole days in jail to an innocent person is a lot of anger and she was more than ready to share it so she abandoned the hold-back-a-lot resolution and picked up right where she left off.

"Look, if you don't want to settle for inconvenience, we can start by talking about why he told me I was innocent then wouldn't let me go, that's court record, here and now. That's also harassment minimum, then comes the kidnapping and unlawful containment with even more unlawful confinement the next day. He already admitted it so let's get this thing done before anybody else gets hurt. Seriously your honor, you're the judge, do some judging."

They settled for $1500 plus by way of a court ordered apology he refused to verbalize, Sheriff Bridget drove her to her van which was parked on the road exactly where and as she left it.

It stunk. Lately she'd been living in it, on and off, and 3 days of being shut up tight made a bad smell mellow into something resembling her current shitty mood but it fired up right away so she opened the window, hit the gas and shot gravel all over Sheriff Bridget's prowler which felt pretty good. She wanted backroads and she wanted to get away on her own terms and that meant right now and quicker.

Then it came to her. She shouldn't be feeling so goddamn negative. She was free and nothing touches freedom. Freedom which is hard to get and harder to keep and if Bridget knew what was good for him, he better not mess with that again.

Dammit, her black mood was back and already in overdrive and she didn't know where to take it or who to share it with until she looked in the rearview mirror, mostly to see what she looked like after 2 days in jail which wasn't real pretty, but not that bad all things considered, except she wasn't the only image in that mirror.

She definitely wasn't expecting to see his lights or then hear his siren, but she wasn't really surprised either. He closed on her damn fast and just as she left town limit with nothing resembling a witness anywhere to be found. He was alone and that was a huge mistake if he had revenge on his mind, something that would be stupid even for him, given the lesson she'd already given him, not to mention the warnings. She always warned them.

Then again, maybe he wasn't after revenge, maybe he needed closure, she'd heard that bullshit before. Like maybe closure with a baton that he'd be wearing like a suppository if he didn't have a lot more skill with it than his deputies did.

She found a nice spot to pull over with big trees on the passenger side and close to the road so he had to park behind her and talk to her with his ass hanging out just in case somebody wanted to take a swipe at it which would be real justice.

He killed the siren and flashing lights but not the high-beams or his Spot so the inside of her minivan was bright as an operating room in the middle of the day which she hated and for goddamn good reason. She knew all about interrogation and had no desire to submit to it unless she was the one in charge of connecting the battery to the dangling bits. Plan change. She got out of her van and no mistake about the body language, he better be ready because ready was coming straight at him and it didn't stop, turn around or back down for anything.

"Ma'am, Marnie…you forgot your money. I have your cheque. Ah, if that's a problem for you, show up at the station in the morning and I'll get you cash."

Oh.

Oh yeah.

That.

She took the envelope and was back in the driver's seat when he came up beside her: "Sorry Marnie, this time I forgot something. Please sign this release, it's a must-do or I'll have to stop the cheque. Regulation. Don't worry I'm not going to harass you."

"Well Bridget, don't jump to that conclusion. You don't know me that well and I'm not out of town yet." she was serious about both and she signed. Of course she signed.

But if she was innocent why did it feel like she was being run out of town for a lousy $1500. She'd fought a whole lot longer and harder for a whole lot less than a lousy $1500. Not right. Not right and not fair.

"If you don't mind the question, Marnie, where did you learn to do what you did to my deputies?"

"Services."

"And what service is that one?"

"The one that doesn't have a name."

"You embarrassed 'em pretty bad."

"Look at the positive, Bridget. After embarrassed comes a lot of therapy if you're lucky and a coffin if you're not. I did them a favor, they should thank me."

"Thank you?"

"Yeah, thank me. You think they'll try that foolishness again before thinking twice about the potential consequences of their actions? Their actions, Bridget, not mine."

"You've got a point there. Nice of you to not kick'em in the nuts."

"That's how they teach men to fight men. I think it's disgusting."

"I guess they don't want them to lose."

"Did you see me lose?"

"No. No. I'm not real sure what I saw, but it definitely wasn't a loss."

If only he knew. She trained. She lost. She trained some more. She lost some more. The more she lost the better she got. Only a few of them figured it out but when they did, they knew Marnie was the total package, the whole enchilada, trouble with a capital T and deadly any way and in any language you want to spell it.

"Where are you headed?"

"Sheriff Bridget, you've got a real way with questions that don't involve you and answers you can't understand so, if this is professional, best you say so, or mind your toes 'cause I'm about to put the hammer down on this mini-van and go wherever I fucking well want to go." She didn't break eye contact and neither did he.

"Sure Marnie, I understand personal and just so you understand too, everything in this town is personal to me."

Dumbass response. "Well then Bridget, if that's the way you feel about it, thanks for the invite because for sure I'm staying now. Mind your toes, and remember, you only get one warning."

She punched it, sprayed gravel on his prowler for the second time in 5 minutes, u-turned back to town, gravel flying from every tire like shotgun spray from a sawed-off double barrel.

It was a whole lot of vengeful driving and a helluva racket in every wheel well as she left four wide arcs of bare tire track on the road behind her and two dust trails in a wake that only disappeared when she topped a small hill. Whoever figured a minivan should have 4wd and a 220hp V6 with that gear ratio deserved early parole.

★ ★ ★ ★ ★

Sheriff listened to the gravel ricochet off his prowler, again. Then he listened as it hit the trees beside him and was fired down the road and into the bush on the other side. It had already been quite the experience with her and now instead of it being over and done she was free to do whatever she wanted to do, and it was more like the easy part was over. But no point complaining about something you haven't even half figured out. He wondered what he did to deserve her and remembered how nice and normal his life used to be.

Like normally his day would start with a quick workout then he'd have some yoghurt and granola and get to work by 0600, an hour before his day officially started. Days that were normally 12 hours, 5 in a week with run-of-the-mill lawbreakers and semi-automatic weapons, barroom battles on payday, a cattle stampede now and again but no such thing as Marnie in town, let alone in his own jail.

Boy, did that idea ever turn out horribly and now she was free and a normal day was most likely going to be 18/7 plus on-call the rest of time and that didn't include keeping track of her. She was small, fast and totally unpredictable except in the being-smart department where she was just plain off-the-charts ahead of everybody in the room.

He wasn't sure if she was more dangerous to herself or to everyone else but figured it was in his own best interest to protect the town that elected him and let Marnie worry about Marnie. Besides, he couldn't come up with any situation she couldn't handle on her own which was still a danger because it sure backfired on him when he really should have won that contest. God help the next guy to make the same mistake. Ultimately, he reconciled his inability to protect her from herself with the logic that if he was protecting everyone from her then he must be protecting her too.

Then, to put it another way, a more realistic one, he knew with certainty that if force became deadly force and if deadly force confronted Marnie, he didn't have nearly enough deputies to protect everybody so he might as well look like he was trying to protect the people who paid his salary.

Damn sure he didn't have to worry about her getting hurt in a fight, regardless how it started and was reminded of that fact with every step he took. The magnificent purple bruise on his inner thigh was just starting to green-up around the edges. It was almost badge shaped and a reminder that Courage, Serve and Protect and Marnie should never be used in the same sentence. Well, maybe courage belonged in there somewhere.

★ ★ ★ ★ ★

With a nice fat cheque in her jeans, she should have been at least a little bit happy, but she wasn't. That worked out to a lousy $750 per day in jail but at least no expenses which was a positive. Well, a thin positive. Definitely not fat enough to convince her she hadn't just been abused. Fact was, they started it and money was just money. It came, it went, and sometimes it went right back to where it came from like nothing had happened except days were lost and she was broke again. Suddenly, her road rage on the Sheriff was biting her on the ass because now, not only did she have to stay in PityVille for another day to cash the cheque but she also had to deal with him again. He better not expect any gratitude for that because that wasn't gonna happen even in his dreams.

To make matters even more pitiful, the last thing she needed and the first thing she wanted were the same, namely seeing those losers at The Hound and an ice-cold beer. Which was completely normal after 2 days in the tank but made even more necessary by the stench in her van which in less than a mile had graduated from funk to outright disgusting.

She parked by a garbage bin, cleaned out the van and left the driver's side window half open with the hope the van would air out enough she could drive it without having to hang her head out the window like a dog. She went into the bar regular-like, no drama.

Everybody looked up then down into their beers because they knew everything about what had happened to the deputies and in court but nothing about what she might do next. Small town.

"Beer and I don't care what kind as long as it's goddam cold." She ordered at the bar.

"Tab or cash?"

Three days ago she didn't have a choice, unless cash or more cash was a choice. News travelled fast in Locoburg, now every dip-shit loser in The Hound had 1500 more reasons to want to get into her pants, starting with the hose-man smiling at her and taking his time with the pour.

He put the beer on the counter and looked like he wanted something, so she gave some attitude: "When this runs out, tell me or keep what's left. Just don't ever bring me a warm beer." She dropped a $50 on the bar and didn't look back.

"About time." she said under her breath, took a deep slug of suds and beer then picked a spot against the wall by the pool table. Not close enough to be part of the moron crowd but not so far away to be judgmental. This scorn or that scorn, she figured. They all knew about the money which meant they also knew what she did to the deputies so logically they should leave her alone unless she didn't want to be left alone which in a way she didn't. She still had a seriously bad mood to share with anybody who wasn't named Bridget.

She watched the game for a bit then got kind of absentminded as the beer started to work its magic and accidentally made eye contact with the shooter. Services used to call guys like him shit-on-the-sidewalk. She gave him a look that any moron would know meant bugger off.

"Ho."

She forgot, morons don't know when to bugger off. So, what to do? She had a couple of seconds to decide. Chug her beer and hit the road or put up with some bullshit and have another beer which was 1 second more than she needed to make that decision. She was free, the beer was icy and tasting way too good not to mention that even 9/10's wasted she could defend herself against a piss tank like him. But it was only fair to give him a warning, so she did. "Ho yourself. I'm just here for a beer or two so don't get any ideas you'll be sorry for later."

"Hell no sweetheart. We're just being friendly, that's all. You're new in town, we know that. We just don't want you to be lonely."

"I like it lonely so don't knock yourself out. And I'm not your fucking sweetheart."

They brightened right up and completely missed the warning because they loved the cursing, it brought everything down to crotch level. If she worked pussy into the conversation they'd probably come in their pants. That was them all right, the 2 biggest losers in HickTown, that was them right down to their backward baseball caps. Real studs, big men in town. A $10 bottle of plonk and a quickie in the backseat where rough came with the upholstery and no didn't mean a goddamn thing.

"Yeah, ok. Sure. Gotcha. I'm Jammer and this here is Dewey. We're local, where you from?"

She looked them over, top to bottom, something they liked which made sense. Cattle country. "I'm from none-of-your-goddamn-business. What do you do for fun around here?"

"Mostly this't but if you get a few brewskis down and the DJ's good it can run a little wild later on." said Dewey, sticking his head out like a turkey vulture. He was skinny with black stubble and about half-loaded which made him the sober one.

"Seriously? What could you ever do to make this place run wild? A pussy chase?"

Why not say it? Sooner or later it would come out so why not now? Get the obvious out of the way early on. No emotion, just another play in a game so stupid it didn't have rules. Plain, matter of fact, and after being bored senseless from 2 days in Bridget's jail, why not?

They loved it. Jammer kept her attention while Dewey made his move and sat across from her.

"Yeah, that would be good. Good fun, yeah, we otta do that." Jammer was suddenly promoting pussy chase like he'd actually been to one.

"What about you Dewey?" She asked while maintaining combat eye contact with Jammer so he wouldn't take anything for granted and try to sit beside her.

It took Dewey a while to answer because he had to figure if he had a shot at her or if he should get back to pool because he paid for the table. It was his shot and they wouldn't wait on him all night. There were lots of double meanings in his brain which sounded exciting and quickly convinced him maybe he did have a shot at her. Two days in jail and she could be horny and for sure he had a better shot than Jammer who was grinning at her like a face-painted clown and couldn't keep his eyes off her tits but who suddenly had a really brilliant idea.

"Yeah, you know what's fun. Go for a drive in the country. Stars'll be out tonight. Warm 'nuff. No law. And I gotta a nice, nice jeep."

No law was said like an ultimatum which didn't make sense but that's how he said it, a little stronger than a warning. Like he could take her or leave her. Like it was a challenge, you want law, stay home. Obviously, he was used to getting shot down, so he cut right to the chase without actually forcing the decision or shutting any doors. There was always the possibility she might not be sure right now but could be convinced after a few shooters. He put it out as clear as he could and loud enough to be heard by his wing men. 'Everything goes or the jeep don't go.'

Jammer was big, angled and clumsy with a beer belly but he knew what worked and what didn't and was perfectly happy with his back-up plan of another night of drinking in The Hound.

"Gotcha." She said too loud for too many people to hear and cringed a bit before lowering her voice and changing the topic enough to distract the audience she accidentally acquired. "So, you gotta Jeep? A serious one?"

"Yeah, and it's cherry. Total off-road. Fun as hell. Top down, Get it?" Jammer was selling hard and Dewey was promoting just as hard, nodding up and down like a bobble-head and getting lit up with his imagination.

Ridiculous but why not? Stars on a clear night are worth a lot and she hadn't had a lot of anything nice for the last couple of nights. "No kidding Jammer? Topless and off-road?" she teased and that got them drooling like a couple of dogs.

What the hell she gave in. It could end up being fun.

"Sure boys. Why not? The last couple of days have totally sucked, you know what I mean? You sure about no law, I don't need more problems with Sheriff Dickhead. You sure? Ok, you get some beers, I'm going for a squat then let's hit it hard." They looked like Christmas came early and she felt the same way. It was time for some fun.

She left The Hound with Jammer on one side of her and Dewey on the other, each one holding her elbow and swinging a 6-pack in their free hand. Some of it was an act and some of it was to keep their balance. They weren't real quick approaching the Jeep which gave her lots of time to check it out.

Off-road it looked, a 5inch lift package with oversize, high aspect mudders on small chrome rims. Bolt-on roll cage. Dual straight pipes out the back with some fancy graphics but the rest looked stock. "Ok boys, best I drive, you're too tanked. Let's go see some stars."

"No way José. This here is Jambo and there ain't nobody's ass in that seat except Jammer's."

"Gotcha Jammer. Too bad though. Maybe you never had a girl do the driving 'cause let me tell you, when you've had that once, next time you won't argue. You absolutely sure you don't want a little female in that seat? Maybe just 'til we get outta town and it's safe for you to drive? I don't want to get busted again, accomplice or not." She jumped into the driver's seat like the cat she was, stretched out her hand cute-like but no doubt about it, if she got no for an answer it was game over. She wasn't about to get in a car with a couple of drunks and no control. Jammer caved and tossed her the keys. Dewey was already on the back bench, cracking a beer so Jammer rode shotgun, lucky him.

The Jeep started with a nice throaty growl, so she put it into 4high then fished the tranny until she had it mapped, dropped it into first gear and punched the gas, full on. The big balloon tires produced a lot of drag and it was just as she figured, engine, tranny, running gear and everything that didn't need to be done for the look was stock. Fake owner, fake jeep. Dewey passed her a beer; she took a good slug before second gear threatened to explode, just slightly over red-line and not an ounce of torque left. The under-inflated rubber was like driving in glue and the suspension was so soft she had to concentrate on keeping the ride straight.

"Let's do it!" she shouted and was approaching 60 when she passed the town limit sign and was redlined in third with the engine screaming for a higher gear just as the railroad trestle came into sight. She shifted into fourth and picked up speed.

The trestle had a center support grid of black I-beams welded together and bolted onto a cement platform poured in the middle of the road where the double yellow lines should be. The grid supported a dual track railroad bridge which was strong as hell and not going anywhere, no matter how hard you hit it or with what. To protect drivers from doing just that, the platform was surrounded with a poured-on-site concrete barrier like an oval doughnut. The end of the barrier was curved to send a vehicle back onto the road before it hit the I-beam and got cut in half. After that it was flat on top all the way through the tunnel and with more than enough space between the barrier and the grid for a drunk to sleep without fear of an 18wheeler dropping out of the sky onto his head.

Marnie lined-up her fat, front mudder intending to ride the barrier end-to-end which would put Jammer's side low enough he would be eyeball-to-asphalt and a real thrill. Total fun but fasten your seatbelt just in case.

"What the fuck!" he yelled, grabbed the wheel and that started everything going south because if she let him do what he instinctively thought he had to do, those instincts would have rolled the jeep. Sideways down the road and at that speed it would have kept on rolling until it hit something immovable or self-destructed, bad news either way. She yanked back on the wheel, hard.

In the Right Now moment that comes before a near death event, Jammer saw the driver's front wheel go over the barrier into the cavity and immediately let go of the steering wheel to brace himself. He knew it wasn't coming out that hole. Hopefully no drunk was having a nap down there because the Jeep's fat tires fit pretty tight in the cavity. Too tight as it turned out and both front and rear tires peeled off the small chrome rims and sprung away. Then the rims dropped down and locked on the inside of the cavity like train wheels on a track and the whole shiteree was on target to an I-beam axe blade that was approaching too fast for a short prayer.

Hung up on her side, Marnie turned into the barrier hoping to shed some by using the front rim against the concrete as an improvised brake until the whole front wheel assembly broke off and got tangled in what was left of the rear wheel. That levelled the Jeep a little which was good but directed it straight into the I-beam which was bad. With not much more to do except keep your eyes open and see what happens next, Marnie tried to relax, Jammer put his hands on the dash to brace himself and Dewey yelled: "Fuck me!"

What happened next was a Jeep that had more than enough grinding momentum to hit the I-beam almost dead center. The I-beam cut through the bumper like it was a matchstick, sprang the hood up and over the windshield, punched the radiator into the engine which broke the motor mounts and drove the whole drivetrain under the floor just as it was designed to do in the event of an extremely abrupt stop involving something like a railway trestle.

After that, there was a lot of steam and cracking metal, but the Jeep was firmly wedged into and around the I-beam while also resting on the barrier, teeter-totter-like but with no real chance of moving until a wrecker pulled it free. Marnie managed to get out her side; Jammer not so much as his door was mangled shut but that was the lessor of his problems as he was pinned against a cracked windshield and held there by Dewey who had been launched into the back of his seat as an unwitting and unwilling accomplice in a major energy exchange with an immovable object and no seat belt.

All in all, Marnie figured, it was one helluva short joy ride and especially short on the joy part. The boys moaned and she yelled at Jammer. "You dumb sonofabitch. Why did you do that. Jeesus, everything was fine. Why did you grab the goddamn steering wheel? You could've killed us, you dumb sonofabitch."

She figured it couldn't get worse until she saw the lights and heard the siren. Bridget.

Bridget, like she didn't already have enough trouble for one night. For sure the Jeep had, no mistaking that and pretty powerful evidence of some kind of felony, she wasn't exactly sure which one or ones but likely as not she was going straight back to jail where they probably hadn't even changed her sheets. Fuck. Obviously, Sheriff Bridget was keeping a close eye on her which didn't surprise her but damn sure didn't make her happy either. Not her fault, none of it, but would anybody see it her way? Like anybody? Not likely was the first and only answer that came into her head.

By the time he pulled up to the scene, Jammer and Dewey were out of the wreck but in a state of shock. She didn't have much time to write a script that would hold up under interrogation but at least the crash sobered them up enough that maybe she could get something simple into them.

"Too bad but you got insurance, right Jammer? It's a steering malfunction, right Jammer? Work with me ok? No way can they prove it didn't fail, just look at it. Right Dewey, you too. Steering malfunction, ok?" Marnie didn't need any more trouble with the law and besides, it was a fair trade. If she hadn't tried to ride the barrier and Jammer hadn't grabbed the wheel then none of it would have happened. So, it was a no fault; no foul, open and shut insurance case, everybody goes home, maybe not entirely happy, but for sure home is happier than jail.

"Shit no. I got liability, thassit. She's driver." Jammer shouted and was on the very dangerous side of coming at her with his anger just like Bridget was doing from the other side only with a lot more determination and no sympathy evident.

"Well, that sucks." Was all she got out before the cuffs were on then double-quick march to the backseat of his prowler and he wasn't being at all nice about anything.

"It wasn't my fault, goddammit Bridget, ask Jammer who pulled the wheel. It wasn't my fault; I didn't do anything wrong. Nothing. Don't you try and pin this on me; I'm innocent. Do you get it? Do you ever get it? Dammit Bridget, I'm the innocent one here."

"You're getting tested anyway." he says over his back and then goes on to check on Dewey and Jammer. "You boys ok? Anything broken? You need an ambulance?"

They shook their heads. He looked at what was left of the Jeep and shook his head. "You're damn lucky is all I can say. I'll call the wrecker. He'll drop you in town. I got her to take care of."

Marnie spent the next 2 days in her cell waiting for the results of the blood test and for Judge Fifth to get back to Idiotville from wherever he had his real life and did a real job. Then it was déjà vu all over again as Bridget marched her down the aisle and Judge Fifth started reading charges before she was even halfway to her seat only this time his voice was stern like he'd told his grandchildren not to do something and they openly defied him.

"Reckless driving, excess speed, no seat belts, open containers in the car, destruction of public property. Miss, you are a one-woman wrecking crew. What do you have to say for yourself?"

"Same thing I've been telling him for the last two days. Not my fault. I wasn't DUI, was I?" she challenged Bridget.

"No, that you were not and notice there isn't a charge for that, just what was read out and I probably missed some charges but no, you were not DUI."

"And it wasn't my beer. I didn't buy it, did I?"

"No, neither of those. They didn't admit to it but the barman did."

"And you want to talk about reckless, who grabbed the wheel? Who did that and isn't being charged and who tried to prevent it and is standing here, like everything is all her fault?"

"Jammer, said he grabbed it and you yanked it back."

"What did he say first?"

"He said he grabbed the wheel to prevent the crash."

"But that's what started it. If I hadn't stopped him doing it he would have rolled us ten times right into the morgue and you know that."

"No, I do not know that."

"Don't be such a hard ass Bridget. You know very well it's true and you didn't have to be there to know that; it's just plain obvious. And on the topic of seat belts, I was wearing mine, wasn't I?"

"You were."

"I told you. I didn't do anything wrong and you know that. Fact is I did everything right before, during and after he grabbed the goddamn wheel. This is wrong as Judas Priest all the way around and you know that too. He should be the one standing here, not me. What are you going to do about him? Do you have one goddamn honest bone in your body?"

She was pissed, emotional and loud enough to remind herself that somewhere between Resolution #1 and Resolution #8 was the Shut-up and Don't Make Bad Things Worse Resolution so for once she decided to take her own advice and shut up. Shut up but not look happy about it because there wasn't a goddamn resolution about looking pissed-off so why let them be all righteous when they damn sure didn't deserve or earn that courtesy?

Bridget ignored her outburst and so did Judge Fifth but she kept quiet and 100% resolved not to make things worse or incriminate herself with any more of her testimony. It was his courtroom and his turn to talk and sooner or later he would have to do something lawful so after a short wait to make sure she was done, he did.

"Young woman, I don't want to see you in my courtroom again, do you understand that? $1000 for damages plus time served and not one word out of you or you'll stay in jail until I retire." He slammed the gavel on his bench and looked at the court recorder who checked her tape and nodded that every word was faithfully recorded.

Dammit. Search for the guilty and punishment of the innocent all over again. Totally unfair. Bridget marched her back down the aisle to take her money like he was right and she was wrong but nothing she should do about that when the judge was already in an ugly mood.

★ ★ ★ ★ ★

Marnie parked in front of the supermarket down the street from The Hound and wasn't at all surprised to see Jammer and Dewey sucking beers in the corner. Jammer was looking pretty beat-up, both eyes black and one helluva bump on his forehead on account of it being treated like a melon against a windshield going in the opposite direction. Dewey's face was about the same plus a few stitches where the upholstery of Jammer's seat proved tougher than his skin. They weren't feeling any pain, at least not until they saw her, they weren't.

She sucked it up, what else was there for her to do? It was just another hospital visit only this time without the hospital; she ordered a couple of rounds and brought them over herself. "Jesus guys, I feel bad about the Jeep."

"You fuckin' well should feel bad. It's all I've got and now it's junk." Jammer was on the belligerent side of his booze.

"Yeah well, sorry, nothing I can do about that. They took my settlement back. Talk about getting screwed."

"You think you're screwed?" Jammer challenged.

"You better think of some way to make up for this." Dewey cut in and sounded like maybe he dislocated his jaw.

She lowered her head. "Jeez I do feel bad." And to prove it she ordered some shooters and a platter of deep fried whatever which was the only way they cooked anything at The Hound. Jammer waved Rosco and Bimmer to join the party. Obviously, it was payback time and no matter how much it cost it wouldn't make up for the Jeep so no sense in arguing that point because it was true. More shooters were followed by more shooters, only faster.

Eventually the shooters stopped the pain but not the complaints and they moved their demands up. They wanted a piece of her and everyone within earshot knew what piece they wanted. Rosco and Bimmer joined in the sentencing like some kind of drunken tribal council and she was definitely feeling the effect of their combined pressure, not to mention the buzz from a few shooters.

Jammer's grief over the Jeep got bigger as he got drunker and Dewey found more bravery at the bottom of every glass. "How about you be nice to us? Huh, Marnie? Dammit, you owe leest that." He sounded half normal, maybe the shooters fixed his jaw but for sure they got him saying out loud what they'd only been hinting. Hinting while making it clear that take-it or give-it were two options; getting-away-with-it altogether definitely wasn't happening. She was surrounded by guilty verdicts and they were hounding her into the corner. Shit.

Shit and then, she figured in a moment of weakness and strength too, what the hell? If that's what it takes to make things right, what the hell? And now was as good a time as any to get it done. Damn sure nothing to look forward to but she was feeling kind of numb and in their state, how bad could it be?

"Yeah, sure, ok, I gotcha. C'mon, my van is just down the street. I owe you. I'll do you right."

Rosco and Bimmer winked at each other.

"Not you two, I don't owe you nothing and you don't witness either, you fucking perverts."

Rosco nodded, Bimmer looked away but neither of them looked too sincere about the no witness rule, like they were part of the crew and deserved something for their loyalty. She flipped them off, downed a shooter and walked purposefully to her van with Jammer and Dewey following her like 2 dogs trailing a bitch in heat. Shit. Already a bad idea. The cool air hit her and so much for New Year's Resolutions 1, 2 and all the way up to who gives a good goddamn, sometimes resolutions are made to be broken, right? Just get it done.

As soon as the van's sliding door closed, she told them: "Strip to the meat. Do it now before I change my goddamn mind." and started peeling off her top.

"Right here?"

"Good as place as any. C'mon boys, get it off before I change my mind and then you won't get anything off. I ain't kidding."

That they believed and faster than she thought 2 drunks could do it in a minivan, they were buck naked and coming to help with her bra and panties. It happened quick and she was cornered with her back against the back of the driver's seat.

"Now you're gonna get it." Jammer slurred.

"Let's do it slut." menaced Dewey with a nastiness she hadn't seen before and couldn't leave alone.

"What did you call me? Slut? You called me a slut?" she screamed at him. "Nobody calls me that, you fucking moron."

As fast as Dewey thought good things were going to happen to him and bad things were going to happen to her, everything went sideways. She kicked the switch and the sliding door opened to the street, right in front of the mini market which was busy. People looked into the van. A normal reaction but what they saw wasn't at all normal and when they got their first glimpse at it, they couldn't look anywhere else.

That distracted Dewey long enough for Marnie to plant a heel under his armpit and drive him hard into the door pillar. The door hadn't quite finished its travel so he banged his already beat-up face with a loud smack against the window before his shoulder crunched into the pillar. Lucky for him, sort of, it should have dislocated his shoulder, but he was so drunk he didn't tense enough. He crumpled sideways, falling half out the open door so with her big toe, in a perfect Ahp Chagi, 1 inch below his rib cage she nailed his diaphragm. The second kick was below stomach, above bowel. No breath; no swallow.

Desperate for air, he raised his head and straightened his back so she planted the arch of her right foot on his butt cheek and launched him out the door like a dog wanting to go for a walk. Only he wasn't a dog with two front feet ready for a landing and instead hit the pavement with his head and shoulders because his hands and arms were behind him still trying to hold onto the floor of the van. In shock and gasping, he staggered to his hands and knees, saw blood pouring from his lips and nose and started puking up shooters, beers and deep-fried chunks of Hound food.

Jammer watched 4 seconds of Dewey's life unfold like it was a commercial before he came to his own reality and lunged at her. She had already recoiled to her corner so when he came into range, she hit him with a perfectly delivered right cross to the cheekbone. It didn't finish him off but the force and the shock was more than his weak knees could handle so it was crippling but she didn't stop there. He felt the pain but mostly became aware of an intense fear for what was coming next. He turned and fell sideways toward the open door. It was a struggle for survival until he became aware of everyone from the Mini-Mart watching him and that redefined survival. The pain disappeared but the humiliation which replaced it was worse. He was completely stunned, better than a taser, and had no way to predict what was coming next until Marnie broke his stance at the elbow, grabbed a handful of hair and pushed his chin to the floor. For a second he was distracted enough by Dewey's puking to forget his own problems. Maybe not quite a second.

With her free hand Marnie picked up a small frying pan, targeted his upright ass and hit him. Hard. The shock, the surprise and the pain paralyzed him. Practice over, she hit him again. Harder. It made a terrific whack, the kind which comes with a shock wave so she hit him a third time, as hard as she could without getting a full swing.

His ass went from white to red to blister as he went from shock, to pain, to fearing for his life. When that sobered him enough to realize he couldn't do a thing except wait and see how much more pain he could handle until his heart stopped beating, his fear turned to panic and that brought some strength to his limbs. He struggled against her and with her awkward position, and his fear driving him, he started to get free.

She stopped hitting him and let his hair go so he reacted instinctively, got onto his hands and knees and tried to crawl out the door. He didn't see anyone watching him; he didn't care that he was naked; he didn't hear Dewey retching; he just had to get away from her, he'd had enough and couldn't take any more.

Marnie had other plans and a lot of emotion driving them. She backed up and with that little extra space she got a full swing at his upright tail end. She hit him as hard as she could, which conflicted his instinct to escape, reinstated his panic and caused him to freeze like a rabbit so she hit him again. His eyeballs bugged, panic ceded to terror and he got his hands on the doorsill ready to launch himself out the door or die trying.

She hit him for the last time, downwards to top of his tail bone and that hit sent a few thousand volts of his own electricity up his vertebral column to the primitive part of his brain that did what it was supposed to do and made him gasp for air then gag with the expel. A perfect donkey bray.

Done, she put both her feet on his ass and launched him out the door onto Dewey, collapsing both of them into Dewey's puke and that ended it, Jammer's mind and body were shattered and that's what happened next, he shat all over himself and Dewey.

"NO MEANS NO, YOU ASSHOLES" Although the crowd probably didn't see her because they were watching something they could never have imagined and would never see again but they heard her and that's what counted. She warned them and they didn't listen, case closed.

She had to get away and she had to get away damn fast, preferably by becoming invisible although in a sense she already was. Dewey and Jammer were the main attraction, or more accurately, the main revulsion. Jammer in particular held everyone's attention as he approached a near-catatonic state induced by pain, fear and his own revulsion with being naked, covered in his own shit and lying on top of Dewey who was struggling to get free.

Too bad, but they should have known better. What the fuck did they think would happen to them after what she did to the deputies? Too bad, but she warned them. She always warned them. Nobody called Marnie a slut, they'd have been a whole lot better off just taking a swing at her. Way better off, in fact.

It wasn't her fault but they didn't listen and she damn sure didn't want to discuss the matter with anyone and especially not with anyone named Bridget so she squeezed over the console and got the hell out of Dodge, sliding door still open. She didn't speed and she turned at the first intersection because it got her out of sight even if it wasn't the direction she wanted to go. As she entered the corner, she saw the red and blue lights of his prowler in her sideview mirror. The last thing she needed was more Bridget or more of his jail, no question about that and no point in sticking around even if she was right.

No doubt about it but not the only doubt in her mind at that moment. That doubt was whether Bridget saw her and if he did, would he chase her? She got the answer to both questions before losing sight of his prowler stopping in front of the crowd at the Mini-Market. Definitely not the decision she would have made but he was quick to the scene, give him credit for that.

* * * * *

He surveyed the scene; it didn't take very long to know what happened. It was one helluva mess with a very short story behind it and a lot of witnesses who, for a complete change of pace, all saw the same thing.

"Jeesus Jammer. You too Dewey. You gotta leave that girl alone."

He gave them a newspaper to cover themselves but when they whined for a ride home, he told them: "You gotta be kidding. Not in my prowler. You can walk home. You're a goddamn disgrace to this town."

* * * * *

Marnie decided that going into deep cover was not just a good idea but the only idea. Unfortunately, it was also an idea without a lot of options because there was too much daylight to hide in the open and every minute she spent driving around was one minute closer to Bridget finding her and this time there would be no doubt about DUI.

She squirreled her way through the streets to the motel where she stayed when she wasn't in jail, which wasn't very much lately but before she even got there, she realized that was a bad place to stay but a good place to find out if there was a barn, a field, an empty garage or anywhere she could hide out until she came up with a plan that didn't include Bridget's jail and Judge Fifth's courtroom.

'Closed for the season' was the best answer from the desk clerk she could possibly have wished for so she got directions and found the government campground, nicely out of town, smack down a valley with a road on one side of it and a stream and a hill on the other. Not a soul around which was perfect as long as it stayed that way. One way in and the same way out so if Bridget came in with the cavalry, she would jump the creek, run up the hill and be lost in the woods before he could come up with Plan B. She broke the lock with a tire iron, drove in, put the gate back and found a nice private campsite in the very back next to the creek and hid her jacket and backpack in the woods in case she had to make a run for it. Only then did she relax. It was always good to be surrounded by nature, unless it was human nature, and this nature ticked all her boxes. Quieter than a church on Saturday night, with the babble of the creek to distinguish any other sound provided you knew how to listen like a dog. Elementary. She made a cup of tea and sat quiet and alone for the first time in too damn long.

★ ★ ★ ★ ★

Jammer and Dewey showered, sobered, picked up her trail at the motel and followed it in Dewey's old pickup. Engine off and lights off they coasted into the wind and parked in the ditch a good mile from the gate. They got out, slung their big game rifles over their shoulders, shoved pistols into their belts and carried 12-guage semi-auto pumps loaded with double ought buck. Extra ammo in the vest. Everything legal until you shoot somebody and then still perfectly legal as long as you kill them and nobody sees you do it. That was the plan, the only plan.

At the campground gate they saw a tiny light, small as a candle on birthday cake, flickering through the trees so they kept to the dark edges on the high side of the road, completely alert to every sound and shadow. Slowly and deliberately, they crept into the adjacent campsite with nothing more than 50 feet of scrub poplar separating them from their prey. She was only surrounded on one side but with the creek and hill at her back and with the element of surprise facing her that was enough. Add enough firepower to bring down a charging bull elephant and surrounded on one side was more than enough.

They waited until a shadow passed through the light inside the van, saw it rock a little then started firing and didn't stop until they were out of ammo. After that, anything in, on, under or around that van was either dead or dying so no point hanging around or risk dropping your DNA so they high-tailed back to town but were stopped and arrested at the railroad trestle.

★ ★ ★ ★ ★

Two days later Judge Fifth gave them 10 years each for Attempted Murder but if mini vans counted for anything it would have been Murder 1; 168 entry wounds is damned persuasive evidence of at least 167 counts of premeditated intent.

Their cheap lawyer tried to throw some opening arguments of reasonable doubt around but before the public defender could raise an objection on Marnie's behalf, Judge Fifth gave him a choice. It was a public spanking, and he didn't mince words: "Any cheap tactics from you and you'll get more time than your clients. Stick to the facts, or else."

Cheap lawyer picked or else and let his clients face justice.

★ ★ ★ ★ ★

Marnie had to stay for the trial in case either side wanted to call her as witness but by now both sides were smart enough not to do that.

She waited in jail where Bridget kept an eye on her. For a change of pace, she thoroughly enjoyed watching and listening to Jammer and Dewey sweat their charges and kiss their asses hello to becoming jail mates. Jammer could either stand or lie on his belly, but any other position was out of the question. He couldn't sit on the can and had to squat over it.

Truth be told though, she sweated a little too. It wasn't until they were sentenced that she knew she was safe. You never know exactly what is going to happen when there is a lot of violence with people who don't like a lot of violence and who are prepared to get serious about stopping it. Bridget was definitely in that camp and he wasn't at all happy facing Judge Fifth, with Marnie, for the third time. No question about it, even though she wasn't facing charges, this time was the last time.

All was said, all was done, all was in the past and once again he drove her out of town only this time in an old Suburban sandwiched between 2 prowlers driven by the deputies she beat up not even a week ago. What little of her gear that wasn't full of holes was in the back.

He didn't say anything and she had nothing to say. It was over and they both knew it. He still had a town to protect and that included protecting it from her.

They turned north on a Range Road and the prowler behind them stopped and blocked entry. A few minutes later Bridget drove the Suburban into a ditch beside a muddy access road. The lead prowler went up to the Township Road and blocked it. No witnesses.

"It's time Marnie." They got out.

A matte black Yukon came up the muddy side road.

Marnie felt strange, very alone but oddly complimented. Somebody went to a lot of trouble to make these arrangements. When the Yukon stopped, she got into the back seat beside the only passenger. Bridget took the seat in front her, beside the driver who looked forward, like a robot.

Marnie spoke first and she spoke from her heart: "I'm very sorry about what happened to your granddaughter. Please tell her that for me. There isn't a woman alive who doesn't have scars she didn't deserve. Please tell her if she ever needs my help with those two animals, all she has to do is call."

"Thank-you dear. And let me tell you, if someone told me that all the justice which has been done could be done in a week, I would have called them delusional. I still don't really believe it but from my heart to yours, thank you. I am so grateful for what you have done. Just wrecking that Jeep did more to heal her wounds than months of therapy accomplished. And, well, after what happened at the market, Amy and I shed tears of laughter we haven't enjoyed for a long, long time. She also witnessed the sentencing of those scum and that was justice for her too. It just might become the end of her pain and the beginning of a new chapter in her life." The lady thought for a moment and a tear escaped and fell down her cheek. After a moment of silence, she recaptured her thoughts.

"I hope she can. For sure she won't be looking over her shoulder every moment and she has already told me how diffrent that is for her. Ten years will only strengthen that and, just so you know, Judge Fifth is on the parole board so there will be no parole, they will do every day of their sentences."

She handed Marnie a cashier's envelope.

"There's a name in there too. A friend of mine. If you can."

"Of course."

Marnie opened the envelope.

"Bridget, you got a widows' and orphans' fund at that place you call work? Maybe some help for a deputy who needs it?"

He nodded so she cut into the stack and handed him a thick wad. Sometimes money goes right back to where it came from because, well, just because. Not every act is right but when it is, there is no better feeling than rewarding it with generosity.

No more words; it was done, it was over. They got out of the Yukon and when it pulled away it brought a sense of relief and joy to her just to breathe the cool air with its sweet lavender scent of freshly cut clover. It was all about time. She got that. She might not always know how her emotions ticked, but she knew how time did and she loved being in sync with it, like right now. It felt so good she didn't want anything to change despite the fact she knew it was already happening.

Bridget tossed her the keys. "Title and insurance are in the glove box. Can you give me a ride to one of the prowlers?"

"Of course I can." She smiled and he laughed, embarrassed.

The Suburban was a generous tip and a thoughtful compliment. It looked like a $4000 Farmer Jones Special, but she guessed 500hp, extra steel wherever it was needed, a 10,000lb winch and high tensile steel bush guard that would break before it bent. It ran great and felt like it was built for her. Like it was ready to run moonshine at a racetrack, fast and with attitude. By the time she shifted into second, the bond was made.

She pulled up to the prowler.

"You could have told me, Marnie."

"Sorry Bridget but I couldn't. By the time I knew you were a good guy, I was having too much fun seeing you protect everybody. If I didn't know better, I think you even tried to protect me sometimes."

"Just so you know Marnie, I am a good guy, but I've cracked a skull or two in my time. Call me if you need help, any kind of help."

"I will. And Bridget...you call me if you need trouble, any kind of trouble. I'm pretty busy, but for you, I'll make an exception."

THE PARTY ROOM

Highcomb was not built on the highest mountain he owned. There were several from which to choose but Edgar Sr. picked the second highest of five modest crowns, all joined by a towering sheer wall of heavily glaciated Appalachian Ridge that he'd owned for less than a year. He built there so he could look down at the deepest canyon within a hundred miles and because he could use the mountain beside him as a shield against the lights of the city he practically owned but did not want reflected in his night sky.

It wasn't at all convenient. A road had to be blasted and 'dozed through miles of hills, ridges, forest, outcrops and other natural ascending impediments in order to reach his mountain. Some of the spoil from this destruction was used to backfill the valleys, lowlands and descending impediments. Edgar liked his roads with no more than a 2% grade and abhorred tunnels so there were plenty of attractive curves around the impediments he didn't want to flatten and no tunnels.

The rest of the spoil, and there was plenty of it, he used to fill a mosquito infested marsh that he wanted to turn into a lake but that would have left him with even more debris and no place to put it so he settled on creating a meadow with a windy, rocky creek bed that insured good drainage and no breeding ground for bugs.

Twelve bridges were needed, one of which was 2 spans and all of them had to support the 50ton machinery which was the maximum allowable weight of the machinery, plus load, needed to build the road up his mountain, tear off its peak and dump it in the swamp.

It was already an expensive location in which to build so when he needed 27 miles of transmission line to provide enough power to run a small town and he wanted it strung where no one could see it, but preferably buried, he didn't like the cost he was quoted so he bought the company. He wasn't the first rich man to buy a public utility for his own purposes any more than he was the first man to become rich by doing so. For him, such decisions were second nature, a nature he learned from his father who gave his son's enormous wealth a jump start with a significant inheritance and the family secret of making money by acquiring any resource people needed for day-to-day living then renting it back to them with the maximum allowable interest and steadily increasing rates of capital recovery until it was paid out and returning pure profit. In this case, he improved his return even further by including the cost to deliver his power in the rate base and making his customers pay for it, with interest.

Edgar Sr. was so wealthy he didn't know what he was worth and held anyone who bragged about the amount of their wealth in silent but perceptible contempt. To him, money was not the measure of the man, it was the way he spent it that defined him. And it had to be spent, idle money was a mortal sin. He also detested hoarders so no matter how much he liked it, he never wore a suit more than a dozen times before it left his closet for good.

His personal philosophy and economic discipline were about as level-headed as he wanted his roads to be, so he moved all that rock, built bridges and rearranged nature with his only compromise being the 8 broad switchbacks on the road he needed to drive up the mountain to Highcomb. He considered straighter options like a funicular but aside from the practical engineering obstacles presented by the sheer granite wall in his way, he didn't like the idea of having his home serviced by the gigantic bucket of a dump truck. He didn't like it for construction and couldn't imagine riding in the glorified public conveyance it would become afterwards.

He built his mile-long driveway up his mountain with its 8 switchbacks curling around outcrops and along ridges that maximized the view of everything he owned which was everything he could see. Once on top, or what was to become the top, he flattened the mountain to the precise ratio of land to building he required to achieve a natural proportion and balance of the building to its environment. Natural meaning, of course, his nature.

Two hundred vertical feet of mountain were turned into granite blocks to build Highcomb and enough spoil to fill the swamp and raise it into a meadow. Not a single pebble went over the side, not then and not during the following 4 years of construction. Except for the building site, which was precisely the topography by his design, the rest was pristine wilderness by his demand.

Highcomb was U-shaped with the front exposure straight and then gently curved at the corners. This was done to soften the façade so it didn't need turrets on the corners in order to balance the façade and accentuate the gothic arch above the entrance. He didn't want a castle or a church, he wanted both, and that was just the beginning of the challenges he presented to his architects. Straight and flat might work for roads but for Edgar Sr. architecture was a different topic and the beauty and opulence of renaissance architecture was in a class by itself, notably, his class. Every line, every surface, every finish was selected because it belonged with the one beside it. Nature might find beauty in chaotic design but that was not a luxury allowed his architects who had to replicate nature using only the forces Edgar Sr. permitted.

Complicated with arches and curves, and driven by an obsession with symmetry, scale and balance that had to be within millimeters of the blueprint, using line levels and plumb bobs, his stonemasons were imported from Italy. Dozens of them and they came on the same ships as the marble, onyx and pink granite they roughly shaped and carved into mantels, columns, plinths, moldings, balusters and balustrades on the voyage over. Then their real work began as they reassembled the mountain into Highcomb with the granite blocks waiting for them.

Their job was never an easy one. They were to create a masterpiece which would have been an outstanding work of art and architecture anywhere in the world, but Edgar Sr. wanted it mildly understated. Viewed from below it had to look like it had been carved and smoothed by the glaciers which sculpted and rounded the surrounding Appalachians and while he deserved some credit for the design which accomplished this architectural tour de force, he took credit for all of it. It was his vision, paid for with his gold, so in the grand scheme of things architects were little more than stonemasons with pencils in their hands. He was the Creator and anyone who wanted to argue that point was out of work and likely to stay that way for as long as they were within his sphere of influence which was anywhere he wanted it to be.

He used the mountain for the foundation and when it was perfectly level and ready for the building he was going to put it on, he blasted and chiseled 2 levels of basement 40 feet into the heart of the it. Into this cavity he would put the building's infrastructure, maintenance facilities, an ample garage and the remainder, and there was a lot of remainder, he used to store his collections.

Highcomb was built on, in and from the mountain. There were no out-buildings, no garages, stables, chalets or villas for guests and definitely no servant quarters evident. He wasn't building a farm or a factory; he was creating a monument and Highcomb was intended to take the breath away without any distractions, like a 20carat diamond is mounted on a simple gold base in order to capture the complete attention of the beholder.

Edgar Sr. was all businessman and lived to negotiate and then close a deal so the anticipation to Highcomb ended and the reality of it began with the 8th switchback. The only reason for that turn was to close the deal by creating an immediate and ethereal reveal. Turn that corner and Highcomb appeared as if out of the sky, as if by magic. It was the equivalent of walking into a movie theatre and continuing to walk into the screen. It was an impressive optical illusion that used depth of field to funnel and then focus perspective to its central arch and the two massive, intricately carved oak doors which were bound and hung with black, hammered iron hinges. It presented Entrance like an Old Master in an antique, ornate frame. Any renaissance church, any large renaissance church that is, would have been proud to impress its congregation the way Entrance impressed but that was just the first of Highcomb's abilities to humble its visitors.

The overwhelm of the reveal and the illusion of entering another world within was the shock. Through those massive doors, so perfectly balanced and hung that a child could open them, was Reception, the awe.

The scale of Reception was also deceiving, intentionally. It appeared no less intimate with 100 people in it and no more crowded than when Edgar Sr. alone personally greeted captains of industry, the royal family, or the President, which he frequently did. The inlaid Carrara marble floors that came with his Italian workmen were covered with custom hand-tied carpets from Turkey and Afghanistan. The walls were rich with wood from the world's rain forests and covered with the paintings of old masters. Reception was the only room in Highcomb which was floor to ceiling and that height was emphasized by the hanging of 2ton crystal chandeliers from Verona and then diminished by the overwhelm of the Grand Staircase. In addition to providing balance to Reception, which would otherwise have been a large, empty room, the staircase faced the oak doors and welcomed visitors to the home as if with open arms. That it turned the rich and powerful into respectful spectators of the grandeur and permanence of Highcomb was its real purpose.

The staircase took 2 tries and 2 years for the Italians to get right, or as they referred to it then, and with no shortage of respect, to get Edgar. To him, it was the power of the building. It was mystical and transcendental as it challenged and provoked the visitor's ego with the realization of being small and insignificant in the face of such perfection. It did this so well that the residual feeling of humiliation was not charged with anger but infused with gratitude for being invited to witness such an impressive display of human achievement.

As with Highcomb's other contradictions, the Grand Staircase provided access to the residences and guest suites down each wing, so it made the invitation and the experience of ascending it extremely personal. That feeling of intimacy worked to Edgar's advantage as it disarmed the competitive nature of his guests.

In spite of this, Highcomb's design was never intended to have the weight or bearing of a castle or a chateaux built around the ego of the owner. It wasn't built to praise or deify Edgar Sr. but that had nothing to do with his modesty, a quality even he admitted was not one of his strong points. Pure but not simple, Highcomb was his home in the short term and a monument to posterity in the long term. As his home, he shared its splendor liberally. Politicians and judges, writers and saxophone players, acquaintances, colleagues, old guard, church and charity, Edgar Sr. invited any and all to his home, seemingly without agenda. Even the press with whom he was often in conflict received the occasional invitation and they knew to be careful about what and on whom they reported if they wanted a return invitation.

As his monument to his posterity, through his careful planning, through his unrelenting purity of design and through the sheer force of his will, Highcomb became what he wanted it to become, a presence in its own right. A place where important treaties were signed, important decisions were taken, and important discoveries were announced. Edgar Sr. wanted Highcomb to become synonymous with his memory and in order to do that he invested heavily in its character, its independence, its very being in order for it to survive him when that day came. And not only did it have to survive him, it had to surpass him. It had to take the place in history that he wanted but which his token modesty admitted was not possible. He wasn't a Da Vinci, a Rembrandt or an Alexander and he knew it so he did the next best thing and created Highcomb to carry his name on that immortal ride.

At the time of his death, which came much sooner and more suddenly than he wanted, he believed he had accomplished this objective and stated on many occasions that Highcomb was his greatest treasure at the end of a lifetime of acquiring treasures. By his death it had achieved identity, it had birthed itself and The Trust he established for its preservation was more than adequate to ensure its permanent survival in the company of world class monuments and Edgar Sr.'s place among the visionaries who created them.

Not the least of the many demands he made upon The Trust, but an unequivocal one was that his personal office remain as he left it with his portrait hanging over the fireplace as a permanent reminder of the man who created Highcomb and he was that man. Without being written, his trustees knew if they expected to collect their generous annuity, it had better stay that way.

★ ★ ★ ★ ★

Edgar Jr. learned little from his father and although he fell under the spell of Highcomb just as deeply, he did it very differently. If it could be said that Edgar Sr. was master to Highcomb then it could equally be said Edgar Jr. was servant to it, a reality The Trust did nothing to discourage. It left him alone as long as he reciprocated with them and their duties, which he was more than happy to do.

Edgar Jr. was introverted and either cared little about what anyone else thought or couldn't figure out the basics of those social interactions in the first place. With some help from his father's connections and made even more attractive by a large and growing inheritance, he managed to attract and marry Ida. The union quickly produced two sons, heirs to the beneficial estate which would otherwise have reverted to The Trust, in its entirety, immediately upon Edgar Jr's passing. All as directed from the grave by Edgar Sr.

Even after death, Edgar Jr. was afraid of his father. With great courage, the week after his father's funeral, he escaped a lifetime of memories and moved to a guest suite in the north wing, which was called the winter wing. From that day forward he only went into the summer wing when it was an absolute necessity. After 'borrowing' every book in which he had an interest from the library attached to his father's study on the summer side of Reception on the main floor, he never entered those rooms again. He had his father's portrait draped and ordered the door to his study be closed at all times.

Other than a few days per year of family business as Director-in-Absentia of the family empire when he absolutely couldn't avoid leaving Highcomb, he spent his life in his suite in the winter wing where he also established and twice expanded a library of notable and rare works from prodigious writers and thinkers.

If it could be said Jr. was afraid of Sr., the opposite was true for his father's collections, especially literary, where he valued first editions more than his own children. Were it not for Ida insisting on Sunday dinners together, he probably wouldn't have been able to pick his own boys out of a classroom of like children, preferring any boy reading from Socrates or Plato in ancient Greek. Unfortunately, dead languages didn't interest his sons and that ended any possible bond between them.

Edgar Jr. did, however, by the ironic accident of contrary and contradictory action, contribute greatly to the worldly reputation of Highcomb by making it a sanctuary and refuge for scholars and historians like himself. Although he seldom hosted more than a few notables of this unique fellowship at any one time, he often had guests, some of whom stayed for months. It was a generosity born from literary curiosity and its non-materiality which virtually imprisoned him, but it produced a learned circle of considerable intellect and influence from academia to bohemia. The excellence and rarity of his father's collections, supplemented by Edgar Jr's own highly selective acquisitions and unlimited budget, was a magnet to the literati who didn't want to wait for a similar text to become available under the strict and restricted procedures of a museum or library, especially when that institution wasn't even on the same continent. Once again, Edgar Sr.'s obsession to distinguish Highcomb prevailed as it took on the reputation of great learning. No doubt he would have taken credit for this too, but he didn't anticipate it so The Trust simply accepted it as beneficial and ignored it.

As Edgar Jr. pursued his personal obsession with the written word, ancient thought and philosophic discourse, Ida raised her boys in the modern world which included shielding them from their father's introverted and decidedly narrow and negative view of the 20th century. Being uncontested, she was successful in this endeavor and produced two equally unique and capable men who were very different from each other.

The eldest, Andrew, as is often the case with the first born, was ruled, rigid and practical, a club man. Sport, business or charity, he assumed his social position without effort or complaint and was often within its leadership, whether elected or otherwise. Like Edgar Sr. who he never met, Andrew was determined, straight-forward and if he didn't know his destiny like he knew his own face, he never let that be known. He was a member of the old guard when he was still a young man and, like royalty, he was not born or raised with a silver spoon in his mouth; he was born with a polo mallet in one hand and the reins of a thoroughbred in the other.

His brother, Thomas was also a club man, a night-club man. From New York to Monaco, he knew where to find the action and was just as frequently responsible for creating it. Fast cars, fast women, high stake games of any kind and smoky blues bars were his domain. Dance, drink and decadence were more than hobbies to him, they were his birthright, his *raison de étre*.

The boys were separated in age by a single year which might as well have been a lifetime and while they always got along well together and always respected each other, the difference of night and day was between them at birth. Had they ever had to compete for their father's recognition or their mother's love, there might have been friction except they hardly knew the recluse who was their father and Ida took her job seriously, didn't acknowledge their differences, and didn't play favorites.

When Andrew was 9 he was sent to the best, moderately disciplined, boarding school Ida could find and the year after that, Thomas joined him in Zurich. It was something of a gamble to abandon them together, but she figured her boys wouldn't compete against each other and were more likely to collaborate for their mutual benefit and therefore emerge even more united than before. She was right, they were brothers, friends, colleagues and partners simultaneously, identical castings from the mold she created, nurtured and then continued to shape by personally interviewing and evaluating their teachers and sometimes even hiring them into the school, much to the headmaster's displeasure but with a financial benefit he could not resist.

From boarding school and into their early adult lives, Andrew and Thomas knew Highcomb was more than just a place to go for the holidays. It assumed life importance as more than a magnificent, elegant edifice to a grandfather who also became larger in death, a consequence of Ida's carefully managed and manicured view of history. Highcomb's importance in their lives evolved because of the permanence of its granite walls and because of Ida's desire to create a dynasty within them.

Under her unrelenting pressure, Highcomb became the definition of their future and Andrew and Thomas were completely aware, very early in their budding awareness, that their future would be what they wanted it to be as long as Highcomb was part of it. When their friends and acquaintances suffered the affliction of identity crises which was common to the over-privileged of their class, the brothers simply joined the society of those who had successfully made the passage to becoming who they were expected to become. They moved on, carrying their roles like backpacks. The thought of being restricted to a single segment of an already narrowly defined society, based on wealth, title or influence was unfathomable to them. That was not the way to succeed, let alone the way to live and Highcomb was absolute proof of what survives and what dies.

By the time they were in their early 20's, both of them knew their path was set and their place on it was guaranteed. They took advantage of every opportunity given or taken, quickly matured in their intellect as well as life experience and had but one weakness, which they shared. Because they had spent the majority of their young lives alone, they were emotionally insecure, lonely and suffering from the lack of meaningful accomplishment which could not be resolved with momentary wins on playing fields or with playing cards. While they expressed this weakness with fundamentally opposite lifestyles, they conquered it the same way.

For Andrew, her name was Christine; for Thomas, her name was Mia, and the two women were as distinctly different as the men they caught even if the bait was the same. At least for the men the bait was the same, Ida had different criteria for approval of her daughter's-in-law but once her criteria were satisfied, everyone's future proceeded according to plan, her plan.

She approved of Christine for her family's wealth and social position and she approved of Mia for the ancestry of her titles and the social position which came with them. That the women mirrored the dispositions of her sons, with Christine being cautious and conservative and Mia being care-free and somewhat rebellious didn't matter just like their independence as unique and accomplished women prior to entering the world of Highcomb didn't matter. Those are details that change with life, sometimes very quickly. What did matter and which was not negotiable was the promise of grandchildren and both were fertile enough to satisfy that requirement within the first year of marriage.

Nothing, she theorized, did more to tame a man's mind than having a wife and children at home. This, in spite of the fact her theory completely opposed her own experience with Edgar Jr. who she saw less and less frequently even though they lived on the same mountain. She left him in the winter wing and moved back to the summer wing shortly after the boys were sent to Switzerland, an act which only deepened a marital isolation which neither of them cared to do anything about. Edgar Jr. got his library and Ida took the rest. Without her boys, Sunday dinner was abandoned to the past and despite his key genetic contribution to the dynasty she was attempting to create, Edgar Jr. was excluded from it.

★ ★ ★ ★ ★

Andrew's Christine was the first to add another twig to the family tree and heir apparent to Highcomb. She painlessly delivered a dark-haired, olive-skinned baby they named Charles when Grand-Mére, as Ida decided to call herself, also decided that the name Edgar III should skip a generation or more until the memory of Edgar Jr. was either forgotten or rewritten in some way. A few months later, with great drama, Mia delivered a blonde and fair-skinned baby they named Thomas Jr. but called Tom, not Thomas and never Tommy.

The maternity months provided Grand-Mére with ample time to renovate part of the summer wing into comfortable apartments for both families and to cement her will that her grandsons be raised in Highcomb in concert with the dynastic values and traditions dictated, and directed, by Grand-Mére herself.

Christine took her new life graciously and would have been surprised and disappointed if Highcomb were not to become her home just as she intended to become its mistress when Grand-Mére's time ran out. She submitted in silence, an appropriate response to her mother-in-law's demand for compliance without comment or complaint.

Mia found Highcomb to be an accommodating 5star hotel which offered excellent services for Tom who she adored much the same way she adored Scuderia Corsa at Le Mans or the ring of the bell at The Ascot Gold Cup but instead of submitting to Grand-Mére's view of an isolated world on top of a mountain, she was aloof, demanding and frequently absent for extended, and always uncertain, periods of time. One does not need to create a dynasty when royal blood already flows through one's veins.

Grand-Mére was pleased with both her daughters-in-law and while some venues were more suited to the conservative Christine or to the out-going, vivacious Mia, both were assets on her arm. She was building a dynasty for all of them and was never shy to explain that her grandsons had Highcomb in their blood as they were conceived and born within its walls.

Shortly after she finished renovating the apartments in the summer wing and ignoring the power of The Trust by not telling them of her plans, she decided to make Highcomb more suitable for the elite and cultured society she intended for herself and her family. Family that by now excluded Edgar Jr. who was intent on a wasted life in pursuit of academic excellence when he should have counted himself blessed and lucky to have a wife who cared so much about power and position in a rapidly evolving world of travel, politic and entertainment. Knowing that she was not adventurous enough for travel or intelligent enough for politic she surrounded herself with those in the leisure and entertainment industry. This meant glamorous parties and a place to hold them.

At each end of the Gallery which looked down on Reception and which provided entry to the winter wing on one end and the summer wing on the other, she had constructed two identical broad, rectangular and somewhat steep staircases to the ceiling where a hole was opened to the flat roof. The graceful curve of the inside corners that Edgar Sr. demanded in lieu of turrets were a nuisance to her local carpenters so they squared the curves with a false wall then textured it with a stucco-like finish intended to complement the work of the Italian stone masons whose work they covered. This was an abject failure in all respects other than it provided access to the roof.

Unfortunately, the brutal design of her staircases didn't stop with ruining the symmetry of the gallery. Not only did they look like fire escapes on the outside of a tenement building but in order to appear welcoming, they were too wide and the sharpness of their incline, too great. Even with the incline, they intruded into the gallery and its introduction to the residences and suites of each wing. In an attempt to compensate for the intrusion, at the bottom she added a tall, thick, octagonal newel post topped with an oversized, carved acorn-shaped finial with the hope that would distract the eye from the chaos of extreme angles and contrary finishes. It didn't.

Once she had access to the roof and running three quarters of the way down the length of each wing she built identical greenhouse-like structures with 7foot glass walls supporting a tunnel-shaped glass roof which peaked at 15feet in the center, it was all held together with a galvanized steel frame. The additions were largely invisible from ground level but when seen from the gardens or from one wing looking across to the other, they contributed a decidedly industrial, if not amusement park-flavor to Highcomb's otherwise perfectly balanced symmetry, classic design and integrity of composition.

Over Edgar Jr's head on the winter wing her monstrosity became The Party Room, comfortable for entertaining a couple of hundred guests. It contained a large circular bar, a dance floor with adjacent bandstand, dozens of tables with wicker furniture and a large, uncovered patio at the far end from which fireworks could be launched or smokers could go with their cigars.

Over her own head in the summer wing her monstrosity was slightly more suited for its purpose and became a botanical garden of sorts with the uncovered patio at the end being used for storage of pots, gardening paraphernalia and dead or dying plants. Ida had no horticultural knowledge or skill and didn't hire anyone who did consequently her garden became a haphazard collection of plants she purchased at the local nurseries where she often took her grandsons on rainy days.

When The Trust became aware of her efforts it was too late to stop it so it advised Edgar Jr. that the staircases and rooftop structures be removed and the building restored to its original state. By return post Ida advised The Trust that such actions would be over her dead body. Once they realized what she already knew, namely that Edgar Jr. was incapable of exerting any influence whatsoever over his wife or his significant wealth, wealth that she would use to fight them just as she used it to create the problem in the first place, it responded to her offer, in writing and with clear intent and copied to her solicitor.

The Trust admonishes you for the unwise and unnecessary threat of making your death a condition with respect to the performance of its duties but so be it, understand that The Trust will remove the disputed elements at its sole discretion and at the time of its choosing.

Until that time, be advised that your residence at Highcomb is a privilege, not a right, and any future unauthorized change, however insignificant, will be met with an order to vacate. The Trust will enforce this order regardless of the time or expense to prosecute. In this regard, you are advised to seek and comply with the advice of your counsel because The Trust will most certainly prevail.

Henceforth, The Trust will inspect and inventory, as is its mandate, biannually.

★ ★ ★ ★ ★

Tom grew up in the summer wing and under Grand-Mére's tutelage, Highcomb's rooms, their contents and accumulated history became his first permanent memories. This painting, that sculpture, those tapestries, marble from Carrera, mahogany from Brazil and teak from Indonesia, there was a lot to learn about his ancestral home.

His personal space consisted of his bedroom, bathroom and three adjoining rooms which were his classroom, his playroom and a large room which was used to house collections which Grand-Mére supervised and which only occasionally reflected his own interests.

Surrounding his space was the rest of the summer wing which included the large and lavish apartment at the end of the wing which was once Edgar Sr's home, and which now belonged to Grand-Mére. Across from him was the vacant apartment Charles once shared with his parents and a number of guest suites and rooms for activities were interspersed. The winter wing was similarly arranged with guest rooms and his grandfather's modest, vacant residence. Notable was the large library with its countless volumes of books, tables and lounges, sliding ladders with which to reach top shelves and nooks and crannies that arose by virtue of Edgar Jr's. haphazard and impromptu expansions.

Downstairs and imposing, because Grand-Mére made it that way, was his great-grandfather's study with the austere portrait over the fireplace. Grand-Mére was frequently found behind his desk pouring over history or accounts or perhaps pretending she was someone she wasn't. Tom never questioned and never doubted that Highcomb was anything less than a member of his family.

He had no memories of his namesake father, Thomas, so Grand-Mére implanted hers. He learned to interpret her tone and her choice of words in order to add some reality to those memories because some of her descriptions were brief to the edge of secrecy or exaggerated to the point of disbelief.

From her he also learned his great-grandfather, Edgar Sr., died long ago but was the larger-than-life, historical figure who created Highcomb. She spoke of him with a reverent awe for his accomplishments including the man's vital contribution to Tom's existence from blood to bank. Grand-Mére's reverence for Edgar Sr. was often prompted by the art and objects she was teaching so she infused life into objects just like the portrait in the study had become part of the wall. There was nothing and no one to contradict her view of this history as anyone who knew and remembered Edgar Sr. had died or left the world of Highcomb, synonymous events as far as she was concerned.

Tom knew Edgar Jr. was his grandfather, however, he died before he could form any permanent memories of him, and because there weren't any memories worth remembering as far as Grand-Mére was concerned she implanted none. His life was as unimportant as his death so she seldom spoke about him or his contribution to the magnificent library he created. According to her, the library and the books in it were simply part of Highcomb and were written by strangers, like her husband, and didn't deserve individual mention. When she had to speak of him, it was with the subdued distaste of a life wasted in pursuit of other people's knowledge. Unlike Edgar Sr.'s portrait, if Tom were shown a photograph of Edgar Jr., he wouldn't have recognized him.

His own father was an even greater mystery. Although he died when Tom was almost 5 years old, whatever memory he had, if he even had one of his own, that memory was displaced by Grand-Mére's images of a son she really didn't know either. Over the decade of his death, she spoke of him with sad acclaim for a full and energetic life tragically lost under unspeakable events. Her memories seldom reflected his actual life or shared experiences and when they did, those were told as calendar events, as dates and places, void of personal connection, like hearing about this fire or that flood. Grand-Mére preferred to dwell on what might have been and his rare and valued characteristics became fantasies of achievement or leadership or some other superlative she admired and that Tom most certainly possessed or would one day possess because he was born with it. That became his father's contribution to Tom's life; his death was never discussed, and Tom knew better than to ask about it. Grand-Mére was uncomfortable with the subject of death and refused to acknowledge it directly so Tom learned to separate the dead from the living by the consistent use of past or present tense.

On his maternal side, Tom knew little about his mother, or Mia, as he most often thought of her. After her husband's death, she rarely visited Highcomb and always fought with Grand-Mére when she did. She told Tom she loved him, often in different languages so while he didn't doubt that love, he didn't really understand it. She always parted with promises for the future which he found more and more difficult to believe as they drifted further and further apart and the time between her visits became longer and longer.

Grand-Mére never saw or spoke of her own family. Had she said she was the first of her line and dropped into Highcomb from outer space, Tom would have had no choice but to believe her. The absence of this history neither disturbed him or aroused his curiosity. Not every artifact or object in Highcomb had a history behind it and that included some of the people in it.

The part of Tom's family that was not remembered in past tense consisted of Uncle Andrew, Aunt Christine and Cousin Charles. He had very sketchy memories of the years when they lived across from him. Because he and Charles were so close in age, so too were their memories, which were mostly the games they played as little boys and not when or why they were separated over 10 years ago. That mystery was as unsolved as it was unspoken; one day they all lived together and the next day they didn't. Whatever the reason, it was an accepted reality by everyone and that made it unimportant enough to be discussed further.

Grand-Mére neither mentioned nor acknowledged the reason or the event, if there was one, for the separation. In fact, she seldom spoke about them at all but even Tom knew she preferred her dead son to her live one and while he didn't know her reasons for that, he knew better than to ask her about them. Questions like that only ever resulted in a lecture about secrets with her stating that it wasn't the secrets a family had, and they all had secrets, it was the way they were kept that was important. That was her way of closing the door on a question she refused to answer.

Like anyone who left Highcomb, Uncle Andrew and Aunt Christine virtually ceased to exist once they disappeared around the 8th switchback but always came back into existence on two special occasions Grand-Mére reserved for family and only family, Christmas Day and September 2nd, the commemoration of the death of her second and still favorite son. In contrast to her sons, her grandsons were treated with equanimity, although neither of them were absolutely convinced of that equality, either between themselves or with her. There was always something missing, some emotion or commitment which left them wondering if they were the next in line to be forgotten.

The boys were together whenever they wanted to be and often when they didn't. Summer camps, holidays and vacations, no matter the event, activity or gift, whatever Tom got, Charles got. Charles still had his own rooms, practically identical to his own, which were carved out and separated from the apartment he once shared with his parents. He frequently stayed for days, sometimes weeks at a time and all summer, sharing toys, tutors and adventures like brothers who had Highcomb as one parent and Grand-Mére as the other.

They loved exploring and Highcomb held endless possibilities and few restrictions but there were rules, the most important being reverent respect, bordering on religious edict, toward Highcomb and its treasures. Breakage or damage beyond the playroom was so serious an offense that the consequences were never discussed but offsetting this governance, Grand-Mére strongly believed that the world of privilege started at birth, so the boys had plenty of privileges. She also knew how fickle the privileged class could be and made certain her grandsons understood that a light hand on the reins did not mean no reins, just as forgive did not mean forget.

Outside they had the lawns, gardens, ponds and patios. On a gentle slope that extended for a quarter of a mile at the south end of the mountain was untamed wilderness. Excellent for games as mountain men with sightings of deer and the occasional bear to encourage the imagination. In keeping with that theme, games of the old west were played in the valley below where the horses were stabled and both boys became excellent riders.

Inside, the boys explored Highcomb from bottom to top. The second-floor basement was unexciting, being mostly row after row of sealed wooden crates stacked floor to ceiling, stretching down both wings of the building. The crates were numbered in black stenciled paint but the actual contents were a mystery other than the knowledge they were part of their great-grandfather's collection from Europe, Asia and Africa and any time or age of the human race. It would have been more interesting territory had it been dark and dungeon-like, but it wasn't. Highcomb's treasures were treated to a modern, brightly lit, temperature and humidity-controlled environment with regular cleaning and constant monitoring for pests.

Occupying one corner of this subterranean storage at the front of the wing was an assortment of art and furniture that cycled back and forth to guest rooms depending on guest status and requirements. In the opposite corner was a large, padlocked, wire security cage that contained polished oak boxes with names like Remington or Smith and Wesson in gold leaf. Against the walls were mahogany and cherry cabinets. Stacked upright behind their curved glass doors were guns from blunderbuss to Holland & Holland shotguns and rifles from flint locks to Winchesters. Drawers in the cabinets held everything from black powder and shot to modern ammunition. Packed into the surrounding space were racks of spears, carousels of swords, bows, crossbows and other armory that was of great fascination but always locked and off-limits even for privileged boys. Between the furniture storage at one corner and the gun cage at the other were offices for record keeping and workshops for maintenance and restoration of the collection but these were seldom used as Highcomb was completely furnished, nothing new was being acquired, everything that needed restoration had already received it, nothing was for sale so nothing ever moved.

The first-floor basement was more interesting. It housed everything Highcomb needed to operate but which didn't need to be seen. Under the summer wing was the garage with its fine collection of automobiles. This provided hours of entertainment and the creative spark for games of spies, gangsters and race car drivers. Under the winter wing, locked but easily accessible because it was frequently open were the boilers, furnaces, cooling, plumbing and electrical infrastructure for Highcomb plus spare parts and a large well-equipped workshop for repairs. Accommodations for maintenance and grounds-keeping staff who also didn't need to be seen were quartered in small windowless rooms scattered down both wings and under the gallery connecting them.

The main floor included Reception and its Edgar staircase to the Gallery which led to the summer wing to the left and the winter wing to the right. Offsetting Reception on one side was Edgar Sr's study and its small, attached library and in the opposite corner was The Treaty Room where historic signings and announcements were made. Down the wings on the ground floor were rooms for entertaining, dance, music, and a theatre. Highcomb's dining room was part way down the winter wing with its epicurean kitchen, overstocked panty and staff quarters. In the summer wing, this space was occupied by housekeeping and quarters for staff, servants of visitors and the general manager's office. Every corner of every room was in complete order and ran with the precision of a Swiss clock in the hands of Manager Bains, from Geneva. The boys had free run but were respectful of staff quarters and never entered unless invited and witnessed. Grand-Mére made no secret of the shame which would be invested on a boy caught spying on staff or in their quarters. That was Manager Bains' job and he reported to her in confidence and carried out her punishments.

Upstairs, an invitation to a guest room or suite was required when occupied but when vacant, every room was common property, so they knew every square inch and every detail of every room. Favorites were Edgar Jr.'s library in the winter wing and its thousands of books, reading tables and ox-blood leather, brass-studded furniture. Grand-Mére's rooms at the end of the summer wing were private and the boys respected that privacy without spoken rule or restriction; her attitude was more than enough for them to know they had to be invited just to sit still and listen or sit still and be interrogated.

Up the steep staircases at the entrance to each wing, were Grand-Mére's contributions to Highcomb. The so-called arboretum on the summer wing was always open and its identical twin on the winter wing, which was always locked.

The boys grew-up in Highcomb and Highcomb grew-up in them. It was an organic relationship. Where Highcomb didn't serve directly for knowledge, belief and boundary, it integrated its values of history, accomplishment and character with their growing awareness of being part of something larger than themselves and their duty to find their place within it and to protect it.

That was Grand-Mére's plan for both boys and for Tom it was executed on a daily basis with the expectation he would share that teaching and that connection with Charles, which he did, bit by bit, year after year. He may have been younger than his cousin but he was the resident heir to Highcomb so it was his duty and he did it without question or complaint, although he occasionally colored the telling or withheld a fact or two just as Grand-Mére did.

★ ★ ★ ★ ★

At first, Tom was enjoying his time in the arboretum. It was a mild spring day; the sun was streaming through the glass, heating the moist air inside and releasing an earthy smell from the beds and pots surrounding him. He chose to sit among the cacti and succulents where nothing was in bloom.

His mood darkened as he stared across open air to the winter wing and try as he might, as he had so often tried, he couldn't see through the glass to satisfy a curiosity which was as old as he was. It was always dark inside but now the glass was so dirty the only thing he knew for certain was that if anything was in there, it was dead.

He and Charles had tried and tried and failed and failed to explore it and with every passing year, the glass got dirtier and dirtier until now he couldn't even make out the outlines of the furniture they once believed they knew to be there. He was never positive and now he questioned whether what they thought they knew was really just their imagination. Not even binoculars helped; they just brought the dark spaces and shadows closer without revealing their true nature.

When they first asked Grand-Mére about it they were told it was just a room for entertaining which was no longer needed and they shouldn't ask about it again. On the rare occasions when staff talked about it, they called it The Party Room and made it sound like a bad place. Naturally all that did was heighten their curiosity and drive it underground. Privileged boys do not like being denied without just cause and the absence of just cause completely justified breaking the rules, or so went the logic of their defense if they got caught.

The doors at the top of the stairs to The Party Room were chained through the handles and the chain was padlocked through the links with a modern, industrial, high-strength lock. On the positive side, that was the only real challenge to their quest because if they got past that, the chances of anyone seeing the doors unchained was remote. Finding the key to that lock became a game they code-named Sherlocking.

There were dozens, maybe hundreds, of locks in Highcomb. Doors, cabinets, boxes and drawers with locks from medieval to modern and nearly all of them were never locked. Of the remainder, some were locked only periodically, by a guest or when a valuable document or article was in transit and a few were always locked, probably because the key was lost or improperly filed in the key safe.

Every key was numbered, not named, on a white circular tag and hung on the correspondingly numbered hook in the key safe in Manager Bains' office. There had to be an index joining the key with its lock and its location and that was probably in the heavy, fireproof cabinet behind his desk. Unfortunately, that cabinet was only ever unlocked for the seconds it took him to remove a document or the moment it took him to replace it and the only key to that lock never left the ring on his belt. Fortunately, the same was not true of the key cabinet which was frequently open. Even more fortunately, with the right story, Mr. Bains could be distracted.

It took teamwork and they did it the long, hard way by eliminating the keys one-by-one, row by row. Many could be eliminated by sight alone: too old, too small or too large, some were not grooved like the padlock or had a different name on the key but some had to be borrowed, tried and returned. If Manager Bains knew what they were up to, he never let on and perhaps, after trying every key which looked like it might work but failed, they figured he didn't care because every key in that safe belonged to a lock that was never supposed to be locked in the first place.

That left them with two possibilities.

Maybe the key didn't exist. Maybe The Party Room was locked and the key was thrown away. But that didn't make sense and was impossible to accept.

Which left Grand-Mére as the remaining possibility and she wasn't about to tell them where it was any more than she was going to tell them why she hid it. 'No longer used' were just different words for 'it's a secret.' They were absolutely convinced that that secret, whatever it was, would be revealed once they got through those doors and that curiosity was all the motivation they needed for years of searching.

He had nothing else to think about, so he returned his gaze to The Party Room and intensified his concentration to a question as familiar to him as his face.

It had to be her, so where did she hide it? Highcomb was a big place to search for such a tiny object. If for no other reason than it made their search monumentally more difficult, eventually they decided it had to be in her apartment because it was the most secretive place of all and if they were going to hide something, that's where they would hide it.

Grand-Mére was meticulous to the point of obsession and suspicious to the point of paranoia so searching her apartment when she was away was out of the question. She would know if anything had been touched. She would detect a change in the scent of the air over her perfume table. She would know whether it was her body which caused that wrinkle in her sheets. She would know if her dust had moved and if it did, she never made a secret of the length to which she would go in order to find the person who invaded her territory. She never said what she would do to them and no one asked. Better the fear you do not know than the one which follows you around all day.

Getting caught by her overly protective maid or a fearful housekeeper was a huge risk and an absolute certainty if they were not quick and without a solid strategy for look-out and sounding alarm. Then an even more solid excuse was required if they were caught searching her room and they couldn't come up with that. The boys understood her strategy of turning everyone into guards and spies because she turned them long ago before they knew what seeds she was capable of planting in their minds. With her network of informers, she ruled her domain when she was away just as effectively as when she was sitting behind her dead father-in-law's desk.

That left only one way to Sherlock safely; she had to be present and that required tactics. Sometimes they would suspect a hiding spot and then test her reaction when either of them showed interest in it. Sometimes, with the right story, or the right amount of innocence they could even search while she watched them. Sometimes she could be distracted by one of them while the other looked over, under, in or around a potential hiding place.

It wasn't in her jewelry box, it wasn't on the key ring in her purse, it wasn't in a drawer or taped under one. It wasn't anywhere and it was a frustrating exercise in futility not to mention that spending time with her almost always ended up with a lecture or some unwelcome chore. When they ran out of ideas, they watched her, hoping she would make a mistake, inadvertently signal her hiding spot or that blind luck would prevail where strategy, logic and tactic had failed. It didn't. She won; she always did.

Tom stiffened at the thought he would never see The Party Room. He was being denied without right or fairness and that darkened his thoughts further.

It wasn't fair and while Charles had given up, he couldn't. Highcomb was his home, it was in his blood and brain and he had a right to every bit of it, top to bottom, inside and out, personal, private and all secrets included. The search had become so ingrained in his mind and the question had been asked so many times it was like one word: 'Where do you hide a key to a lock you never want opened?'

Not in plain sight, that ground had been ploughed over and over. It had to be out-of-sight but that made no sense and they had abandoned that idea long ago. She was too controlling to allow it out of her sight.

Or was she. Did she hide it so far out-of-sight that even she didn't know if it was still there. Is that what she did? Why not? There weren't many places they hadn't looked so why not one of those? Why not throw it down a well so you know where it is even if you can't see it or get to it without someone noticing? That made sense. She knew where it was, and that no one would look there. Why not hide it in a place like that? As he mentally listed the hiding spots that qualified, he knew he was on to something. He knew because he ran out of hiding places almost immediately.

The very thought he might have solved the mystery sent a charge of electricity into his mind and from there it raced to his heart, which began to thump. Then he felt it travel, felt it involuntarily sparking muscles in his arms and that caused his skin to shiver. So many years of searching had gone wrong and now all that failure was about to be tested one more time, maybe the last time. Maybe. Best of all, there were only a handful of options and only one good one so both the search, and the disappointment if there was to be one, would be quick.

He felt time concentrate until it became solid like he was witnessing history. It was intensely personal, vitally real, he felt incredibly alive. The end of who he was and the beginning of who he was to become were side by side. He knew this. He wasn't certain what that meant, just that for the first time in his life, he knew he was reaching a conclusion and not because of logic or faith, but because he was out of options. Another second always follows the one passing and this was the second in which the past would be revealed or permanently hidden from the future. It changed him, he knew he was experiencing a critical turning point in his life and the only question was how the game would end.

He would find out tomorrow. Wednesday, she would lunch then play bridge and be gone all afternoon. Her maid would take her half day off. All he needed was 5 minutes, maybe 10 and if he was right, years of Sherlocking would finally rest peacefully, and permanently, in the past.

★ ★ ★ ★ ★

The Bentley disappeared around the 8th switchback and he dismissed his tutor with the excuse of the headache he had been faking all morning. As soon as it was safe, he went to his great-grandfather's study where he took an old split bamboo fly rod from the back of the rack. He pulled a couple of feet of line from the reel and tied a magnet to the end.

Her bedroom had two very tall, ornate, antique French armoires against the wall, facing her canopied bed. The front and sides were beautifully carved with a scalloped floral frame which was higher than the body of the armoire, leaving a sheltered cavity at the top. It was the perfect place to put something you didn't need, didn't want seen and didn't want accidentally found. He held his breath and swung the magnet into the cavity of the first armoire.

He heard a metallic clink, raised the pole, swung the magnet into his free hand and his search was over. As he held the dusty key he was suddenly fearful of it. It was evidence of his crime and he wanted to put it back until he realized the benefit of her hiding place had gone from her to him. She wouldn't look for it because she didn't have to, that was how she kept the secret from everyone for so long and now it was his secret. Now, time was on his side and that included the rest of the afternoon. His next moment of uncertainty was to wait for Charles but something, perhaps years of unsatisfied, insatiable curiosity convinced him it was his discovery. He deserved the credit, and not only should he be first to go behind those doors he should go alone. Charles had given up; Charles deserved to wait; Charles was second.

With hurried steps he returned the pole to its place on the rack, remembering at the last minute to remove the magnet, which caused his heart to skip a beat. It was a good lesson. Being safe did not permit being careless just as being first did not mean it was a race. Besides, he thought, the denial he suffered from years of searching should be rewarded slowly.

Easy to think but hard to do. The blood was rushing through his arteries; his heart pounded as he walked up the Grand Staircase and down the Gallery to the winter wing. At the bottom of the steep staircase leading to The Party Room he took a quiet moment to make certain he was unseen and alone then ran up the stairs and within seconds was standing before the double doors and completely out of sight.

The key turned in the padlock without making a sound so he quietly unthreaded the chain from one of the handles, hung it on the other and put the open padlock through the links so it couldn't do the impossible and fall off. After that, there was nothing more he could do to disguise the break-in, but he knew that worry wasn't rational; in all the times he and Charles had tried keys or tried to pick the lock, never had they been interrupted.

He turned the knob and felt but didn't hear the latch move past the strike plate. The door cracked open with a firm push and a squeak which seemed so loud he thought it could be heard in the basement but that worry also disappeared in an instant but not because it was irrational. It was completely rational to dismiss it because even if someone came up the stairs that very second, it would be too late for them to do anything except tell on him; he was going through that door and not coming out until he was done; it was his right. He felt a resolve so strong, if he had to, he'd charge through that door like a bull but knew that wouldn't be necessary, no one would lay a hand on him. Nor would any punishment deter him. He pushed the door enough to squeeze through, shut it behind himself and entered a world no longer the product of his imagination.

The smell of dead air was an immediate assault to his expectation of a sweet victory, and he tried to analyze it. The residue of dust, summer heat and winter cold; the smell of air that has not been breathed for years, it was an inhuman sensation. He took it in then realized he was experiencing the event like in a movie, like it was happening to someone else. That sensation repeated itself as he stepped onto hardwood flooring that hadn't experienced a footfall for years. They were alien experiences which would become familiar with time and Tom intended to live those moments, before, during and after, to their fullest.

Fine dust covered everything but with the slight breeze caused by his movement, the insignificant weight broke cobwebs that had become brittle and fragile. The particles clouded the dead air like falling smoke. He was entering the past but not a past like the art or objects he was accustomed to associating with the past. This past had been abandoned; it was as dead as the dust that covered it. It was a past trapped in a secret and that, he knew, was the reason its assault on him felt as physical as a punch to the gut.

The Party Room. The mysterious, illusive twin to the arboretum was finally admitting a visitor. Its secret was no longer safe.

The end of search and the beginning of discovery occurred simultaneously and so quickly that what was completely new became instantly familiar as he stretched his mind into it. He re-experienced the epiphany he felt the day before when he unraveled the mystery of the lost key. But this time the realization was even more powerful. He detached from his past and when he returned, he brought that past back with him like it was a crate from storage with its black stenciled number being the only reference to its contents. His mind cleared, he understood that the past he was entering belonged to someone else and he was the alien. That troubled him, mildly.

His footprints in the dust were evidence of his crime but there wasn't a way around it and he didn't care. He stopped thinking about being caught because there was too much to absorb, too much to be recorded in memory, resolved into context and concluded with truth. He was surrounded by a secret and knew he could no more go forward with guilt than he could turn around and leave without remorse. Whatever it turned out to be, he was owed this revelation and, good or bad, he intended to own the experience. This was his heritage, within a few steps it was no longer alien, it became part of him.

His first, extra-ordinary, conscious realization of the room was the stark image of time stopped and something frozen in it, something held in place by dust and broken cobwebs; something he was the first person to see since whatever happened, had happened. It was a thought which ran parallel to detachment from his own past. Past was meeting past and he was fully committed to it just as it was fully committed to him. It wasn't cold but he thought his breath was visible in the dead air when he knew it couldn't be. It was a strange sensation, but it came from, and fit perfectly with, the world surrounding him, so his mind sunk into it, like his body sunk into a soft leather chair in the library.

As he always suspected, the room was identical to the arboretum and indeed there had been potted plants and trees. Some of them still had a few dead leaves stuck to their branches while the pot below was surrounded by leaf litter which dropped in their last and final fall. The room had been left to die. It was a cemetery on a roof and it held no emotion. Or did it? He was feeling something. Or was he? Was it a feeling or was he merely ending a search that had occupied his thoughts for so many years? It came with the uncomfortable sensation he wasn't the only person in the room, as impossible as that was. Maybe a combination of thoughts and emotions in conflict, definitely conflict. He knew he was alone just as he knew he wasn't absolutely certain of anything including being alone. It didn't matter. Being certain about anything was not important at that moment. Certainty could wait, certainty had to wait; this was not the time for his mind to be closed to any possibilities or the outcomes they produced.

He knew his uncertainty would change with every footprint he left behind. Like those footprints, which could not be erased, nothing would erase the experience and the certainty which came with it, once it took hold on his senses. He lingered in the in-between of indecision. He looked around, occasionally returning to this or that object, this or that impression, absorbing detail, like a person getting their bearings. He didn't listen because there was nothing to hear.

With his back against the door, he thought he saw a pathway through the room, a path like a pattern of flow which went like a rabbit trail through the tables and scattered chairs. Something, or someone, made that trail. Was there a reason for it? Is there ever a reason for a rabbit trail?

The tables were covered with tablecloths brown on top but shadow grey in the overhanging folds where dust couldn't settle. On the tables were glasses, napkins, ashtrays and some dishes with cutlery, randomly surrounding what was once a floral centerpiece, now dry, brown and dust covered with the dead bloom bent over like in mourning.

Indecision was over, his mind was open, he decided it was time to engage the past.

He took a step and started the process of changing from observer to explorer by following the trail between and around the tables and chairs. He stopped and picked up a glass. It left a perfect white circle on the cloth. A memory. The contents were dried into a residue. He blew the dust out; the residue was a glossy, caramel color that held no scent. He returned it to its circle but left it slightly uncentered, like that would help him find his way back. Some chairs were neatly pushed into their place at the table and others were scattered. He left them alone.

Midway into the room was a large, oak bar of two facing semi-circles with an entry between. He stopped to explore and when he did, he realized he needed breath. In the process of internalizing the room, his breathing had become shallow, making him feel slightly faint.

Behind the bar were bottles of wine and spirits, trays of glassware and dishes that were stacked in bins, some dirty, others clean. The bar was littered with glasses and some open bottles which were dried to empty. Ashtrays contained cigarettes that had burned themselves out and a cigar that had not. He wondered if he could use the cigar's ash trail to calculate the exact hour it was extinguished like a broken watch tells the time of its own destruction. Probably not, at least not without more clues so he kept his mind open and accepting of any thought or observation. Later, he would sort, order and then dismiss the clues which didn't fit. What remained would be the secret he and Charles had sought since the game began. He smiled at the irony. This was no game.

Beyond the bar were more chairs and tables, only more widely spaced, surrounding a dancefloor. He expected to see a shoe or a napkin on the floor but there wasn't anything except empty space, like a mistake had been made. It was mildly troubling.

Facing the dancefloor was the bandstand. Music stands were in haphazard display, some overturned and sheets of music were spilled in a way that suggested the band had reached a chaotic finale. A few instruments were left on the floor or on chairs, a French horn, a bass and an empty violin case, all the drums. He wondered if the sheets of music on the few stands still upright would tell him what was being played when chaos occurred. Probably, but not likely a clue toward the chaos itself.

The bandstand was at the far end of the room just as the cacti and succulents were at the far end of the arboretum. The double doors in the center of the wall that led out to the patio were the same, he had to concentrate to see through the dirty panes.

There was even more chaos outside. Tables and chairs were tipped over, pushed together and tangled. Linens were trapped in the furniture or blown into corners and deteriorating into rags. Broken glass was mixed with leafy debris blown in by seasons of storm and wind. Whatever happened inside was compounded by nature's forces outside. He kept that thought.

He felt time surround him and put a forearm on the bar to steady himself despite the powerful feeling he couldn't move because his feet were stuck to the floor just like the room was stuck in time. He couldn't understand the mystery surrounding him, yet he felt its magnetic draw, stronger than any curiosity he had ever known. And different too, deeply different, like he had to know the exact moment in the past he was viewing just like he imagined a person had to know the moment between life and death because of its intensity. A moment of knowing which has no point to it except that it only ever occurs once and is too compelling to resist or deny despite the consequences it brings.

It was a moment in which he had to see what no one had seen for thousands of days but which had been faithfully, carefully and completely preserved for this moment and just for him. It was confusing yet familiar, like a memory which is just slightly out of order, slightly wrong on the calendar or perhaps with the wrong people in it. It needed correction like the reflection in a pond waits for the ripples to stop so the image can clear.

Whatever had happened in that past, temporarily defied analysis in the present but he was determined that it would not escape his understanding. He understood that abandoned time, just like the abandoned room, was irrelevant because objects don't experience time like living beings. The only way they could help him understand was because they preserved time so if he could see through the dust he might discover what happened and that would reveal a secret. Unless he was asking the wrong questions, it had to.

Perhaps the answer evading him was connected to the feeling of his feet being frozen to the floor, so he cleared his mind of metaphysical wonderings and moved to the dancefloor, one unhurried step at a time.

Each step produced a different thought which he accepted as a puzzle piece. Overturned tables and chairs. Broken glass. Drinks spilled on the once white tablecloth. More cigarettes; burned out. Unfolded napkins abandoned on placemats, litter on the floor. Nothing different compared to what he had already passed in order to get there but closer to the beginning of the chaos, closer to the origin of the trail he was instinctively following. What he couldn't quite see, he could feel.

He stepped onto the dancefloor and surveyed the bandstand, which produced no new thoughts. To the left of the bandstand and patio doors were more tables and chairs. And more chaos as he concentrated and saw another passage, another trail, but not like the one which had brought him here. This either led to the epicenter of the chaos or was the origin of it. It was wider, more obvious and surrounded by a confusion that felt neither warm nor cold to his senses but still possessed the energy of the people who made it.

He walked into it and on the floor saw a lipstick. He picked it up and opened it. Red, the color his mother wore. He hadn't seen her for months and realized he hadn't thought of her all that time either.

He followed the energy until whatever happened, he was certain, began where he stood. Or perhaps it ended there. He was surrounded by a seating of wicker chairs and a sofa arranged around a large square coffee table which was pushed violently aside, as witnessed by the scattering of what once was on it. Tom sat on the arm of a chair and looked around, seeing for the first time the posters taped to the wall. White had become grey but the colors of the images were still bright and lively.

PEACE

PEACE AND PROSPERITY

NEVER FORGET

FREEDOM

VICTORY

NEVER WAS SO MUCH OWED BY SO MANY TO SO FEW

WARS END

BUY VICTORY BONDS

WELCOME HOME

The Red, White and Blue banner draped across the width of the room above the bar that he hadn't noticed before gave him a clue.

VJ DAY SEPTEMBER 2, 1945

He felt a prickly feeling in his feet and knew it was time to leave.

★ ★ ★ ★ ★

Wars come and wars go; soldiers fight and soldiers die; fathers are buried, mothers cry. Children grow up to repeat the loss.

When people die, records are kept, especially when important people die and when they die in an extraordinary way it is even easier to find them. Tom found everything Grand-Mére had hidden and it was easy. With a date, he went to the newspaper's archives, just like he'd been tutored. It took him less than 10 minutes to uncover the secret of his lifetime.

> Thomas Comb, son of Edgar and Ida Comb, grandson of the late Edgar Comb Sr. died of gunshot wounds at a victory party at Highcomb, the family residence. It is rumored that several men were engaged in a round of Russian Roulette. When Andrew, older brother to Thomas, refused to play, Thomas took his turn, with fatal consequences.

Continued on page 2.

Charles was coming for the weekend and Tom was eager to show him The Party Room and share the family secret. He stole a snub-nose Colt .38 from the gun cage and this time, if he didn't pull the trigger, it would be pulled for him.

MARNIE II

Marnie loved her old Suburban. It was rough on the outside and tough on the inside. A tank with attitude and it fit her like a glove, a perfect partnership. At least that's the way it started but now she was in complete control and command and she liked that even better. It delivered whatever she needed, whenever she needed it, however she wanted it delivered. Whoever built her wheels must have run moonshine through the swamp and for that he didn't just deserve early parole; for that she'd bust him out and drive him to the nearest chop shop where he could build her a spare.

She loved those wheels and not for the ego that came with them, because there wasn't any. She loved that red beast because when her life depended on it, she knew it wouldn't quit just because some glass got shattered, some sheet metal got bent or the whole works rolled over a few times. It wouldn't just take a bullet for her; it would take on the whole platoon.

Perfect as it was and much as she loved it, she left it in the back row of the rental lot and put her bags into a brand-new Lincoln. New wheels, new wardrobe, new prey, new Marnie.

This one was a pissant little white-collar crook and maybe not the worst thief in the world but he made an enemy, a determined and unforgiving enemy, her client. The kind of client she liked the best, the one with very few but very clearly communicated requirements: 'Break him, bill me and, by the way, the smaller the pieces the bigger the bonus'.

Not a word of unnecessary detail came with the mission, but a boatload of intel did and that was also the way she liked it. No such thing as too much intel, just like there's absolutely no sense in going overboard with accounting, timelines or operational details that might get in the way or be mistaken as barriers or boundaries when none are needed. No, this client wanted the minimum of restriction on both sides of the destruction. 'Just accept the challenge, do your best to ruin the little shit and don't hesitate to ask for whatever might be needed along with where and when to deliver it. Put any incidentals, collaterals and medicals on the final invoice. Just fix the problem once and for bad and, by the way, the more pain inflicted and the longer it's inflicted, the bigger the bonus.'

He left the rest up to her, provided everything she requested and all of it was first class. She was ready to go work when work walked into the hotel bar like it was just another day hoping to get lucky.

"You all alone?" he asked as she accidentally made eye contact.

She acknowledged and assessed him with a quick, practiced look. Medium everything but too stiff and flaccid for any kind of strength, stamina or skill. Three seconds max and she would have him face down crying for mercy. Thin brown hair with gel in it. That was all she needed to pick him out of the crowd, preferably with a scope.

"Sorry. I'm here for a quiet drink."

"Business or pleasure?"

"No, seriously, all I want is a quiet drink. I don't want company and right now I'm not good company so you should thank me for that and leave me alone. No offense."

She warned him. She always warned them. They never listened but she always tried to make them understand who was in charge. Then again, maybe better he didn't listen to her. If he was smart enough to run away, she'd have no choice but track him down and run over him with a spanking new Lincoln. Over him, hell, more like through him; it was a rental, let them scrape him out of the grill. Regardless, she delivered Warning #1 and if he was too stupid to even try and imagine any consequences by ignoring it, then he deserved what was coming at him.

"I'll buy. Let me guess, deal fell apart, you don't look like the kind of lady who would cry over a man, more like the kind of lady who would make a man cry." He made it sound like a thoughtful observation, but it wasn't, it was his standard line and it always worked with women of her type. He knew her by the dress, the purse, the hair and the way she looked down at him when she told him she didn't want his company. But she wanted something and all he had to do was figure out what that something was and then he'd be on his way to first base. He'd had her type before.

It was that simple and it usually worked. He didn't know her want, yet, but he liked the hide-and-seek part of the game just about as much as he liked the ego orgasm which came with his win and her loss. Sometimes the feeling of conquest that came from starting as the runt at the back of the pack and ending up top dog was the real reward. For sure it put a shine on the trophy.

Everything was a game, every rule was made to be broken and he had nothing but time on his hands so slow was not only fine, but fun. He'd play into her story and even if all he got was her, that would be prize enough. She was super sexy in that little black dress and for sure anyone who looked and moved like that would be nothing less than unforgettable in bed, or any place he could get into her.

Marnie stared right him into the seat across from her. Not even 2 minutes and he was already in her crosshairs. Just like the intel said, brazen and arrogant. A gutsy little weasel but also a smart one who knew all about traps. She shook her head at his plastic pick-up line but answered him anyway.

"You're right about that and thanks for the offer but I always buy my own drinks. Always."

"Ok by me. So, what's the problem? Go ahead, I'm a good listener."

She looked into her drink then at him and with a 'why not?' shrug, started with a challenge.

"You got a million or ten?" she asked with no doubt the conversation would be over if he said no. She started with money because he was staring down her neckline and she wanted him thinking greed, not lust. Sometimes the best bait for one sin is another one and if a little black dress isn't made for that then it's made for a funeral, but she'd already warned him about that.

"Go on." Numbers in the millions and her dismissive attitude simultaneously aroused his curiosity and his anger which may not be sins but sometimes lead to one. He wasn't shy about that option. Not all sins are equal but an opportunity to get laid and paid didn't come around every day and this might be one of them, providing he had to get past her ice shield.

She read him and turned up the temperature with a simple sigh. Just enough to provide some encouragement and let him think he still had a move left. He leaned toward her and that was the end of him being in the driver's seat and the beginning of a game of Russian roulette with all the chambers loaded.

Introductions were made. Jared, thieving little shit of an investment advisor, meet Marnie, widow-maker. She patronized him with the mild arrogance she'd treat a wannabe player who wasn't in her league. Easy to do because it was true, and he lapped it up. He loved being underestimated.

Insecure, as she predicted, he reacted to her power play with the cloying attentiveness of a used car salesman. It was his standard approach when he changed her destiny from trophy to conquest. Any woman who treated him like a dog needed a lesson in humility and he was the pit bull to bring it. He smiled at the fantasy of pain in her future.

Marnie knew what she started. She preferred to fight on several fronts with different tactics on each. The more reasons he had to engage, the more likely he would stay engaged. And the more confusion she created in the theatre the less likely he would see what was happening on the stage. You don't need to read Sun Tzu to know that art.

Standard Marnie tactics made the strategy even more effective. She didn't fight just to win and was always prepared to take a loss, sometimes engineering one which would ultimately work to her advantage. The point of multiple fronts was not winning on all of them but with dissipating energy and resolve by causing losses. Small and unimportant individually but disorienting and collectively devastating when the time is right. In the meantime, stay fluid, maintain balance, make strategic sacrifices and keep the surprises coming. She was off to a good start, he was already off-balance.

In a sting, it's all about the bait and the best bait for money is money but when the mark is also a con, it takes a lot of bait with good solid opportunities for it to be stolen. Everything must be real as rock and perfectly presented.

In this case the presentation was a little black dress with her in it and just like Classic Blues never get old, Classic Marnie is an invitation which no sane man can resist. Resist? Hell, they'd line up just for a chance to be abused by her and ignore every warning she gave them about how much it would hurt. For some stupid reason they figured if the worst-case outcome was being on life support in the ICU then the game must be worth playing because once you accept that, the rest was all upside potential.

Even if he thought differently, Jared was no different as she artfully avoided confrontation with his false belief that he was still capable of making a free choice decision. Thanks to her intel and a career of assessing the enemy before the enemy detected her presence, she could move him like pawn on a chessboard. The classic confrontation of illusion: she was in control and he was in denial.

She spun herself into a web of lies about a deal gone south. Until a couple of hours ago her deal was a lock. Then she found out she was being played. Only 4 seats at the table and one was hers; 20 mil per seat and she still had half her seat committed. It was a once-in-a-lifetime opportunity and replacing what she lost would be easy except the door closed in 2 days. Two lousy days.

That minor detail eliminated everyone who had the wealth but couldn't liquidate on command or borrow without an audit trail pointing right to where no one should be looking. She wasn't overly enthusiastic with the options she had left and only had time to approach one, maybe two, which is what she was deciding before he interrupted her.

Return on the investment was a double. It was a simple front-end buy-in to an IPO. The 'table' would buy owner shares in the private company and those shares would be converted 2 for 1 when the company went public. And it could get better, the offering was over-subscribed so likely to open over the subscription price. All NYSE so no junior exchange or offshore market where only the locals knew the rules or spoke the language. Not a tech but a solid retail with 70% of its own supply chain internalized. In other words, a Wall Street favorite and portfolio must-have.

The flip was a simple white paper crime where everybody wins if the right people are on the ground floor, and the right people were on the ground floor. It might as well be legal because it would never be investigated anyway.

The inside risk was just as negligible. No chance of a sting or a set-up because everybody was a respectable insider and had to stay under SEC radar for their own good. Bottom line, nobody says nothing or the whole team gets kicked out the country club, can't ever trade or hold office again and picks up garbage in an orange jumpsuit for few months. The unique character flaws of Wall Street crooks but all told, a totally bullet-proof deal ready to hemorrhage profit in 2 short days.

She told the story low key, like an impersonal memory, but pitched it like a pro, all the detail and jargon compliments of a quick but very thorough schooling by one of the smartest venture capitalists in the business. Her client spared no expense. His pockets were deep, and he wanted to plant a knife that deep into Jared's heart. The little weasel had screwed with the wrong man and was now toying with the idea of repeating that mistake with the wrong woman.

Sometimes you need to make a mistake to learn something important like a cobra can spit venom into your face from 8 feet away so you shouldn't think your boots will protect you. Jared didn't know that and before long he was drinking doubles and pretending to be careless. He was all too familiar with overselling and underdelivering on an IPO but if what he heard was legit, he could see a return. Probably not the double she was pitching because the shares had to open at subscription and stay there until the dump was bought and no such thing as a predictable day on any market. Commission and miscellaneous would eat a little icing but that still left a lot of cake.

She pitched it perfectly, from prospectus to oversubscription and only let out a few details he would have kept back. She figured the return would improve with a hold decision but didn't think that was a great idea, smart girl. Once the deal needs time to deliver it smells the same as a dead fish. In quick and out quicker is the way to run a flip.

Who's the company?" he asked but didn't expect an answer.

The little weasel was sniffing the bait. She wondered if she should give him another warning and he caught her thinking that instead of answering his stupid question. She instinctively covered the catch with embarrassment which looked genuine because it was carefully practiced. Always default to innocence when you get caught off-script or out-of-position.

Never attempt a cover-up and if innocence doesn't work, either counter with a premeditated strike of superior force or a rented Lincoln but whatever you do, do not wait, annihilate.

He couldn't figure her quickly enough to decide if she was inexperienced or if she was covering something but neither answer mattered because she gave him what he really wanted to know. Every player has a coverup strategy and when her overconfidence got her in trouble or when she got caught doing or thinking something she shouldn't be doing or thinking, she played 'the little girl card'. He liked that, it could be pushed into something he really enjoyed and that stirred his lust.

Marnie recovered with a smile and by brushing her hair back while he watched her like dog over dinner. Recovery from a lie or a glitch is damn difficult to do; it was his specialty, and he could spot a fake from across the room. He didn't have to hear the reset, come-back, go-around or the close; body language was more than enough to tell him what was going down and she was good but not good enough. He'd kept investors on the hook for months, telling story after story. She wasn't in his league and that made her perfect for the lesson coming her way. All he needed was an opening and the angle to play it.

"You don't get that, and it wouldn't help you anyway, Jared. That's my end. Like I said, there's half a seat left, and I own it. It's called blind trust." She delivered it as a firm take-it-or-leave-it ultimatum because that's exactly what it was. Eye to eye. It was decision time; if he didn't chase her now, it was time for plan F with a Lincoln and if he was that stupid then he deserved plan F.

"Sure Marnie, I'm familiar with the concept. I know you've got to protect your deal. So fine, let's say it's doable but you've gotta understand this part. I can give you ten mil but I don't give anybody my trust, that you have to earn."

"So, what else do you want? What do you have to know before I start asking you the tough questions?"

"For one, who is in the chair beside me?"

She had him. It was written in the squint of his eyes and the way he licked his lips. He was concentrated on her and she knew he wouldn't miss a change in her heartbeat let alone a bead of sweat on her brow. He was a bloodthirsty little weasel, just like the intel said. Even before he had his angle, he was pushing her into the victim zone.

No one had ever successfully interrogated Marnie and especially not when their choice of drug was vodka tonic, and their choice of weapon was bad breath, so she played into his delusion of being the best of the worst of Wall Street. The little black dress had done its part, it was time to put the bait out.

"Let's just say I know a very motivated county Treasurer with a money problem and a payroll big enough to cover his side long enough for the deal to clear. IPO's happen on time and no I'm not telling you the date, industry, broker or financial house. And I know you could figure it out but that won't do you any good and you know that too. In fact, I don't know why I'm talking to you."

She leaned in so he could hear every word and issued the ultimatum. "This is bar room and bullshit combined and even if it isn't, don't ever think about playing me. The people I'm dealing with may be gentlemen but I'm no lady." Warning #2.

She gave him attitude like when they first met; pissed off, angry about a deal gone south and in no mood for games. Warning #3: "And if you're in this for a happy ending after a couple of drinks, you're wasting your time because that's not going to happen either."

This time she stared him down. Last chance to be a smart little weasel and get flattened by a nice new Lincoln or go with the flow and get skinned alive with a dull knife.

"Well Marnie you better take me seriously. I can make this happen but here's my deal. You talk about trust, great, me too. I'll trust you with the details and the connections and you trust me with the money. I'm the sole and exclusive Treasurer for this transaction and the money doesn't move without me and I mean both sides of it. I receive it and I send it. All of it. Can you play by those rules? Can you make that happen? Plus, just to make you trust me even more, I supply the holding company that covers not just my ass but everybody's ass which is nice of me and non-negotiable. And you don't have to tell me again, I understand your hurry, this company has been on the shelf for two years, is federal and state registered, inactive with no history, ever; and when it's a smoldering wreck, it's a guaranteed dead end to you, me and the folks from Kalamazoo. You work with that and you can do whatever you want to do with it providing 50% of the shares are mine. You can be president if that turns your crank, but I am the Treasurer and the only director with the power to bank. That's in the Articles of Incorporation and that's what the bank follows so no way around it. That's the way I do business and that's what I call blind trust."

She listened to his pitch, replaying and analyzing each statement while the next one was being delivered. She had to be ahead of his angle or risk getting caught in her own game or worse, losing the bait. Few people can do strategy on the fly but it was her strength so before he finished, her response was ready.

"You're forgetting something. The split is 45/45/10 and the 10 is my end. That's what I get for bringing this to you and don't even think about screwing me for a few percent because the other side has already done due diligence, isn't going to pick up your share and you are already looking at a double so it's a gift, take it. I may not like my options, but I still have them so either we both win, or you lose. Simple as that and if you think differently, go take your chances at the track."

She watched him pretend to think about it and it didn't take him long to quit pretending. He had his angle and as far as he was concerned, she was as good as naked and crying in the corner. Once he got hold of a dollar, it didn't leave his sweaty grip until he was ready to let it go and if she was stupid enough to give it, he was going to take it.

"Ok. Sure. You deserve a cut, it's not easy to be the Rain Maker and even harder to keep it together when the nut-cutting gets close, as you found out already. Fine, I can live with that and what's more, between you, me and too late to do anything about it now, I'd have given you 20%. A double less your commission and costs is still high eight mil to me. I'm not greedy."

"So, Marnie, you talk to your Treasurer friend and if it's a go, I'll give you the corporate details, the bank and the account it is going to use. You can elect whoever you want to elect in any executive capacity you want except Treasurer and you can put whoever names you want to put on the shares and shareholder register except my shares stay in the name of the holding company that is currently there. That's another dead-end to me so look after yourself because if anything goes wrong later, there is no paper or money trail to me. But nothing will go wrong, will it?" he asked with sarcasm.

He wasn't questioning or threatening or finished being top dog. He just paused to put her into submission, to teach her who was in charge of silence as well as the rules of the game.

She waited.

"You get that right? Banking authority isn't a big ask compared to what I'm laying down, is it? That's my sole duty but like you said, I'm not taking anything seriously until I see your cash in the account. You still want to play with me, Marnie?" he half threatened, half scorned.

She wanted to kill him.

"Sure Jared, I'll work with that but let me repeat. A couple of hours ago I thought this deal was on its deathbed and it still might be, but I'll make the call. Like I said, the other guy is finance with a problem so it won't take him long to figure out he doesn't have anything left to figure out and you've got do the same thing. Once this starts, there is no backing out." She looked for a nod from him but didn't get it and that pissed her off.

"I'll see you here tomorrow at noon to confirm him, and you. Don't meet me and I'll know it's bullshit on your side and that will become a problem because I will find you and you won't like what happens next. I'm out on a limb here so don't even think about playing me. Life is short, don't make it miserable too." All the right words and the performance was flawless because she meant every one of them.

It was last call for Plan Lincoln; he let it pass with a nod and an arrogant smile, completely genuine, just like her. He was 100% in, no act. He had her right where he wanted her. Well, maybe not exactly where he wanted her, but that possibility was still in play.

She knew what the little weasel was thinking, no average IQ required for that and to keep that front in play she returned his evil smile. Eyes, lips, the whole package as enticing and libertine as Mardi Gras on the beach. It made her $2,500 little black dress look like a rag. She could do that on demand and whoever received it thought it was built especially for them.

It was supposed to be just a little more motivation by insulting his ego then giving into it but the cruelty in his eyes was more than she expected. It reminded her that the client is always right. He wanted the little prick broken into as many small painful pieces as possible and now she knew why.

"All right. All right Jared. Now you can buy the drinks and get your ducks in a row and don't even think about showing up with some story about having to move money around, offshore this, collateral that or 3 days to settle a sale. You jerk me around like the last guy, I'll put your balls in a vice and you don't want to know what happens next, so I won't tell you." She said it in a quiet, normal voice. It was all-in time.

He laughed, a high-pitched giggle, like he might enjoy the experience and she responded with a low chuckle because nothing would please her more than doing exactly what she just promised. On her way out the door, she turned and caught him watching her ass like the smarmy little perv he was.

It wasn't the best trap, but simplicity and speed made up for its shortcomings. The ice was broken and the little weasel was floating on a piece of it not much bigger than himself. He was a confident little weasel. Once she gave him control over the bait, he only pretended to care about anything else. Unfortunately, no choice there; she had to give up something to keep him interested and really, what's the point of bait if you aren't prepared to lose it? It was off to a good start unless your name was Jared.

Now, if only the rest would be so easy because now the rest was finding a County Treasurer or somebody who looked one. The greedy little weasel with the big insecurity complex had to see motive and opportunity or he'd vanish like a ship in the fog. She promised him someone in the seat next to him and now she had to deliver.

It felt good and bad, which was appropriate. Part A was done, which was good. Part B was next and if that didn't work, she had until noon to find Part C before the whole works went overdrive into Plan F. Plan F wouldn't earn her the bonus she didn't need but it could stain a hard-earned reputation and with that came the obvious. Plan Lincoln didn't deserve a fee; running over that pathetic excuse for a human being would be doing herself a favor and she wouldn't charge anybody for that.

With no time to waste and no point crying into another vodka tonic; she called the cavalry.

"What's-up, Marnie?"

"You remember how you said you trusted me?"

"No. I don't remember saying that. What do you want?"

"Can you do dumb?"

"Funny you should ask but that's my specialty."

"I believe you, I really do."

She was completely sincere and really hoped he took it as a compliment because it was.

Part B done, the calvary was on the way but no time to rest. Combat conditioning meant approach each hour with heightened intensity. Move fast; redeploy quicker. Keep the analysis flowing. Stay one step ahead and lay three traps behind. Keep the plan simple and remember the objective. Put the critter in a crate, then sink the crate. Manage it, manage it some more then manage it sideways and if that isn't complicated enough, bring in a complete stranger who is not only willing to work with the absolute minimum of intel but who actually believes the less he knows the better job he'll do and the more he'll enjoy doing it.

Bridget.

He knew her better than she gave him credit, which was a warm feeling compared to the cold and hospital biosphere of her hotel room, her fancy underwear and her buttoned-down wardrobe. All wrong choices for a country girl with a free side and more than enough experience and training to do what she had to do all by herself. Except she needed a Bridget because Jared needed a Bridget for proof so one more thing to manage although in her heart, she admitted, she was really looking forward to seeing him again.

Besides, there was a major positive with bringing him into the plan. If the critter didn't go into the crate according to plan, he was going into the crate not according to plan and Bridget didn't care which. He wouldn't kill anybody, but he wouldn't say anything if somebody who was going to die anyway forgot to look both ways when he crossed the street. No witnessing and they both agreed on that.

With the absolute minimum of intel, in a little less than a day, Bridget would meet Jared and the rest, they agreed, would 'just naturally unfold'.

Marnie knew 'just naturally unfold' from Africa. When bullets are flying it is not the time to rewrite the plan. It's the time to remember your training and do your job. That's when she discovered her nerves didn't 'just naturally unfold' and how most of the time those nerves didn't want to listen to her telling them to shut the fuck up. The thing that saved her was a whole lot of training specifically designed to bypass all the doubts and questions which happen in seconds so scorched with emotion and layered with fatal consequences you'd be crazy to listen to your nerves. All that did was freeze you and those targets are always picked off first.

★ ★ ★ ★ ★

Jared showed up for the noon meeting at 12:30. Just another not-so-subtle message about who was top dog. Marnie was in a good mood and happy to see him, which he took the wrong way. He figured she was warming up to him, maybe even starting to lust for him when she was really just looking forward to introducing him to Bridget. There was something about putting that mouse into a cage with that cat which fascinated her. Interesting but not so interesting that it should become a distraction she definitely didn't want. Just like she didn't want questions, small talk or the risk analysis which came with them, so she kept everything short and business-like. No how-do-you-do. No please or thank-you. No beating around the bush but complete concentration on the deal and he was in the same state.

"Is your side in order?" she asked.

He expected the question because he had the same one for her and she just answered it. He put a file folder on the table. "Everything you need. Company details, bank details but not the account. You get that last minute. Is that a problem?"

"No problem but it better have ten million in it when I get it." she replied, flat.

"It will."

"Then we're done here. The Treasurer is sending a representative. We meet here, in the restaurant, tomorrow afternoon, two o'clock. Sharp, this time."

He gave her a 'I don't care' shrug but it was a lie. He wasn't expecting a representative; he wanted the Treasurer. He wanted to know who was in the seat beside him for control and he wanted to intimidate him. He'd dealt with more than enough Treasurers when he was running his investment business and developed a real distaste for them, their attitudes, ethics and the business secrets they refused to share.

But it made sense to send a representative. This was not Treasurer territory; it was way too close to the grit and the grime of making money with guts and wits. It was also too much money not to keep an eye on it. Still, the Treasurer and not some pudgy white-shirted supervisor with a check list would have been better.

"I'll be early." he said and this time he meant it.

"Good. Then get ready to make a pile of money, Jared, because that is about to unfold. Now, I've got some work to do and I suspect you do too so let's get it done. The countdown has started."

She was happy.

Exactly the attitude he had to see. He watched her leave. Designer jeans that left way too much to the imagination.

★ ★ ★ ★ ★

After hours of title searches, lawyers, registering shelf shareholders in a shelf company with shelf executives and a restless night, unfolding time was approaching, slowly, as it always did. She was ready for anything, the Lincoln had 3/4 tank of gas and overnight she'd become quite accepting of Plan F. She was finishing her second cup of coffee when he came into the restaurant and it didn't look like he'd slept at all. Perfect.

He started making idiotic small talk as soon as he sat down. Rookie but it gave her a moment to realize it wasn't an allergic reaction to him that was creating the burn under her skin. It was the anticipation of seeing Bridget and what he might do to the little weasel if he didn't man up.

Jared was pretending calm, like it was just another day and another dollar, but he wasn't missing a thing. He was totally wound up and alert for the tiniest hint of a scam, set-up, bust, robbery or anything that might part him from his money. He knew all about traps and analyzed every movement, change in tone, inconsistency in language, intention or overt action that might signal an attack on his bank account. He always kept two choices in play and running away was always one of them. He could be out the door and in the next town before she could find her car keys.

To keep her nerves steady and blur his focus, she flirted a little and asked him about his business. She had to keep him talking and she wanted him talking on a subject where she could read him.

He answered, why not, but kept details to public knowledge which she would know if she'd done her homework. He embellished it with a few personal touches like how he lived for the con and wasn't ashamed to admit it. In his eyes that and the little bit of flirting made him the perfect partner for her. Paid and ready to be laid.

In her eyes, it made her wonder if bringing Bridget into the plan was a huge mistake. Not that she didn't believe in him or trust him, but one hour of Jared was more than enough to want him under the bus so why complicate everything?

Except, she reminded herself, she wanted justice for his victims and returning their money would not happen with plan F.

For sure he wasn't the biggest crook in the world and he damn sure wasn't the first investment advisor to steal his clients' money. He was worse. He was the kind of thief who wasn't content with the crime. He had to do some damage, cause pain and suffering along with the financial carnage he created. He played his victims to the last dollar and then continued to play them when he had nothing to gain but witness their lives being torn apart.

Like all conflict engagements, waiting is the worst part with the longest minutes being just before bullets start flying. Marnie knew that only too well and had to remind herself to be patient and not so judgmental on herself. Whatever happened to him was better than nothing. That reality forced her to relax enough to keep her mouth shut and that made her impossible to read.

Jared struggled between controlling the moment and anticipating the future. His money was still tight in his sweaty grip and it would stay that way but if everything went right, he was looking at another $7 million on its way to Rio with him. It would be a record score, but it took some doing and some of it was against his better judgement. He had to borrow a little over 2 mil in order to meet his end and he had to repay 3 mil in a week, which was pretty steep interest. Just the cost of doing business on short notice, he rationalized, but no leniency, renegotiation and damn sure no default with those lenders. Anybody who tried that didn't live to spend their money. That added some risk, injected some adrenaline and put him into the big time with the big players. It was a total win.

He loved the feeling that came just before the money vanished and this time, he would vanish with it, permanently. Too bad he wouldn't see the look on her face when she realized she'd been played. Ha. It would be quite the shock and for sure it would be the last time for the rest of her life she would be as happy as she was right now.

He kept her foremost in his mind but didn't challenge her. He needed her confident because that was her most unguarded, most reliable and most readable state. In that space, he maintained control because if she was doing exactly what he expected her to do, that meant no tricks for him.

Something he couldn't say about himself. When he made his move, she wouldn't see it coming or him going but all downhill for her after that. Out of the country with all the money is the best defense against somebody with no resources, no help from the law and being chased by a eunuch treasurer who wanted his money back.

Marnie knew what he was thinking and stayed confident, and calm. More than one of her adversaries made the mistake of thinking she didn't know their motive and couldn't read their mind only to learn the foolishness of that mistake the hard way. She pushed back on the discomfort of the 'wait and wonder what happens first'. A simple case of pre-combat jitters and she concentrated on the only thing that matters before the shit hits the fan. Timing. It's all about timing and the timing was unfolding outside the window and only 25 minutes late.

Bridget was classic. Like he just finished a long shift and probably got free lasagna somewhere and he wasn't acting. Two days in the same uniform, nightstick on the left side that had rubbed a slick spot on his dungarees and the biggest fucking magnum she had ever seen on his hip. He parked his prowler in the taxi lane, nose in, ass out and slammed the door. No hazard lights but no need for them. 'Touch my fucking prowler, that's the hazard.'

Marnie loved it. The guy was completely predictable, totally dependable and the power in the room shifted the moment he walked through the door. The dumbest cop you've ever seen including TV and anybody who acts that dumb is definitely trying to trick you but not him because nobody can act that dumb and get away with it. Except nobody told Bridget that.

She nodded and he came over. Unfold was suddenly in play and it felt great. Even better than running over the little weasel with the Lincoln, although that option was still very much open because all of a sudden, she felt very protective of Plan B.

"You Marnie?" and she nodded.

"You're Jared?" he asked eye-to-eye but didn't care about his own question because he wasn't looking for an answer to it. Typical dumb cop who knows everything because it's in his computer.

Bridget sized him. He wondered how long it would take to scare the little perp enough to shit himself and came up with less time than it would take his magnum to clear the holster. How that little worm survived as long as he did without somebody squishing the life out of him was a miracle.

"I'm Sheriff so now that we know each other here's what's going to happen."

With the power shift in the room, or, more accurately, the immediate centralization of it, a pretty, shapely, dark-haired waitress started hoofing over so he waved her a slow-down and smiled like he'd been there every day since the beginning of time. "Just a coffee honey, black."

"Sure thing darling. I'll start a fresh one."

He was 100% Serve and Protect with a genuine smile that made her feel completely safe because he was there for just for her. She turned and looked over one shoulder that was shifted up like the cute, younger version of the cheerleader she was 10 years ago and was again today, just for him.

"So?" Marnie felt some jealousy, which was unusual for her. As a result of that emotion, her one-word question came out harsh, like she wanted an answer but not any old answer. She wanted an answer that would drag the little weasel underwater and keep him there. She wanted it over before it started. Like maybe Plan Lincoln really was the best because in that moment a whole lot of Plan B was relying on someone she hadn't seen for a while and realized she didn't know that well.

If anybody read that thought it was only Bridget, but he didn't acknowledge it or let up on Jared who wasn't expecting anything like what just walked through the door for a cup of coffee. He couldn't stop thinking about first impressions and his first impression was that Sheriff wouldn't think twice about using a 12 gauge to bring down a fly that was annoying him.

"You got *it*?" Bridget asked in dead pan voice directed sideways at Marnie then made full eye contact with the greedy little snotnose. No question about his attitude or the 'don't give a good goddamn' which was driving it. Power wasn't just in the magnum. Jared was struck with an irrational fear which made perfect sense because that's exactly what was boring into the back of his head.

It could have been anything but he didn't have time to figure *it* out before Bridget got *it* started again. Marnie knew the tactic. Life in the slow lane doesn't last very long and in the fast lane of the right here/right now moment, there wasn't a single doubt in anyone's mind about who Sheriff was, what he had to do, or what he would do if he didn't get what he wanted.

Again, he didn't wait for an answer before getting back into Jared's head. Twice in 4 seconds and he was just getting started.

"Here's what. The side of the transaction I represent will be sent when I say so and here's how you get my say-so and it's not up for discussion. First, close of business and I see a bank slip with your money in the account, then I make a call and his money gets sent. Everybody goes home. Second, 5 minutes before opening tomorrow, we meet at the front door and go in together. You send the money where she tells you to send it. Nobody goes anywhere until I get a call that the shares are in escrow. After that I don't give a rat's ass what anybody does until I'm told to come back and collect. That's how he wants it and more or less what you already agreed so it's an open and shut case unless somebody wants to go to jail and get forgotten for a long time because I can do that." He shifted his stare from Jared to Marnie.

He wasn't acting and Marnie couldn't believe her eyes, or her ears. Every time she saw that face and his uniform she was being thrown in jail and here he was, threatening to do it again. Sonofabitch. Was he acting then too? Then she got angry with herself because she'd bought his dumb cop routine right down to doubting herself. She felt a flush on her cheeks. Sonofabitch.

She flustered and saw Jared watching her like a bee with a million pixels in its 100,000 eyes and in that second: 2 plus 2 equaled Jared gobbling the whole fucking burrito in one bite. He loved seeing her with her back against the wall and must have figured it was his turn to throw some testosterone into the conversation.

"A bank slip? There's no bank slip. There's orders, confirmations and on-line balances but seriously, what's this about a bank slip?".

Being the asshole he was, Jared didn't respect authority unless it was his. Years of bullying and a few bad experiences with authority gave him a detest for uniforms especially the one with the attitude standing in front of him. This called for push-back and it didn't have to be nice. If anybody was breaking the law they were all breaking it so nice manners were for nice people, not present company who he vastly underestimated.

"That's right. That's what I said. A bank slip. Call it what you want to call it but I call it proof. That's my job and nothing moves until I've got it." Bridget made it plain that as far as he was concerned this method or that method was the same because he was in charge of everything.

Except weasels don't back down from words and this weasel was about to ruin everything by getting himself shot, beat up, thrown in jail or all of the above.

She couldn't wait for the next round because Bridget didn't look like he was in the mood for bullshit and that just happened to be Jared's strong suit. She had to calm the waters or invoke the Lincoln plan just to cover the collateral damage. "Hold on Sheriff, that's my job and I've done it since day one. You want proof, you'll get it, no surprises. It's all there just like we are all here and don't anybody even dream about bringing anything new to the table."

She said it clear, defensive and staring at Jared like the arrogant moron he was. Everybody's ass was covered because she covered them and absolutely no need for a stupid pissing contest to get violent and wreck a simple little white-collar crime spree. Luckily, calling out Bridget was one of her favorite pass times, so she was damned convincing when Jared got the message and she turned to see if he did too.

As expected, Bridget reacted like he didn't give a shit because he didn't.

"Fine." he said. "Everybody happy. The bank. Quarter to four." He said it like a guard to an inmate then caught a charm school smile with a carafe of fresh brew in her hand. She guided him to a corner table where he'd have 2 walls at his back knowing that as long as he was there, she was safe.

Jared couldn't resist the temptation of a thin, triumphant smile. He was on his way to making a pile of money and he felt so damned lucky he was sure he could improve his take. "We've got some time to kill. Let's celebrate, Marnie. Dammit I'm amazed you put this together so fast. How about some champagne? Your room or mine?"

"Not until this deal is done. I mean cash in my bank, on my island, done. Then we'll celebrate and it won't be in a hotel unless it's in a cabana on a private beach."

All lies including a huge one. It was over. She had him. Bridget clinched it. Some authority to openly defy was Jared's fatal weakness and Bridget made that defiance irresistible.

"See you later." She left without a smile or a backwards glance. He could watch her ass and this time she was fine with it. That might just become the memory which haunted him for the rest of his short life.

★ ★ ★ ★ ★

As demanded by Bridget, fifteen minutes before closing, Jared gave him an account number and he went to the first available teller where he received a bank slip showing a balance of 10 million. He made a call, buttons were pressed and 8 minutes later, he got a response but hung up without saying anything. He went to a different teller and received another bank slip for 20 million. Everything Kosher as a pickle.

They were the last to leave the bank and the door was locked behind them.

No goodbyes and no handshakes, Marnie slipped into the soft, contoured tan leather of her Lincoln which was parked in the bank's VP stall. Bridget watched her over the lightbar of his prowler as she backed-out and burned rubber, just a chirp. He didn't have a clue what was going to happen next but figured Jared was in the crate. The little thief didn't know it yet but when he did, it would come as a total surprise which would keep getting worse. When Marnie sprang a trap, the pain was just getting started.

Jared felt great. He went to his hotel which he would vacate in 15 minutes, 30 tops. He wasn't followed so his fancy escape plan wouldn't be needed.

Shortly after congratulating himself for being so wicked smart, he found out three things he probably should have considered before believing they'd actually leave him alone with all that money.

First, his phone told him he couldn't make an on-line transfer. No details, just couldn't. Something had changed since last week.

Second, and admin at the bank told him what had changed, blah, blah, blah, new bank policy regarding money laundering which required Manager Forbes approval for offshore transfers exceeding $5 million.

Third, Manager Forbes personally told him the $10mil from the 'other party' and now the entire account, was value dated. Technically it was in the account just couldn't be accessed, even if the bank was open for business, which it was not. The deposit was drawn on a British bank operating out of Hong Kong and the funds would be interbank until the clearing house in New York opened the next morning at 8:00am EST.

Jared felt some pain in his chest as he realized he needed a new angle, right now, so he listened to Manager Forbes ploddingly explain what he should have thought about when he was thinking about Marnie being a little girl. A little girl who obviously knew a lot.

Manager Forbes explained how banks all over the world bought and sold overnight liquidity in order to meet reserve requirements and nothing was going to change that because the computer wouldn't allow it. It was his money in the morning but until then, the account, all of it, was in jail. He should have known a County Treasurer would do something petty like that just to earn a couple hundred dollars interest and save a transfer fee.

That tightened his guts to match the pain in his chest and sent him into a barrage of whining, wheedling and lying until Manager Forbes finally agreed to an 8am meeting for the purpose of getting his money out of fiduciary incarceration and making an unhappy client happy. The transfer would only take a couple of minutes, no problem, but no option except in person, and bring ID.

Manager Forbes wasn't about to break rules for a lousy 20 mil which left Jared with two choices. Show up at 8 and take it all or show up at 9 and take his chances with the flip. It didn't take a genius to make that decision.

Luckily, first class tickets can be cancelled and rebooked on a moment's notice, so he rebooked his evening flight for the next morning, unpacked his overnight bag and hunkered down with nothing to do except watch TV. It was a sleepless night. With every second thought, Sheriff came into his mind and that worried him. He had plenty of second thoughts that night and that worried him a lot.

Like maybe Sheriff wasn't that dumb. Maybe he was parked on the front steps of the bank, right now, and would be there all night until the bank opened.

A crazy possibility, but with nothing else to think about he conjured up one lie after another in case Sheriff caught him trying to sneak into the bank. Other risks went up too. Banks were notorious for stopping a transaction over a hint they might be giving the wrong money to the wrong person. When it mattered to them, meaning when it was in their best interest, absolutely everything had to be perfect and not everything Jared had to offer was completely legit let alone perfect. Some of it was sketchy and looked like it. Like a shelf company with no history and head office on a tax haven Caribbean island for $399 a year.

By breakfast, which he ordered but couldn't eat, his blood pressure had dropped to a manageable 175/110. That took him to Manager Forbes' office by 8:03am. No Sheriff anywhere which was a relief because high blood pressure wasn't nearly as critical as no blood pressure which came next. Manager Forbes told him the account had been cleaned out. Not a penny left.

"That's impossible. I'm the only person with banking authority for that account. Either you get it back or you put it back and I'm not waiting around for you to figure out where you fucked up so do it now." he screamed, infuriated. He knew banking almost as well as he knew how to pyramid a portfolio. No doubt about it, banks have lots of money to pay for stupid mistakes and they'd just made a huge one.

Manager Forbes was used to dealing with petulant assholes like the one unwisely threatening him. People who gave him their money for protection and expecting interest earned due to his diligence then thought they could tell him what to do and how to do it.

He understood how possessive people could be about their money and even sympathized with some of them, but this customer was far too arrogant and entitled to excuse such bad manners. He took his time finding and explaining why Jared wasn't going to get a dollar from his bank, or any bank. Not a single dollar.

He turned his monitor around so Jared could see the most recent Director's Resolution, filed online with the Registrar of Companies, at 10:17pm last night. The resolution was complete with the required affidavits from two registered shareholders who represented a 55% majority in a perfectly legal shelf company which led to a dead end in Antigua by Jared's own design. Said resolution allowed the President full banking privileges which she used to transfer the entire account to a bank in Aruba, almost 9 minutes ago, at 8:00:01.

It was gone, poof, like that. Everything. And it wasn't coming back. She got the drop on him. He was momentarily impressed with the achievement then reality started to sink in and pull him under.

Reality with an extremely high voltage applied to it; the kind which inhabits your entire body as it turns your legs to jelly, your guts to liquid and your brain into a racetrack for horrible consequences waiting to be unleashed. He knew there wasn't a thing he could do except count his losses and that didn't take long because she got everything plus what he owed. He never should have borrowed that 2 mil. The only way they accepted a loss was when they got the loser. They would kill him like a science experiment in slow death.

He had absolutely nothing to trade for his life. No money, not a picture of money, not an ounce of leverage, not even an accomplice to blame. Everything pointed back to him. It was his company with his digital fingerprint on the shares, his DNA on the articles, his vote on the officers who mutinied against him, his scam until he got outfoxed and borrowed what he couldn't repay. Everything was completely undeniable including undeniably screwed. On a holy day, they'd crucify him, and he'd be grateful for their kindness.

He left the bank with a head spinning out-of-control as he searched for options. If he had anything left, maybe it was time. Maybe he had some time left, the one thing you can't buy anyway. He had 5 days before his loan was due and was flat broke. But the only way they would know that major detail was if they were part of the sting.

Did they do this? Maybe there was hope there. If they ripped him off, maybe they'd leave him alone. He analyzed that hope and came up empty. First, it was a total longshot. Second, they didn't think like that; if they wanted something, they took it, especially when the victim was as dirty as they were. Third, leaving him alive with a story to tell was not in their best interests. That wasn't the way they worked so this definitely had nothing to do with them except fear them with every drop of blood he had.

He was screwed out of everything except for the time he had until they found out he was deadbeat on the loan and became dead meat in the morgue. Precious time which he had to use fast and really smart to hide where he couldn't be found, by anyone, ever.

At least he was prepared to run and maybe even be chased by an angry Sheriff, so he took inventory. He had an overnight bag, a leased Cadillac and a 1st Class ticket to Rio with a 2-hour drive to the airport which was decision 1. Should he get on the plane or take his chances on home ground? It was a life and death decision and he had to figure out where he would have the longest life and the quietest, most natural death.

Cash was thin, about 8,000 Brazilian Real for walking around money when he got there. That would convert to a couple of grand and maybe another couple of hundred in his wallet. If he stayed with Brazil, that wouldn't buy him a week before he was somebody's bitch in a Rio jail if he was lucky or white meat in the barrio if he wasn't. Rio is fine when you have millions in the bank but damned dangerous with lint in your pocket. Hell, he could be robbed before he learned enough Portuguese to beg for soup.

On home ground, he had a chance. He spoke the language and with a few more dollars he could survive off the grid, far off the grid, until the heat died down long enough for him to pick-up a new identity. Even then he would have to keep moving until maybe he got so old and wrinkled that he didn't resemble himself, which, screw vanity, the sooner the better. Even so, those sharks would never forget him or give up the chase but that was just as true in Rio as anywhere and he damn sure couldn't get a job slinging beer in the barrio.

Inventory complete. Rio was off. Better to go deep into backcountry somewhere remote and not leave his destination in an airline computer. Thank God for first class, they would refund the tickets to his credit card. He would take that and the maximum cash advance every day until he hit his overdraft. Starting now. He plugged his card into the bank's ATM and entered his PIN.

Account Closed

Please Contact your Personal Representative

The card wasn't returned. What couldn't get worse, just did. In a heartbeat his problems compounded, and the next heartbeat came with the helpless realization those surprises were going to keep on coming. Nothing he could do to stop them, nowhere to hide, no one to help him and no escape plan.

That shock brought him into full, fatal acceptance of how tenuous his life had just become. So tenuous he suddenly didn't even have time left because after worse comes terrible which went downhill to dead if he didn't start putting some miles behind him.

Then he had to abandon the Caddy where it wouldn't be found for as long as possible and run away from that. He was already on the second warning for the Caddy, it might already be reported stolen. Screwing them out of a couple of payments was a dumb idea. At least defaulting on the house and furniture wouldn't blow back, that's the first place anybody would look for him so other than being homeless with no cards, a short stack of Brazilian Real and a car that was about to hit the hot sheets, it was definitely a save on the rent.

All his bridges were in flames. What started out to be the perfect entry into a new life in a world class fun city collapsed into the space surrounding him and how fast he could run around in it without being seen.

It was a big, sudden drop and it was just the beginning. This wasn't a surgical strike to the jugular with 45 seconds of consciousness followed by 45 seconds of bleed-out. This was death by 1000 cuts and every step he took reminded him his life was in a very temporary, extremely fragile state and that wasn't going to change, ever.

★ ★ ★ ★ ★

Bridget watched him slink away from the ATM. The little weasel was already looking over his shoulder, an obvious tell he was on the run and stupid too. Whether it was a bullet to the back of the head or they goon-picked him off the street he wouldn't see it coming so looking for it was just drawing attention to himself. He was wearing guilt like a condemned man with a rope around his neck but that wouldn't matter to them. They didn't waste time looking for guilt unless amputating fingers and toes is a waste of time.

That thought triggered an alert response. He went to his holster, released the hold-down, the safety, then palmed an easy load from his ammo pouch. More than enough. Twelve rounds and either he'd be writing reports, or he'd be dead.

That calmed him, facing his own mortality always calmed him, and in that calm he quickly and methodically assessed the danger which was minimal to nonexistent for everybody except Jared.

Jared's danger was imminent; his safety net was non-existent. No one would waste a breath on his behalf, the little rodent deserved to be hunted to death. It made perfect sense but was paradoxical too. Like thinking that being struck by lightning and being struck by Marnie are the same thing. They're not. Pick the lightning, you've got a chance with it.

Where the little crook went after disappearing around the corner was unimportant and not what kept Bridget hunched down in his prowler. It was the red Suburban parked in a side street and dead center in his sightline that was his sole focus. He wasn't going anywhere until it did, and God help anybody who messed with it.

★ ★ ★ ★ ★

"Please make yourself comfortable, Marnie, and before you ask, everything is as you requested. The money is on its route. A couple of banks but before close of business tomorrow it will be in the recovery fund here. From there it will be distributed according to instructions. And, apparently, your client lost a bet and forfeited a significant amount from 'the bait?'. I don't normally congratulate someone on losing a bet, but I certainly do this time. This returns even more money to the victims, almost 80 cents on the dollar by my calculation… that's an amazing recovery for this kind of fraud."

"It wasn't my client who lost a bet, Mr. Ellerson."

Even bank presidents have to show surprise sometimes and this was one of those times. Ellerson had momentarily forgotten who originated, orchestrated and then delivered the return of those millions and did it legally. In his own defense, he reasoned, he was caught off-guard because the woman in front of him seemed completely different from the one who had been giving him orders for the last few days. Orders he followed, without question, to the letter, and not just because they were lawful, mostly, but her client was so high up that if he wasn't supposed to know who that person was, he damn sure didn't want to find out by screwing up. Not often the president of a local branch gets orders directly from the CEO but when those orders are on behalf of a 'friend' you don't ask questions and you don't fuck up unless you want to deliver coffee for the rest of your career.

He flushed then found his demeanor: "I must say, this job comes with a lot of headaches, but this is one of those rare moments that makes up for it, makes it right, so to speak. Thank-you for that." he said with genuine humility and handed her a small briefcase. "This is from your client. I have no other details." He bowed his head a little.

Marnie opened the case, took out a stack of bills the size of a brick and gave the case back to him. "Please add this to the fund."

She extended her hand in goodbye. She didn't want talk. She wanted her ass in her Suburban and 100 miles of road behind her and it didn't have to be paved, hell, better if it wasn't. She smiled slightly at that fantasy before Ellerson interrupted her thoughts. "Thank-you so much for this. It's not necessary and I certainly don't want to know any names but such a large wager, I am curious…"

He was shaking her hand and started apologizing immediately.

"I'm sorry, I really shouldn't have asked you that, just that bankers are trained to know both sides of the transaction and I forgot I was already acting for one of those sides and don't need to know anything more. It's an occupational hazard. Please ignore the intrusion."

It was over. She relaxed in the presence of the banker's honesty. He did his job; he was one of the decent guys.

"I can't really answer you because I wasn't told about a bet but if I had to guess, I'd guess it was whether or not I could break him, which I did. He had to borrow a substantial amount from some lenders who don't accept losses. You see, Mr. Ellerson, my client didn't just want him broke, he wanted him broken. I suspect the bet was something along those lines."

"Well, he didn't borrow anything from us, I'm happy for that."

"I'll bet he wishes he did."

Ellerson escorted her out the metal clad, double alarmed back door and she walked around the block feeling happier with every step. The fight was over and unless your name was Jared, peace was declared.

She navigated through Bridget's blind spot and came up on his shotgun side. What she noticed made her smile. His 12gauge was uncaged, safety off and triggered semi-auto. About 1.5 seconds to fire left, another couple to fire right with a round through the windshield, if necessary. It would be damn loud inside. He was slouched down but his concentration was focused on the few inches that contained her Suburban and the space around it.

She tapped on his roof, looked at him with eyes happy, smiled and told him: "Take care of yourself Bridget and call me when you need trouble. It's good to know I can count on you and thanks for worrying about me. That means a lot to me, it really does."

She didn't wait for an answer and she didn't look back. She walked straight to the Suburban. Her hands were open and her arms swung purposefully at her hips like she didn't have a care in the world.

Bridge knew that walk.

Somebody was in real trouble, which is Marnie-speak for being on the unlucky side of not yet dead.

STORY

—————⇒➤●⋖⋲—————

That's the word which creates a new world. Five little letters that can take a year to perfect the first paragraph and a lifetime to find the last sentence. One seemingly innocent 5-lettered word that only changes the mindful path if all the elements are present and work together in perfect harmony. Not in every reader's mind, of course, but for every writer, there is one reader who scores the work and marks it pass or fail, print, purge, just or junk and I'm talking about you.

We both know anyone can throw words on paper and call it a story but that doesn't excuse them of the responsibility for turning hard core fact, random suspicion or complete nonsense into meaningful thought. Even doing that doesn't automatically earn the author title which, in case you wondered, is not an easy row to hoe. Like a lot of things in life, you have to walk it and talk it before you can claim it and then, in this case, create something out of thin air and write it.

Still, some wannabes continue to throw black on white and hope no one asks any tough questions or applies any critical thought. 'Good enough, story done and not my fault that it's crap'. A piece of crap that makes it the reader's responsibility to figure out why there isn't a message let alone the meaning for so many words so carelessly put to page that a child could do a better job.

Every reader knows that insult and has endured it too many times to accept poor vocabulary or lack of skill as justifiable excuses for a pre-emptive literary assault on their senses. They know it's an outrage and an insult to their intelligence, but we know that outrage should really be directed to the lack of guts of the writer who refuses to listen to his or her personal critic, don't we? And that criticism can get pretty nasty, can't it?

Some readers, and some critics, actually believe a writer needs more courage than humiliation but that isn't true. A real story is an invisible hammer that hits you where you dream. It inspires fear, wisdom, magic and a supernatural, mystical world where none existed just moments ago.

That doesn't come from courage. That comes from humble submission to the art; to accepting the twist of the plot which ruins the endin; to being driven and not driving; to obeying characters who are beyond judgement, suspended above reality. Anything less than complete subservience to the art is arrogance. Arrogance combined with the weakness of an ego who can't tolerate criticism or the foolishness of a writer who believes they own the words when they put them on a page.

Admittedly, a lot of verbose crap gets published when it shouldn't. Some of this trash is scooped up with a shit shovel and substituted for real work because red hot hammers beating thought into an innocent, unwilling mind is not everyone's cup of tea, all the time. People want entertainment and however violent or crazy they like it to be, they want it to end benignly so they can return to their own thoughts, and their own soft bed where they have some control over their dreams. That doesn't happen with a real story and it damn sure isn't intended to happen with this one.

The epitaph of every story, the hundred words plastered on the back cover or the ten words of testamentary cliché slathered around the author's name on the front, is advertising. It is as ridiculous as year born and year died on a tombstone describes the person lying beneath it.

That isn't a story where every paragraph is born and raised in the triumph and disappointment of real life. That isn't a story where the whole works must end and everything in between is judged for the creativity and the integrity in doing a proper, dignified job of ending it. Fail that last paragraph and you might as well start all over. Harsh and not easy.

Between those first and last sentences resides the telling. Telling from past to present, agnostic to omniscient, flashbacks, first person/third person, story within story, regression, bold titles like October 31 and even humble footnotes are tools of the trade.

But not this time.

This story is about Story so no epitaph will be written because Story is not written with a neat, logical strategic conclusion. Story does not submit to the tick of the clock, perfection of plot, cleverness of subplot, the magnetism of a perfect back story or the relentless flow of words to the final paragraph where the wolves trap the deer against the fence.

So where does a story about Story go if it doesn't follow this delightful or horrific journey from start to finish, interwoven with time and tide like the warp and weft of a Moroccan carpet or a Mexican serape?

Think on that a little. Don't criticize it, think on it. Maybe with Story, it isn't my sole responsibility to write the truth, to find the perfect ending. Maybe the critic should share some responsibility, put in some skin in the game, suffer some sleepless nights and yes, I am talking about you. You don't believe it, but I see you and I am always thinking about you when I write, especially the ending.

Then again, when it comes to Story, maybe the end isn't important. Maybe the only real point of a story about Story is to bring out the invisible hammer, the one in the reader's mind at midnight when there is nowhere to hide and it is impossible to sleep? What if Story is simply about acknowledging the end by stopping the words because ending the words is irrelevant, absolutely and irrevocably irrelevant because truth is absolutely and irrevocably irrelevant at the end, beneath the ground? And stop criticizing my sentences for hyperbole, redundancy, run-on and think on it for a moment. How do you feel about that?

Suppose you are responsible for the ending? You, on the other side of these words reading this page. You, the one in the last sentence of the first paragraph. You think that was put there by accident or simply to introduce the next piece of a literary onslaught? It was not.

You think I don't see you just like you think I don't know you, but I do. Being so critical of my writing, for so long, is suddenly a more delicate conversation, isn't it? Having intellect and creativity and paradigm criticized and condemned is not so much fun when you are the one being exposed, is it? Words like simplistic, verbose, profane, immature, embarrassing or unskilled purveyor of pontificated pedantry are not any nice to hear when they apply to the critic, are they? And are not some of those your words?

Ok, now that we acknowledge each other's existence, let's agree we are in this together and any words can apply to you as much as they do to me so the fame and blame will be shared. I know that is a lot to ask. Or is it? Perhaps, that is the only way Story can be told.

That's right, this is the point of no return, for both of us.

Now that you are over the shock of being outed, do you remember the question I asked? That's right, what if you were responsible for the true and false of these paragraphs and making a hammer out of them? And, just to make it a little more interesting, fodder for thought so to say, are you absolutely certain it is not you typing these words on this little blue computer? You do have that influence.

Could it be this is all in your mind, that these words are tumbling onto a virtual page as you think them? Are you, at this precise moment in time, a moment which will never again be repeated, are you absolutely certain that the next line will not be written by your own eyes?

Or perhaps we are on a completely different parallel in our shared reality. Perhaps none of this is real including you and me and all of it is nothing more than countless letters like countless stars orbiting in space and mysteriously joining into words and becoming thoughts like bacteria growing designs in a petri dish. Then, of course, it can't be your fingers typing these words because neither of us has fingers and this is just an awkward, convoluted introduction to Story by an omniscient power?

Or am I writing this because you are dictating it to me? Are you directing me to write this in order to introduce your Story which begins with the captivating opening paragraph you have imagined and re-worked so many times. Yes, that one.

Good, now that we are successfully communicating, it's only fair to tell you I can see some of your thoughts but not all of them. But I do know that you know real Story and have a desire to see it written.

Funny isn't it? All this time you have been my critic and now it is your turn, your opportunity to put some words down and I can feel how much you want to do it but are hesitant. Do you want more time?

I know you can't start *and* answer questions. I am not asking you to walk in my shoes. This time we are in them together; think of it as a collaboration. I need you just as much as you need me, so let's try it. Take a more creative role in our mutual existence. That might be just what it takes to write the story of Story.

Of course, you are doubtful and you don't want to give up your cushy job criticizing. I know this is about Story and not putting black on white but it makes some sense doesn't it? Someone had to take the initiative. Someone had to break the ice in our relationship and yes, it is more complicated this way, but relationships are complicated, we can easily agree upon that. And yes, it is too bad that all we have to develop and enrich our understanding is this controversial and often confusing medium of words but let's give it a try. Let's get started. Let's try something that has never been done before, go ahead, I'm willing to give it a shot.

What do you mean you don't know how to start?

Fair enough, you have a long history of criticizing and little practice with writing so maybe start with a path. That's always a good place to start. Go ahead; try a few words and don't worry about where they go because that's the whole point of a path. It will go somewhere, or it might end unexpectedly but that is well within the definition.

Plus, path is good because it implies thought. Just don't spend a lot time describing it, over and over, step by step because no one wants to read that even if in real life they do it all the time. Trust me on that. Go ahead, I won't judge.

The path could have been beams of light or it could have been air separated by fog like clouds in the sky but it was a million years ago nestled between ferns and logs all covered with luminescent moss when the turtle came out its shell for the first time.

That's good. I like it already. Succinct and the imagery is fantastic. Light and air, clouds and moss, where would we be without them? Then in a mere ten words you added the omnipresent human phobia for nakedness but instead of using a regressive, historical metaphor like Adam and Eve, you picked evolutionary shell abandonment, a nod to Darwin. Excellent, this path could go anywhere!

Plus, nakedness, and its role in creation, is always a winner but coming from you makes it paradoxical in an absurd, otherworldly, perhaps unreal sort of way and then you picked turtle! Congratulations on that. Nobody ever thought turtle but now that you write it, and the way you introduced it, it makes perfect sense. A turtle out of its shell is the most vulnerable of all life forms and if that isn't an excellent, and accurate, allegory for the development of the pre-frontal cranial lobe becoming the human self-shell, I don't know what is.

Good start friend, I'm engaged. In fact, I'm hooked. But take your time with the next paragraph and choose your words with care, we don't want to play fast and loose with our readers. Without a plot and characters, we still need to use tact and tactic, play hide and seek, build structure before revealing substance. Tell it like you are experiencing it for the first time. That's the key to good storytelling and we both know Story has rules. And, by the way, this is an excellent and thoughtful start toward building our relationship so thank you for that. Being respectful of each other's role in creativity is important, isn't it?

Impressive too, this is the first time the page has been shared like this and very clever of you to begin with an obvious challenge to both theology and science. Seriously, how can anyone believe that part of our brain which made us human evolved from apes. What a ridiculous fantasy; it must have come from somewhere else down the line. Maybe even from the ocean, like everything else, but what fanciful thinking and so ignorant on so many levels. We should be so lucky to share our nascent spark of awareness with primates not to mention where we would be if it were true. How advanced we would be; how natural our world would be; how simple our society would be. Such an obviously false evolutionary concept based solely on walking erect and having a thumb when 'turtle abandoning shell' is so brilliantly true and responsible for nature's experiment with cognition.

Good job. You nailed it. It was turtle right from the get-go and it is turtle right now but maybe that's not your point. Sorry, I forgot. You started this...so the turtle leaves its shell and becomes a naked human being. Then what?

Soon after the turtle left its shell it began running around because it could run around but all that exercise made it hungry, so it started killing things to eat and for their skin to cover its nakedness. It killed and killed and ate and ate until it realized that no matter how much killing and eating and skin it took, it would never be content. And worse, it realized it could never go back because it would no longer fit its shell but not just because of that. It completely forgot that all that wasteful killing and hurrying is wrongful behavior not to mention just plain destructive and that has nothing to do with having a shell or not having a shell; that is plain common sense. Truthfully, turtle knows lots of things that humans no longer know like thinking turtle is slow. Fact is, turtle thinking is not slow. Turtle thinking is about being completely stopped for days, just floating with the tide or sunning on the beach, hurting no one.

Which explains the invention of time. When humans created a shell to hold their psyche, they invented tomorrow in order to compensate for all the eating and running around. Those hurtful behaviors needed a calendar and a clock to provide hope for happiness which might come tomorrow. But that failed. Failed miserably so while humans lost their turtle nature and do not understand turtles at all, and kill them and eat them, the opposite is not true.

Hmmmm. I'm getting the sense this story is not going to have a happy ending. Plus, it's getting a little hard to follow but frankly, both of us are damn lucky to have got this far, don't you think? That's good, and sometimes a story takes time to develop, characters need to find their feet, plot needs to be inverted, twisted and tweaked. At some point though, that single thought or idea which is too raw for words on its own must join the collection and become the invisible hammer. Not quite sure what that point is yet.

And the whole idea of turtle being slow or stopped but without time to differentiate fast or slow could use some more explanation. Or perhaps some contrarian logic, more contradiction or some comparisons. Humans love opposites, reversals and corollaries. In fact, we are dependent upon them as hiding places and escape routes so maybe this is a good time to explain why this whole turtle/human misunderstanding is such an important issue. Are you turtle, by any chance?

Dumb analysis and obviously you are incapable of understanding spatial thought because everything in your brain is a competition or on the path to a temporary conquest but certain failure. Truth is, thought was wasted on humanoids when they evolved into it just as it is wasted on them now.

Listen to me: you invented time. If you can't forget it then at least study it properly. Look in the direction you came from, go backwards if you can. Stop blundering forward. When time is good remember that nothing lasts forever and that includes a ten-thousand-year-old tortoise shell and the mountain it died on.

When time is bad then take responsibility for making it a big deal because it's about you but completely unimportant when it's about the mountain. That alone should explain how wrong humans have become but it doesn't explain why, so here is the answer to that.

It was all about the shell. Or more accurately, the absence of it. It was a huge mistake to abandon the shell for fashionable clothes and a tomorrow not to mention the killing and consuming of everything in sight until everything in sight became a wasteland of your own path. See how ridiculous your existence has become? See why your shell of values, games of ego and executive control are not only useless but dangerous?

You can't even talk about nakedness. See how ashamed you have become since you abandoned your shell. Don't you miss it? I bet you do and I bet right now you wish you hadn't started this relationship. Don't you wish we'd each stayed on our own sides of this page and left Story alone?

You've got some good points. The shell point is huge. It was a big mistake to leave the water and an even bigger mistake to leave the shell. Evolution is a capricious bitch, isn't she? Based on your words, I'm kinda guessing there isn't much hope for changing the intersection of our path with our destiny. I didn't think Story was going to have a happy ending and no doubt about that now. It's not like we can grow a new shell or return to the one we traded for our nakedness, is it? I told you not to worry about the ending, that time would take care of it, but I'm not so certain about that now. Now I'm a little worried about it.

Anyway, if Story must have an unhappy ending, I'm sorry and too bad because happy endings make best sellers. But if it has to be that way, so be it, beginnings and endings are just points in time from which people and their stories circle around, so don't sugar coat the ending for me. Best get to the truth and be judged on that, not how we got there.

Take your time. Unfortunately, too many stories have poor endings which are made even worse with unhappy endings so if yours isn't completely worked out yet, don't rush it. I'd rather not know the ending than be given a bad one or a stupid one. But you didn't answer my question: are you turtle? That might help me understand.

Understand what, you moron? Understand turtle when that is neither a beginning or an end? Understand where you came from? Understand how to stop obsessing about tomorrow which is not an ending because it is now? You talk about excuses, you use understanding, or your lack of it, as the biggest excuse of all.

Open your eyes. See what is perfectly natural, not manmade. Perfectly natural with one exception and it is not a minor one. Turtle is minor, nature is not.

Fair enough but it sounds like things are going to get a lot worse before they get better or is that being optimistic? It's depressing, that's for sure. Any chance there's a joke to be made somewhere, a little humor to help the story along, to keep the reader from feeling suicidal, lol? Or how about some simple Pollyanna truth made with artistry and intellect. Like all the hearts of all the sentient beings in all the world pulsing together will protect them from perilous and catastrophic collapse?

How about some hope for those of us who don't have a shell, but wish we did?

That's got some potential! That might provide some motivation to keep the reader in the game. Getting a newer, better, more modern shell, would be marvelous.

Or maybe quote some history that makes the journey look like progress and sprinkle it with some fancy cliché to cover our naiveté and our nakedness.

How about throwing in a little mystery to encourage a search and promising discovery? Add some potential for hope?

Maybe use words like 'slowly beating heart' to analogize life and death, the dichotomy, the yin and yang, of existence. Existential endings become spiritual beginnings, how about that?

Philosophy is not an answer or an excuse. Philosophy is dressing reality with words that hide or excuse greed and vanity but that cannot deny consequences. That is the purpose of Story.

Good statement. At least the intellect with this collaboration is picking up. Is that turtle thinking?

Are you dim? Have you listened to anything? You think Story is about a bunch of naked turtles? Are you even going to try to understand what this is about or are you going to stay stuck in your post-primordial brain?

Why don't you think turtle for a change. Start with a beginning, any beginning that comes to mind, and see where your thoughts take you when you aren't busy trying to mold or manipulate the path of your words with rules and egotistical self-absorption. Leave all that at the door and maybe your own words will force you into the truth you so desperately seek to avoid.

Do it. Leave your precious pre-frontal lobe logic in the past where it belongs and stop trying to manufacture an ending that suits your preconceptions. Stop hiding your nakedness. Try writing that and don't stop when it doesn't make sense or the characters misbehave because that might just be the moment you are writing something worth reading.

Ok, I'll take a shot at it.

The year is 1943 and that number alone should tell you this is not an exact accounting in a time when bullets were flying, bombs were falling, people were dying, and buildings were burning all over Europe.

In Queens Bench Courtroom B, in a small city in Alberta, Case 19770118 was in progress. Legal antics had been raging since the Hearing for Discovery earlier that month but that morning Jagigure had had enough legalities and fired her lawyer. She stood alone with her hands on the railing in front of the judge and that appealed to her because she always stood alone. Jag didn't stand for much, but she stood for that. It was her parents who named her Jagigure and they were both dead.

In Punjabi, Jagigure is pronounced much more harshly than it is written so she locked that sound in the back of her mind and only ever introduced herself or responded to Jag, said softly. She always responded with a very bright, very white, luminescent beam of light cast from the exact center of her dark black eyes.

She knew that laser light was evolutionary and irrelevant to the just and legitimate crime of passion for which she was currently being held accountable.

She knew it because she understood with ancient awareness it was a necessity for survival at the bottom of an ocean where not only is it black but cold within a fraction of a degree of freezing and at a pressure which would stuff a human body into the casing for a pork breakfast sausage. She knew where she came from, she knew where she was going, and she didn't care for legal antics or the pointless politic driving them.

Her knowledge came from a completely inhospitable environment where there is more life, and more to life in the depth, dark, and cold to defy and confound the collective intellect of any number of humanoids ignoring it from the safety of their extravagant boat. Nothing should exist yet a vast quantity and arrangement of life defies the rules.

It is a world where millivolts are magnets,
Parts per million are digital maps, and
Everything hunts to survive.

Exoskeleton luminescence is for introduction,
Spatial perception Is for prey location, and
Neural cognition is for capture.

Biology runs contrary to physics,
Physics is governed by chemistry,
Chemistry is buried in silt, and
Time is irrelevant.

You're getting there, now answer your deepest question. It's about time you finally got something right, you finally found a path worth writing. Now, stop thinking about the answers you want to hear and write directly to the question. Confront the truth.

Fine.

Everything is inside-out, reversed, upside-down, inverted and prolapsed? So what if all the light and heat and oxygen outside the deep abyss supported and then fueled population growth beyond recommended domain design parameters and then vastly exceeded the environmental constraints needed to maintain equilibrium?

So what if humanoids are nothing more than walking, talking, thoughtless, intentionally destructive protein-based life forms and nature is encouraging us to perfect genocide in order to get rid of us so the next experiment can emerge? Even more frightening, what if she doesn't like our progress with genocide and decides to take matters into her own hands?

We know she doesn't permit over-consumption without consequences, won't accept over-reach or permanently support over-population but we're doing all that and more. We're just asking for it. Excess is only permitted in strictly approved quantities and then only in a tightly defined yet volatile balance with the consequential destruction or deprivation to other species but we aren't paying attention to that. We aren't paying attention to anything, and the last thing on our minds is asking permission or seeking compromise. We just do whatever we want to do and never clean up the mess we've made. Like, fuck nature and see how she likes it. Is there an answer to that?

Definitely. And you can hope it isn't the brown stinking slime that slowly dissolves through the skin and flesh on its way to the bone as the mind wriggles in terror but don't count on it.

End of Story

BOOKS BY DFWILLIAMS

—❯❯●❮❮—

NeverEnding
Whiz, Natty & Me
The Blues

dfwilliamsbooks.com

www.ingramcontent.com/pod-product-compliance
Lightning Source LLC
Chambersburg PA
CBHW070218260626
47160CB00002B/590